Praise for Valdur

"A merrily anachronistic adventure... Beal keeps the action
balanced expertly with complex political machinations."
Publishers Weekly

"Beal is a storyteller who can handle plot adeptly
enough to create a hugely compelling narrative... terrific fun."
SFX Magazine

"An excellently gripping story of thievery, betrayal, piracy, and
adventure... a fantastic and satisfying read."
SciFi Now Magazine

"A cracking piece of salty fun. If you're a fan of Michael Moorcock
and Fritz Leiber, you will most likely love Clifford Beal;
The Guns of Ivrea proves that Beal can deliver addictive, page-
turning pulp with fun characters and nifty world building."
Starburst Magazine

"Clifford Beal's novel will suit those who want something
somewhere in the middle of Scott Lynch's *Red Seas Under Red
Skies* and George R.R. Martin's *A Game of Thrones*...
A highly readable, fast-paced, fun adventure novel that somehow
manages to be all of that without ever sacrificing on character
development, authentic descriptions, and vivid world-building.
Great reading that will keep you guessing until the very end."
Fantasy Faction

"Fast-paced, intelligent fantasy action.
A fascinating tale of intrigue, magic and war."
Adrian Tchaikovsky

"Beginning with a deadly temple secret and leading into a pirate
rebellion, Clifford Beal proves you can't go wrong with a heavy
dose of adventure and intrigue... From sea battles to subtle mental
tricks, the fights are played out in many different ways and end

Tales of Valdur:
Book Two

The Witch of Torinia

Clifford Beal

SOLARIS

First published 2017 by Solaris
an imprint of Rebellion Publishing Ltd,
Riverside House, Osney Mead,
Oxford, OX2 0ES, UK

www.solarisbooks.com

UK ISBN: 978 1 78108 512 7
US ISBN: 978 1 78108 513 4

10 9 8 7 6 5 4 3 2 1

A CIP catalogue record for this book is available from
the British Library.

Designed & typeset by Rebellion Publishing

Printed in Denmark by Nørhaven

*To Lorraine,
for bestowing the magic of books*

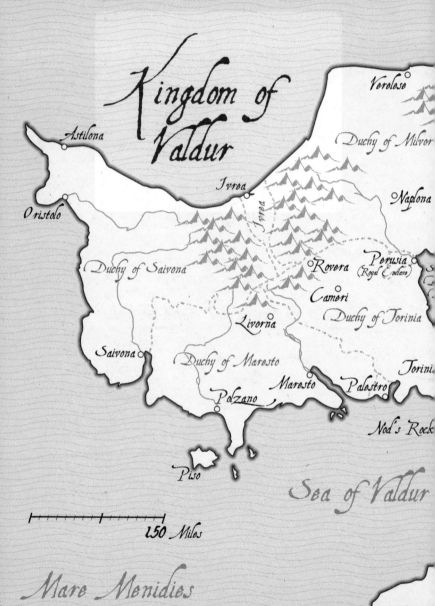

Imperium Serica
(the Sinae)
and lands East

N
W   E
S

Gorviatas

Duchy of Colonna

Miluorna

Colonna

Telas

Tetrarchy of Kores

Kerespura

Darfan

Azilas

Naaman

Kingdoms of the Southlands

One

THE DEVIL KEEPS his bargains. Men, on the other hand, do not.

Biagio sniffed and pulled his lower lip between thumb and grimy forefinger. He could see them on the crest of the hill ahead—two horsemen astride their mounts as still as stone and partially obscured by the silvery leaves of a ragged grove of alders. He saw a cloud of steam billow from the mouth of one of the horses, the crispness of the early dawn giving them away, if anyone else was bothering to watch. But at his back, he knew most of the little town of Persarola was just awakening on this spring morning, the promise of rain on the air obvious to those stumbling from their beds. He rubbed at the itching scalp underneath his grubby linen coif and turned to his companion, an equally rustic countryman whose nose was streaming snot down his hairy lip.

"They're waiting," Biagio said, a note of sourness creeping into his voice. "Just like they said they would be."

His companion wiped his nose across the sleeve of his tunic and gave him a baleful eye. "Did you really expect them to lose interest? They're soldiers, you had better have the right answers on your tongue."

Biagio's fingers tightened on the hazel staff he was poking into the ground. He shot a glance back to the walls of Persarola and the town gate. Several crows cawed at him from the fields on either side, adding their own chastisement. "You just let me do the talking, Pandolfo. It's my arrangement. And you're lucky I let you in on it to begin with. Even if you are my sister's husband."

Pandolfo twisted his mouth, unconvinced. "If you say so. We'll see if they deliver the coin. Don't hold your breath."

They set to scaling the grass covered slope, a few low scraggly bushes giving them handholds. They sidestepped the gravel strewn clefts made by the incessant winter rains of Valdur, slipping and cursing as they made their way up. At last, they reached the crest. Below them, Persarola sat snug in the valley surrounded on three sides by farmers' fields: richly brown, ploughed and sowed. Beyond this vista, the Duchy of Maresto sprawled westwards as far as the eye could see. Away to their right, northwards, far distant mountains, purple-grey, could be seen melding with the dark sky. In the foothills of those mountains lay the free city of Livorna, home to the One Faith and the Temple Majoris that stood ancient upon the rocky plateau of Ara.

They walked towards the grove, the mounted men still sitting rigid in their high saddles but now observing them in an almost detached manner. A few miles further, eastwards, across the undulating plain spotted with copse and field, ran the frontier with the Duchy of Torinia. And that was from where these mounted soldiers had come. Biagio could feel his breaths coming faster even though he had completed his climb. He saw one of the horsemen cinch up on his reins and turn his mount slightly towards them. God knew he was used to seeing soldiers and armies, living as he did in a border hamlet, a border that seemed to move as frequently as his bowels. But he never trusted them, particularly *these* mercenaries. The Company of the Blue Boar. *As contrary as a rich whore at a fair.* And now it was too late to turn back. He had made his deal and now he had to stick to it come what may.

As they approached the gently swaying branches of the alders, Biagio swiped his sweat-stained coif from his head and gripped it between both hands. His companion hurriedly followed suit, doffing his brown woollen beret and breaking into a disingenuous grin of abject good humour.

"Well, what joy do you have for me?" said the closer of the two horsemen.

They were both arrayed in white harness, shining dully in the colourless overcast of the dawn. Both wore long slender swords at their hips, simple cross guards and round pommels protruding at their saddle bows. The visors of their sallet helms were unlatched and raised, revealing hard faces; the faces of men who knew command and war. The other officer—one as yet unknown to the peasant—was a few years older than his companion, and wore a blue satin sash over his breast and backplate. His long face, with angular features, was as smooth, pale, and unblemished as a maiden's, despite the man's age, and lacked the usual corpulence that Biagio saw in men of wealth and position. His armour was far grander than his companion's. Breastplate, paulders, vambraces all edged in fine rolled brass with a mirrored finish. His helm, tapering back to a sharp point behind his nape, was decorated with swirling filigree, blackened upon the steel to give it impressive relief. Surely, thought Biagio, this was the commander of the company of the Blue Boar himself. Despite the queasiness welling up in him, Biagio managed a smile and a bow of his greasy head to the more junior officer.

"A good morrow, my captain sir!"

The officer's mount stamped and snorted. Biagio took half a step back as the horse's black eyes fixed him. Captain Janus smiled as he leaned over and looked down on the man.

"He always knows who he wants to trample. And today he seems to like *you*." The smile evaporated. "Now, what intelligence do you have for me? Any changes to the militia?"

The peasant nodded, his eyes darting to the other officer—captain-general or Coronel—who sat staring at him as his horse gently shifted its weight. "No more than a hundred men. At least a fair number of them old. Mainly glaives, a few swords, some round shields."

Janus leaned back against the cantle of his saddle. "So, they haven't beefed up the garrison. And what about the gates?"

Biagio smiled—more sincerely this time, proud of his cleverness. "My man drank the gatekeepers stupid last night. When we crept out a while ago the gates were wide open and all of them asleep in their clothes."

The captain nodded. "You haven't seen any companies of Maresto of late?"

"Only a few squadrons of *rondelieri* horsemen that passed by more than a week ago, on their way north. No more than that, my captain."

"And what flag flies from the temple tower?" the older officer asked, voice laced with impatience.

Biagio crushed his cap in his hands and stuttered. "The... *flag*, sir?"

Coronel Lupo Aretini, commander of the Blue Boar's two columns of cavalry, both heavy and light, looked to his captain. "Is this man a half-wit? I ask him a simple question and he gives me one in return."

"Around here we'd consider ourselves most fortunate to find even a half-wit," replied Janus, gently tugging the reins as his mount stamped again. He turned back to the peasant. "The *Temple* flag, you fool. The one with the sun upon it."

Biagio nodded. "Aye. It flies even now."

"How many rays lie upon the sun? Tell me." Aretini edged his horse closer.

The two peasants exchanged worried glances and bumped shoulders. Rotund Biagio balked again, words somehow failing to emerge from his throat, only an incoherent gurgle of confusion as he looked to Pandolfo for support.

Aretini's right hand leaned heavily on the pommel of his sword. "Sweet Aloysius! Is it *that* difficult? Seven or ten rays on the sun? Come now, you dolt!"

Biagio felt his balls shrivel as he turned again to his comrade. "Did you notice how many?"

Pandolfo stepped forward with some bravado, bowing his head. "There are ten, sir. Ten spokes upon that sun flag."

The Coronel nodded. "So, there are *Decimali* preaching there now."

Biagio forgot his reticence. "*Decimali*, sir? They look like the same black-robed priests as always."

Aretini's white teeth flashed for a moment. "You are not a regular worshipper, are you, my man? De... ci... mali. *Tenners*. The new heresy out of Livorna."

The peasant blinked and shot a glance over to Pandolfo.

Janus leaned over his saddlebow. "They have added three heretical commandments to those of Saint Elded. Distasteful unholy truck with the merfolk. Commandments that encourage open dissent to the authority of the High Priest and Grand Curia." He got little reaction. "Do you live in some hole in the ground? The old High Priest was murdered last summer. There's a whole new lot in charge of the Great Temple."

Both peasants nodded, if somewhat dubiously. "Her-e-ti-cal," mumbled Biagio.

The captain raised an eyebrow, now doubting his earlier decision to employ these two as his *devastatori*—ravagers to be unleashed after the Blue Boar was finished with its work that day. He looked to Aretini who shook his head at the lack of perspicacity of the villagers. The Coronel waved a hand to signal that he proceed. Janus unlooped a small leather purse from a horn on his saddle and hefted it in his gloved hand. "You two still have how many in your little band of brothers?"

"Forty-three sturdy men, sir!" Biagio proudly proclaimed.

"And you remember what's expected of you after we clear out the town? Drive out every last pig and cow. Every chicken and goose. We'll trammel as many of the fields as we can but you're welcome to tear up or thieve whatever else you might find. Torch what takes your fancy. We'll give the rats a way out by the west gate but they'll have damn little reason to come back after we're gone." He leaned over again and lowered his voice. "And your gang is going to make sure of that."

Both peasants gave a vigorous nod and the mercenary tossed the leather pouch down to them. "That should keep all of you happy enough. But make sure you do a thorough job."

Aretini had raised himself in the saddle and was peering at the red tiled roofs of the tightly nestled houses. His pale eyes, the same colour as the listless sky, settled upon the tall white stone, four-square tower of the town's holy temple. From a pole lashed at its top, a standard billowed. "Foolish that they would not change the flag entirely if they are so keen to recast the One Faith," he said. "I mean, how is one to tell enemy from friend?"

The captain followed his gaze. "And preaching new commandments beyond the seven... after all these centuries. *Ten* commandments supposedly delivered by the Lawgiver—and then conveniently forgotten?"

"That's three more commandments than I need," said Aretini.

"And the priests down there?" asked Captain Janus, thrusting forward his stubbled chin.

"Heretics. Kill them all." He sighed and jerked the reins of his mount, turning it away. "Aye, well, it's not proper battle I know. Unfortunate business. But Duke Ursino's will be done. Give the order to advance."

And without bothering to dismiss the peasants, the horsemen rode back over the crest of the hill. The peasants exchanged a look of relief and Biagio, feeling he was about to leap from a precipice into a swirling sea of shit, breathed a heavy sigh. He knotted the purse around the thin worn belt of his jerkin before pressing his coif back on his head. They followed the horsemen at a respectful distance then stopped dead as they looked beyond. Hundreds of mounted men were now trotting through the vale, preparing to gush forth from its widening throat. They came on, four abreast. Lightly armoured in studded leather brigantines and open-face barbute helms, every man bore a short lance and a sword at his hip. The column pounded across the spongy ground, taking a wide turn still in good formation. Biagio watched as the captain galloped down the hillside to catch them up while the Coronel cantered towards the rear of the force, some five-hundred strong. Further back down the column two great standards whipped taut, borne aloft by dizzily garbed soldiers dressed in flowing dag-toothed coats of red and white. One was painted with a dark blue charging boar upon a white field, the battle flag of the mercenary company. The other bore the crest of the duchy of Torinia: two red towers flanking a golden bull above which shone a seven-rayed sun in splendour. Biagio saw the captain raise his drawn sword to be immediately answered by a trumpeter, the peal echoing across the valley.

Biagio and his brother-in-law stood and watched as the vanguard narrowed to two files and dashed through the gates at a canter, lances couched. They did not have to wait long for the cries of alarm, swiftly followed by screams.

"We'll be rich," remarked Biagio quietly. "But I'll be moving to Torinia after this is done. Because we'll be dead men if we stay hereabouts."

Pandolfo wiped his nose on his sleeve. "Aye, you're right in that. Too bad. Your sister loves that little house and yard."

THE BLUE BOAR cavalry pounded down the High Street, hooves slipping in the mud, riders breaking off down alleys to pursue folk, whooping as they dug in their spurs. A few of the town militia, jerkins hastily laced, ran to engage, clutching rusty glaives and spears. They were spitted where they stood. By the time the captain trotted down the street, well behind the vanguard, looting had begun and grim games of hide-and-seek with the womenfolk of Persarola had broken out. He pulled up short and cursed loudly as a dismounted soldier cut past him, pursuing a screaming chemise-clad woman terrified for life and honour. When he reached the square he saw that a group of thirty or so militia had formed a hedgehog of pole weapons, backs to the large square stones of the temple. Some of his men were laughing and harrying them from horseback, their lances clattering along the shafts of the glaives and spears.

The captain swore and gestured to a contingent of mounted crossbowmen who were just entering behind him. "You lot! Over here! Take these men down."

The bowmen dismounted, lay quarrels in their stocks, and took aim. Once the strings began to speak their muffled twang it was quickly over. Two defenders, crossbow bolts protruding from their gambesons, made a desperate break but were hacked to the ground by the press of mercenaries. The large studded oak doors of the temple gave way to the combined muscle of half a squadron of grunting soldiers and the mass of men fell inwards, the cries of those inside now spilling out to the captain's ears. A few moments passed and a soldier came running out, sword in hand.

"Captain, sir! You should have a look at this."

"Elded's bollocks!" Janus muttered, swinging his leg out of the saddle and jumping to the cobbles with a metallic jangle. He threw his reins to a mounted comrade and drew his long slender war sword, spurs jingling as he strode to the doorway and crossed the threshold. Tall, narrow slit windows cast some feeble light into the great hall but at the altar end, iron candelabra blazed upon the raised platform, illuminating something he had not expected to see.

Two crumpled black forms lay in the aisle. Dead priests. Further on, at the apse, a last stand of sorts was being played out. Three black-robed priests and a younger, clearly terrified greyrobe were backed up against the brocade-shrouded altar itself. And standing in front of them, shoulder to shoulder, stood two defenders with feet braced, bearing round shields and swords, their heads bare. His own men had retreated from the altar, swords poised and waiting for orders. Janus tilted his head slightly in bemusement. Here were two lads up for a fight but they were no town militiamen. Most strange of all, their heads were shaved bare at the back and sides, leaving a mop of unkempt locks on their crowns. A smile parted his lips. They were monks. *Fighting* monks.

"Easy, my lads! Have a care! We haven't seen the likes of these in our travels, have we?" Captain Janus said, easing forwards, sword drawn.

He looked at the tabards both monks wore. White linen with a sun in splendour embroidered in yellow. A sun with ten rays spreading across their chests. The rude wooden buckler shields they wielded in front of them carried the same symbol. Janus's veteran eye immediately took notice of the drooping rims held nowhere near high enough to make a tight defence. Their sword arms were held high, too high, blades waving nervously. It was abundantly clear these two had little benefit of training.

"A fine defence, brothers! Now, just who are you? Monks playing at soldiers?"

One of the men (they were both young but not striplings) shouted out a reply. "We are of the Order of the Temple of Livorna! And we will die defending this holy place and our brethren!"

Janus pouted. "Ah. I see only a band of apostates dressed in robes. And it is the order of the Duke that all heretics and profaners of the One Faith be put to death."

"That you disregard the truth of the revelations is your own affair," yelled back the monk in reply, his voice quavering. "But this is the Duchy of Maresto and we give not a fig for what your Ursino says."

The captain smiled. "Today, my friends, this place *is* the Duchy of Torinia."

"We defend this temple under the authority of the High Priest himself and the Council of the Nine. You are nothing more than brigands." He banged the pommel of his sword on the face of his shield. "We will not surrender it to you!"

Janus hefted his sword. "We are not asking for your surrender."

The monk nodded and spoke softly. "Elded's will be done."

JANUS RE-ENTERED the square, now quiet since the short sharp business had been performed. He took the reins of his horse from his man and mounted up. The sky was even darker now and a fine misting rain had begun to anoint them. The smell of acrid smoke touched his nostrils. Border raids were tedious and brought little chance for distinguishing oneself, but, that said, he was paid the same. So too, he was perceptive enough of a soldier and tactician to understand what the Duke of Torinia was up to with these attacks on the fat and complacent northern reaches of Maresto. The company were but the wasps goading the bear, fully intending a larger response from Duke Alonso in the south. Full and open battle was the goal, nothing less. Carving out a swath of new territory between Maresto and the free city of Livorna would do well for a start. But now, bloody fighting monks from Livorna of all things. Coronel Aretini will love hearing that one, he thought as his horse clopped away across the cobbles and the sated Blue Boar began to reform outside the walls of Persarola.

Two

BROTHER ACQUELONIUS GALENUS, captain-general of the nascent fighting order of the Temple of Livorna—still called Acquel by most of his brethren—sat poised at his writing table. The goose quill pen in his hand had not moved for more than two minutes, a large purple blob of squid ink now starting to thicken upon the paper. His thoughts were reeling far afield, nowhere near to the task at hand. The sheaves before him, spread out in disorder detailed supply orders, poll counts, regulations, and all of the other mundane but necessary details of organizing and running a small army.

Although the winter was now long past, the events of the previous summer played over and over again in his head—the murders at the Temple Majoris and at the Ara monastery; his discovery of the amulet of Saint Elded and the secrets it carried; his flight and pursuit.

His theft of the amulet, rashly done with little thought, led to the revelation that the great Lawgiver—dead for centuries—had been half mer. He had also rediscovered the lost commandments of the great Saint, part of the so-called Black Texts, suppressed by the Temple priests since late antiquity, deemed the final works of Elded, aged and enfeebled of mind. But it was the deaths that preyed upon his conscience most. The innocent monks caught up in the Magister's plans to hide the discovery. The High Priest himself, murdered in his own bedchamber, and Timandra, the woman who had aided him in his flight, who had guided him and fallen in love with him (and he with her). Timandra Pandarus of the Company of the Black Rose. Her tanned, green-eyed face filled his vision and Acquel exhaled slowly, his heart filled to bursting with sadness and remorse that he had not been able to save her. Remorse that the evil the Magister had unwittingly released by employing treacherous allies had not been destroyed after Timandra sacrificed herself for him.

It had all begun when Acquel had fled from the cavern crypt under the Ara monastery. The Magister had scapegoated him for the murder of his brethren, and when news of the terrible deeds reached the town that clung to the Ara, his mother had succumbed to grief and shame. Now he was truly alone.

He had thought then that he knew what the Lawgiver expected of him—spread the lost Word that had been rediscovered; defend the One Faith from the ancient worship of twisted gods and those who denied the truth of Elded. He had agreed a *modus vivendi* with the Magister, Lucius Kodoris: that the Magister should take the mantle of High Priest, adopt the truths of the Black Texts, work to disseminate them to the faithful, and Acquel would not reveal his role in murder and subversion. For himself, Acquel would found a fighting order to protect the Temple and the truth of the new Word. Bringing light to the kingdom would require strength and strong defences. Yet still, it was all founded on deception. Necessary perhaps, but deception nonetheless.

Acquel touched the small round amulet lying against his chest. It was quiet, far different from months ago when it had flared with heat, warning him of approaching danger. His visions had also ceased—visions of the Lawgiver himself in ancient Valdur. He did not truly yearn for their return but he felt rudderless without them. Why had the spirit of the Saint, who had chosen and guided him, suddenly abandoned him?

Acquel put the quill down and blotted the paper. He took up the bronze blackwood-handled seal of the Order. The metal was still orange and shiny, practically virgin from the forge. He stared at the seal: the ten arms of the sun, each long ray separated by a shorter wavy one, an upright cross-hilted sword lying upon the face of the sun. He turned it over, thumped the seal down upon the table, and clenched his jaw. It was nothing, nothing but an example of his folly, a folly made manifest. The last fighting order in Valdur had been disbanded decades before after the last great dukes' war. He had recruited 400 men in six months, a third of those from the old discredited Temple Guard, men he had let sign on as lay brothers because he needed those who actually knew something of fighting. But it was a phantom, untested and untrained. He was making it up as he went along and everyone around him knew it.

He slid down from the high stool and straightened his surplice, emblazoned with sun and sword—more like a tabard than a monk's *scapular* for it delineated him a soldier, not just a holy man. He took in his surroundings: a high-ceilinged chamber, ornately decorated and with a black and white chequered floor. All a world away from his bed in the dormitory a few months ago.

He left the room, entering a wide corridor in what, centuries before, had been a simple monastery, now grown as grand as any ducal palace. Other blackrobes nodded greetings or gave the blessing as they passed. He was not shunned for the horrors of the last summer, now known by all in monastery and temple, but he was feared. Acquel believed he knew why. He had robbed the brethren of certainty by bringing a new age of revelation upon them.

Once in the cloisters gardens, the high stone wall and arches rising up around him, he found his feet taking him along the path to the centre where a stand of *nutaris* trees, branches intertwined, standing vigil over the simple grave of Timandra Pandarus. No other had ever been buried in the gardens but he had demanded it, and Kodoris had granted his wish.

"Brother Acquel!" It was a young greyrobe, his sandals slapping on the paving stones. He stopped himself a few yards from Acquel and gave a polite bow. "Your pardon for disturbing you, brother. His Holiness has requested your presence."

Acquel nodded in return and silently made his way back towards the west portico and towards the great white stone archway that led to the main staircase.

Two monks of his new order stood before the great studded oak door to the High Priest's apartment, white tabards with a golden sun in splendour over their black robes, swords at their hips. They bowed deeply as Acquel approached and he raised two fingers of his right hand to his forehead in a gesture of both greeting and blessing. One of the men turned the great iron ring and pushed the door open, admitting him. Acquel stepped into the perpetually cold and austere antechamber, hung with ancient tapestries of the saints.

A page, a boy of about twelve in black livery, smiled and bowed and then led the way to the High Priest's private chamber. He struggled briefly to push open the heavy carved blackwood door after having first knocked.

"Brother Acquelonius, enter. We have much to speak of."

Lucius Kodoris was standing, smiling, hands clasped, draped in his robes of purple velvet, the great medallion and chain of holy office upon his breast. He was old—bushy grey hair and thick eyebrows to match—but he was tall still and vigorous. Acquel was yet wary of him after the events of the year gone by. Even so, they were strangely beholden to each other. Kodoris, realizing his terrible mistake in the undercroft of the Temple Majoris, had returned to the light of Elded and slain the man who would have killed them both. For his part, Acquel gave the alibi that would allow Kodoris to ascend to the purple. He needed Kodoris to pave the way for the dissemination of Elded's new revelations, something impossible without the support of the High Priest and the Grand Curia of the Nine Principals.

Kodoris's smile quickly faded as the High Priest gestured for Acquel to take a seat. The room was as expansive and ornate as his own—even larger—a great casement window at one end flooding the room with light. It was the very chamber where the last High Priest, Brachus, had had his throat slit. Acquel's eyes drifted to the floor near the great table. The porous marble still held the evidence of that horrid night: copper-red bloodstains upon the white tiles.

They seated themselves across from each other. Acquel's hands nervously wrapped about the gilded arms of his chair, sinuously carved and terminating in eagle claws grasping golden balls.

"I'll make no bones about it," said Kodoris, his voice rough. "The One Faith is descending into chaos. We may have moved too quickly with our reforms... with preaching the Black Texts. The people are not ready."

Acquel's face remained impassive. "Many have joyfully accepted the new Word. Even the king and the prelate of Perusia. So too will the others in time."

Kodoris nodded. "That may be so. But at this moment there is strife across the kingdom. People are taking sides. You've heard what happened at Persarola? They singled out the priests for death. All slain, including the defenders you sent there."

More deaths laid at his doorstep. He had sent them before they were ready and they had given their lives. Acquel swallowed. "That was Duke Ursino provoking Maresto. The Torinians were bent upon war before all this started and Ursino is using the Faith as cause. You know that."

"And it is clear he means to cut us off up here at Livorna from friends and allies in the south. Ursino himself has rejected the new commandments as heresy. If he sends an army here it will be to kill us all and restore those three Principals that fled to his court for protection."

Acquel fought back a wave of helplessness. He shifted his weight in the chair, thinking of what to say next. "And what does the High Steward have to say about all this? Has he sought to recruit more for the militia?"

Kodoris harrumphed. "Marsilius is younger than me but he may as well be a hundred for all his vigour. He's looking to *you* to lead the defence of Livorna. He has a hundred of his own retainers to guard his palazzo plus another two hundred in the town militia. That is the extent of his army."

Acquel leaned forward. "And that is why I have asked for the aid of Duke Alonso in Maresto. My men are not yet ready to face an army led by Torinia's mercenaries. Nor are there enough of them."

"The Duke has answered your call," said Kodoris, his large brown eyes boring into Acquel's. "I have received word this day that he is sending one of his own mercenary companies to meet with you, in your capacity as captain-general. They arrive on the morrow."

"Do you know who is coming? Is it the Black Rose?"

"It is the Company of the Black Rose—or at least a contingent."

"Who leads it?"

"The letter did not say. But the Lord's mercy shines on us if they will remain here at Livorna. I do not know how soon Torinia may strike. After they sacked Persarola, the soldiers moved on to other villages nearby. We are only at the start of the campaigning season. They could be at the gates within weeks. But there remains the other threat."

"Lucinda della Rovera," said Acquel, a bitter edge to his voice.

"Yes. Wicked as she is, she is an incomparable beauty and the Duke of Torinia has taken a strong fancy to her since the death of his *duchesa*. She may already be guiding him for all we know."

"A convenient death that I'll wager she had a hand in. Did none of your entreaties to him about her duplicity—her murders—move him to cast her out?"

"Her poison has already seeped into the court. Ursino rejects our accusations and claims it is me—and you—who have usurped the Great Temple and the One Faith. She has told him that it was my own hand that slew Brachus. There is no doubt that the creature is urging him on to make war upon Maresto and Livorna."

"Her dark arts are yet at work here. We still cannot kill the roots of that infernal tree she gave life to in the crypt. Fire and quicklime worked for a time but now it has sprouted anew. How can we stop her?"

"I was praying that you would know that," Kodoris said quietly. "Has not the amulet sent you further guidance? Has the Saint not come to you again in dreams?"

Acquel looked down at his knees. "I fear he has not. The amulet sits cold on my breast."

Kodoris sighed. "Her game must be to splinter the faithful through war. It is pitting those who adopt the ten commandments against those who embrace the seven. But her true aim is to resurrect the Old Faith and cast us all down. I fear that prayer may not be enough. Worse—" he paused, shaking his head.

"What is it?"

"There are reports that the tree of the Old Faith is sprouting across Maresto and Torinia. Everywhere one had been felled centuries ago now shows new shoots rising, black-green and with a sickly-sweet scent."

Acquel smoothed his scalp, his hand resting upon the nape of his neck. "Elded preserve us," he whispered.

Kodoris looked run down, tired. There was a long silence before he spoke.

"You know I am a man in penance, from now until the day I die. I cannot undo my actions—the lives I took—and permitted *her* to take. But you must know that I am with you Brother Acquelonius, in body and spirit and with all my heart. I have embraced the revelations."

Acquel stared back at him, his mind swirling, tormented by conflicting emotions. He could never trust Kodoris fully, yet he needed him just the same. He nodded slowly. "Then we share the same goal, your Holiness, and the same mission. And our first task is to safeguard the One Faith and the Temple."

Kodoris rose from his seat, knees cracking. "Then, by the grace of God and his saints, that is what we shall do."

ACQUEL SLEPT FITFULLY THAT night. He had been a long time getting used to sleeping in a room alone after four years in the vast dormitory of the novices and greyrobes amid laughter, whispers and farting. The silence of his chamber had initially been unnerving, but now, months later, he had grown accustomed if not exactly comfortable with it. He had awakened in the early hours, a chill upon the room, and his body in a sweat.

His dream was as horrible as it was vivid. He was in the undercroft again, down the wide winding stair deep beneath the Temple. He lay on his back on the slab stone floor looking up at the cantilevered brick ceiling above him. There was silence all around but soon a hundred whipping green tendrils, a monstrous beanstalk that erupted from the cracks, enveloped his limbs and torso. Dark, darkly verdant and almost black, leaves waxy and thickly scented, the plant embraced him and tightened. The tendrils had sought out his face, his eyes, nose and mouth. And he had shot to wakefulness, sitting bolt upright in his bed. She had poisoned the foundations of the Temple with her black magic, causing the ancient stump of that pagan tree to sprout anew, and now it was battle unceasing to keep it at bay. He knew as he lay there, eyes wide open, that no further rest would come and it being close to sunrise and morning prayer, he gave up and threw his legs over the side of the bed.

He broke fast alone, his thoughts consumed by doubts. Had Saint Elded abandoned him? How was he to defeat not just the armies of Torinia but also the rise of the old worship? Those ancient gods his own ancestors had sacrificed to: Andras, Beleth, and Belial. That unholy trinity now had a powerful mortal champion. Lucinda della Rovera could turn men's minds to her will. Although a lay canoness at a wealthy priory, somehow she had hidden her true beliefs from all. Her abilities as a Seeker, deemed a gift of God and given the blessing of Kodoris, were anything but God-given. In his mind's eye he could still see her shining pale face, coldly angelic, the night she had set about murder at the Ara.

About mid-morning, his head in his hands, sheaves of papers spread around him, a knock came upon his door.

"Your pardon, Brother Acquel. The delegation has arrived from Maresto." The blackrobe gave him a weak smile and bowed.

"I will meet them in the chapterhouse. See that they are guided there and given refreshment."

Acquel donned his tabard, smoothed out upon his shoulders the hood of his robes, and buckled on his belt and dagger. He briefly regarded himself in the tall looking-glass in the corner. The embroidered sun-in-splendour with drawn sword shone garishly upon his chest, and he felt a charlatan.

When he pushed open the heavy double oak doors of the chapterhouse, he already had a likely idea who would be in the chamber. He was not disappointed. There, at the long refectory table at the far end, backed by the enormous tapestry of Elded and his disciples, stood three soldiers, all dressed in high boots and brigandines. The tallest among them he recognized immediately: Julianus Strykar, captain of the *rondelieri* column of the Black Rose. By his side stood his lieutenant, Poule. The other soldier he did not know. He rapidly closed the distance between them, the sound of his footsteps swallowed by the intricately carved and gilded wood ceiling. He reached the delegation and bowed.

Poule was beaming at the sight of Acquel but Strykar's face was without emotion.

Acquel smiled. "Captain Strykar, I'm grateful that you've come. It does my heart good to see you again."

Poule chuckled. "Hello holy man! See that you still have the dagger I lent you last summer. And the captain here is now raised a Coronel of the company."

Acquel looked again at Strykar and bowed. "I did not know. Your pardon."

Strykar fixed him with a hard look. "And you, brother monk, have had advancement of your own I hear. Captain General? A bit hasty for someone of your tender years who's never swung a sword in anger, no?"

Acquel ignored the jibe. "I do not know your other comrade, Coronel."

Strykar lifted his hand and gestured to the swarthy man with large dark eyes next to him. "This is Captain Cortese, who now commands the *rondelieri* in my stead." Cortese inclined his head ever so slightly, his eyes meeting Acquel's.

"Your servant, Captain Cortese," said Acquel, bowing again.

Poule stepped forward and grasped Acquel by the arm. "It is damned good to lay eyes on you again, my boy!" he said. "We did not think you would ever be seen again."

Strykar set down his wine goblet on the table behind him. "Shut it, Poule," he said quietly.

Poule frowned and backed up a step, folding his arms across his chest.

Acquel looked at Strykar, the man who had saved him from death on the road from Livorna eight months earlier. The mercenary had since shaved his unkempt beard and his cheeks had filled out over the winter. He had deeper crow's feet perhaps, but it was the same man he had come to both fear and respect.

Strykar met his gaze. "I want to hear from your own lips what happened, Brother Acquel. Why is it Timandra Pandarus is dead and you're not? Was it a mistake that I released you that night in the camp outside Maresto?"

It could have been a knife through his heart the words stung him so. "Your cousin saved my life, but I could not save hers. That is the truth of it and my shame. She swore to stand by me when we searched the crypt for the Black Texts, just as I wrote to you. I had been disarmed by that renegade, Flauros. She attacked him... wounded him sorely... but he stabbed her. She gave Magister Kodoris the time needed to put a sword through him." Acquel swallowed hard as the terrible images filled his mind once again. He thought he could see Strykar's eyes welling up for a moment and he heard the soldier sigh before turning and seizing his goblet again.

"Would that *you* were a better swordsman, holy man," the mercenary said.

"I swear to you I would have done anything to save her."

"And why didn't you strike Flauros while she struggled? Did you freeze?"

"He struck my head with his hilt, and I went down."

Strykar took a deep swig of wine and wiped the corners of his mouth with thumb and forefinger. He waved the goblet towards Cortese. "I have shared with Captain Cortese here, and old Poule, my conversation with Duke Alonso. The one we had after the Duke had read your letters." Acquel nodded expectantly. "Who is this noblewoman—this new enemy—you speak of?"

"She is not what she seems," replied Acquel. "Lucinda della Rovera is skilled in the black arts. She came here to kill the High Priest and unleash something in the Temple. She seeks to overthrow the One Faith and restore the old ways—the old worship—the Tree."

"Della Rovera?" It was Captain Cortese who spoke, his voice like gravel. "The great beauty who has captivated the court of Torinia?"

"The same. And 'captivate' does not begin to describe it. She is twisting Ursino's mind, bending his will to make war not just on Maresto but upon the Faith also."

"What of this tree you speak of?" asked Strykar.

"The Great Temple was built over the remains of a sacrificial tree," replied Acquel. "A terrible tree that Saint Elded himself cut down when he drove out the worshippers of Andras, Belial and Beleth. Lucinda della Rovera has given life to the tree once again after all these centuries by drenching it in the blood of High Priest Brachus. We have worked to destroy it down in the Temple undercroft these many months. Still, the thing sprouts again within days. It needs no sunlight."

"Aye," Strykar said. "I've seen a tree of my own. In Ivrea. A tree that devoured human flesh and whispered evil tidings. Thriving in a dungeon chamber. Is this what you speak of?"

Acquel nodded slowly as Strykar's news sunk in. So there were already even farther afield than he had been told.

"And now you say this noblewoman plays the Duke of Torinia like some puppeteer?" said Cortese, his words tinged with disbelief.

"I am saying exactly that," Acquel said. "She slew the High Priest and God knows how many others. Even her own sister when she finally rebelled. And she has an unnatural power to make others do her bidding. I have seen this with my own eyes."

Strykar glanced over to Cortese who in turn raised a bushy eyebrow. "I've seen a few things these months past that would freeze your blood," growled Strykar. "Things that are neither good nor godly. And Torinia rests heavy on my mind and Duke Alonso's."

"You yourself have seen her, Strykar," said Acquel. "On the quay at Perusia. That evening when Gregorvero and I were attacked."

"Aloysius's balls. *That* was della Rovera?"

"It was. And when she fled Perusia she came here to Livorna to pursue her plan against the One Faith."

Strykar did not reply but twisted the stem of his goblet in his hand, thinking.

"She will seek to split Livorna off from the south," continued Acquel. "They will cut Maresto down the middle and then turn to finish us off here on the Ara. I need more than the men of my own Temple Order to defend against a Torinian army."

Strykar chuckled. "So you're an intelligencer and a strategist too now?"

"Do not underestimate her. This is more than just about Torinia grabbing land. You yourself must know this to be the likely move. I need your help to meet the threat."

"And I suppose the fact that the new commandments you've adopted—that already, I might add, seem to have split the faithful down the middle—these have no part in all this?" Strykar set his goblet down. "Place your cards on the table, brother monk. Tell us what you want."

"I need a detachment of the Black Rose here in Livorna to stiffen the backs of the militia. And I need armour and weapons for my four hundred fighting brothers. And... I need Lieutenant Poule."

Cortese swore an oath under his breath. "Coronel, this upstart monk is seeking to pinch my officers right under my nose!"

Poule blinked a few times and would have melted into the wall behind him if he could. But Strykar held up a hand to silence his captain's outburst.

"And what does the High Priest—or the High Steward for that matter—have to say about this?"

"Both have given me responsibility for the defence of the town and the Ara."

Strykar shook his head and smiled. "You have come a long way, my boy! If my own tongue were only half so convincing I'd be on the throne of Valdur."

"I am not a fool. I'm no soldier and I know it. I've tried to train the brethren with a few of the more artful guardsmen I disbanded but they're not up to the task."

"So... Poule here is the answer to your prayers," replied Strykar, trying to suppress a laugh.

Acquel pushed his shoulders back. "I know and trust him. He's a good fighter and a good teacher."

Poule grinned at the praise and inspected his feet.

Cortese stepped forward, champing at the bit. "Surely you can't consider leaving us in a goddamned monastery for garrison duty?"

"The Duke has given me complete discretion to do as I wish," said Strykar, keeping his eyes fixed upon Acquel. "And I haven't yet decided. As for your request for arms, that I can meet. I have two wagonloads with me outside the walls as we speak."

Acquel bowed low. "Strykar, I am most grateful."

"Tell me. That amulet of yours. Does the Saint still guide you?"

Acquel touched his chest. And then he lied. "The amulet guides me still."

Strykar nodded. "So much change in the world and in so short a time. I often wonder what we've done to deserve it." He paused. "I will consider the remainder of what you ask. Come down to the encampment tomorrow and we will talk further. Bring a few of your most promising recruits."

Cortese folded his arms in a sulk but kept silent. Strykar placed his hand on the hilt of his sword. "I think that is all we have to discuss, for the moment." As the double oak doors creaked open and Acquel ushered them into the entrance hall of the monastery, they were met by two liveried 'Templars' as the members of the Order now called each other.

Poule leaned close to Acquel and whispered. "Very pretty tabards, brother monk. Sun and sword. Very good that."

Acquel smiled. "Brothers, escort the officers back to their camp."

Strykar slowed a pace and turned back to face Acquel. He gently laid a hand upon the monk's wide sleeve. His words were softly spoken and heavy with regret. "I do not know if I can forgive you, Brother Acquel. But I will try."

Three

Travellers say that memories of Palestro will linger in your mind like the smell of old fish in your nostrils. Captain Nicolo Danamis, admiral to the king and born and raised in the ancient port of Palestro, never subscribed to that cynical a view. He stood on the long quarterdeck of his caravel, the *Vendetta*, his heart swelling as the long and low warship entered the walled harbour of the city. Cartmen stopped and waved from the quay as the ship glided past, a gang of ragged boys ran full tilt from one side of the docks to the other to catch the ship where it would moor. Fishwives mending nets stood to watch his progress, their calloused hands shielding their eyes. Even old Edolis, his father's captain-of-the-forecastle on the *Royal Grace* when he was just a boy, sat on his customary bench outside the chandlery saluting with his crutch held high.

Danamis had just completed his second voyage to the free city of Ivrea in as many months, his hold now ballasted by the new marvel of the age: guns of cast orichalcum. It was these that had, eight months gone by, allowed him to defeat the mutineers that had taken Palestro from his control. Harder than any other metal known to the world, orichalcum guns could throw iron balls faster and farther than any hoop-bound, cast-iron cannon that fired stone shot. And it was he who had forged the alliance with Ivrea, the only place that held the secret of their making. It had made his fleet the most powerful in the kingdom of Valdur overnight.

The vessel eased its way to the east quay under tow by rowers, all canvas furled, his ship's master barking out commands as they neared. Seamen heaved out the thick cable to those waiting on the dock. Danamis's eyes scanned the terraces of the city, each one rising up steeply behind the other. It was late in the afternoon, the sun reflecting its orange glow off the whitewashed stone houses. Palestro was built into a hillside, its ramshackle wooden houses clinging precariously up to the summit. The high plateau above held his palazzo and those of the wealthier sort of Palestro. All was ringed by a great stone wall, a gate at north, east and west. The joy of completing the voyage halfway around Valdur and back was tempered by what he knew awaited him: his father. Lord Valerian Danamis, a pirate turned mercenary who then turned ally and friend to King Sempronius, had returned from the dead eight months ago even as Danamis had defeated his enemies. It was Nicolo who had ruled as High Steward and Admiral after his father had not returned from a voyage to the *Mare Meridies*, gone for six years and assumed lost at sea. Valerian Danamis was a ghost he was still coming to terms with.

"Thinking about your reunion?" It was Gregorvero, the master, who had climbed the stairs to the quarterdeck, now that the ship was made fast.

"Which one?" replied Danamis, shaking his head forlornly.

"I know the one you prefer, my friend." Gregorvero reached his side and stood with his arms on the railing. "You will see her soon enough I am sure. But give your father good tidings of the voyage and the guns first."

"I thought after all these years he would have changed. Seeing the places and things he has seen. Being away from Valdur for so goddamn long." He turned to the portly sun-scarred seaman and smiled. "But, after all that, he's still a bastard."

"Aye, but he let you remain the king's admiral. He could have taken that back too."

"He has other things on his mind these days. Fighting Southlanders and Torinians isn't high on his list of priorities. I hope that the merfolk village fares well since we've been away. Lord Valerian is not a great believer in its fortunes. Truth be told, it hasn't been an easy alliance of late, him and me." The colony was just another excuse he had given his father to lambast him on his return from death. Danamis had allowed the merfolk of Valdur to create a village next to Palestro, the first in centuries after their flight to unknown sanctuary off the coast. He had done this in return for a great deal of treasure— and more active help in defeating the mutineers. But centuries of animosity between men and mer cannot be forgotten in a day—or months. Relations were delicate. All depended upon the mermaid Citala, daughter of the merfolk king. That too was a point of contention with his father. All of Palestro suspected—and many knew for certain—that Nicolo and the merfolk king's daughter were lovers.

"All the more reason to visit then, eh?" Gregorvero winked at his captain. "Now, what are your instructions for offloading the guns? The warehouse or the towers?"

"Into the west tower and under guard. I doubt that Duke Ursino would try a raid into this harbour. He's painfully aware of our new firepower, as the holes in his ships attest. He'd dearly like to have a few of these wondrous sakers for himself."

Gregorvero nodded. "And I hope that the Ivreans take seriously your warning about an attack upon them. There are many princes that would have such guns at their disposal."

Danamis clapped the ship's master upon the shoulder as he turned to make for the stairs down to the main deck. "The Ivreans are no fools. Their council has assured me that the militia will be doubled, even if they have to press some of their miners." As he descended, he raised his right arm in a mock flourish. "And so, off to bend my knee to father. If you need me, send word to the palazzo."

PALAZZO DANAMIS, RECENTLY renovated since the depravations of the mutineers and still smelling of pine, paint and linseed oil, lay behind tall stone walls in the upper town. Ransacked in the search for the Danamis treasure, the once glorious manor had been brought low: silver and tapestries stolen, windows smashed, walls knocked in, beds shat upon and the fireplaces used as piss-pots. But they had not found any treasure. Danamis dismounted at the open gates, a liveried retainer taking his reins. He knew where his father would be, in the great study on the first floor, denuded of most of its books, scrolls and charts. He paused and looked up at the yellow sandstone edifice, its magnificent oak door scarred by billhooks but still standing solid. Inside, the palazzo had been lavished with attention over the winter, Lord Valerian spending a thousand ducats on replacing what was stolen or destroyed. Expense hadn't been an issue: he had made his unexpected return with a cargo hold fair stuffed with raw gold and gemstones from lands beyond the *Mare Meridies*. The haul Nicolo had made, trading his intoxicating myrra leaf for sunken treasure salvaged by mermen, paled in comparison. Most of that was gone now anyway, in payment to the Ivreans for the guns that saved his skin and to Maresto for ships and men.

He climbed the great wide marble stairs leading to the upper storey of the palazzo, already dreading what news his father might have in store. He'd been away for a fortnight. That was long enough for anything to happen and time enough for his father to plan some new venture that would undoubtedly commit him as well. A retainer hurried ahead to announce him, his shoes slapping on the black and white tiles.

Nicolo entered the chamber to find his father standing at the huge table that sat in the centre, mullioned windows bathing the study in warm sunlight. He was bent over a freshly pressed paper chart, calipers in hand, carefully rotating them to measure a distance. He did not turn to greet his son but his gruff voice barked out.

"How did you fare then? A goodly success I hope."

Valerian Danamis was as tall as his son but his shoulder-length mane and short beard had turned snow-white since Nicolo had bid his father farewell six years ago. Nicolo approached the table and moved to the opposite side. "It was, my lord. Ten more guns for the fleet."

Valerian Danamis grunted. "Very good. And the alliance? It still holds? The council likes you well enough but what of the new High Steward there?"

"The alliance is secure. The Council of Decurions and the High Steward are in complete agreement. Our alliance is their best insurance against encroachment by Milvorna or Torinia. They know that full well."

Valerian chuckled. "Don't presuppose to know the heart of anyone. And none are more fickle than those who rule." He set down the calipers and looked intently at his son. "I would have thought you had learned that lesson last summer. The city in mutiny, three valuable ships burnt to cinders and my loyal castellan killed defending this house."

Nicolo felt the child within him recoil. He raised his chin. "I didn't appoint the treacherous sack-of-shit commander who led the rebellion. You did, father."

Valerian did not blink. "Six years is a long time. Time for any man's soul to change and blacken with envy and greed. Giacomo Tetch changed on *your* watch, not mine."

Nicolo could feel his cheeks flush. He leaned over the table and pretended to scan the large map spread out before him. "I reckon his heart was always black, father. Just better concealed when you were last in Palestro."

Valerian picked up the calipers and resumed his measurements. "Well, my son, it is past arguing the point now. I merely raise the issue again to impress the lessons upon you. I am more concerned about the mer colony you have seen fit to plant on my doorstep."

"A decision we have discussed at *length*, sir, these past few months." Nicolo pressed the edge of the blackwood table, his fingernails turning red. "It was the price of regaining Palestro and the fleet. And with the new holy commandments announced by the Temple, the colony is in keeping with the spirit of reconciliation. Saint Elded tells us so. Why shouldn't they live among us now?"

"Yet they don't want to buy myrra anymore."

"And you have been told the reason that Citala forbids it here."

"Yes, you have told me." Lord Valerian twiddled his calipers while he moved to pick up his stylus and dip it into an inkpot. "And your dalliance with her is a complicating factor in these affairs."

"You have no idea what we have shared together. She saved my life. "

"Well, my lad, others appear to be trying to follow your fine example. Some of your men have tried to procure mermaids of their own, luring them out of their camp with promises of love and fortune. We are likely to have a goodly crop of bawling half-breeds come the end of the year."

Nicolo had already foreseen this himself. "They are free to choose who they wish to be with are they not?"

"Not if it leads to vice. *You* should be more concerned with finding a count's daughter to marry and start producing some sons. If you take a cannon shot or a Naresis sword in your gut in the next few months, where does that leave our house? And don't tell me you're contemplating taking the mermaid to be your wife."

Nicolo bit his lip. "Let us speak of other things, father."

Valerian grunted as he continued tracing the outline of an island upon the map he was drafting. He tapped at the chart with his forefinger. "If you had only seen *this* island, my boy! Populated by one race only, the Blemmyae. They have no heads but instead the organs of the senses—eyes, ears, nose, mouth—all lie in their chests." He shook his head. "To look upon them takes a strong stomach—and they are quick to anger as well. It is a shame the one we captured died on the voyage home and we had to throw him overboard."

"It will be a rousing tale in your manuscript I am sure, father. But I would hear news of Palestro and of the war with Torinia."

Valerian raised his head, eyes flashing. "Do you think I will let my knowledge be forgotten? This map will be the only one of its kind in Valdur! Piero Polo may be the discoverer of the east but I am the discoverer of the west! And by Elded's holy beard I swear Palestro will be sending another expedition to the *Mare Meridies* before another year goes by."

Nicolo stood back and folded his arms across his chest. "As you wish, my lord. That is your prerogative. But we have other concerns at the moment that require your attention. How we administer the merfolk outside the gates for one."

"Impudent little—" Valerian tossed the calipers onto the map.

"I can answer that, if I may, Admiral Danamis."

Another had entered the chamber. The merman moved towards them, his blue silk-like robe shimmering as it reflected the sunlight.

Valerian turned. "Ah, Necalli. Yes, you explain things to the lad before he gives me a spasm."

Nicolo gave a curt bow to the merman. This mer was not of Valdur, he had come back with a handful of his kind from the distant islands of the far western seas. Valerian had found these merfolk inhabiting a vast kingdom, Atlcali, a place of far greater culture and sophistication than that of the merfolk of Valdur—and perhaps far more ancient. With Valerian's return, this mer had eased himself into the role of a trusted but informal advisor, a position vacant since the death of Escalus, the castellan of House Danamis, killed during the late mutiny. He had acquired the Valdurian tongue rapidly, aided by the months spent on the voyage, though his men seemed to have had less success in speaking it. He had been the captain of his vessel, a commander in his own right, before it was lost with most hands.

To Nicolo, Necalli looked the same as the Valdurian mer, perhaps somewhat shorter of stature but with the same hairless head, bluish purple complexion, thin lips, small nose and ears and large eyes. But his cynicism and craftiness rivalled any human's.

"They are as children," continued the merman, "and I fear your experiment will come to naught. They live in poverty, cannot build, and have no skills other than weaving and fishing. What do you expect to come of this? A flourishing trade?"

"I expect peace and amity to come of it, Necalli. Citala and her people have stood by me when I most needed allies," Nicolo said. "This was her wish and the wish of those who join her in the village here."

Necalli blinked rapidly, a habit most mer had. "In your absence, some of them have found this leaf called myrra. And you know full well the effect that has on them."

friend of ours. He and his folk think themselves better than we. He looks like mer but he does not act like one."

"I don't trust him either. But my father does. And there could have been a lot more of them had their own ship not foundered on the voyage here. But, is there truth to what he tells?"

"Somehow, some of the seamen from the ships found some myrra. They have traded it for coin delved in the harbour by a few mer boys. Some of your seamen would trade it for our she-mer too."

"I will not permit that. And I will seek out who is supplying the leaf."

She shook her head. "Elded be thanked there is not much thus far and only a few mermen have sought it. But I fear more could fall back into the myrra if the men persist. And... I am beginning to worry that perhaps too much time has passed since we last lived upon these shores."

Nicolo leaned back. "What do you mean?"

Her long webbed fingers gently closed about his arm. "Our peoples have grown apart over the centuries. The gap is so large I fear my people will never understand your world now."

"Citala, it is early days yet. Give it time. This is what you wanted—the agreement that was made."

"There is more. A mer chariot arrived a week gone by— from Nod's Rock. The messenger told me my father is asking for another shipment of myrra from you. We did both agree... to gain your freedom... but it will kill me, Danamis, to fulfil that promise."

Nicolo touched his forehead to hers. "Perhaps... perhaps we could give him a small amount. Like weaning an infant. I have Strykar's last bundle stored away. After that I'm not even sure I can obtain more. At least not quickly—not with the border war."

"He will be expecting more. Much more." She released him and moved outside, her silken kirtle dragging along the rush-strewn floor. Nicolo frowned and followed.

"I know my father well," she said. "If he does not get what he wants he is likely to come here to demand it—in force."

Nicolo spoke quietly. "That, Citala, he must not do."

"I know. That is why I must again convince him to forego the leaf. It is slowly killing us." She turned away and looked down to the beach where the stockade palings were pulled away so that the mer could enter the sea. "I have been filled with disquiet these past weeks. I keep sensing something— something out *there* in the sea. Something watching—a presence. Neither good nor ill, just there."

Nicolo put a hand on her arm. "It is worry, that's all. It will pass." Citala looked at him and returned a weak smile. "Perhaps that is so."

Nicolo looked about the settlement. A group of children fought over a broken human doll one of them had found. Two mermaids, clothed against their nature in muslin, dragged the broken remnants of a blood-stained fishmonger's table into the village to make some poor use of it. Where before he had seen simple tranquillity, he now saw the beginnings of discontentment and squalor. A people cut off from their roots, eking out an existence on the edge of a great and unruly city filled with seamen, thieves, and merchants, good and bad. He remembered Necalli's words. *They are as children*. And he began to see what the real danger to the merfolk was. Not myrra. Palestro.

Four

SHE THREADED HER way down the narrow passageways of the lower city, her plain woollen cloak and hood, obscuring her identity. She carried a canvas-wrapped bundle clasped to her bosom. Lucinda della Rovera, of late a lay canoness of the Abbey of Saint Dionei and now a guest of Duke Ursino, knew well the alleys and streets of Torinia. Although she came from the far reaches of the duchy, daughter of a northern baron, in her youth she had made several trips with her father to the great city. She and her sister had explored the various markets each specializing in a single commodity whether meat, fish, spice, cloth or ironmongery. Their favourite had always been the little street market that sold books and manuscripts, its wooden stalls crammed closely together in the shadow of the modest red brick temple dedicated to Saint Giacomo. Now, after many years, it was there that she was headed again.

It was only just past the hour of prime, the sun still low in the sky. Booksellers were busy laying out their wares or tying their awnings securely against the breeze that blew down the cobbled street. Lucinda pushed past the merchants, handcart men and street sweepers and entered the little square that fronted the temple. She cast a quick look behind her and walked past the colonnaded marble portico and down an alleyway leading towards the south doorway. Standing there was a black-robed priest, his arms wrapped around himself. He fidgeted and rocked slightly, clearly uncomfortable. He saw the woman nearing him and he straightened up, arms dropping in anticipation. Lucinda stepped up into the doorway and he folded his long wide sleeve about her shoulders and ushered her inside.

His voice was almost scolding. "I thought you would not come. Or that you had run into trouble."

Lucinda threw back her hood and smiled at the priest. "How could you doubt me, *signor*? My faith is strong." Her long hair was dressed high and covered by a cream linen kerchief. Her simple dress gave her the look of a maidservant but her voice said otherwise. The priest had no idea who she was, highborn or low, but he knew the fire of the new revelations burned fiercely in her and his eyes fell expectantly to the bundle she held.

"You have them! Elded be praised you have been safely delivered. May I take them?"

They were standing in a small entryway of carved stone, the studded wooden door still ajar slightly to help let in the light. Lucinda watched his eyes and hands move to take the bundle, an excited child about to receive a present. She moistened her lips and held out the string-wrapped parcel.

"I have obtained ten copies, newly printed at Livorna, *signor*. As I promised."

The priest, middle-aged and balding, grinned in appreciation as his hand pulled out a palm-sized brown leather-bound volume. "Brave child. You serve the One Faith well."

Lucinda smiled and the priest found it difficult to take his gaze from the deep blue vibrancy of her eyes. "They are slim works," she said quietly, "but they contain the Ten Laws and some of Elded's epistles to man and mer, as were so long suppressed. Give them one each to the congregations where they meet."

"Oh my child, have no fear on that account. You have taken great risks here in Torinia since the revelations were declared heretical by the Duke. He has already imprisoned many who will not recant. I will see that all of the congregations receive them."

She reached out and grasped his arm tightly. "The Word must be spread further—and the Truth of Elded's teaching with it. Far and wide across Torinia."

He nodded. "I will give my life for the One Faith if need be."

Lucinda released her hold and smiled. "I know you will, *signor*." She pulled up her hood again and turned away.

"Be safe!" called the priest after her. "The Duke's reach is long and he has many ears."

Lucinda's long, fine fingers pulled aside her hood as she replied. "I know exactly how long his reach is, *signor*. Have no fear." And then she was gone.

LUCINDA RETURNED TO the palace by way of the servants' arch on the west side of the sprawling crenelated pile of ugly red stone. The brainless but well-meaning handmaidens given to her by Duke Ursino were still abed when she had reached her apartments, no doubt aided by the draught she had administered the previous evening. And after tongue-lashing them for oversleeping, she set them to work upon the clothes she was to wear that evening in the Great Hall, making sure that the golden lace and pearls on the gown were just as she wished. Lucinda herself kept to her bedchamber, running through her mind the myriad of stratagems that jostled for priority. To see a full invasion of Maresto was her goal, but Duke Ursino was a cautious prince and would not be goaded into an unwise campaign. She had seeded his duchy with the heresy but still the Duke procrastinated in crushing it fully by striking at Kodoris and invading the Ara. The fracturing of the One Faith did not dismay her in the least; she hated all of it. The sooner it shattered into competing sects the sooner the old religion could rise anew. Her honeyed entreaties to the Duke had continued, yet as far as she could tell, Ursino had only partially unleashed his mercenaries in the north, subject to tight rein.

There were other pressing worries that ran through her mind as she sat embroidering a Valdurian griffon, warm sunlight streaming through the tracery of an arched window. Her visitations by the spirit of the Redeemer, Berithas, had become fewer, his whispers softer, half-imagined. It was as if the spirit had abandoned her and she prayed to the trinity of the old ones—Andras, Belial and Beleth—that their favour would not be withdrawn. He who had guided her, who had helped her renew the Tree of Life, who had given her the power to bend the minds of men; he had become a wisp of the night. So too, she sensed, the second sight taken from her dying sister did not shine so brightly in her as it once had. But Berithas had told her to take it—to *kill* to take it—and she had done so. Now, as she sat alone, pulling needle and thread, she was confused. The more she dwelt upon these thoughts the more it became clear that she would have to become bolder in her deeds. Bold enough to convince Ursino to make war. Bold enough to make him love her. Bold enough to bring Berithas back to her.

*   *   *

THE KNIGHT LEANED in with an aside directed to his comrade. "I still think he makes too much with his merriment for one so recently widowed. I mean, it's not seemly."

"Agreed, Messere Lazaro," replied the other. "Four months is not long enough for mourning in Valdur, I'll give you that. But look at the incentive he's got to forget the past. Can you blame him?"

They watched as the Duke of Torinia, expertly guided the Lady della Rovera two steps left and then two to the right in the *bassadanza,* his graceful movements perfectly in time with the tabor, the shrill yet melodious sound of shawms large and small filling the Great Hall with music from the gallery above. Forty courtiers of Torinia looked on as the Duke danced with his fancy, the men among them wishing it was their honour and not his.

"And what about *her*, Messere Claudio? Was not her sister murdered at Livorna only a few months ago?"

Lazaro winked to his companion as he adjusted his unwieldy and slightly out of fashion *chaperon*. "Perhaps they are comforting each other in their grief." The two men stood by a long table laid with platters of sweet delicacies, fowl, fruit and silver ewers of red wine. The Duke, without pausing, gestured to another couple to join the dance so to make a four. He was tall, with a bronzed face, all angles from his squared chin to his high cheekbones and dark eyes, deeply set in a prominent brow; a look more striking than handsome to most. His near shoulder-length hair was black streaked with grey about his temples, swept back over his ears and contained under a wide velvet cap. Its ornamentation of pearls and golden stars shook as he moved and gave strange animation to his slow deliberate steps.

Claudio smirked. "Have a care, Lazaro. It wasn't three years ago that he sent you on your arse at the tilt. Daresay, he would do it again if you give him half a chance."

Lazaro chuckled despite the dig. "I was lucky I got up again with the speed I flew off that horse. But I doubt he will have time for sport this summer. Has he asked for your service yet?"

"No, but I stand ready with thirty men-at-arms should he ask. And I do think he will ask. Very soon."

"Agreed. He'll need more than a company or two of his mercenaries if he plans on invading Maresto. The Blue Boar are formidable soldiers but an easy mark like Persarola is no Maresto or Palestro."

Claudio nodded and raised a goblet to his lips. "Somewhat tougher nuts to crack to be sure. And sieges are so boring and expensive. Better to take them on the open field. The Duke will lure them out. Of that I am certain."

The music came to an end and the dancers gave reverence to one another. Lucinda's smile shone brilliantly and the courtiers next to Ursino saw his own bloom in response to the Lady della Rovera. He still held her hand raised high as they looked at each other. The Duke turned and guided her across the floor as they slowly promenaded, the guests parting to make way. Above them, the musicians, after a false note and the sound of a crumhorn clattering to the floor, resumed. The music drifted down again to echo across the great hall.

Lucinda turned to the Duke, her eyes wide. "My lord, I would take some air on the balcony with you. I find it grows close in here."

The Duke nodded and they continued their progress to the far end of the hall where a large open arch led to a heavy stone balustrade facing out over the inner courtyard of the palazzo. The sun was nearly set and the sky in the east a deep purple. The night air still held a chill, a faint reminder of the winter past.

Lucinda sighed as they stepped out. "Such a beautiful revel on a lovely Spring eve. Why is my heart so heavy?"

Ursino placed his hand over hers and gave her a quizzical look. "Why so, my dear lady? Have I not afforded you every comfort since your flight from the heretics?"

"You have, my lord, and more. But as a canoness of the faith, the spread of the *Decimali* heresy wounds me. The One Faith is riven. The wound is deep."

"Not in Torinia. You know I have outlawed the *Decimali* catechism—at your urging. I've stuffed the prison full of priests who will not disavow it."

"It is the rest of the kingdom I fear for. For the holy places at Livorna. Even the king appears to have embraced the heresy or at least tolerates it." She turned to face him, her hand gliding up the skin-tight sleeve of his green satin doublet. "It is Duke Alonso—that spider in Maresto—who stirs the pot at Livorna. I have seen this. He and the High Priest are thick as thieves. That meddlesome monk too. The one who claims visions from Saint Elded."

Ursino snorted. "Maresto has plagued me for years. Those trumped-up pirates in Palestro too. They hit my shipping so I hit them back in the north. The Blue Boar is doing its good work there with the Sable Company to follow shortly. Maresto will soon see sense."

"But it is Livorna that needs liberation, is it not my lord?"

Ursino's face suddenly changed from an expression of gentle amusement to a harder cast, his eyes fixing Lucinda. "In time, dear lady, in time."

"But if you attack Livorna, surely Maresto will come out to challenge you in open battle. You will defeat them."

"A campaign must be planned—carefully. It is not—"

"But if the heresy spreads unchecked it will be even harder to stamp out—even here in Torinia. You are a true champion of the Faith. The sooner you engage the enemy the sooner the One Faith can be healed. With Maresto vanquished the heretics of Livorna will have no sanctuary."

The last traces of a smile left the Duke's face. "And who has appointed you my counsellor, Lady della Rovera? Do you suppose to know my intent? My heart? I bestow my affection upon you and you prattle about politics?"

She could feel his back stiffen and she withdrew her hand. "I am sorry I have given offence, your Grace..."

"Perhaps I have been too forward in my attentions to you, my lady. Fate has kindly rid me of one trying woman and I would not find myself saddled with another of similar nature."

Lucinda felt a chill move through her. For the first time he was questioning her and her motives. If his affections waned, then what? Almost without thinking, and in near panic, she pushed into his mind. Their eyes were locked, her probing intent like invisible fingers caressing his distrustful soul. She carried thoughts of love, of lust, to his heart. Gentle prodding, pushing on the open door that lay deeper down inside him. Behind them, the music rose higher, a peasant dance now upon the floor, the courtiers laughing as they whirled in a circle. The Duke was motionless, his face frozen as he stared into Lucinda's eyes. Slowly, a faint smile reappeared on his lips. He blinked and dropped his chin slightly, as if he had forgotten what he was about to say.

He reached for her hand. "We must not have words, dear lady. I care too much for you to ever wish a wall of even the thinnest gauze to come between us. Let us re-join the fete and the guests!"

Lucinda exhaled in relief. "Good my lord, that would please me well and truly!" And the Duke lifted her hand and pressed it to his lips.

AT MIDNIGHT HE came to her. Not the Duke, whom she had thought might knock on her chamber door, but the One whom she worried had abandoned her. As she stood by her bed in her chemise, combing out her hair, the familiar tingling began. Its source was the pink wound below her collarbone, what some might take to be a healed burn or even a brand. But it was more, a dark secret that no one knew but her. Those that had shared in the knowledge of her mark—her parents, her sister, even her last paramour—were all now dead. She felt the wound part, a soft sucking sound, and then the voice came. It rose up to her ear a hissing, urgent whisper, but this was echoed deep inside her head as well, a stronger musical voice she recognized well.

Daughter. You have laboured well these past weeks. I have been here, with you, seeing you.

Lucinda closed her eyes and let the voice of Berithas wash over her. To her, and the few remaining followers of the old ways, he was the Redeemer. To those of the Temple Majoris and the One Faith, he was the Deceiver. Unmasked and cast down by Saint Elded nearly a thousand years before.

You will bend the Duke to your will. To the will of my masters. And this man's earthly armies will further divide the people of Valdur until they see the Tree is their only salvation. I must set you a new task...

Lucinda nodded. "Tell me what needs must, Berithas," she whispered. "Tell me and it shall be done." The blood thrummed in her head, her ears. The voice filled her mind.

I will send you two servants of Andras who will do your bidding. You will send them to Livorna. There they must take the reliquary of Ursula. The hand of silver. That which lies in the treasury of the Ara.

"Why, my master? What use will their powerless relics hold for such as you?"

You shall deprive them of one power they yet possess. Hope.

Her chin lifted, eyes still closed, and a thin smile appeared on her perfect red lips.

"How do I gain entry? Surely the treasury room is locked and guarded."

Seek out the new Magister of the Ara. He holds the keys. Do with him what you will. The servants of Andras will be as your eyes and ears.

"And what of the monk? The one who is shielded. Shall we destroy him now?"

There was a sound in her head like the tinkling of a fountain. For a few seconds the voice was silent.

Strike him down, my daughter. Do not let him stop you in this task. His purpose is nearly served out now.

"When will the messengers of Andras come to me?"

Be ready at this hour on the morrow. Here, in this place.

Lucinda opened her eyes and watched the moon through the great arched window. Berithas had sent her a vision, a glimpse of what would visit her a day hence. She smiled.

Mark me, daughter. This is but the first task I set you. There will be another to follow. Something is about to happen. Something that will hasten our return to this world.

Staring into the middle distance, her eyes widened as another vision filled her mind. Her lips moved and silently she mouthed: "The crown... the *crown*."

Five

Bartolo Poule pushed his palms into his eyes, his fingers digging into the fringe of his wild mop of greasy hair. "By the sacred merkin of Dionei! No, no, *no*!"

A young monk stood before him, rather gormless and discomforted in breastplate, gorget and gambeson, a sword held drooping at this side. His head hung low as the lieutenant poured his scorn on him. Another young Templar stood next to him, also looking sheepish and embarrassed by their lacklustre performance.

Poule growled in exasperation and picked up his mug of watered-down wine from the trestle table. He threw it back into his mouth, wishing it was stronger stuff. "You are supposed to keep your eyes *open* when you strike your opponent! What are you afraid of for godsake? Do you think having your eyes shut will stop him from lopping your head off?"

Acquel stood off to one side, watching the proceedings and feeling more dejected than usual. Coronel Strykar had agreed to his request for training more than a week before but not all of his recruits seemed up to the profession of a soldier monk. Although many had met his call to join the new order, it appeared that the right temperament was lacking in many, some of whom were probably better off pushing a quill than swinging a sword. He too had joined in the training this morning, sweating in his padded gambeson and breast and backplate. And when he donned his chain mail hauberk, greaves and barbute helm it was all he could do to raise his arming sword and round shield. Fighting in full armour had to be practised long before the battlefield was reached, Poule had lectured, for one could never adjust to the added weight unless one became accustomed to it. He had assured the monks that eventually it would be a second skin to them—one they would be grateful for. But practice in merely a gambeson was simply not good enough.

There were fifty of the brothers assembled out on the wide plateau that lay in the shadow of the Temple Majoris, the only area with enough space for martial training on the Ara. Each day Poule took the brethren out in groups, monks and lay brothers alike, teaching basic footwork, how to hold and roll a shield up and down to fend a blow and how to deliver a blow from a hanging guard. Six oak pells had been driven into the ground for the men to learn how to strike high and low, channelling might to their shots by twisting their hip and thigh as the blow was landed. The din of steel on wood echoed across the Ara like the sound of a forest being cleared as the monks lay into their targets, arms aching. Acquel winced and hitched a hand into his gorget to clear a snag on his gambeson. He tried to console himself as it had been only a few days since training began. They would get better surely. But when would the enemy be at the gates of Livorna was the question that gnawed at him. Would they be ready in time?

Poule set his mug back down and stood away from the trestle, hands on hips. He glanced over to Acquel and then turned again to his pupils, waving them off. "Alright, go hit the pells. And keep those eyes open when you swing! Pretend it's some baby-eating Torinian intent on gutting you."

Acquel hefted his sword and ran a gloved hand along its blade. It was, said Poule, a good weapon though nothing special, one of hundreds knocked out for the militia in the armouries of Maresto. But it was well-forged and would do good service for someone who learned how to wield it. Even his untrained eye told him that this weapon had most likely seen battle. Ground-down nicks gave the sword an undulating edge, the price of sparring at practice or of a hard-fought fight to the death he could not say. Already he was wondering if he would yet draw blood with it now that it was in his charge. He lay it on the table, near the disordered sheaves of paper that was the latest roster of the Order. Poule flapped his unbuttoned doublet to cool himself after his rant.

"Remind me, Brother Acquel. What is your total strength as of this week?"

"Four hundred and thirty two. A hundred and thirty six are from the old Temple guard."

Poule nodded. "Well, those I can tell straight off. It is the others I'm worried about."

"They all believed enough to take the oath to fight," replied Acquel. "I would give them the chance to learn the craft. I can't give up yet. Not when I know what lies ahead."

"You I am not worried about. You can swing a sword already from what I have seen in the past few days. Most of these old guardsmen you've signed on are lazy but they'll do." Poule put a hand on Acquel's shoulder. "I understand what you are trying to do here, to defend the monastery, but, as an old soldier I have to be honest with you, holy man. A lot of these lads will never be soldiers."

Acquel wiped away a bead of sweat that had dripped into his eye. "If the Saivonians did it at Astilona then I can do it here. That holy order was respected in the last great war."

Poule smiled. "And it has been done but once. But if you think you can get lightning to strike twice then who am I to complain. We will keep trying. But a word of advice to you, Captain-General. You would be better served by three-hundred competent swordsmen than four or five hundred poor ones. If some of your monks can't fight we can still use them to help arm the others. Look after the armour, mend, tend to supplies."

Acquel looked out over the field. Some of the brethren indeed looked hopeless, struggling to heft their weapons or raise their shields for more than a minute without tiring. Others, though, seemed to have some spark, a keenness of spirit that kept them swinging, attacking and defending, their faces fixed in concentration and intent. Perhaps Poule was right. Maybe not all were up to the task. But he knew that most of them were. They would sweat and they would bruise but they would learn the skills—as he would alongside them. He had made a vow to the Saint himself that he would see his new Order rise, even if it was destined forever to be small. But he would never submit to the enemy without a fight. A fight he knew was coming, one driven by the greed of Torinia and the evil of the old gods and their earthly servants. And one he believed a godly punishment for the forsaking of Elded's teachings by the misguided zealots who had hidden and perverted the truth.

"And what does Strykar think of our efforts, then?" he asked as he lifted his sword again.

Poule shrugged. "He has given you your arms as you have asked. And he's let me remain here to beat your brethren into some form of army. But I reckon he thinks it's a fool's errand." Poule reached for his mug and took another long swig. "Maybe we can prove him wrong. At any rate, I'll give you a band of holy men that will put your old Temple guard rabble to shame. It may just not be as big as you wanted."

"What about my request for a contingent of the Black Rose? Has he confided in you?"

Poule looked up at the sound of horses entering the inner gate near the north side of the Temple. "Well, you can ask him that yourself. Here he is with the captain."

Acquel groaned inwardly. He had not wanted Strykar to see his brethren this soon, awkward and green as they were. The two horsemen slowed their mounts to a walk and dismounted as they reached him. Strykar gestured for one of the nearby monks to take and hold the reins.

"Brother Acquel, the Captain-General! How goes it? Is valiant Poule proving his worth as you hoped?" Strykar pulled off his riding gloves and approached the trestle. He ran his finger over the roster of men, his hooded eyes running over names he could not possibly recognise.

"Lieutenant Poule has just begun his work with the Order. It will bear good fruit, in time."

Strykar didn't reply but scanned the field in front of him, watching the comical sparring of some, the cautious but inept attempts at technique by others. One of the monks was desperately yanking at the grip of his sword with both hands, having buried it deeply in a pell.

"Yes, I can see that from here. I suspect the fruit will be a long time ripening on the vine though."

Captain Cortese grinned. "And perhaps a bitter harvest."

Acquel bore it as well as he could. "No one knows better than me what a long road it will be, Coronel. But every journey begins with the first step as is often said. We will make good progress."

Strykar nodded. "That you may. You have surprised me before. I have come to tell you that I am heading south again on the morrow. To see the Count of Malvolio and the Duke."

Acquel cradled his blade in his arms. "And what will you counsel them?"

"The towns on the eastern border must be garrisoned. Beginning with Palio and Istriana. They are already fortified and putting in troops there may discourage the Torinians from making more mischief. Any march on Livorna would by necessity take the road that runs past both of them."

Acquel quickly saw what was coming next. "Then you will leave me no men of the Company to guard the Ara?"

Strykar fixed him with a stern gaze. "No. I'll not divide my force. If the Torinian armies strike in any great numbers in the coming weeks then I will need every one of my men. And Livorna is not the frontier despite what you may think."

Acquel watched Poule raise his eyebrows and shuffle his now empty mug on the table.

"I see," said Acquel, hiding his disappointment. "When will you depart?"

"First thing in the morning. I will advise the Duke to send the entire Company of the Black Rose back to the north—the cavalry and all the men-at-arms they can scrounge to send up here. Preferably under the command of Malvolio himself, the better to keep his overfed knights on their toes. We should be able to muster some two-thousand lances."

"And Lieutenant Poule?"

Strykar nodded. "Poule can remain and work with your brothers. I suppose I owe you that much. I cannot tell you how long it will be but I expect to be back in less than a month." The mercenary pulled on his gloves and gestured for the horses. He then turned again to Acquel. "Brother Acquel, I do wish your enterprise well. It is a bold one. But if war is coming—and I believe it is—your efforts will be but a drop in the ocean, however well-meaning. You should not lose sight of that."

Acquel gave a curt bow. "I thank you for giving me the service of your officer. I would ask that you take a letter from me to the Duke thanking him for the gift of the armour and weapons. I will have one of the brethren take it to your camp tonight."

"I will see that he gets it, Brother Acquel." He took up his own reins as Captain Cortese mounted his horse. "Poule— keep your nose clean!"

The lieutenant pressed his thumb to his brow and nodded. "Rest assured of that, my Coronel!"

Acquel stood by Strykar's horse and patted its neck. He looked up at the man who had saved his skin a year ago but who now probably blamed himself for having done it. "This war that is coming. It is about more than just a contest between two dukes. It is about saving the kingdom from falling into a terrible darkness, one as once was generations ago. You yourself saw a tree of death. In Ivrea. Torinia is but a pawn to the forces that serve that tree and the others that have taken its place."

Strykar cinched up on his reins and Acquel stepped back. "That is what the coming war is about," he continued. "It is what Timandra fought and died for. She saw what was happening around us. I for one will not let her death be in vain."

The commander of the Black Rose looked up and out over the field, avoiding his eye. "Don't presume we are not in agreement, Brother Acquel. But my road is a different one than yours. That said, I will consider your words—and your warning. You can be certain I will do honour by my cousin's memory. Fare you well."

He spurred his horse and rode out, Captain Cortese at his side. Acquel watched him go, saddened for a friendship that unequal and doomed as it may have been, was now as good as lost.

As HIS DREAMS went, it was not a bad one. Acquel was with Timandra again, the sutler's widow, sitting cross-legged in the trampled long grass outside her wagon. Laughing without care and discoursing upon the fate of dukes and kings. Suddenly he felt himself pulled up and out of the dream and wide awake. He pushed himself up in this bed, wondering what time it was. The darkness outside his window told him the moon had set a while ago. It was either near to or just passed the hour of Vigil where whiterobes and greyrobes would be attending at the Temple, giving silent prayer. But something was wrong. In the blackness of his chamber his mind's eye flashed disjointed images: the corridors, a colourful tiled floor smeared with blood, and then a fleeting glimpse of a golden casket surrounded by holy relics in their various receptacles of silver and gold. It was but a moment upon him, a rush of scenes, then it was gone. Yet he had glimpsed the treasury of the Ara, he was sure of it.

Just as soon as the vision passed he felt the amulet grow hot upon his chest. He grasped it and it seemed to be pulsing. Warning him as it had done nearly a year gone by. For months he had sometimes hoped, sometimes dreaded, the guiding hand of Elded would come to him.

He climbed out of his bed and groped to strike his flint to fire the rush-light on the little table. He hurriedly dressed by the dim glow, pulling his robes on over his head followed by his tabard. He slipped on his shoes and lastly, reaching to a hook on the wall, wrapped his sword belt about his waist, fumbling with the double-tongued buckle.

Outside in the long corridor, a lone torch sputtered, shedding imperfect light across the stone floor. At the far end, where the colonnaded loggia began, he saw one of his Templars on watch. He was leaning against the wall, hands resting on his sword pommel and head down. Acquel walked briskly down the corridor, his shoes slapping loudly. The young monk snapped upright at the sound, turning to recognize the face of his Captain-General.

"Brother, come with me!" said Acquel quietly as he reached him, grasping his elbow. "I think something is amiss at the Temple."

Too stunned to utter a word, the youth nodded and followed as they marched down the long covered loggia to the staircase leading to the ground and cloisters. The breeze that blew across them was chilly, the cloudless sky a canopy of stars. Acquel could feel the amulet burning his chest. Without stopping, he reached inside his robes and shirt and pulled it out, letting it drop on the outside, bouncing upon the golden sun embroidered on the tabard. They descended the great staircase, pace quickening.

"Brother Acquel!" called the Templar in a raised whisper. "Where are we going? What is wrong? Are we under attack? Thieves?"

Acquel's heart was racing as if he had already seen what threatening them. "We're going to the Temple, to the treasury chamber!" he called out, breaking into a slow trot, hand on his sword grip. They were now making their way along the flagstone walkway that led to the eastern entry of the Temple, its huge tympanum now visible by the lit torches along the wall of the monastery. They were alone and Acquel reasoned that it was too soon for Vigil, for no other brethren were to be seen. He reached the great oaken door—ajar— and drew his arming sword. A quick glance from Acquel and the young Templar did the same, the lad's eyes now grown huge with alarm.

They entered, cautiously, moving along the soaring stone columns by the light of a brazier left burning after the prayers at Nocturne. The treasury lay at the south end of the Temple Majoris on the east side, entry gained through a large doorway which in turn led to a second door of oak and iron. There was silence in the cavernous Temple except for the jangle of their swordbelts. Acquel held up his hand as they reached the doorway. Like the eastern portal, this too was open—wide open. Acquel moved cautiously forward and his foot shot out from under him. He had slipped. Reaching down he wiped his fingers on the tiles. In the dim orange glow he could see it was blood, sticky on his fingers.

The youth had a hand on Acquel's shoulder. "Sweet Lord, is that—"

Acquel raised his hand again to silence him. He was listening. Laboured breathing could be heard in the antechamber beyond but the darkness was absolute. Acquel turned to the brother behind him. "Quickly, grab a torch and light it from the brazier."

Acquel's fingers reached for the amulet. He flinched; it was near to scalding. The intruders had either come and gone or were yet within. But someone was hurt and still inside. The young Templar returned and handed over the burning willow bundle to Acquel.

"What is your name, brother?" asked Acquel.

The young blackrobe swallowed hard, his voice sticking in his throat. "I am Carlo."

"Carlo, stay by me. But not behind. Move off to the side as we enter. Do you remember your low guard—the plough?"

Carlo nodded. They moved inside at a crouch, ready to defend. Acquel held his sword low, the torch in his left hand. As they entered the antechamber, the light of the brand spilled across the floor and walls. Carlo gasped. Upon the floor, off to one side, lay a monk, sprawled, his robe slashed and covered in blood. Acquel could see the gore smeared like a trail from the entry way to where the poor brother now lay, but he was not dead.

Acquel handed the torch back to Carlo and bent down. It was the new Magister of the Temple Majoris, Brother Lodi. The wound across his stomach looked grave. He was babbling, eyes wide in terror, darting madly from one side to another and then toward the treasury. As he recognised Acquel, he tried to lift a hand.

"Lie easy, brother! We shall find help."

Behind him, he heard the sound of claws scrabbling, like a dog running across a stone floor, followed half an instant later by Carlo's painful cry suddenly cut short. It all happened in the time it took Acquel to wheel around. Shadows rippled across the chamber as the torch flew to the ground and Acquel had a fleeting glimpse of a large figure driving into Carlo and sending him flying back out into the temple. Acquel gripped his sword with both hands, poised to spring to Carlo's aid, but another sound stopped him. Something else emerged from the portal to the treasury, a creature of the likes he had never seen in his life. His heart flew into his mouth and he began backing away. It was partly human—a woman from the waist up, a muscular torso of grey with pendulous, swaying breasts. From the waist below it was a bird-like thing, feathered thighs ending in huge yellow talons, three enormous claws on each foot. Behind it he could see its wings, now folded, rising up over its back and head. They brushed the archway as it stepped into the room, talons clacking on the hard tiles.

Acquel could not take his eyes from its face. Lucinda della Rovera. At least it had appropriated her features, but the womanly beauty had been twisted, elongated such that it was not human anymore. Its hair was a wild riot of blonde locks that shook as it made its almost hesitant progress into the chamber. Somehow, it had not seen him. It was clutching something in one of its long thin black-nailed hands: a shining gold and silver reliquary garishly embellished in dozens of tiny gemstones that sparkled in the torchlight. The object looked almost a living thing: a splayed metallic hand and forearm. Acquel recognised it instantly—the hand of Saint Ursula, one of the most sacred artefacts of the Ara. The creature's head jerked and swivelled, searching. He froze as it stared directly at him. The Magister groaned behind him and the thing's attention immediately snapped to the wounded monk.

Acquel only then became aware of Carlo's desperate cries without, as he battled this thing's companion. If he could put himself between the creature and the entry way, he could bar its passage. His feet slid across the tiled floor as he moved, still half in a crouch, sword held out before him. The creature turned its attention back to him, its eyes moving. It hissed in frustration. Somehow, he realized, it could not actually see him. It could hear him and no doubt smell him, but he was invisible to it. Yet it was clear to him that these creatures could see. They had pounced upon the Magister and Carlo and were here to search out and steal the sacred relics of the Ara—their vision was keen enough. It was the Saint who was shielding him and him alone.

Carlo cried out again and he heard the sharp metallic ring of sword on stone. No time to hesitate, he thought. *Elded save me.* His thrust, unsteady as he was, ran along the outside of the thing's left arm, piercing its bicep. It howled, and kicked. Acquel found himself lifted off his feet and landing hard on his backside, his hip in agony, robe ripped wide. He scrambled to rise, his blade scoring the tiles as he staggered up, arms moving into an unsteady guard. The creature clutched the reliquary to its chest with one hand and lashed out with the other blindly. Acquel watched as it tilted its head listening for his movements. He raised his sword in preparation for a downward cutting blow. He would have to make this blow with all his strength, driving the sword deeply into the thing's neck and shoulder. And then it spoke. In her voice.

"Where are you, holy man? Beloved of Elded." The voice was husky, unnatural, half-human and half the rasp of an animal.

He raised his arms higher—and his scabbard and belt shifted on his waist, the sound barely perceptible, but she heard it. As he brought the sword down, the creature had leapt to one side and the blade cleaved air. She had moved, closer to the Magister's prostate form. Acquel turned and ran through the door back out into the side aisle of the Temple, while behind him he could hear the terrible sound of those huge talons scratching the floor as she pursued. Carlo cried out again and Acquel ran towards the sound. The soldier monk was swinging wildly at his foe as its great wings beat frantically, holding it aloft. It dropped down, trying to rake him but somehow the youth was keeping it at bay, his garments ripped and blood-stained from the slashes the creature had already inflicted.

Acquel joined him and thrust with his sword as the thing dropped down again, screeching. He saw its face but a moment, reflected in the light of the single brazier. It too, had the likeness of Lucinda della Rovera. The creature kicked his blade away but a thrust from Carlo bit, slicing into its thigh. A thin, high-pitched howl echoed across the holy place as it beat its black-feathered wings faster, rising out of harm's way. The other creature had now also taken to the air, landing on the cornice of one of the massive stone columns of the Temple. Acquel could see the reliquary glinting in its arms. He grabbed Carlo by the shoulder. "Are you hurt?"

The monk held up his hand, his fingers covered in his own blood. His face appeared unbelieving of what was happening. "I am cut, Brother Acquel," he said quietly. He leaned against the column and slowly slid down onto the flagstones.

"Brother Carlo!" Acquel raised his sword again to defend them both. The creature above them flew to the other pillar and joined its companion. Acquel watched them, dark shadows high above. His heart was beating hard, and he could feel the blood pulsing through his hands as he gripped his sword. The beating of huge wings again sounded and Acquel tensed, ready to receive their attack. He then heard a scream from the east portal. He dashed to where he had entered, sword ready. There in the porchway, stood a greyrobe, his lantern held limply at his side. He saw Acquel and dropped the lantern to the floor.

"Harpies," he said breathlessly. "They were *harpies*."

SOME TWO HUNDRED miles away, in the ducal palazzo of Torinia, Lucinda della Rovera crouched naked on all fours in her locked bedchamber. She raised her head and closed her eyes for a few seconds before opening them again. She breathed deeply and brought her legs up, pulling herself into a seated position on the bare but ornately tiled floor. She was angry, frustrated, and confused. She had felt the blackrobe's presence but her gift could not perceive him, unlike the other monks there. It had been like trying to swat a quickly moving shadow, or seize a will o' the wisp. Despite seeing through the eyes of Andras's servants it was as if she were peering through some dense black gauze. She rubbed at her left arm, still painful though it had not a mark on it. *Bastard*, she thought. That was not the first time such a thing had happened where Brother Acquel was concerned, but she had not thought it would be an issue this time. Yet it had been. She hoped that Berithas would not withdraw favour for her failure to kill the blackrobe. But the reliquary was on its way to her even now, carried through the moonless night high over the plains of Torinia. And the Ara would be needing yet another Magister she was sure. But once the One Faith discovered what had been lost to them then that would seem like a small problem indeed.

Six

He held her in his embrace, tightly, but with no fear it would crush her. She returned it, giving equal strength, her long arms grasping his back, pulling him in towards her. Their mouths touched again. Danamis was surprised that his passion for Citala had not diminished in the past few months. Perhaps it was all the voyaging, the weeks away to the northern shore of the kingdom that fired his desire for her. But deep down, he knew it was more, and that he knew also presented somewhat of a problem.

Citala's lips pulled away from his, but her deep violet eyes lingered upon his face. "I must leave now, Nicolo. I have been here for more than a day and a night."

He understood she needed the sea. The memory of last summer's adventure in Ivrea and her near death there had never left him. She would always need the water. Without it her body would wither like a flower left in an empty vase. He nodded, trying to smile. Somewhere across the cavernous palazzo halls, alive with newly painted frescoes, his father was bellowing at a servant.

"I do not think he likes my visits here," she said.

"Not altogether sure he appreciates my presence either. Despite my attempts to placate him."

"It is because I do not please him."

Danamis squeezed her. "I care not what he thinks, and he usually thinks of only himself. He wants me to marry so he may make a match that serves his plans. He has suggested the daughter of the High Steward of Ivrea."

She raised her eyes a little and looked askance. "Noble blood? Is mine not noble enough?"

"It is the guns of Ivrea and the wealth of that city that he hopes to secure. That and an elevation of our family to the aristocracy of Valdur. A mer princess cannot confer that in his eyes."

"But the treasure we dredge from the depths for you is considered most acceptable." She gently pushed away from him, holding his hands in hers. "And it was your father who began that arrangement. Now I must try and heal the wound that myrra has inflicted on my people."

Danamis lowered his head. "You are leaving still, to see your father then?"

"I am."

"Citala, take a small bundle of myrra at least. If it is like strong drink is with us you must do this thing slowly. I will gladly give it to you from the stash locked in the storehouse."

"I have considered that. A small amount would only serve as a prize to be fought over."

Danamis squeezed her hands. "Think again, my love. You yourself told me that Atalapah would come here with his warriors if they run out of the leaf. What do you think will happen then? If they attack the city they will be destroyed. Our bowmen will see to that. You gave your people the choice of returning to Valdur without myrra or staying at Nod's Rock to remain as they were. They have made that choice. Give them the myrra."

She blinked, that slow way the merfolk did, that which he had once thought a sign of confusion, he now knew to be one of irritation. "You think I should give them the means to poison themselves?"

"If it is their choice. Save those who wish to be saved. Many mermen have already joined the colony. Others yet could."

She suddenly backed away as if a sound had disturbed her. But Nicolo heard nothing.

"Citala?"

It was only then he glimpsed Necalli ascending the great marble staircase to the hall of apartments where they were standing. He glided towards them and gave a court bow, the voluminous sleeves of his elegant silk-like robes swallowing his hands fully.

"Captain Danamis, I give you greetings of the day!" He looked at Citala, his wide thin-lipped mouth breaking into a smile. He spoke to her in the mer tongue and bowed once again. Citala returned the bow—barely—and answered him. He blinked once and replied, but in Valdurian.

"Until I am ready to return. Or when Lord Valerian wishes me to or when he decides to voyage once again. I still have much to learn about Valdur. I was once an explorer even as is Lord Valerian."

Citala looked aside to Danamis. "I asked him how long he planned to remain in our kingdom."

Danamis laughed, uncomfortably, knowing Citala's distrust of the South Sea merman.

"I might ask you the same question, Citala," said Necalli. "The fact that we speak the same tongue—after a fashion at least—tells me that your people were once among mine. Perhaps, sometime, we could affect a return to your homeland."

Citala stood straight, shoulders thrust back. Nicolo gently reached for her forearm, warning her. But she smiled broadly at the merman. "We might weigh the possibility that the origins are the other way around."

Necalli chuckled. "If you could see my kingdom you would be in no doubt of the truth of my words, and the mistakenness of yours."

Citala voice dropped lower. "Then we must leave it there until one may prove it to the other."

Necalli bowed again. "I go to see Lord Valerian now. He needs more details for his chart of the southern sea." He turned and walked down the hall, his long-fingers twitching from out his sleeves like curious snails.

"*Hahthlxi*," she mumbled. Danamis didn't ask for the translation. "I will take you to Nod's Rock," he said, grasping her hand again. "You can bring myrra with you, or not. As you choose. But you should see your father again. And your people."

"Perhaps you should go back to pirating again as you once told me. Leave the rule of Palestro to your father. There is a world out there and many ships for the taking. We could be together upon the seas with no one to tell us what is not possible."

Danamis kissed her cheek. "My Citala, that is a dream and a wish most inviting."

She stroked his fine, close-cropped beard. "Then make it come true."

THE CITY OF Maresto was bursting with soldiery: half-trained city militiamen armed with spears and bills; cynical mercenaries of three separate companies (as happy to scrap with each other as much as the enemy), and Duke Alonso's own haughty men-at-arms, each one trailing a legion of grooms and attendants. Dressed in his black-etched breastplate worn over his fine woollen robes and wearing a pair of tall riding boots, Coronel Strykar was following his commander, Malvolio, and his guard of honour across the piazza that led to the main entrance of the ducal palace. He looked up at the edifice he knew so well. The russet sandstone walls, crenelated and dagged, always reminded him of some giant beast's jawbone, jagged teeth raking the sky. Had he been born on the right side of the blanket, it might also now be his home. Even so, he knew the place well now that his half-brother had come to depend upon him. Or was it merely blood loyalty, bastard though he was?

He had been held at arm's length his whole life. Gifts arrived for him every year, a pony when he was ten. But such things only made him the butt of jealousy by others even if his benefactor was only guessed at. He first met Alonso when he was twelve. Brought to the *palazzo* once a month by his unseen father to amuse the elder half-sibling lord, to play, to learn about the court. Yet he was ever the outsider. The three-year difference in age was a chasm, and Strykar bore it as best he could: all the jibes, the insults, the condescending *curiosity* about who—or what—he really was. Alonso knew he was blood, even if not quite one of them. In the years to follow, the distance between them remained, an invisible wall. Maintained even when all the court knew who he was. He was an oddity, a relation without purpose. His father's last fall from a wild destrier brought Alonso to the dukedom and Strykar closer to Alonso. His life in the Black Rose had hastened that change too. As Strykar's reputation had grown, so had the wall begun to crumble. A Valdur duke needs loyal swords to keep a coronet on his brow and shared blood is better than none.

The great oak gates swung inward to admit them, a dour party of ducal guardsmen ushering the Count and Strykar deeper into the cavernous palace and up a staircase that was wide enough to encompass twenty men—in armour.

Malvolio turned to Strykar. "What will he decide, I wonder? You seem to have his ear more in the last several months. More than I do, it seems."

"I will tell him what I told you," replied Strykar over the din of the clanking guardsmen, climbing the stairs. "What I've seen up north. A bloody shambles of the border towns. Torinia need to be taught a lesson—and soon. Ursino has had an easy run of things until now."

Duke Alonso was waiting for them in his private conference chamber, fire blazing in the hearth. Three heavy grotesque armchairs, sparkling with gold leaf, was all the furniture within. The soldiers of the Black Rose bowed low and Alonso beckoned them to be seated. Two guardsmen took up station near the door, their polearms thudding as they stood to attention. Strykar immediately noticed that there were no advisors with the Duke, not even Lord Renaldo, his most trusted. That could bode well or ill in equal measure.

Alonso leaned back after they had seated themselves. "Well, what news has the Black Rose of the north?" Malvolio, a short, wide man built like a bull mastiff cleared his dagger and scabbard which had become stuck in the arm of the chair and bowed his head again.

"Your Grace, Coronel Strykar has briefed me upon his return and I would leave it to him to tell what he has seen on his travels."

Alonso looked over to his half-brother. "Coronel?"

Strykar cleared his throat. "It's a sad tale to tell, your Grace. Persarola sacked. Most every village within ten miles of it raided as well. Most folk have fled to Palio and Istriana."

"Who led the invasion?"

"The standard of the Company of the Blue Boar was sighted by many. This was no raid by rogue cohorts. It was organized—well-planned. It was intended to terrify the inhabitants. To drive them away to remake the border. I saw a pedlar who had come through Persarola not one week ago. He told me that new folk were coming from the east to take over the surrounding villages and hamlets."

Alonso looked up to the rafters in what Strykar thought was a silent cry to heaven. Or a curse. "We no sooner put an end to the mutiny in Palestro and the threat to the wool fleet and now we are rewarded with this."

"There is more, your Grace. I have seen the High Steward of Livorna and also the new Captain-General of the Temple Majoris—Brother Acquel."

Alonso's brow creased. "Yes. That awkward monk who accompanied you and Lord Danamis last summer. Still can't fathom how he merits his command despite his visions from the saints."

"He is convinced that Torinia is bent on invading Livorna and overthrowing the High Priest and the Nine. If that is true, it would cut Maresto off from that city and give Ursino control over the north. Ursino has already declared the new commandments heresy. His excuse to clean out Livorna to his liking." He reached to his belt and produced a folded piece of parchment. "Brother Acquel has given me this letter for you."

Alonso plucked it from Strykar's fingers but did not open it. "Well, I have given him what he asked for—arms and armour to support his new military order. What else could he want?"

"He asked for troops from me. He fears his own force will not make ready in time to defend Livorna and the Ara."

"Will it?"

"I wouldn't bet on it."

Alonso waved the packet in his hand. "All, no doubt, explained in here."

Strykar nodded. "He is greatly worried. And he fears a wider war what with the faith now splitting at the seams. And he may have cause, I must admit."

"I'm not bothered by these new commandments or the rediscovered texts. I like the merfolk. Why Ursino has to shout and bluster about heresy I don't understand. He's a trumped-up, self-important fool."

"Aye, well the monks say that Ursino's heart is hardened by a canoness who is a witch in disguise. She guides his hand. Maybe even through the dark arts."

"You expect me to believe that?"

Strykar shrugged. "Your Grace, there are strange reports across the north. And what I witnessed in Ivrea last summer made hard men weep. This woman, whether witch or not, is bending Ursino's mind and it is to make war upon us."

The Duke turned to Malvolio. "What forces do we face over the border?"

"Our spies say there are three full companies in the north and another two billeted outside Torinia itself. He also can call upon his own men-at-arms. Combined force in the north perhaps seven or eight thousand men. In the south, six thousand—maybe more."

Strykar leaned forward. "Your Grace, let us take the fight to them. Over the border."

The Duke of Maresto arched an eyebrow at his half-brother. "To match their numbers in the north we would risk leaving the city exposed. What makes you think they won't try striking us here in the south after they have lured you into the provinces?"

"Because they want to take the north from Maresto," replied the mercenary, irritation rising. "And we owe it to the folk there to save their women, their children and their homes. The insult of Persarola cannot be allowed to stand!"

Malvolio stood, harness jangling, and turned on Strykar. "Have a care, Coronel! You forget your place."

Strykar slumped back into the overstuffed chair. "My passions run ahead of me. I beg your forgiveness."

The Duke raised a hand and motioned for Malvolio to be seated. "I am used to his outbursts by now. But mark me,

Strykar, your passions will be your undoing. I know vendetta burns in you—for your family—but do not let it master you. Let the Blue Boar come to you."

"Is the blood debt not to be repaid? I have waited ten years to have Coronel Aretini's head on a pole. That is a long wait to see justice served for a murderous reiver like him."

"Your Grace speaks wisely, as always," said Malvolio, more than a hint of oiliness to his tone. "The last thing we need is to get bogged down in a siege in Torinia. We know they are preparing another thrust into the duchy, maybe further north towards Livorna. We can be ready to take them in the field in open battle."

Strykar's jaw clamped shut and he held his tongue. The Count's implication was clear. A few more villages and towns would have to be sacrificed to lure the Torinians deeper into Maresto in order for them to choose the most advantageous ground for battle. But Strykar had never believed in giving ground to an enemy. Nor would he start to do so.

"I will sanction any battle you can bring against the Torinian companies," said Alonso, "but use your best judgement in doing so. I cannot give you more than your own lances, spearmen, and *rondelieri*—plus those of the Company of the Scarlet Ring. Maresto city must be safeguarded so my men-at-arms will remain here."

Malvolio bowed his head in acknowledgement.

"And we must look to our allies," continued Alonso. "Now that the *old* pirate is back in Palestro, the younger Danamis should have plenty of time to strike against the Torinian fleet. That will keep Ursino occupied. His coffers must already be getting low with half his trade taken in the last few months. And we should pursue these orichalcum guns for our own army. Why should Danamis and the Ivreans be the only ones to benefit?"

"Why indeed," agreed Malvolio. Strykar said nothing but bridled at the man's arse-licking puffery. He wasn't sure just what arrangement Danamis had with the Ivreans but he was sure that his pirate friend would not be keen to sell any orichalcum guns—not even to an ally. He had seen first-hand how the cannon could turn a stout carrack into kindling in minutes.

"Shall you convene a battle council, your Grace? With the other commanders? Time is crucial and the season well under way. The roads are dry up north now."

"I have already given Lord Renaldo orders to do so. For the morrow. And Coronel, I would like you to go to Palestro before you take your column north again. Admiral Danamis is your friend. See if he will not part with some of his artillery for our sake." Strykar prevented his jaw from dropping by giving a nod. Was he supposed to negotiate a price on his own? And that was even assuming his old business partner and sometime friend would countenance parting with part of his valuable arsenal.

The door at the far side of the chamber opened and a round-shouldered Renaldo entered as if he had heard his name. Clutching a piece of paper, he scuttled over to the Duke's chair and bent to whisper in his ear. Strykar saw that the old man was as white as a ghost, his eyes fairly bulging with excitement—or concern. And as Renaldo whispered urgently, he watched Alonso's face fall, a veil of disbelief descending on it. Malvolio had noticed it too, throwing a concerned glance to him and shifting on his cushion. Slowly, the Duke reached for the paper that Renaldo's shaking hand was offering. Alonso's eyes squinted as he read. He lowered his arms and looked at the mercenaries before him.

Malvolio leaned forward. "Your Grace?"

At length, the Duke found his voice. "The king is dead. A few days ago."

Strykar sat upright and Malvolio began to stutter. "What? How did it happen? He was not ill."

The Duke's eyes went to the letter again. "He was bitten. By that damned cockatrice he kept as a pet. Bit his hand and he was dead after one night. I did not know they were... venomous." He trailed off as all the implications began to sink in.

"Sempronius dead. Saints preserve us," muttered Malvolio.

"Queen Cressida has declared herself regent. The prince is only ten."

Strykar remembered his meeting with the king in the last summer. A fool more interested in his gaming and sport than his kingdom. And he himself had given that damned cockatrice a sideways glance as it had skulked around the halls like some hungry dog, its beady blood-red eyes never blinking. But this news was badly timed indeed. And then he suddenly remembered the royal hunt where the cornered satyr gave his prophecy of coming war—a war that he said the king would not live to see.

"Your Grace. Does not Duke Ursino have some blood claim to the throne? Cousin to Sempronius?"

The Duke looked up, distractedly. "Yes, I believe he does. What are you suggesting? That he would challenge the succession to Prince Sarant?"

"Now would be the time to make his move."

"Unlikely when he is otherwise occupied with us," added Renaldo, annoyed at the mercenary's boldness.

Alonso shook his head firmly. "No. What would be his cause to make such a claim for the throne? Even if he is of the blood."

Strykar looked over to Malvolio, and then back to the Duke. "Bastardy... for a start."

Renaldo laughed explosively, before he remembered his place and bowed low to the Duke. "Forgiveness, your Grace. But that notion is nonsense."

"I know," replied Strykar, "that Nicolo Danamis was close to the queen before her marriage to Sempronius. The boy was born just nine months later. It *could* have been his. Few alive know any of this, and Danamis's romance was quickly quashed by the House of Guldi. But I would bet good money that Ursino has somehow found out as well. More to the point, the queen handed Danamis a sack of gold as big as a boar's head when we left Perusia last summer to fight the mutineers. Without the king's permission. She made quite a show of it."

Alonso shook his head. "Bastardy could never be proven."

"With respect, your Grace, it does not have to be. The suspicion will give him cause to challenge. Torinia sits on the edge of Perusia. The Queen's household has no more than two thousand soldiers, I warrant. He could lay a siege without breaking a sweat."

Malvolio continued the line of reason. "Then it would be civil war. Every duchy and the free cities taking sides."

The Duke arose and Strykar and Malvolio hurriedly followed suit. "Tell no one of this event. Nor a word about the whiff of bastardy either. We will have the bells rung and the announcement read tomorrow in the market squares. Just pray that Ursino's appetite for a wider war is not whetted. I must go and write to the queen. And Strykar..."

"Your Grace?"

"Get me those damned guns."

His HEAD STILL whirling, Strykar left the palazzo and after bidding his commander good fortune until the morrow, headed to the merchant's row and down the alley where the apothecaries carried on their trade. The sight of a lone soldier was not an unusual one here, for it was often the destination of lovelorn men looking for a potion, a powder for crab itch, or a cure for a surfeit of drink. But the Coronel of the Black Rose had an altogether different purpose in mind.

"Messere Strykar, sir!" cried the old apothecary, hurriedly wiping his hands on his leather apron. "Your arrival is most propitious!" He pulled the mercenary into the deeper recesses of his shop, the rafters a stinking collection of weeds, dried herbs, and dead birds, snakes and lizards, carefully preserved. "It's taken me longer than I expected but the results have surprised even me."

Strykar found himself among a tangle of copper pipes and vessels, long-necked glass jars, scales, and two dozen burning candles to illuminate the workspace. The apothecary raised a finger dramatically then reached over to his bench to retrieve a small dark blue glass flask. "The elixir is ready."

Strykar smiled. "This better not kill me."

"My lord, may the saints strike me down if that were so. I have tasted it myself and do pronounce it most... appealing." The little man held out the flask to Strykar. "It is as clear as the purest *acqua vitalis*. But the taste is altogether more challenging—and rewarding."

Strykar took the bottle and sniffed. It had virtually no scent whatsoever. But then again, myrra leaves didn't either. Although chewing pure myrra could knock down a horse, he had always suspected that *distilling* the leaves might afford something better. Now he would see if that was true. He raised the bottle to his lips and took a cautious sip. His tongue felt the bite straight away, and then a taste of burnt honeycake that lingered but a moment before fading into a warmth that enveloped his mouth. His felt a jolt, a brief exhilaration, as the warmth slid down his neck. He took a longer swig and felt the effect again. He lowered the bottle and broke into a grin.

The apothecary, who had the bulging eyes of a frog, beamed as he watched Strykar's reaction. "The first batch gave my apprentice a headache for two full days but I have remedied that with an efficacious addition of essence of birch bark. In after-effects, it is no worse than any tavern-brewed *acqua vitalis*. In my humble opinion, sir, it is the finest elixir I have known. A cure for fatigue and veritable courage in a bottle."

Strykar nodded, smacking his lips, his head slightly euphoric. He had given the apothecary a small sack of leaves but he still had a bundle with Danamis at Palestro for safekeeping should the merfolk decide to trade again. And he knew the hillsides where the myrra trees grew on the edge of the border with Saivona. He could get more—or perhaps send someone else to get them. "How many leaves do you need to make a full flask of this stuff?"

The apothecary scratched his cheek. "The leaf is remarkably strong in its properties. The yield is good. I would reckon a bushel to make twenty flagons, possibly more."

Strykar quickly did the sums. No one would need buy more than half a cup of it, sold in a little flask with a stopper.

"*Acqua miracula*, yes?"

Strykar smiled again. "*Acqua miracula* it shall be. Agreed."

"What do you propose to do with your elixir?"

"To do with it? Why you're going to brew it and we're going to sell it. War is coming, master apothecary. Everyone is going to need a strong drink."

Seven

AFTER THE NIGHT of terrors, a pall fell over the Ara with the coming of dawn. What had happened in the Temple Majoris could neither be wished or explained away. As news of the attack spread through the dormitory and refectory, a quiet sense of dread enveloped the monastery like an invisible fog drifting across the flagstones. Something otherworldly and evil had entered the sanctuary and done murder there among them. Acquel knew that the brotherhood was now looking to him. For both blame and deliverance. He had spent the remainder of the night with two other monks, tending to Brother Carlo's wounds. Acquel had Carlo carried back to his own chambers in the palace and had woken the blackrobe who administered the dispensary. He followed with a basket of unguents, wych elm bark, and *acqua vitalis*. Grim-faced, they washed the slashes on the young monk's torso, thankful that they were not deep wounds. Two long downward slashes from a claw had gone through his belly fat but no deeper, while another two had ripped across his ribcage cutting into the muscle wall. Carlo was near delirious with the shock of it all, babbling and raising his arms to ward off the flying things that still bedevilled his mind's eye.

The Magister was dead. Acquel, sword still in his shaking hand, had re-entered the treasury antechamber after the fight to find Lodi had bled out, the open eyes of his grey face staring at the ceiling in death. As Acquel had bent down to examine the old monk, the harsh torchlight revealed glistening loops of bowel protruding through the gaping wound in Lodi's belly. It was an image Acquel could not rid himself of even hours later. He told no one that the Hand was stolen. It was clear to him that this was the reason why the harpies had come. Brother Lodi held the keys to the treasury and that was why he was taken and killed. It was a message from Lady della Rovera: she could touch them at will and take what she wanted. But what use would she have for the most sacred relic of the One Faith?

He had sent one of the Templar guards to wake the High Priest soon after he had seen to the care of Carlo. Kodoris had arrived quickly, wearing a blackrobe habit he had hurriedly pulled on, feet sandal-shod. The brethren in attendance all bowed as he entered the chamber but Kodoris barely acknowledged them, his eyes settling on the wounded monk who lay moaning upon the bed.

"In the name of all the saints what has happened?"

"We were attacked, your Holiness." Acquel's voice was quiet.

Kodoris looked again to the heaving chest of the wounded monk, now salved and bandaged and then turned his gaze back to Acquel. "Come with me, Brother Acquelonius."

They went out into the corridor and Kodoris grabbed Acquel's arm. "Who did this thing?"

"The Magister is dead. Murdered in the treasury."

Kodoris started. "How is that possible?"

"Two fell creatures entered the Temple—flying things. They were as beasts of old. From the texts—harpies. I had a premonition, a vision of the treasury in my dreams. I awoke, and somehow... knew something was wrong. The amulet was burning upon me."

Kodoris shook his head, incredulous. "Creatures..."

"I found Brother Carlo on guard and we went to the Temple and found the Magister upon the floor and the treasury open. We were attacked by these things, talons like cockerels—tall as men... but, sweet God, they were female. It was Lucinda della Rovera—her face."

Kodoris lowered his head. "The Seeker turned sorceress. So she has declared war upon us."

"There is more." Acquel said. "These things stole the Hand of Ursula. Brother Lodi held the keys to the treasury and somehow she knew that. Once they had it they fled."

Kodoris seized Acquel's arm. "The Hand? That reliquary has forever been carried at the vanguard when Valdur goes to war. She meant to deprive us of it before the battle has even begun."

"I have told no one else."

Acquel watched the High Priest's lined face, his large brown eyes staring across the corridor, mind working.

"Good. No one need know—yet. Does Brother Carlo know of the theft?"

Acquel shook his head. "I am sure he did not see it, he was fighting another of the creatures. It was the one I faced that held the reliquary."

"Then we must look to the defence of the Ara next. Your Templars must be on guard—in strength—each night. If more of these things should return, then what?" Kodoris looked back to Acquel and he could see the look of desperation in his face. The leader of the One Faith, bereft of a plan to save them from what was coming. "We had better hope that steel is enough to stay them. Steel and prayer alone."

Acquel was not so sure. If the sorceress could summon such terrible creatures, what else could she do? "Will you address the brethren this morning? We can gather in the refectory."

"I will tell them that the One Faith is under attack by those who would bring back the Tree and blood sacrifice. That we must look to the defence of the Ara."

"And tell them that we have no magic of our own with which to fight them?"

Kodoris threw Acquel a look of icy defiance. "*You* are the chosen of the Lawgiver. Not I. And you are the Captain-General of your order. It is you who must open your heart to the voice of Elded. If he will speak."

Acquel felt queasy. What could they do? Poule had barely begun training those who knew nothing of fighting. He himself, hardly a competent soldier, armed with only a few vague visions of a saint long dead, an amulet that gave warning but not power. What could he accomplish? "You must find a new Magister," he said, trying not to sound hopeless. "A blackrobe the brethren can rally to."

Kodoris looked at him but said nothing. He tilted his head, a certain grimness overriding the worry that his face had worn earlier. "You, Brother Acquelonius, will be the new Magister. Captain General of the Templar order and Magister alike. It is the right thing in time of war. It is you who possesses the blessing of Saint Elded."

Acquel was shaking his head even as the words left Kodoris's lips. "I am too young. I know nothing of being a Magister."

"There is no other. It should have been you after me in the first place."

"Brother Lodi had the respect of all. I have only their fear. They do not know what I bring with me."

"I have killed to safeguard the One Faith. I have sacrificed the innocent," Kodoris hissed. "I am responsible for being cozened by that witch in Torinia. Bringing her here to the Ara to find *you*. I am tainted. Forever. But you are not."

"I am only a man."

Kodoris seized him by his robes and pushed him against the wall, Acquel's mouth fell open. "You, my brother, are all we have! Find your faith, damn you. Unlock the secrets that you bear in that cursed charm. Haven't you asked yourself *why* the Saint chose you?" He loosened his grip and relaxed, stepping back. His voice became quiet again. "See to Brother Carlo. I will see that Magister Lodi is prepared for burial." The High Priest turned and walked away.

Acquel ran his hand along his face, shaking. He was alone. Utterly alone.

THE CHOIR HAD sounded thin, voices constrained despite the soaring height of the nave of the Temple Majoris. There was more than sadness in the air at the funeral of Magister Lodi, there was uncertainty. Kodoris had given the eulogy and offered prayers. The brethren had joined in, praying not just for the soul of the murdered Magister but for their own as well. Acquel had stood at the side chapel, distracted, his eyes drawn to the columns above the treasury antechamber where he had battled the unspeakable creatures less than a week earlier. The brethren around him acknowledged his presence, his authority, but they did not offer companionship. To them, he was touched by Elded and, in turn, untouchable. He had become hardened. Kodoris's vehemence had woken him to responsibility, reminding him that it was he himself who had demanded the role he now held: Defender of the Ara. That day he had taken measures. Every night, Templar monks in breast and back plate and bearing polearms paced the long arcades of the Ara palace. Always in pairs, they walked the monastery and Temple grounds through every hour of darkness until they saw the disk of the sun spread its welcome red light at dawn.

Brother Carlo remembered little of the attack. Nor that the Hand had been stolen from them. Honey and ginger poultices had prevented rot from taking hold, which the brethren had feared would carry the young monk off within days.

How Lucinda della Rovera would next strike he did not know but he worked with Bartolo Poule each day to train those of the brotherhood that had volunteered their lives, oaths sworn, to defend the One Faith. He thought they were making progress: faster reflexes, longer endurance at sparring, the basics of competency with sword and shield. Poule's tirades were never-ending but the men had come to expect them; they offered encouragement in their own way. The day after Lodi's funeral, in the morning Kodoris had announced to the Council of the Nine that Acquel was to be the next Magister. Poule was at his work table in the training yard, watching the exercises with an occasional shake of his head and shouted curses. The sky was pure blue, the sun already beginning to bake the trammelled ground of the yard. At Acquel's approach, he turned and broke into a wide grin.

"Ah, holy man! Another promotion I hear. What next? High Priest?"

Acquel ignored him and slipped on his gambeson and began tying its points. "What is my next exercise, Lieutenant Poule?" he asked. "More longsword today or would you have me do shield work or learn pole-weapon?"

Poule crossed his arms. "What do you fancy, Magister? I think I should give you the choice."

"I want to learn the longsword. Until I get it right. Without thinking."

Poule nodded. "That is the way it should be. If one has to think about a guard or a blow then it's already too late and you're dead." He looked past Acquel, towards the stone archway that led to the yard and lifted his eyebrows. "What's this then?"

A group of around twenty young men were walking towards them, led by a white tabarded Templar. Acquel turned and saw that some were monks, the backs of their heads shorn, while others were not. The guardsman ushered them into the presence of Poule and explained they were recruits from afar who had heard of the new holy fighting order at the Temple and were eager to petition to join it.

Poule rubbed his stubbly chin as he ran his eyes over them. "What do you think, Magister? A good crop?"

Acquel looked at the faces before him. Some fair, some tanned, some untested, others with the look of seasoned tavern brawlers or even bandits that would as soon cut your throat as offer a greeting. "If they will take the oath of the Order than we will be glad of their service."

Poule placed his hands on his hips and his gravelly voice boomed out across the training yard. "Has your worthy guide explained to you what you are signing on for? Lots of fighting, my friends. But, I must be honest with you." Poule gave them all a forlorn look and shook his head. "Your days of wenching are over. Hope you enjoyed them. As for strong drink, it is only permitted when we give it to you." There were nods and a few murmurs. Poule let them die down. "Sweet Lord, you *are* all desperate shits aren't you? Very well then, line up over there and be prepared to sign the articles or make your mark and swear the oath."

They shuffled along, a quiet nervousness amongst them, and took up station where Poule indicated. The mercenary turned to Acquel. "You understand," he said, voice low, "that it's going to take many months to train this lot up like real *rondelieri*. Many months."

"We don't have many months," replied Acquel, finishing his lacing and reaching for his breast and back plate. "You knew that from the start."

Poule smiled slyly. "Yes, I knew what a tub of shit I was leaping into. I can't magick them into real soldiers. But I can make them proficient enough to give as good as they get. That I can promise you!"

Acquel somehow managed a smile in return. Poule's rough honesty gave him some solace and the mercenary now seemed like an old friend, maybe his only friend. "That is all I can ask of you, until Strykar takes you away."

Poule laughed and helped Acquel buckle his armour at the shoulder. "And on that day I ought to ask you to shave my head and put me in a blackrobe. Just to see the look on the Coronel's face!"

Poule slapped Acquel's shoulder. "Fetch your blade and I will test your guards." Behind them came raised voices and they turned to see one of the lay monks, a former red cloak of the disbanded Temple Guard who had signed on immediately into the new Order, shouting at a man who, having lagged behind, had only just now joined the group of recruits.

The former guardsman threw up his hands again and swore. "Look, I told you to bugger off, old man! Are you sun-addled or just mad? Go back to your own monastery."

Poule and Acquel reached them, a muttered curse on the former's lips. "What's all this then?"

The exasperated guardsman turned to Poule and jerked his thumb towards an old monk who stood proud and unbowed before them, a walking staff in his right hand. "This old fool says he's here to join the Templars. I've been trying to tell him to shove off since first this morning."

Acquel looked at the man. He had easily lived through sixty summers and winters and quite probably more. His hair was bone white, the tonsure at the back of his head showed a scarred scalp, the skin towards his nape collecting into yellowed folds. But his face, as lined and worn as it was, showed a ready defiance. His nose was more a rustic bump and as wide as a bull's. The eyes glinted with intelligence, not befuddlement, and Acquel sensed something in the man. Something of interest.

"Come now, brother monk," said Poule politely. "I'm sure your heart is stout but I think you're long past bearing arms. Perhaps the Magister here can find some other work for you... in the library. Or at least give you a decent meal." Scattered laughter rippled through the recruits.

The old monk leaned forward on his staff. He smiled at Poule. "If you think I am too old to bear arms then try me and see."

Poule stepped back. "I admire your spirit, brother monk, but I have work to do here this day. I have not the time to give an old man a beating."

The monk dipped his shoulder and let his satchel fall into his hand. He placed it on the trestle table and moved off to the side, closer to the pells. His hands choked-up on the staff, no longer using it as a support. "Try me."

Poule, smirking still, looked over to Acquel. Acquel was now intrigued and despite his urge to send the old man on his way, something held him back. "Go ahead, lieutenant, let him have a try."

The mercenary frowned, rubbed his nose and plodded back to Acquel. "Captain-General, sir. You want me to break a quarterstaff over this old fool?"

"I want to give him the chance to break a quarterstaff over you."

Poule snorted. "Very well. But you can take charge of him in the infirmary." He motioned for one of the Templars in the yard to toss him a staff. "Well then, brother monk," he said as he twirled the six-foot length of oak, "here's what you have waited half a century for." He stopped about a man's length before he reached the monk and brought up the weapon in both hands, held equidistant from one another. From what he had already been taught, Acquel knew it was rather a half-hearted and weak guard.

The old monk placed his left leg forward and moved his quarterstaff into a low guard, holding both hands towards the rear end, the length pointed straight at Poule. "I am at the ready," he said calmly as he waited to take the mercenary's advance.

There was now an excited babble among the men, and those who had been bashing the pells stopped and began to watch, confused at their commander's choice of opponent. Poule shook his head, annoyed that he would have to go ahead with the game. He stepped forward, made a feint with the left end and then swung with the right, overhand, aiming for the monk's shoulder. But as the blow fell, Poule found to his dismay that the monk was no longer there. The old man sidestepped while at the same time thrusting his staff fast through his forward hand, driving the pole into Poule's belly and doubling him up with a grunt. An instant later the monk had sidestepped again to the right, swung his staff around and hooked it behind Poule's right knee, yanking it and sending Poule onto his backside. As Poule hit the hard dust of the ground the monk's staff whirled again to end up touching the lieutenant's throat, poised to crush his windpipe with a simple jab.

There was silence in the yard. Someone coughed. Poule, still on his back, looked over to Acquel. "Fuck me, " he said. "He's the second monk to put me on my arse."

Acquel smiled, remembering how he and Poule had had a similar exchange one year before. He walked over to the old man as Poule, muttering obscenities, pulled himself up and dusted down his arming doublet. Despite his embarrassment, he was chuckling. "Well done, old man. Well done."

The monk turned to Acquel and bowed.

"What is your name?" asked Acquel.

"I am Brother Ugo... Ugo Volpe of Astilona."

"The monastery at the fortress of Astilona?"

The old monk nodded. "The same, Magister." And, as if reading Acquel's mind, he tamped his staff onto the ground and said, "I am of the last of the fighting brothers of Astilona."

Acquel moved closer. "And why have you come here to the Ara, Brother Ugo?"

"Because you need my help."

Acquel looked into the monk's dark green eyes and could see the answer for the question he was about to pose. "Who told you I needed your help?"

Ugo Volpe smiled mischievously and lifted an index finger up to the sky.

Eight

LUCINDA, IN THE quiet of her bedchamber, regarded the Hand of Ursula, exquisitely wrought but dulled by the ages: silver tarnished to black at the fingers, dirt and dust nestled into the engraved details of wrist, cuff and fingernails. Only the gemstones—emeralds, rubies, sapphires and opals—seemed yet to possess life, winking in the strong sunlight that filtered through her window. Most intriguing (and pathetic, she thought) was the small glass cut-out of now milky opaqueness that was embedded in the forearm of the reliquary. An ulna bone could be glimpsed, wedged within. The last earthly remains of that poor misguided woman now claimed a saint. Never had she dreamt that this object, almost a myth of her devout youth, would ever be in her hands. It was a disappointment. Now she saw it for what it was: a meaningless lump of metal from a deluded faith.

She recalled when the servants of Andras had returned to her, the night before last just on the cusp of sunrise. Their terrible beauty was apparent even in the darkness as they scrambled along the balcony bearing her their trophy from the Ara. As they crouched, silent, long arms resting on their feathered thighs, she watched as their faces seemed to melt into a featureless mask of marble—white eyes, lipless mouth and two oval holes for a nose. But she had seen the visage both creatures had worn earlier when they had arrived at midnight; it was her own face, or that of Lavinia, her sister. Poor dead Lavinia. Her heart was heavy at the thought of her sibling who had once stood firmly by her side and then had slipped into treachery, aiding the false pretenders of the Ara.

The Redeemer had told her to take her sister's gift, the gift of Farsight. Though she too possessed that talent, it was Lavinia who had the superior sight. When she had plunged the dagger into her sister's throat she felt it was right. With her sister's gift now hers, she could always have a part of Lavinia with her, a part unsullied. Even so, it had not worked out as Berithas had told her. She still could not see the blackrobe Acquel, no matter how much she put her mind to it. Nor were her visions as sustained or clear as they had been for her sister. Perhaps, she thought, this would come in time, but she had done what Berithas had asked. The reliquary was hers.

She turned it over in her hands. Such a pretty but ultimately powerless trinket. To think that some artisan had worked this silver long and hard, and painstakingly set the gems to decorate it in semblance of some regal sleeve. She looked at her own hands, long-fingered and delicate. Ursino had told her yesterday she was looking pale and unrested, spending too much time alone in her chamber with her thoughts. He had said today they would go riding and perhaps review his troops assembling north of the city. Sunlight would do her a world of good, he had said. Lucinda smiled to herself. She found she did not always need to leverage his will by using her gift upon him, as she did with others. He had already given his heart to her and all he needed was a gentle push to guide him when he grew recalcitrant. He was proud and did not take advice easily, but pride was also a weakness she could use.

A knock sounded at her door. She quickly thrust the reliquary under the mattress of the grotesquely carved four-poster blackwood bed and pulled the curtains upon it.

"My lady, the Duke is enquiring if you require anything before you set out later. A cloak perhaps?" The handmaiden kept her eyes low. Lucinda pursed her lips. The Duke had made gifts of his dead wife's wardrobe on a weekly basis. Lucinda almost regretted having finished off the woman. If she had stayed alive, sickly, then she herself might have enjoyed a new wardrobe of her own and a mistress's advantage: the presence of an unloved wife to keep the man keen. Still, better to have the path ahead clear so she could become the next *duchesa*.

"I have what is required. Please thank his Grace for his thoughtful consideration of me."

The woman curtsied. "Then I shall return to fetch you at midday, my lady. Unless you would take some air in the gardens beforehand."

Lucinda smiled sweetly even though the servant's eyes failed to meet hers. "No, that will not be necessary. I will stay in my chamber until the time. I have reading to attend to. My holy books."

She shut the heavy door and slid the iron bolt across, gently, and pressed her face against the planks. She did not love the Duke. A few years earlier she would have fallen for him like any young maiden of a noble house. He was handsome, powerful. But such feelings seemed to have weakened in her as her duty to her faith called more urgently. Love was a distant need. Even before the handmaiden had departed, she had felt the familiar tingling in her collarbone, a tickling caress, distracting her from her thoughts of Ursino. Her head grew light and she loosened the tie of her gown, tugging at her chemise underneath and exposing her shoulder. The wound was whispering.

My daughter. Heed me.

She moved across the chamber and stood at the window which overlooked the cypress grove and inner gardens of the palace.

"Speak to me, my Redeemer," she whispered. "What is your will?"

There was a soft moist sound as the mouth at her collarbone parted, followed by a strange genderless voice that carried no farther than her own ear.

I would show you the king of Valdur. Come with me.

Lucinda closed her eyes. Her head swam and she clutched at the stone sill to steady herself. She was in Perusia. She saw the harbour filled with ships, the sprawling red sandstone palace, the hills beyond. The scene swirled, she felt herself falling, and now she was in the palace itself, her view as if she was running through the corridors. Falling through a great door she found herself in a large hall, a high bier at its centre draped in black silk. At each corner stood an armoured guardsman, the pole of his glaive resting at his instep and held out at full arm's length. Several robed and jewelled courtiers stood by, leaning in to whisper into each other's ears. Lucinda could hear nothing.

A body lay upon the bier, arrayed in fine velvet robes of purple and crimson, a golden circlet upon its lifeless brow. It was Sempronius, king of Valdur, and the memory of her vision of a few nights ago—a spinning jewelled crown suspended in the ether—returned. This was Berithas's foretelling come true. The king was dead. She could see the queen, pale and stone-faced, her hand on the shoulder of a young boy. Somehow she knew this to be Prince Sarant, only child of the king and yet too young to assume the throne. The lad was red-faced, cheeks tear-stained as he stood close by his mother, Cressida. A handsome boy, perhaps nine years old, she thought, his hair jet black, the colour of a raven's wing. The vision hazed over and again she felt herself falling. Her knees gave slightly, she clutched hard at the windowsill, and then she opened her eyes.

His house has fallen, my daughter. A new house must arise.

The wound tingled, then the sensation sharpened, a prickling of intent like needles under her skin.

The Duke of Torinia must claim his right. That is your task.

Lucinda stared out at the gardens. "How is that to be when a crown prince lives?" she whispered.

Sempronius has no son of his blood. A cuckoo stands at the mother's side. A new king must come. One of your making. One who will lead Valdur to the old ways.

She swallowed. "Then I will be the instrument, my Redeemer. If you will guide me."

You shall be queen of Valdur, my daughter.

"What befell the king? Is this a foretelling or a shadow of what has passed?"

Sempronius trusted that which he did not control or understand. A creature of the ancient Wood, that which has a venom tooth and an eye of red. A thing of my influence and that of the Others whom I serve. A creature that has served our purpose.

"I will bring Ursino to your revelations, my Redeemer."

And I will give you command over my legions, gifted one.

Her head suddenly filled with a vivid picture of a battlefield and a mighty host arrayed for war. A host unlike any she had ever seen, one that would strike dread into the hearts of unbelievers. A host from an age long gone by.

THE SUN WAS high, its bright rays bathing the meadows filled with wildflowers that lay just north of the city walls. A large flock of golden sheep, the prize breed of the duchy, their wool a deep buttercup covered the fields as they grazed. The ducal party, thirty courtiers and an escort of one hundred men, made its progress over the wide, firmly packed road that led from Torinia and all the way to the border with Milvorna, some two hundred miles distant. Their destination was, however, already within sight: a sea of multi-coloured tents and banners that spread out on the plain before them. Lucinda rode at Ursino's side, her hair coiled tightly and topped with a veil of deep blue satin and a silver circlet. She wore (much to the chagrin of her maidservants) a plain kirtle split at front and back and joined-hose underneath that she might ride like any man in the saddle. It was never for her to ride like a noblewoman was expected, leg contorted over the horn of the saddle. Foolishness. The courtiers were polite enough not to stare for fear of angering the Duke who himself cared not a fig for her mannish equestrian style. Now and then he would turn to her, nodding and smiling. Drinking in her beauty.

He was dressed for the review: short padded gambeson over his dark green doublet and wearing hose and black riding boots. His breastplate—polished steel and gilded with the bull's head from the arms of Torinia—shone blindingly white in the brilliance of the afternoon sun. Upon his head he wore a felted bonnet of red, a great golden jewel at his brow. Bred for battle, his horse was garishly caparisoned in crimson harness, the scalloped reins in suede. As this fine mount stepped high, threatening to break into an excited trot, Ursino's sword bounced and swung at his thigh.

Behind them, rode the favoured knights of the duchy, among them Claudio and Lazaro. There was a certain laziness to the procession, born partly of the heat and partly because it was expected that they do their part as the Duke's retainers—or at least be seen to be doing it. The occasional harsh laugh rose up, a few hushed exclamations, but the chief sound was the clop of hooves as the party moved along the road. As they neared the encampment, the advance guard shot forward on their horses to announce the visit to the assembled great captains of the mercenary army. Their duty this day would be to publicly renew their oaths of allegiance to Ursino after which they would be handed a sack of gold and an emerald ring as reward. The party turned off the road and across a field that sloped gently upwards, a broad plain that stretched for more than a mile, one small stand of oak lying lonely at its centre. A dozen great hunting horns sounded their welcome and a drum tattoo began a steady thump.

Lucinda marvelled at the force on display. Some six thousand men stood, arranged like gaming tiles, erect and in perfect squares. Armoured and bearing spear or shield, glaive or halberd, they all stared straight ahead as the ducal procession rode in and reined in at the boldly striped open pavilion set for the ceremonies. As the swallow-tailed banners flapped in the rising wind, the fanfare continued, echoing across the field. At the entrance of the huge three-sided pavilion, stood the commanders of the free companies: Aretini of the Blue Boar, Michelotto of the White, Carraffo of the Sable and Perotti of the Golden Lance. Lucinda looked on them dispassionately. They were the most skilful of freebooters in the kingdom. Inured to violence, addicted to gold, they would be the hammer of Torinia. If they stayed loyal.

She watched as the Duke dismounted, arms held wide as his commanders paid homage, bowing low. A long table had been set for them all, groaning with platters full and silver wine ewers the size of wash tubs. Ursino's chief gentleman stood at his side, handing out the gold after each commander placed a clenched fist over his heart and recited his oath. Then the remainder of the Duke's party dismounted and joined the feast. He gestured for Lucinda to sit at his side while the mercenaries roared their encouragement to their men preparing for friendly combat in the lists. She gave him a coquettish tilt of her head and slowly lowered herself onto the bench beside him. A tournament between the companies began, the chosen men-at-arms fighting on foot with blunted blades. Even so, men were felled like trees then carried off to be prised out of their twisted steel shells.

Two more combatants entered the list and saluted each other: *rondelieri* bearing stout swords and round shields. One had the blue boar's head of Aretini's company, the other's shield was polished steel that glinted in the sun, sending out bright flashes across the onlookers; a soldier of the White Company. The boars' man wasted no time and raised his shield to his guard position and rushed forward, sword held far back over his shoulder. The other walked forward a few steps to meet the attack, his shield nonchalantly angled and held out in front. They met with a jangle of harness and the crash of shields. The first blow, a powerful *tondo* cut by the boars' man, sailed over the top rim of the other's steel buckler, slicing only air. The White Company man, a left-handed swordsman, aimed an equally forceful blow downwards at his opponent's sword side. The blow glanced off the bottom of the man's armoured knee and smashed his unarmoured shin. A howl of pain reverberated across the lists and he dropped, rolling in the trampled grass.

Aretini snatched an apple from the pewter bowl in front of him and hurled it at the apparent victor. It exploded on the man's shoulder armour and the fellow stood back, confused.

"Son of a whore!" yelled Aretini, stepping forward out of the pavilion. "Low blow! Goddamned cheating Whites! That shall not be counted!" It didn't matter. The soldier of the Blue Boar was already limping off the field, helmetless and assisted by his companions. Aretini hurled a second piece of fruit for good measure before swearing and sitting down again.

"My condolences, Coronel." It was the courtier Lazaro, a big grin on his face. "Such conduct is unbecoming in the lists—even for mercenaries."

Aretini looked down the table. "Eh? Oh, Messere Lazaro, where are your men today? Would have been rewarding to see a few of them getting their skulls cracked."

"Could not be helped. They are guarding the palace while your troops play games here. Someone must watch for the Palestrian raiders."

Aretini snorted and reached for a walnut which he cracked in his fist. "And what will your retainers do then? Bring out some wine so the pirates can quench their thirst?"

Lazaro smiled again and wagged his finger in a mock scold. "I am sure we will all be shoulder to shoulder soon. In the field against Maresto."

"Shoulder to shoulder, my arse. More like dozing and dicing in the baggage train for your lot."

Lazaro's smile went a shade thinner and he raised his goblet to his lips and took a sip.

"Rather be in Maresto now," mumbled the mercenary to himself. "Getting rich on spoils... than all this... frippery." And Livorna would be the biggest prize once northern Maresto was sorted, he thought to himself. A good scrap with the Black Rose was long overdue. He'd thought sure they would have come to blows a few weeks earlier but they had had a clean push through Persarola and the surrounding villages. Maybe Malvolio and his men had gone soft, drinking and wenching on the coast. He glanced over to Ursino who was mooning over his new lady. *That* was the real problem. Dithering. The weather was good and here they wasted time while the enemy gathered more forces to his banner and schemed new alliances. They had enough now to do the job. If Ursino would let the Blue Boar off the leash.

Looking to the far side of the roped-off lists, Lucinda smiled as she watched a few sergeants struggling to prevent a brawl among the two companies. The Duke leaned over, placed his hand over her wrist and spoke quietly into her ear, his moustache tickling her lobe. "Just as well they are using dulled weapons. Otherwise I'd have to recruit another whole army."

She covered his hand with her long fingers. "It is a mighty host, my lord. They frighten me—even at play!"

"Somehow I do not see you being frightened by much of anything." He gave her a tender look. "There is a strength that lies behind that beauty of yours. And that gives me strength too. We are soon to embark on campaign... I would have you join me."

She regarded him with a certain look of intrigued scepticism. "I thought you would prefer not to hear from me on martial matters. You made that most clear."

Ursino raised his eyebrows, recalling his admonishment to her at the revel. "Yes. I was perhaps hasty. Knowing you are a Seeker, I should perhaps have given you more credit for your cunning. I have seen that more in the past days when we talk. You have a confidence I find... alluring."

She laughed lightly. "You like that I ride like a man."

"I like that you seem to know the mind of man or woman. I have a handful of counsellors who barely know what day it is never mind what others are thinking—or plotting."

She locked her eyes onto his own and spoke in a whisper. "Then let me prove my worth, my lord. You will soon receive a messenger. I have seen this."

The Duke leaned in closer. "What are you saying?"

"It is news from Perusia. Tidings that will change everything. And that could have great significance for you."

"You are a Seeker, but I did not think a prophetess. How do you know such things?" She could tell he was debating whether she was playing him or not.

"I possess many abilities. The blackrobe at the Ara is not the only one favoured of his God. I know what I say to be true. I have three things to tell you, one of which you already know. Let me whisper in your ear." He narrowed his eyes but leaned in even closer to her. "First, you are cousin to the king. Second, the king is dead. And the third, Prince Sarant is a bastard."

"That is a bold foretelling, my lady. Bold to the point of reckless."

Lucinda remained expressionless. "But it is done. And... I shall tell you a fourth. The prince's real father is known to you. A close enemy."

Ursino leaned back, still staring at her face. He heard the neighing of several horses and looked up. Three riders had reined in fast in front of the pavilion, their mounts glistening with sweat, nostrils flaring. Palace guardsmen. The lead dismounted and entered under the canvas, stopping and kneeling before he reached the Duke. He bore a leather packet, tied with ribbon which he held out before him.

"A message from Perusia, your Grace. From the palace."

Ursino snapped his fingers and motioned for another guardsman nearby to fetch the packet. He seized it, cracked the wax seal, and unwound the red ribbon binding it.

Lucinda watched, motionless, savouring the anticipation. Ursino unfolded the parchment and rapidly read the words upon it. He folded it, slowly, and turned again to Lucinda. She saw wonder in his eyes, wonder for her, and also a glimpse of a newly kindled fire: unbridled ambition. And then, she felt something rising within her breast, an inkling of something she had not felt for an age. It had been there for a few weeks but she had pushed it back down, denying it, whenever she was with him: an attraction, a longing. She realized that Ursino was not just a means to an end, she was finding a certain joy in his company. Lucinda smiled back at him, lips parting, and the pleasure in her heart overrode the whispers of caution from her head.

Nine

"For Crown Prince Sarant! Vivat! Vivat! Vivat!"

The response from the throng of Palestrians in the market square was, not surprisingly, somewhat subdued as the shock of the king's death rolled across the crowd. The herald threw up his arms with each cheer before rapidly scrabbling the scroll in his fists and stomping off to his next destination to announce all over again the death of King Sempronius, the naming of Sarant as heir apparent, and of Queen Cressida as regent. The mutterings carried from street to street, tavern to tavern and market to market. How did the king die? When would a coronation be held? Need the boy be twelve years of age before he could wear the crown? And who really was Queen Cressida, now dowager queen? Some upstart nobleman's daughter from Colonna and she now leading the kingdom. God save us.

High above the city's steep terraces where the rocky soil levelled out onto a plateau—the moneyed merchants' quarter—Palazzo Danamis overlooked all. Nicolo Danamis again found himself in his father's day chamber, a grand solarium recently renovated after the sacking of the palazzo the previous summer. The message from Perusia notifying the High Steward of Sempronius's early demise and the new regency lay still upon his father's table. It had not moved in nearly a week, merely tossed to the side after it had been read.

Necalli of Atlcali stood near the window but just out of the light, a grey presence in the corner. Nicolo looked again at the message from Cressida that he held in his hands. Delivered that morning by an exhausted royal courier whose bay courser, upon reaching the courtyard, had promptly sank to its knees, exhaled loudly, and died.

Rumour abounds... I do not feel safe here... some of the council have gone missing... I have not left the palace.

Valerian Danamis was leaning back into his chair, the usual look of resigned disgust that Nicolo had always felt was reserved particularly for him. It was something he had not missed in the past six years, if indeed he had missed anything about his father.

"She is newly widowed, for godsake," said Valerian. "What would you expect her to write. She is unbalanced with grief."

"The queen is made of strong stuff, even now. I swear it. She is deeply concerned and this cannot be without some reason." Nico thrust the letter out to his father. "Read it for yourself. The council is beginning to fracture. Rumours are undermining her attempts to govern in the prince's name. God only knows whose side the Chamberlain, that worm Raganus, is taking."

"I may have been away a long time but my memory was not left behind in the south seas. And I remember well your dalliance with her. You might have pressed your suit and now we'd be ruling Colonna as well as Palestro." Valerian sniggered and wiped his forefinger under his nose. He looked up at his son. "Is the boy yours?"

Nicolo folded the letter and did not meet his father's gaze. "I don't know. It matters not. The queen has asked for my help. She is gathering allies around her. Rightly so."

Valerian scoffed. "Doesn't matter? If he is your by-blow then the prince is no more a prince than I am. He's a bastard and not the rightful king. You want to support a pretender?"

"And if he is the king's son? You owe the possession of this city and your power to Sempronius—no matter that he was a useless fool. It is your duty to come to the defence of his heir."

"And what army do you have to defend the queen? You would sail off to Perusia—with our best men and ships— barely a year after the mutiny? You really trust the rest of them here?"

"I'll take only two vessels and a few hundred men. You'll have command of the bulk of the fleet, nine loyal captains who will follow you into hell itself if need be. Be my guest and pull Duke Ursino's beard while I am away. But I am going to Perusia whether you like it or not."

Valerian shook his head. "And what do you hope to accomplish there? When we're fighting a war against Torinia?"

Nicolo walked to the window and cast a long glance at Necalli, who had remained silent during the exchange. "I expect to find who is stirring the pot, father. By God, I don't know who has spread the tale but in eleven years not a word of Cressida and myself, and now this. You know as well as I that there is no better time to make a grab for the throne than now. That spider Ursino was kin to the king. These rumours are kindling for his bonfire. And will Duke Ridolfo in Milvorna support the queen as regent?"

"Bah! It only matters that there *is* a king on the throne. Who that king may be is of little concern."

"And what of Lord Piero Polo?"

Valerian leaned forward. "What of him?"

"He would sell his own mother to gain favour and fortune. I do not trust him."

"He already has favour and fortune."

Nico shook his head as he stared out the window. "His new friends are more than curious about Valdur. What if they took a more active interest in the outcome of the succession?"

"The Sinaens? They have their hands full with their own empire in the east."

Nicolo turned back to his father. "Then why do they keep such a large presence in Perusia and Colonna? Polo is scheming with them. I can smell it."

"Your little mutiny last year has rattled you, boy. Piero Polo has ever been a friend to this house, and to the rightful king of Valdur."

"My queen has summoned me. I am going to her."

"Do you hear him, Necalli? Rashness. Bloody rashness. You had best watch yourself, my boy. Your first duty is to defend Palestro. That is what your warrant as admiral states."

Nicolo thought then about how many times he had wished to put a dagger into his father, since he had been eleven. Fate had seemed to reward him when Valerian disappeared into the distant ocean, but it had laughed in his face when the old man turned up six years later, as cruel as ever. "The city is well defended. I shall not be gone more than a month."

"Well, sod you then." Valerian tossed his quill to the table and ran his hand through his tangled white mop of hair. He then pointed a bony finger at his son. "If you go—and I won't stop you—you will take Necalli with you."

Nicolo froze. "Necalli? Why him?"

"He's as much an explorer as I, indeed a great captain in his own land. He should see Perusia, meet the court. And you should heed his counsel when he offers it."

Necalli gave a slow bow and Nicolo gritted his teeth. "Father, I have my men. Gregorvero will be at my side. With respect to Master Necalli, I do not think it is a good time for a merman to arrive at Perusia. Not with the split in the Temple there about the new holy texts."

Valerian laughed. "The new holy texts? Do you take me for an old incontinent fool? You don't give a shit about the split in the faith. You just don't wish to take my advice, or help."

Necalli turned to face Nicolo with his arms open in a gesture that Nicolo took to be an effort at accommodation. "Captain Danamis, my lord, I would be most grateful if you would consent to take me with you." He blinked as he spoke, his Valdurian accented with an odd sibilance. "I will obey you in all things, and I will fight by your side if need be. It means much for me to see more of your kingdom. Please give me this chance."

Nicolo looked at the merman. He was as smooth as any Perusian courtier and would no doubt fit right in, as slippery as the rest. So very different from the rough and rude merfolk he knew of his world who wore their friendship or enmity openly for all to see. Nicolo turned to his father. "Very well. He can come along, but I leave before the week is out."

Valerian's familiar look of disgust reappeared on his leathery face. "You think you know everything don't you, boy?" He shook his head slowly. "The Xosians are an ally of Palestro now. Some day you might find out why."

LATER THAT DAY, Danamis rode down to the west gate, two of his men-at-arms accompanying him on foot, swords at their waists. He wore a burgundy doublet and red hose, tall boots pulled up to his knees, and a long silver-hilted dagger at his hip. Pushed down low just above his brow was a black woollen hat, pheasant feather and egret flash pinned to the front with a jewel the size of a plum. Palestro was heaving at the port side: fish being unloaded and sold by the loudest people in Valdur; one of his carracks, the *Drum*, offloading wool bundles, taken off a Torinian merchant ship the afternoon before. The smell of hot tar and pitch wafted to his nostrils in the heat of the afternoon. It was a smell he had grown up with, a comforting scent. Those that recognized him stopped to doff their hats and bow. He returned their greetings, his horse's hooves clopping on the cobbles of the seafront piazza. The gate was open as it always was during the daylight hours. The city militiamen went rigid on spying his approach, their comrades rushing out of the gatehouse to join them.

After he passed through the hulking stone arch and towers and over the wooden bridge, he dismounted and handed the reins to one of his men. "Wait here for me," he commanded. A curtain of purple flowers clung to the stonework of the battlements, cascading downwards into the shallow ditch below. He skirted this and made his way down to the mer encampment. The high palisaded double gates were already open to receive him and he strode through and entered a clearing with a fire-pit, a huddle of palm-thatched huts just beyond.

Citala was at centre of a group of she-mer, facing off against two huge mermen who bellowed their displeasure. One kept slamming the butt of his spear into the ground as he leaned forward. Citala was holding firm, her voice raised as high as the mer warriors who confronted her.

"Citala! What goes on?" Danamis stopped before he reached the group, feet spread wide.

The mermen turned and halted, exchanging looks with each other.

"These two have come from my father," shouted Citala in Valdurian. "Making demands."

Danamis was certain what those demands were. He kept his place and put his hands on his hips. "Tell them I wish to parley with them, if they will let us speak for a few moments *first*."

"I have been telling them to leave."

"I can see that."

Citala gestured with her outthrust arm for the mermen to move away. They grumbled but complied, hefting their weapons and moving off to one side. Their eyes settled upon Danamis as he walked forward. He could see that the she-mer had moved around Citala to protect her from the warriors and now they relaxed a little, stepping back to give Danamis room.

Danamis addressed Citala without taking his eyes from the mermen. "They want the myrra, I suppose."

She nodded. "And they want it now. I told them I would be coming back to see my father shortly. That hasn't satisfied them."

Danamis's thumb worried the pommel of his dagger. "Are you sure these two are from your father?"

"Yes. I know them. And they say if they go back empty-handed then Atalapah will come with all his warriors to remind you of your promise."

Danamis exhaled deeply. Citala had been lucky enough to get by this long without having to come to grips with the myrra trade but time had now run out. "Citala, you must let them have the myrra. I have one bundle—well, most of one bundle. They can have that for another chest of gold, as before."

She looked at him, her eyes full of pain. "It is not what I want, for them or for us here."

Danamis reached out and touched her shoulder. "I know that. But the alternative is worse. Give them the myrra. We will figure something else out later."

One of the merman banged his spear, his nostrils flaring in annoyance, his skin mottled from grey to a brighter purplish hue.

"Citala, listen to me. It is the only way. I came to tell you I must journey to Perusia. You can come with me. We will bring the myrra and stop at Nod's Rock. Hell, these two can come with us if they don't fancy swimming back."

Citala muttered under her breath, then paused. "It only prolongs the misery for them. And what happens when it runs out? Strykar has not brought you more leaf in months."

"I can't answer that. But we can buy ourselves more time. Tell them."

"Very well. I must see my father before I find him turning up here. I will go with you as far as Nod's Rock."

She spoke quietly to the warriors, the fight evaporating from her. They, in turn, exchanged a few words before nodding their agreement. Citala pointed to a rack of fish standing near the gates. One of the merman gave a jagged smile, razor teeth flashing, and they wandered off to their meal as if nothing unpleasant ever had happened. Citala gestured for Danamis to follow her into her hut.

"Tell me why you are sailing to Perusia?"

He put his arms around her and she returned his embrace. "Because I must. The king is dead and the queen has asked me to protect the prince. He is just a boy. She does not know who to trust and her enemies are circling."

"Why you, Danamis son of Danamis? Has she not her own army to safeguard her?"

"She trusts me, Citala. That is why."

"You never told me you know the queen of Valdur. She must think much of you to ask such a thing."

Danamis gave her a weak smile. "I have served her husband, as did my father. Now I must serve her."

Citala's brow furrowed. "And then you will return... here, to Palestro?"

He nodded, already feeling guilty that he dare not share the entire story. "We leave in a few days. Two ships. But you must name one of your people to look after the colony while you are away."

"I have a council now. They will do what they must until I return."

"And that means not giving *my* father a reason to cause grief here." He reached up and stroked her cheek. "It will be good to voyage with you again, my Citala."

She smiled and looked down. "Yes, and to swim in the great sea far away from shore."

"There will be another passenger." Danamis paused to steel himself with the courage to utter the rest. "Master Necalli must come with us too."

The force of her two hands against his chest sent him tripping backwards into the thatched wall, as if a charging bull had hit him square on.

Ten

Lucius Kodoris, REPENTANT murderer and High Priest of the Temple Majoris, looked like he had just bitten into an unripe gooseberry. He had never expected to see the man who stood before him again in this lifetime; a reminder of another life, one nearly forgotten and lost to his own past.

"Ugo Volpe." The name slid off his tongue in a tone of disbelief.

"Pax vobis, Holiness." Volpe folded his arms across his chest and bowed low. Acquel stood a few paces behind, watching the High Priest's reaction on seeing his old companion from Astilona. From what Brother Ugo had already told him about the old days, Kodoris's lukewarm welcome was no surprise.

Kodoris turned and walked back into his receiving chamber. "I require no service of yours. There can be no good reason for your visitation."

Acquel followed him in, a grinning Brother Ugo at his side. "I think you should listen to what he has to say, your Holiness," said Acquel. "Of all men he probably knows best what we are facing."

Kodoris stopped and spun about. "That is precisely why we should not seek his aid, Magister! He was cast out of

Astilona for his *philosophy*, as he called it. Black arts more like."

"We were all cast out of Astilona," said Volpe, unperturbed. "I was only the first."

"Yes, when the Duke of Saivona grew to fear our power; our martial power. But the brotherhood was beginning to fear *you*." Kodoris shook his head, looking the monk up and down. "You are an ill wind, Ugo Volpe. What blows you to the Ara now, after all these years? I can only hope you are too old to cause trouble anymore."

Volpe shrugged. "I was not needed here before. Now I am."

"And how do you know this? We have told no one of the unholy attack upon us."

"I had a dream, and a vision. The Lawgiver himself told me to come to defend the One Faith."

Kodoris looked to Acquel. "Am I the only one on the Ara not to hear from Elded? How can you give credence to this... *brother*? Has he told you how he was cast out before the monastery was dissolved? For conspiring to use the very magic that we see used against us now."

The old monk raised himself up. He was now without his staff and seemed to have no use for a crutch. "That is an untruth, his Holiness knows full well. My science does not come from those infernal powers that plague us. It comes from our own faith. A gift of God for those who know how to wield it."

Kodoris puffed out his chest, indignant. "It is blasphemy. It was then. It is now."

Acquel placed his thumbs in his sword belt. "And I say it is not. Show me where in the holy text it says magic is forbidden. I am charged with defending this place and I'll take what aid I can get."

Kodoris flushed crimson. "You would do well to remember *my* office, young blackrobe."

"And you would do well to remember how we both came to our offices... *Holiness.*"

Kodoris swallowed his anger. "You will undertake no action without my knowledge, and participation. Do you understand?"

Acquel gave a polite nod. "That is why we are here, Holiness."

"The power of prayer alone will not defeat the likes of what has come," said Volpe darkly. "Brother Acquelonius has told me of the harpies in the Temple. I can tell you I have seen worse in my dreams. Defence will require more active measures, and *my* science."

Kodoris grimaced. "I do not believe spells and incantations will save us from the unholy. It can only let them in among us."

"Yet I understand it was you who invited a Seeker to aid you," said Volpe. "The same Seeker who has now turned against you and the Faith. I would say it is you who does not understand what rises against us, or its power. Why do you think they took the Hand of Ursula?"

"To deprive us," replied Kodoris. "And to dishearten us."

Volpe shook his head. "Think harder. That relic has been lost and found a dozen times over the ages. It's probably not even Ursula's arm bone. It could be a monkey's for all I know."

"How dare you speak such sacrilege to me," the High Priest spat.

"I am saying, Holiness, that the Hand is carried before the king's army when Valdur goes to war. That is all it is used for. It follows that if war comes this sorceress will attempt to win favour by giving it to the king. Its power lies in the faith it gives to men. It is not intrinsically sacred. That is nonsense."

"The king is dead," said Kodoris.

Acquel's head drew back but Volpe seemed unmoved. "Then that fact gives more weight to my argument. She will give it to the man she *wants* to be king."

"What has happened?" Acquel said, staggered by the news.

"The king was killed by a tame beast at the palace, a cockatrice it is said. Bitten and poisoned."

"Fate or design?" mused Volpe. "That is the question, even though the answer will be much the same. Chaos."

"I do not know," said Kodoris. "The news arrived by messenger from the High Steward only last night. It is a terrible thing, and the prince is too young to rule."

"Let me show you what I can do to help defend the Ara," said Volpe. "We are already at war."

Kodoris looked again to Acquel, who was his only alibi for what he had done—or caused to be done—the previous summer. Only so much truth could be shared before the strands would unravel and damn him. Acquel returned his stare, not giving an inkling whether he had told Volpe everything he knew. Kodoris realized the young monk wasn't so young as to not know the value of blackmail. He himself had never seen Ugo Volpe practise his magic but he had heard of others who had watched and fled at what they witnessed. Now, despite his fears, he had no choice. Lucinda della Rovera had unleashed upon them something beyond his own power to fight. And the sins that lay on his soul made him a fragile and flawed champion of the Faith. It frightened him, but Volpe was right.

He wet his lips. "This is a dangerous course, Magister. Are you prepared to take this path?"

Acquel was solemn. "I believe him. I believe he has been touched by Elded. As was I. We must be prepared to fight what is coming."

"Then God help us. I will come with you down to the crypt... and to the abomination that grows there."

No DAYLIGHT PENETRATED the under croft and crypt of the Temple Majoris. Its thick sandstone walls, seven hundred years old it was said, rose up to the ceiling of the temple floor overhead, some thirty feet high. The three of them descended the wide stone steps, the dank cold striking them and filling their nostrils before they had even made it halfway to the bottom.

Kodoris clutched at his robes, drawing them closer about his neck, and thrust out his torch. He had come back to this place but once after the horrors he had witnessed. He could still hear the sound of his predecessor's blood as it spattered upon the stump of the petrified tree and the flagstones around it. Acquel was out in front, Brother Ugo beside him, each bearing their sputtering tallow and rag torches, the halos of orange light barely driving back the darkness. None of the brethren dared come down to light the iron wall sconces since the harpies had raided the temple a week ago.

They made their way deeper into the crypt, to the northwest corner where the remains of the pagan tree lay; a shrine to Elded's triumph over the old ways. Acquel watched as Volpe's eyes scanned the chamber, his face set hard. He made a grumbling noise in his throat and shifted his leather satchel on his back.

"Can you not smell the sweetness?" he said, quietly. "Not the sweetness of natural corruption. Something else." He turned to the High Priest. "Tell me again. You were here. What did the canoness do?"

"She poured the blood of Brachus upon the stump. Spoke words in an elder tongue. Invoked... Berithas. And she said the roots of the tree grew deep... slumbering."

Volpe nodded and resumed walking forward. "Then what?"

Kodoris looked over to Acquel, whose face was pale. "The ground shook. The paving stones cracked. Then they dragged me away to—" He stopped, not wanting to go further.

Acquel continued. "When we next came here, the shoots had emerged and spread. We burned them with pitch, threw down lime, but still they returned after a week."

Volpe lifted his torch and pointed it towards the nave where the stump was, dimly visible like some giant unmoving spider, legs bent and poised to spring. He looked at the floor and saw the black vines streaming out across the stone, emanating from the dead stump of the unholy tree. "The tree that Elded hewed." He turned to the others. "Your sorceress is quite correct, its roots go deep. Across the land." He stooped down just short of where the tendrils stopped and rummaged in his satchel. He took out a coil of thin rope. Acquel saw that it had coloured ribbons tied to it, spaced along its length. Volpe looked at Acquel and smiled. "But we have talismans, and we have protection."

"Can you kill this thing?" asked Acquel.

"It is growing elsewhere," replied Volpe, uncoiling the rope. "Even as I journeyed here, I came across a sapling on the edge of the road, below the forest and not far from a little village. It was growing as I watched. It had been nourished by followers of the old ways. I could see animal bones around it. Someone had hung a few squirrels from its branches. Its leaves shivered as I approached; foul smelling and slick."

"What did you do?"

"Burnt the thing back to hell." Volpe's eyes widened with fervour. "Not with fire mind you, that is but a temporary measure." Volpe reached into his sack and pulled out a phial. "With this. A distillation of my own making, rowanis berries and a few other things. Long forgotten by those in the Faith."

"Poison," said Acquel as he looked at the little stoppered blue bottle.

"Of a sort," replied Volpe, nodding. "Your sorceress wakened this tree with a powerful incantation and the blood of Elded's anointed representative. I hope that I can put it back to sleep. Here, take this." He handed Acquel the rope. "Take the end and pay it out in a circle, around us."

Kodoris stood with his torch held aloft, watching as the rope was laid out around them. "I pray to all the saints that you know what you are doing."

"Prayers wouldn't go amiss," said Volpe as he followed Acquel around the newly formed circle, a circumference of seven feet. As Acquel completed the circle and coiled the remaining line, Volpe changed the circle by straightening the curves. It became a triangle, the tall apex pointed towards the stump ten feet away.

Kodoris fidgeted, his discomfort growing by the minute. "I hope you're planning on telling us what you're doing before you start doing it, Brother!"

Volpe barely looked up as he arranged the rope to his satisfaction. "Worked last time, your Holiness. You and the young Magister will stay inside the rope." He looped the rope at each corner into a small circle. He then arose and looked at each of them in turn. "Remember, stay inside the triangle. I will now begin. Do not lose heart no matter what may happen."

The old monk's words did nothing to reassure Acquel, whose knuckles were white on the grip of his sword.

"This is madness," whispered Kodoris. "He is playing with fire."

Volpe stepped outside the triangle and walked to the stump, holding the little phial. He cautiously sprinkled its contents onto the thickest of the roots and immediately returned to the protection of the rope. He turned and faced the stump again, arms raised, palms towards the long dead wood. His lips began moving, without sound, as he appeared to utter some prayer or incantation.

Acquel became aware of the smell—something acrid and foul—and saw what looked like a spreading whiteness upon the top of the stump where the vines sprouted forth, like a frost. The whiteness spread along the vines and the smell grew stronger, akin now to a whiff of strong drink, of spilled *acqua vitalis*. Volpe's voice rose as he chanted in a language that Acquel did not recognise but thought might be old Valdurian. He suddenly felt very cold and the hairs on his neck stood up. He suppressed a shiver and looked at the High Priest. Kodoris stood grim and stone-still with his torch aloft. Acquel saw a small cloud of condensed breath emerge from his mouth.

And then the swarm was upon them.

Small black things rose from the stump, like ascending ash, moving towards the rope triangle, darting and diving. They were insects, brown and wasp-like with drooping legs and iridescent, quivering abdomens. They recoiled from the triangle as if it were a wall of glass. One hovered at eye level in front of Acquel and he jumped back in horror when he saw its head. It had a human face and it was crying out, a tinny high-pitched whine of rage. More flew about them, a swirling, enraged cloud of buzzing gossamer wings.

Volpe still stood, hands raised. His voice did not falter, the commanding bellow from his throat echoed across the crypt. Acquel watched as Kodoris swung his torch at the things, his arm passing over the rope as he desperately flailed away. The wasps were on him in a second. He tried to pull in the High Priest, but it was too late. Kodoris let out a cry of pain and dropped the torch. He fell back, cradling his arm. One of the wasps had made into the area of protection and was crawling up Kodoris's hand. Acquel knocked it off and stamped upon it hard, hearing it crunch underfoot. Kodoris sank down, clutching his hand where it had been stung, his eyes huge with fear and pain.

The chant of the old monk had now reached a crescendo, and with it, the swarm receded. It collapsed upon itself and flew, quick as an arrow, into the pagan tree. The last of the swarm, those not quick enough, dropped lifeless on the stump and the stones. Volpe dropped his arms, his shoulders hunched.

"Brother Ugo!" Acquel held Kodoris upright as he cried out. Volpe saw immediately what had happened and grasped the High Priest's wrist. They could see how the hand was already swelling grotesquely. "We have to get him out of the crypt."

Volpe cursed. "I told the old fool to stay inside."

"Those wasps! You did not warn us we might be attacked."

"Well, *that* never happened before."

Acquel turned back to Kodoris. "Holiness, can you help yourself up? Here, put your arm over me!"

As Kodoris lurched against Acquel, the smell of Volpe's tincture lingering, he saw that the vines were now grey-white and brittle. Volpe stepped out of the hempen sanctuary and returned to the stump. He grasped the thickest vine and it exploded in his hand, crumbling into dust.

He nodded, satisfied. "Now that *has* happened before."

ACQUEL STOOD OVER Kodoris's bed, watching him sleep fitfully. The High Priest's hand was purple and horribly swollen. Volpe had tied a ligature below the elbow and had removed the black stinger, fully half an inch long, before lancing the wound and bleeding it. Acquel had watched as the old monk had drawn an elaborate pattern in dark ink upon the chest of the High Priest. It was intricate and dense, taking him nearly an hour, and all the while, as he carefully drew upon the loose pale skin of his one-time brethren of Astilona, he droned his spell. It was old Valdurian once again with the occasional addition of a well-known prayer, even Elded's Prime. Two blackrobes from the infirmary exchanged dubious looks, neither very sure of the sanctity of what they were watching. They quietly backed away and left. The sleeping draught had calmed Kodoris and he had drifted off despite his pain. Volpe had given him another draught as well, something he said was to counteract the venom. Acquel also saw a long livid scar on the shoulder of the High Priest: a sword or knife wound from long ago, perhaps inflicted on the battlefield.

"Will he survive?"

Volpe shrugged. "He is strong. But this is not ordinary insect venom."

Acquel shuddered as he remembered the perfectly formed miniature human face on the wasp as it had hissed at him, cursing him.

"We will have to wait and see," the old monk continued. "I can do no more. She is clever, this witch of yours. She must have laid an enchantment on the tree even as she worked her spell to revive it. A trap for the unwary. Hence my rope."

"First the Magister, then Brother Carlo, and now the High Priest," mumbled Acquel. "And yet she is nowhere near the Ara."

"I need wine."

"For him?"

"No. For me. He will sleep awhile now."

Sitting in Acquel's rooms, within half an hour they had drained the pitcher of cherry-red Livornan wine, most of it quaffed by Ugo Volpe. "You had better send for more," the old monk said, scratching at the stubble on the back of his head. "That barely touched me."

"How can they return now? After these centuries. The old gods."

Volpe chuckled. "Gods? They are not gods. They're opportunists."

"But Elded threw them down. Beleth, Belial and Andras. All of them. If not gods what are they?"

"They are powerful entities. But they are demons, not gods. There is but one God. Elded is his prophet and lawgiver."

Acquel drained the last few drops from the jug into his goblet. "But they were worshipped as gods by the people centuries ago, and now it begins again."

Volpe grumbled, stood up, and walked to the entrance to the chamber. "Hoy! Get an old brother a drink here!" he yelled down the corridor to two Templars. "Not like any monastery I'm used to!" He waddled back and resumed his seat at the small work table beside Acquel.

"These entities are not of our world, but when given the chance they enter. They are let in by the ignorant, the gulled."

Acquel looked at him, unconvinced. "And how do you know that? Your *philosophy* as Kodoris called it?

"My science," Volpe replied sourly. "Of which you know nothing. These demons seek to imitate gods, but their only desire is to sow strife and war—which is what they draw sustenance from. As well as from human souls."

"Will not the Lord help us then?"

Volpe laughed weakly. "I am afraid that God does not intervene in the affairs of men. He empowers others to do that. For us, that was Elded the Lawgiver. Think of it as the Lord giving us a gentle push from time to time. A push in the right direction."

"Your science, again?"

"No. My philosophy."

They were interrupted by a white-robed novice bearing an even larger clay pitcher of wine. "About bloody time. Here now, there's a good lad," chirped Volpe, seizing it and filling his goblet.

Acquel was growing annoyed with the old monk's frivolity. "So what are we to do? How do we face these entities as you call them? And all the terrible servants that they seem able to muster. How do we *fight*?"

Volpe took a long swig and set his goblet down, the wine dripping down his dimpled chin. "You must remember, these great demons need followers—and sacrifices—to gain entry to our world. I don't believe they have attained enough yet to come into the world entirely, but they must be close. Their lesser servants can come and go, directed by, or directing, their human faithful. Like this renegade canoness of yours, Lady della Rovera. Poor deluded bitch. Something must be guiding her." He took another drink and shook his head.

Acquel placed his hand over Volpe's goblet, holding it to the table. "So I ask you again, brother: how do we fight them?"

Volpe grimaced. "She wishes to destroy the One Faith in order to drive our people back to the old ways, thus opening the gates to the unholy trinity from beyond. So, she will seek to destroy us here, on the Ara, the centre of the true faith. Unless we find a way to strike at her first. Either way, young Magister, we will meet her. We must match her, magic for magic, spell for spell."

Eleven

"WHAT ARE YOU staring at, Captain Cortese?" Strykar asked his second-in-command, a sparkle of amusement in his eyes.

Slack-jawed, Cortese was ogling the group of she-mer that had emerged from the stockade gate, all with long hair of the starkest white like the sands of Polzano. "Sir, I have never before seen merfolk. Ever." He twisted around further in his saddle as two mermen, towering creatures with skin glistening bluish grey, emerged bearing spears. "Elded's beard, they are taller than I thought they would be," he muttered. He smiled and turned to Strykar. "Imagine a regiment of those devils in the Black Rose!"

"Well, if we fought all our battles within pissing distance of the sea, aye, might be helpful. But when is that going to happen, eh?" Strykar still could not believe that Danamis had followed through with his promise to the mer princess and allowed a settlement on his doorstep. He was looking forward to hearing from his friend about just how well the enterprise was proceeding. It looked peaceable enough to his eyes, but the thought of the myrra stash that Danamis was still holding for him quickly came to mind. With his new-found liquor—*acqua miracula*—perhaps he would not need to push the leaf onto the merfolk any longer. He quickly realised that the price they were willing to pay, with salvaged treasure dredged from the depths, was far greater than any soldier could offer for a little flask of his new elixir. Maybe, just maybe, he could carry on with the illicit trade schemes, if Citala could be convinced to see the positive side of things, with the help of Nico's silver tongue, of course.

Strykar had left his detachment encamped on a ridge overlooking the western walls of Palestro. Two hundred or so of his men, all on mounts, and a few empty gun carriages, ready to receive their shining new pieces of ordnance, courtesy of Admiral Nicolo Danamis. He knew that Danamis had already returned to Ivrea for more orichalcum cannon so the sale of two—perhaps even three, if he was lucky— would be no hardship for the pirate fleet. As he and Cortese passed through the hulking gatehouse and under the raised portcullis they were challenged by four of the town's militia. These four had been joking and laughing at the doorway to the gatehouse tower but had stopped their slouching and gripped their pole arms when they saw the armoured horsemen approaching.

One of the guards moved forward and raised a hand. "Hallo, friend! What business have you in Palestro this day?"

"My business is with your lord and master. I am Coronel Strykar of the Company of the Black Rose. Escort us up to the mount or over to the *Royal Grace*—wherever he is. Just let us be on our way."

The guard nodded while his comrades admired horse and armour. "I've heard of you, Messere. You've voyaged and fought alongside the admiral. But I will have to call for an escort before you and your companion can go on up the hill. The Lord Valerian would insist on it."

Strykar leaned forward in his creaking saddle. "I am here to see Admiral Danamis, not the High Steward."

The guardsman pushed up his rusty barbute with one hand and leaned on his halberd. "Aye, well, he ain't here no more. You missed him by a day. Sailed off again."

"Sailed off to where?" asked Strykar, his voice lowering in annoyance.

"He's gone to Perusia, sir. Two ships."

Strykar looked over to Cortese, who toyed with his reins and gave a shrug. "Suppose we'd better see the old man, then."

Strykar cussed under his breath. *Perusia?* And then, like a cold bucket of water thrown on his face, he remembered his friend's short but fiery romance. *Sweet Elded's beard. The king's dead, the queen's in trouble and Danamis is back in Perusia. That will put the cat among the pigeons.*

AFTER THEY HAD been announced through the iron grating on the ship-timber gates of the Danamis palazzo, they waited, and waited.

"I'm sweating like a pig in this armour," grumbled Cortese. "Least they could do is give us some water." And it was light armour at that: brown quilted gambeson and only a breast and back plate plus his sallet helm. Strykar was dressed similarly though his body armour was far more elaborate, a lavishly wrought and tooled piece that portrayed a battle won in the distant past of Valdur. He was hot but not yet irked. The delay, which he knew was no unintended slight, at least gave him time to think about how to make his requests; requests put to a man he had seen only twice before and that more than six years ago.

They suddenly heard the bar being lifted on the far side of the double gates, an iron peg being pulled, and then the gates swung inward. Liveried attendants, armed with curved Darfan blades at their hips, took hold of the bridles of the visitors' mounts and guided them into the large courtyard of the great house. They dismounted and were ushered inside to the cool of the palace, a leafy loggia at its centre, a fountain tinkling contentedly off to one side.

Footsteps on the wide marble staircase focussed the attention of the mercenaries and they watched as Valerian Danamis descended in long velvet robes of crimson. He was flanked on either side by lanky, taciturn mermen, each armed with the same Darfan steel scabbarded at their hips. They wore loose fitting tunics of blue silk, their long feet unshod. *So that's how old Danamis is keeping the merfolk busy*, he thought. *He's pressed them into service.*

"Captain Julianus Strykar. I remember you, sir. From long ago."

Strykar gave a court bow. "My lord, thank you for seeing us unannounced. I have been of late promoted to the rank of Coronel of the Black Rose. This is my captain of *rondelieri*, Giovani Cortese."

Valerian bowed in return as he reached the bottom of the staircase. "I welcome you to Palestro. It is a shame that my son has left the city, he would have been very pleased to have seen you again."

"It is unfortunate, my lord. For I have urgent business to discuss. Duke Alonso sends his fraternal greetings to you."

The voluminous sleeve of Valerian's robe waved as he gestured for them to take a seat in the loggia. Already, the mercenaries could see silver wine ewers and goblets being set down near the ornate gilded table and chairs.

They waited until the High Steward had seated himself before they took their own. Cortese grasped a goblet, a bit awkwardly since he was still wearing his riding gloves, as it was proffered by a retainer. He smiled, awkwardness leaching out of him. He couldn't but help keep his eyes from the mermen who had taken up station behind Valerian. He found them oddly man-like though they were clearly not men at all with small, almost under-formed nose, lips, and ears, but overly large and glassy eyes the colour of lapis stone. As if God's hands had left their clay unfinished.

Valerian had noticed the object of Cortese's intent. "You have not seen merfolk before, captain? These are my bodyguards brought back by me from the islands of Atlcali in the South Seas. They are Xosians."

Strykar took a sip of his wine. "I thought they were perhaps from the settlement beyond the gates, my lord."

Valerian smiled tolerantly. "No, Coronel. They are not."

One of the mermen slowly folded his arms across his chest as he watched Strykar, eyes unmoving.

"My son was manoeuvred into a rash promise to the merfolk outside the city gates. But I think you were aware of that situation, were you not, Coronel?"

Strykar took another sip of the cool wine before replying. "I was. It was how he won his freedom. A debt owed, I believe."

The old pirate changed the subject. "I thank you for the tidings from Maresto. But what is it that brings you here? My son has again not controlled his impulsive nature and has gone to Perusia, despite my protestations. He seeks to meddle in the unfortunate affairs of the throne. So, I am afraid you will have to make do with me."

Strykar nodded and set down his goblet. "I have come at the request of the Duke to enquire of the orichalcum guns. The guns that I told Nicolo about last year. The guns that I helped him negotiate out of Ivrea."

Valerian smiled broadly, his big yellowed teeth showing. "I wasn't aware they were borrowed from you."

"My lord, the Duke would ask that you sell him a few of these guns, at a price I negotiate. We fight the same enemy, allies in a war that Torinia has thrust upon us. I have seen these guns fire in anger. They would serve our army in the field a hundredfold better than the artillery we now possess."

"Then why not procure them from Ivrea yourself? The guns that my son has bought equip the fleet that defends Palestro, and the port of Maresto I might remind you."

"With respect, my lord, Palestro is much closer than Ivrea. We only ask for three. Which we will compensate you for handsomely. As friends."

Valerian shook his grizzled head. "Ah, the problem is that we are forbidden from selling orichalcum to anyone else. That was the terms of the agreement with Ivrea."

Strykar swallowed and nodded. He could feel the anger welling. Nicolo had not exaggerated. His father truly was a bastard. "Then an agreement between friends. To let us *borrow* the guns, until we can come to an arrangement with Ivrea."

"The Ivreans do not wish to spread these weapons further than Palestro. If Duke Alonso had but written me I could have saved you the journey."

"This is an insult to Alonso and to the Black Rose!" Cortese spat, leaping to his feet.

He was barely out of his chair, before a merman forcibly pushed him back into it and held him there. The other merman's hand flew to the hilt of his sword, poised to draw.

"Cortese, hold!" shouted Strykar. He turned back to Valerian, eyes flashing. "Release him, my lord."

Valerian raised his left hand and gestured. The merman lifted his hands from Cortese but remained half a pace behind his chair. Captain Cortese's face had gone deep red with embarrassment and rage. "This is my goddamned house," said Valerian quietly. "I demand respect of my guests. From my friends and my allies. The guns are not for sale or loan, Coronel. Nor would I seek to undermine the admiral of Palestro in his absence."

I'm sure you're really concerned about that you fucking old sea rat.

"If you have made up your mind, my lord, I will not remain to trouble you. And I will tell Duke Alonso what you have said." Strykar rose slowly so as not to alarm the vigilant mer. "There is one more thing though. There was a shipment of myrra leaf. Myrra that is mine until I am paid for it. Nicolo was holding it for me here. I would take it now."

Valerian's brow furrowed as he shook his head. "Myrra? Leaf that was yours, you say? I know only of one bundle of myrra in the city. That was in my son's keeping and I have been told he has taken it with him aboard ship. Something about keeping Atalapah happy."

Strykar sucked his teeth. He was not used to leaving anywhere empty-handed but this time he been truly plucked and trussed.

STRYKAR WATCHED FORLORNLY as the horses were hitched up to the thick-wheeled and iron-shod gun carriages: all still empty. The beasts didn't know how lucky they were. The encampment above Palestro was being broken up, the small force readying for the trip north to rejoin the main company of the Black Rose: mounted lances, spearmen, bowmen, and *rondelieri*. Every last man.

Cortese joined him, buckling on his harness. "This won't go down well with Malvolio. He was counting on you and the pirates being as close as brothers."

"You're lucky you're still here standing next to me. You realize that merman could have ripped your head off your shoulders as easily as you'd wring the neck of a rabbit?"

Cortese chuckled. "I'd have had the fishman before he got the chance."

"I've seen these mermen in a fight. Believe me, you would have been killed. And I would be talking to my new captain of *rondelieri* at this moment."

Cortese pretended not to hear. "Saw that you did well in the city with that *acqua vitalis* compound of yours. Your camp servants sold more than a few I heard. Folk coming to blows over the last few bottles was the story."

"*Acqua miracula,*" corrected Strykar. "Now, get your men into the saddle, captain. I'm ready to leave." He pulled himself up onto his mount and adjusted his reins as he surveyed the scurrying soldiery. Malvolio was going to rip into him when he told him the news. He knew that the Count was no great admirer of artillery—more trouble than it was worth he often carped—but the Duke's expressed desire to possess the new guns was reason enough to push for them. Danamis might have been cajoled into giving up a pair, but never the old man. At least he had nearly two days' ride to come up with a convincing explanation.

The drivers whipped up the horses pulling the gun carriages and the whole force began its slow march north, up the rising grassy fields and towards the ancient road to Maresto. Strykar kicked his horse off from the main body of *rondelieri*, shields slung over their backs, and took one last look at the walls of Palestro.

Fucking Nico. Of all the times he could choose to run off and play champion to the queen it had to be now. Showing up in Perusia now would only stir the cauldron even more.

He shook his head. Below him he saw a lone horseman riding full tilt towards them. He whistled and signalled to a few of his mounted men before trotting to intercept the newcomer. It was a merchant, sweating profusely on an old palfrey, a brace of baskets slung over its cruppers.

"Good soldiers! Your captain please!" he cried as he pulled up near Strykar.

"What is it you want?" bellowed a sergeant who put himself between the merchant and his commander.

"I would buy more of that efficacious medicine what was sold in the market by the men of the Black Rose. It is all gone already. Sold like it was mother's milk! Have you got more before you leave here?"

Strykar gave a sly smile. "See the man who drives that wagon over there," and he pointed it out.

The merchant nodded vigorously and jangled the big leather purse that hung from his neck. "I have the money, good captain!"

Strykar nodded and turned his horse northwards. He reached down to the small leather bottle at his saddlebow and retrieved it. He took a judicious sip of the *acqua miracula* and replaced the stopper, letting the flask dangle again. A surge of quiet elation went through him, a joyous confidence that filtered through his body down to his toes. "By Elded's own cods," he muttered, "that is fine spirit indeed." And rather than thinking about his report to the Count of Malvolio, he began dreaming about making more of his marvellous liquid.

THEY SAT SIDE by side in the bower of the palace's most private garden. One reserved for the Duke of Torinia alone. Lucinda della Rovera looked again into the intelligent dark eyes of Ursino and reached to touch her lips to his. When they met, she felt a desire that had been long in abeyance. One that surprised her. She gently pushed him away, though he was still eager to taste her.

"I have a gift for you, my lord"

He smiled and tilted his head. "A gift? It is I that bestow gifts upon *you*."

She pulled out a large square of folded linen that she had concealed in the slashed sleeve of her green brocade gown. "A gift before we ride north tomorrow. To victorious battle."

Ursino took the cloth and opened it. An approving noise rumbled from his throat. He held up the embroidered square to admire it. On it were two golden griffons, their details embellished with black thread. "You have a talented hand for needlework, my lady. And the royal beasts of Valdur as your subject. Are you trying to make a point?"

Lucinda laughed lightly. "You already know my counsel, your Grace. And I think you have made up your mind. It is to attack Maresto first then pursue the crown."

"Then you know my conscience. But do you know my heart?"

She knew that too. But worryingly, she was starting not to know her own. She reached over and gently grasped his hand. "I believe our hearts share the same beat."

"My love for you grows each day. You know that, do you not?"

She nodded. "Then you will be by my side as we ride north on the morrow. And I wish you by me in my bed."

Lucinda lowered gaze. "My lord. I am yours." But her mind was suddenly seized by the thought of how Berithas would judge her. Was this man not just a means to an end: the return of the Old Faith? She pushed down her feelings and moved on to the real matter at hand. "The embroidery is but one part of my gift to you."

"How so?"

"First, do you trust me and my powers? What you have seen since you have known me? For me to impart my next gifts you must implicitly trust me, and believe me in all I shall tell you."

He folded her hand in his. "Lucinda, I have witnessed your skills. I will trust you in more, yea, with my heart and my fortune in the days ahead."

"The rightful king of Valdur should have the symbol and the power of that right with him upon the field of battle.

A weapon that no enemy can stand against. I can summon these powers to your side, and I will do so."

Ursino's eyes gleamed. "Can you truly do such a thing?"

"I can, my lord. And I looked down upon your enemies on the march, as does the eagle in the sky. Something that Maresto could never hope to do, nor the scheming heretics of Livorna. I need but one thing for it to happen."

He sat upright. "Name it, my love. I will afford it if it is in my power."

Her eyes were now so intense he could not look away from them. For a moment, he felt lost. "Name it," he repeated, his voice a hoarse whisper.

"I need your promise. A promise to serve the Lord and Redeemer. And a few drops of your blood upon this piece of cloth. That is all."

"A blood sacrifice to the Lord. Is that what you mean?"

Her eyes widened. "Yes. And to his *true* servants."

He reached to the narrow belt at his waist, studded with gems, and carefully drew his dagger. Lucinda nodded and spread the embroidered cloth upon her knee. Ursino looked at her for a moment before running the tip of the blade deeply across his left palm. Lucinda watched the dark blood pool. The Duke held his hand over the griffons and his lifeblood rained upon it, a spattering of crimson. "I make my promise," he said softly.

"Then it is done." She folded his hand tightly. "When the time is right the old forces of Valdur will rise and stand with you against the enemy."

Ursino looked down at his wounded hand, fist clenched. "How will these forces manifest?"

"You will know when you see them. Let it be a wondrous surprise."

His brow furrowed. "Then first Maresto and Livorna. The throne in Perusia will follow. I have already gained assurances from the Duke of Milvorna who may be sending me a little gift of his own." He nodded to himself and then gave Lucinda a look, a look that said he was searching for reassurance. "I will trust you in these things."

"And there is yet one more power I can afford: the Hand of Ursula. Stolen from the Ara by my servants. This will go before your army into battle against any who stand against you."

Ursino's look of surprise subtly changed to one of almost wonder. "The sacred hand of Elded's disciple. You are indeed sent by the higher powers, and I will capture Maresto as quickly as you have captured my heart."

A warm breeze wafted away the faint scent of corruption from the blood-stained griffons before the Duke of Torinia could smell it. And Lucinda della Rovera, former canoness of Saint Dionei, rapidly folded the cloth and tucked it away.

Twelve

KNOWING THEY WOULD be parted again soon, their lovemaking was urgent, almost wild. Entwined in passion and ensconced in the great cabin of the *Royal Grace*, they felt the gentle rise and fall upon the swell as the ship drifted, just beyond sight of shore some twenty miles off the coast of Torinia. Citala had become inured to the stink of the captain's berth with its miasma of sweat and mildew, yet it was the only privacy that Danamis could afford her while on his ship. She much preferred (as did he) to make love in the bosom of the sea but both knew this was hardly feasible this far out upon the water amid the rolling swells. The cramped confines, the stench, the creaks and groans of the vessel, she forgot all in the arms of this man whom she loved above all else.

Danamis marvelled at her physique: Citala was lithe yet possessed of incredible strength. In the soft light of the lantern that swung from the beam above them, he traced the sinews of her legs with his hand, feeling the powerful muscles of her thighs, the tightness of her calves; all a delicious blue the colour of pale lavender. Looking into her violet eyes, framed by her strange coarse hair, whiter than white, he was lost to her and more deeply in love than he had ever known.

Sated, they lay silent, listening to their own breathing. Danamis could see the first light of the day showing through the tiny half-moon windows of the stern. Above them they could hear the stomp of feet and the voices of men as the ship came to life again.

"We will make Nod's Rock by mid-morning," said Danamis quietly, moving strands of hair away from her small round ear. "I will stand well off, that none may guess your destination."

She nodded.

"I know you have much to discuss with your father, difficult things that you must tell him. But I will wait for you at anchor for a day and a night, should you wish to join me again."

"In truth, I do not know how he will take to me. To see such a small bundle of myrra. And I'm afraid, afraid for what has happened to the settlement in the time I have been away. My father has never had much of a conscience. I've had to be his conscience for him."

Danamis shifted his weight and leaned on his elbow. "Fathers. They suffer us and we suffer them. My father beat me near every day when I was a boy. I suppose there would be nothing in that if I'd merited punishment. Most of the time I did not."

"We strike our children when correction is needed. Humankind is not alone in that."

Danamis laughed lightly. "Justly so. But to turn an hourglass and tell a boy that he will be beaten *after* it has run its sands out? To submit one's own flesh and blood to such treatment takes a special cruelty."

She stroked his cheek. "Why did he take such a dislike to you?"

"He already had the son he wanted. And, as I grew into a man, he decided that I was the grit in the oyster that had failed to become the pearl."

"To hear such a thing saddens my heart."

"Then he goes and makes me think he is dead only to turn up again to rain his disappointment upon me once again."

"You are your own man now, my love."

Danamis smiled, kissed her and swung his legs out of the berth. "I have to leave now. See what Gregorvero is up to."

She let go of his hand and a melancholy washed over her. Danamis dressed quickly and sat on the berth as he pulled on his boots. She knelt, watching him.

"Come outside when you are ready," he said. "Your mermen will be looking for you. You can tell them they're nearly home."

"They will know that already, Danamis son of Danamis," she replied, and for the first time, she now knew that home was a place that might not welcome her return.

NICOLO DANAMIS WATCHED the solitary pimple on the horizon as it slowly took form: Nod's Rock. The carrack was making good time with a fair wind on the larboard quarter, the mainsail billowing in full and the spanker on the mizzen straining under its stays. This stretch was the place where he had first carried on the myrra trade with the merfolk; the place where, a year ago, he had nearly been blown apart, drowned, and run-through with a mer spear. The sun was high in the sky, a canopy of azure that met the darker blue of the Sea of Valdur. The deck creaked and popped as it baked in the heat of the day, the smell of pitch growing stronger as the breeze grew warmer. Danamis watched as the two mermen dived over the side and disappeared while the sole Xosian, Master Necalli, watched their progress from starboard. The mermen had done this several times each day, no doubt to cool themselves. He had fed them as best he could, finding that their taste for fresh eels (kept alive in a barrel on the deck) knew no bounds.

Citala walked the main deck, occasionally glancing up at him, yellow silk robe whipping gently in the breeze. She had avoided contact with Necalli as much as she could. She did not trust his motives, and nor did he, but to Danamis's mind he thought she also chafed at the Xosians and their sense of superiority over the Valdur merfolk. He could not blame her. She had probably never even dreamt that another tribe of mer existed. Now she had to contend with the fact that her people were not alone.

Danamis turned to Gregorvero, his shipmaster, who stood nearby on the quarterdeck watching the *Vendetta* as it followed in their wake. "Wishing I'd put you on the caravel instead of this old tub, are you?"

"They are two very different ladies, captain," said the master, squinting as he hung onto a stay-line, his face beet red. "And I can appreciate the attributes of both. Bassinio handles her well. Like he's been captaining caravels for years instead of the *Salamander*."

"You're being too polite, old friend. I know you want her for yourself. You're still drooling."

"What? And give up this venerable old whore who knows me so well?"

Danamis laughed. "Drop us a sea anchor with a spar and some canvas when we're about half a league out from the Rock. The bottom is too deep for our cable unless we're on the ledge."

Bassinio shot him a look full of hurt. "You think I forgot that already?"

Danamis winked and headed to the stairs. Halting short of Nod's Rock was not just to safeguard the location of Citala's home, it was also to give *Royal Grace* a measure of protection. With Atalapah riled about the lack of myrra and threatening to bring out his warriors, he felt it better to keep his distance. He reached the broad main deck of the carrack and saw that Necalli had manoeuvred Citala into a corner at the foc'sle bulkhead, engaging her in conversation. He worked his way around the mainmast and one of the three great cannon lashed to the starboard side, all the while keeping an eye on the mermaid. She was holding her own at least. As he reached the two, the trilling sound of mer speech came to his ears, strange as always and in this case heated.

"Master Necalli, may I join you?"

The Xosian turned and his wide mouth opened in a grin. "Admiral, Citala and I were just talking of her home in these waters."

Danamis gave a cautious nod. "That is a subject we speak little of—for reasons of secrecy. I am sure you will honour that."

"He is mer," replied Citala. "Unlike your folk he can easily guess where my people dwell."

"I understand the need to protect Citala's tribe from the kingdom of Valdur. I will of course keep your confidence." Necalli folded his hands into his long robe. "Would that I could visit though..."

Citala snorted. "I do not think you could hold your breath long enough to make the journey."

Necalli gave a low laugh in reply. "I may not be as soft as you believe. My people are no strangers to the sea despite what we have built."

Citala shrugged. "Maybe so. But why would merfolk need ships to cross the sea? Danamis tells me you build great wooden vessels as do men."

"Such vessels are more practical for hauling goods between our islands than swimming with them under the surface. Surely you can see the benefit of that?"

"Hmm. Not good enough to survive the voyage to Valdur though, it would seem."

Necalli stiffened. "It does not become you to talk of the deaths of my people. It was a storm that could have carried away any ship no matter its size or construction."

Citala seemed to lose some of her steeliness. "I am sorry. It was wrong of me to say those words."

"You do not like me very much, I know that. But you should know that Lord Valerian has told me much of the unhappy history of this land. I admire your people for surviving in it these many years. I would only see you prosper in future."

"And your advice?" Danamis demanded.

Necalli tilted his head slightly. "I am in no position to give advice to the princess. But since you ask…" He turned again to Citala. "I would say your colony on the shore is ill-advised. You belong with your people—*our* people."

"We are one with Valdur," Citala said. "We were once and will be again."

"Citala, those days are gone. They cannot be brought back to a land that has changed. If your people have a future it is on your little island over there… or in Atlcali."

She took step back at his words. "What are you saying?"

"That you would be welcome in my lands in the far west beyond the great ocean."

"That is a bold offer, Master Necalli," said Danamis before Citala could reply. "Bold to assume you can even return yourself."

"You underestimate your father's determination, captain. And mine."

"That would be an impossible journey for an entire people to undertake," said Citala.

"Over time, Citala, nothing would be impossible," replied Necalli. "A great migration could be undertaken. You have already taken the first step yourself, in Palestro. You have merely chosen the wrong place."

Danamis moved to the railing, his eyes on Nod's Rock. "You have spent far too little time here, Master Necalli, to know the peoples of Valdur. We may surprise you."

"Perhaps, Captain Danamis, perhaps. But I know my king would welcome a return of Valdur merfolk to our land. Someday."

Danamis turned to Citala. "You will be able to leave within the hour. My men have sewn up the myrra into some sailcloth for you. Are you ready?"

She smiled at him briefly, gave a small nod, and touched his forearm as she brushed past along the rail. She called out across the water to the two mermen that swam effortlessly in line with the ship. They soon returned and clambered up over the side. As always, the sailors gave them a respectable wide berth as they went about their business, while the soldiers who were on deck grinned and continued their polishing of blades and helms.

When the glass had turned, Gregorvero hollered for all sail to be dropped and for the sea anchor to be let out from a port on the stern transom. The *Royal Grace* slowed to a crawl. *Vendetta* furled sail too, in reply, and after a few minutes launched a small longboat ferrying Bassinio over so he could meet with Danamis. Citala stood by the starboard rail near the sterncastle. She had shed her robe and now wore only her *tapua* braes and a dagger belt about her waist. Her mermen companions bore their spears and between them held a large canvas bundle trailing a length of sisal rope. Citala looked out across the main deck and up to the quarter deck that towered over her. The men of the carrack had stopped to watch, many giving a bow of respect to her as she prepared to take her leave. She knew many by name now, these rough men who once had ogled her but now treated her as almost one of them. She could see the sadness in Danamis's face as he watched her, an awkward, forced smile on his lips. Necalli stood at his side, expressionless.

"I am ready, Danamis son of Danamis," she said. "Until we meet again, God keep you well." She raised her voice loudly. "And God keep all the men of this good ship!" This was met with a rolling cheer and she smiled broadly, white teeth flashing.

"Fare you well, Citala," said Danamis tenderly. "I will keep station here... if you should change your mind."

She nodded, finding it hard to prevent herself from embracing him. A voice entered her head. Faint, but clearly not her own. A male voice, reaching out to her: *Good fortune, Citala*. Necalli. *We will meet again. I hope as friends*.

It was gone in an instant. Flustered, she barked an order to the mer warriors who hefted the myrra sack up over the railings. She had thought only she-mer could communicate by thought. Necalli had gently interrogated the merfolk of Valdur for months in his wanderings about Palestro. It was conceivable he had learned of the she-mer gift. But that a *merman* could possess this too? She suddenly felt exposed, vulnerable to this creature who was one of her own kind yet somehow not. Without looking to Danamis she bounded up onto the railing and dived headfirst over the side. The blast of cool water enlivened her and she kicked hard, down into the depths, her mer guards following close by, the precious sack of myrra bobbing along behind.

Two DAYS PASSED. Danamis watched as the morning sun rose. His men were restless, the ships having drifted lazily upon the gentle sea too long for most of their liking. She wasn't coming back. Whatever had happened with her father, she had either decided to stay or was even now making her way back to the colony at Palestro. Danamis swiped his hand across his short black beard and yelled for Gregorvero.

"Weigh the sea anchor! Raise all sail!"

Gregorvero waddled over from across the other side of the quarterdeck. "Aye, been waiting for that order. Wind's fallen off a bit this morning so she'll be slow. What course?"

"Resume the course for Perusia," replied Danamis, glumness barely concealed.

They hung out every sheet of canvas they had but the wind barely filled the sails, leaving them twitching and rippling like the back of a flea-infested cur. By mid-afternoon they had made little progress at probably no more than three knots. Danamis paced, his thoughts already on what lay ahead in Perusia. He wanted to help Cressida in any way he could but deep in his heart he knew his father was probably right. His presence might add fuel to the fire of the succession crisis, his arrival seen more as an exercise of control over the widowed queen and his bastard son—if indeed he was his blood. If Cressida had lost control of the council and the confidence of the city, he was facing the prospect of evacuating her and the prince from Perusia, with all that such an action would imply. Abdication.

The men of the foc'sle had rigged a striped canvas tilt to shield them from the beating sun, as he had up on the quarterdeck. *Vendetta*, being rigged fore-and-aft, made better speed in the becalmed seas. Danamis had waved her ahead, to take the lead. Slowly, the distance widened between the two vessels. He could see she was making an effort to slow; her foresail was shortened, leaving just her mainsail and mizzen to fill with the warm but mean wind. The afternoon dragged on. Sailors mended, archers rosined bows and fixed fletchings, swordsmen oiled their weapons, and all found what shade they could. A wispy column of smoke rose from the deck grating and Danamis knew the cook was starting his fire for another fish stew.

"Ship!" came the cry from the crow's nest on the mainmast.

Gregorvero hollered up to the sailor. "Where away, boy?"

The sailor's arm thrust out to larboard. "Four points off the bow!"

Danamis had already spotted the newcomer. She was low on the water with practically no canvas out but still she was making headway. It was a galley, and virtually the only galleys were those of Perusia—the king's fleet.

"Gregor, raise our standard."

The master gave a nod and sent a sailor below to retrieve the colours. Fully fifteen feet long, the white and red pennant emblazoned with dolphin and falchion, glided up the line until it reached the top, the two men in the crow's helping to unfurl it. In the paltry breeze, it barely trailed out in their wake.

Gregorvero stood alongside Danamis watching the approaching galley with interest. "Where do you suppose they've come out from, Perusia or Torinia?"

Danamis shrugged. "Could be either. We'll hail them when they're close. Might get some useful intelligence of the situation in Perusia, and what Duke Ursino might be up to."

Gregorvero grumbled. "Not likely to be good either way."

"You're ever the optimist, Master Gregorvero. Nudge us a few points larboard so we may meet them the sooner."

"Ring to quarters?"

Danamis's brow furrowed. "You are a distrustful bastard, aren't you?"

"Trust never got me anywhere."

Danamis rubbed his chin as he watched Necalli ascend the stairs to the deck. "Aye, break out the charges for the swivel guns and get the bowmen assembled. Just in case."

Gregorvero turned to go but quickly pivoted around. "Netting?"

Danamis frowned. "You want them to think we're attacking them? No. Just get the swivels primed. I'm burning to hear what their captain may have to tell us."

"A problem, Captain Danamis?" Necalli said.

Danamis tried to reassure himself. "It is a royal galley, but we're just being cautious."

The soldiery became raucous, chiefly at prospect of even seeing another ship even if it was an ally. The boredom of the last few days evaporated as they chattered, setting to spanning their crossbows or stringing their ash-wood longbows. The cast iron breeches were manhandled into the little falconets mounted on the foc'sle and stern rails while gunners lit their saltpetre match, blowing gently to stoke it. Gregorvero oversaw all, directing the two soldier 'captains' of the stern and the foc'sle to order their men.

When the galley had closed to about five hundred yards, Danamis leaned forward over the rail. The thirty oars on either side of the great galley—over a hundred and thirty feet long—began rising and falling faster.

"Do you see that?" said Danamis.

"Aye," muttered Gregorvero. "What do you suppose they're up to?"

The great square royal standard of Valdur, two golden griffons upon a field of blood red, rippled lazily behind the mizzen lateen spar. Danamis could barely make out the men aboard but it appeared there were many. His soldiers crowded about the larboard side to watch the galley approach, most wearing just their arming jackets, hose and shoes. Many were already laughing and pinching their noses in allusion to the stink that usually accompanied galleys: the reek of seventy rowers in a broiling hull would soon announce its presence downwind.

Gregorvero shielded his eyes from the glare coming off the sea, smooth as blue marble. "There's something swinging up on the main mast. Halfway up."

"I see it. And I think it's someone's head." Danamis could see a gaggle of sailors out on the broad flat prow of the galley. A small serpentine gun was mounted, fixed straight out over the beak of the vessel. Danamis looked further aft. The sun glinted off dozens of polearms and swords. His stomach dropped. The king's galley was attacking.

"Sweet Elded's blood. Get the polearm men over to the railing!"

Gregorvero swore and dashed across the quarterdeck, nearly tumbling down the stairs. Danamis turned to the dozen bowmen around him. "Take your positions, you fools! We're under attack! You! Gunner, get that falconet ready!"

Necalli was now at the railing, watching the approaching vessel intently. "May I be of service to you, captain?"

"I'd prefer you stay here on the quarterdeck, Master Necalli. If I got you killed my father would be even more trouble than he is to me now."

This set Necalli to blinking furiously. "You would not begrudge me a sword, I hope?"

"Arm yourself, but don't leave the quarterdeck."

The cracking boom of a cannon was near instantaneous to the sound of splintering wood as the bow gun on the galley fired. The grape shot ripped across the carved railings of the *Royal Grace* tearing chunks of oak from the edge of the foc's'le. Three men were writhing on the main deck, screaming. Just yards away from them, Danamis watched as a second flag was hurriedly raised up the main mast, joining the royal standard that flew further back. It bore two red towers flanking a golden bull—the standard of the Duchy of Torinia.

Danamis grabbed the captain of the stern castle by the shoulder. "Don't stop firing until your arrows are spent! And keep those falconets firing." Then he was down the stairs and into his great cabin to find his falchion. With no time to don his brigantine he was as naked as most of his men as he ran out onto the main deck to receive the attack. He was cursing a stream, mainly at the foolhardiness of allowing Bassinio to push on ahead. He could still see the *Vendetta* but could not tell if it was turning back. Surely they must have heard the shot, he thought, as he jostled his bill men into position. There had been no time to ready the main deck guns and the low sleek galley was too close to engage now.

The carrack listed drunkenly to the sound of a deep grinding noise before righting level again. They had been rammed. A shower of arrows flew across the deck, most of them sailing high and over the other side. Danamis instinctively ducked and then heard his own guns explode into action. His men, some one hundred, crowded together amidships, crouching instinctively as the deadly steel-tipped rain fell. The galley sat low on the water and the *Royal Grace,* fully laden, rode low as well. They were holed above the water line, the iron-crowned prow having pierced their hull just below the rails. But there were a few precious feet of difference which gave his men a fighting chance: the enemy would have to climb up and over to reach him. Already the clatter of the wooden shafts of dozens of glaives, billhooks, and spears was drowning out the shouts. Danamis felt the air move as an arrow shot past him. A soldier next to him groaned and sank, the bolt of a crossbow protruding from his chest. His death spurned on his men to push back the Torinians. So broad was the galley's fighting platform, a few of their men were already flanking the main hedgehog of combat, scrambling for a handhold up to the carrack's deck.

The screams seemed to be growing louder as volleys from his own bowmen on the high ground of stern and foc'sle sent their deadly missiles over and down the short distance between the vessels. Three Torinian soldiers clambered through a wide cut-out port and over a now useless orichalcum cannon and sprang up, swords at the ready. Danamis was on them, joined by one of his own swordsmen, a small buckler in his left hand.

He seized his falchion in both hands, left cupped around the disc pommel, and raised his guard. The closest enemy rushed him, feinted a thrust and brought a rapid downward cut that Danamis caught, the man's blade sliding down his own to catch on the cross hilt. Danamis pushed forward even as he parried the cut, stamping on the man's lead foot and then slamming his pommel into his face. The Torinian staggered back two steps, dazed, and Danamis swung his blade again, bringing it down diagonally upon his shoulder and neck. A fount of blood erupted, spattering him, even as the next opponent swung at him. Danamis's man deflected the thrust of a glaive, stepped inside while choking up to grasp his blade halfway, and stabbed his opponent in the throat.

Danamis was deep into the heat of the fight, unthinking, moving on instinct and not artfulness. The rest of the battle was far away, unknowable. Two more engaged him and as he deflected the thrust of a bill, it shot past his blade and across his bicep, ripping his shirt and slicing his arm. His opponent suddenly dropped, an arrow in his back. And the other Torinians around him had fallen too. His sword grip felt slick. It was his own blood pouring down his arm. He turned back to the main knot of the battle, the rise and fall of spears and glaives still sounding a terrible din across the deck. But the enemy had failed to breech them yet. Fewer salvoes were coming over from the galley. Had their bowmen run dry?

His eyes shot up to the quarterdeck. Gregorvero was yelling down at him and gesturing over to the galley even as Necalli stood behind, strangely still and quiet despite all that was happening. He staggered, wiping his brow with his sleeve and moved down towards the stern, sidestepping the great sleeping orichalcum guns. He looked over to the galley, now locked in a deadly embrace with the *Grace*. At the stern command deck, under the cover of a red and gold striped tilt, a separate battle was being fought. He froze, horrified, as he watched a single mer fighting with two officers. Even from a distance, he knew it was Citala. She bore a swordfish bill spear, jabbing it outwards and deflecting the Torinian's desperate attempts to thrust her with his light curved sword. Her reactions were faster than any man he had seen fight. He watched her parry a cut and then thrust the officer through his belly, pulling the spear out in an instant and engaging the next.

The oarsmen had emptied their benches, joining the fray and adding their numbers to the press of steel that was pushing hard up on the side of the carrack. One of his falconets roared again and a hail of iron dice-shot cut a swathe of red amidships on the galley.

Danamis's mouth opened as he saw half a dozen soldiers make for the stern platform and Citala. Then, emerging up from the stern, he spotted a blue form climbing aboard behind her—a lone mer warrior. He looked again up to Gregorvero and then over to the galley. The two mer were holding off more than half a dozen soldiers and sailors, aided only by the fact that the narrow decking that ran between the oar benches forced them to advance only two abreast. Danamis dropped his bloodied falchion to the deck. He was up and over the rail in the next moment, half diving, half falling into the sea. He burst to the surface and began digging into the broad low swell with all his might.

The vast galley seemed to go on forever. The banks of oars were raised and locked like some monstrous water bug, towering above him as he pushed himself through the water. His boots, now sodden through, felt as heavy as lead as he kicked. None of the combatants on deck could see him past the oar banks and he worked his way quickly to the stern and the little wooden stairs that reached down to the water. With a groan he pulled himself up and staggered onto the small quarterdeck. The merman wheeled at the sound and made to thrust at him but Danamis raised his hands, palms forward.

"Danamis!" he yelled. "I am Danamis!"

Citala parried a spear thrust and turned her head at his voice, before wheeling back to continue her fight. The merman, his eyes bulging with intent, turned back to help Citala. Danamis looked about the deck. He saw two swords lying near the bodies of the slain, one a Darfan blade. He retrieved it and went forward, legs wobbling. Two Torinian men came at him, clambering over the rowing benches. One shot his glaive forward, aiming at Danamis's chest. Danamis twisted and grabbed the haft with his left hand as it glided past. His light curved blade he thrust forward, burying it in the man's belly. He was aware of a noise behind him. Shooting a glance over his shoulder, even as another Torinian lunged at him, he saw four or five mermen pulling themselves up over the stern, each armed with black swordfish bills.

The mermen launched themselves into the fray, pushing past a startled Danamis. The lead mer tackled a burly soldier, tossing him into the oar bank like a plaything. And then the others were stabbing and leaping across the benches, dispatching men with a frenzy that caused Danamis to stop dead and stare in stunned amazement. The mer warriors were head and shoulders taller than the galley men and twice as strong. One merman took a spear thrust in the thigh, paused only long enough to pull the spearhead out, hefted the weapon, and then swept the deck like he was shooing chickens.

At the bow, the Torinian push had stalled. A few more well placed shots by the swivel gunners on the *Grace* and they lost heart. In threes and fours, they began falling back from the prow of the galley and as they lost momentum, the surrenders began. Polearms began clattering to the blood-slick deck, bodies sprawled along the rowing benches. The sight of the mermen was enough for some to throw down their arms and raise their hands. By now, the *Vendetta* had arrived, having husbanded every scrap of wind she could find to make it back to aid the *Royal Grace*. Danamis looked to the main mast of the galley. He was now close enough to see what was indeed a human head dangling from a rope, tied by its hair, face as grey as cold ashes. It was Captain Alandris, the same man who had come to his rescue a year ago; not far from where they were now. His crew had apparently decided that the rightful heir to the throne of Valdur should be Duke Ursino—and had taken rather forceful measures to convince him to surrender his ship. He moved his eyes from the grisly trophy to the mermaid.

"Citala!" he called, his voice hoarse.

She walked to where Danamis stood dripping, his chest still heaving. Hefting her spear, she reached out and took his hand, her face beaming. "Danamis son of Danamis, I am not letting you out of my sight again!"

Thirteen

ACQUEL STOOD WITH his arms folded at the foot of the High Priest's bed as the shafts of sunlight pouring through the stone window traces projected strange and beautiful shapes upon the coverlet. Kodoris was propped up by pillows, his hands cradling a cup of water which he brought slowly up to his lips. His colour was improving each day, the poison having been cleansed by the unconventional skills of Ugo Volpe. Now, Kodoris was merely pale, dark bags hanging under his eyes and a week's worth of grey beard on his cheeks.

"It was Brother Volpe that saved you. You realize this do you not?"

"I accept that," he said grudgingly. "But he's probably damned my soul with his... methods." He pulled away the collar of his white shirt and peered at his chest. "He's *painted* me, for the love of Elded."

"You would have been dead otherwise."

Kodoris fixed him with a look that carried worry, even fear. "In my delirium I saw things. Terrible things. So vivid I can see them still."

"And what sort of things did you see, Holiness?" It was Volpe who had entered the large bedchamber. "I am glad to see you are made of sterner stuff. All that vile refectory food in Astilona in your youth must have hardened you to any poison."

Acquel smiled as the monk shuffled forward and stood at the bedside. Whatever Kodoris thought, he was beginning to believe in the old man's methods. He had killed the tree and he had cured Kodoris; that was two contests won thus far, and it seemed to him that there was more to the powers of this refugee of Astilona, much more than that which his own amulet could offer.

Kodoris looked at Volpe. "What medicine did you use? "

"A woodsman's medicine, using some of the extracts that I carry, and… a fair amount of prayer. *Old* prayer. You have no doubt noticed the talismans I inked. But I asked you a question, your Holiness: what did you see?"

Kodoris pushed his head back into the pillows, his eyes staring up at the dark embroidered canopy above him.

"Things that even now I cannot rid my mind of," he replied. "Terrible visions that were fantastical yet so real I could have reached out and touched them. As if I was there rather than lying asleep."

"Perhaps you were there—for a time," said Volpe. "That venom—like the creature it came from—was not of this world. You have glimpsed the darkness beyond our plane."

Kodoris swallowed and shut his eyes. "I saw a white wolf come towards me from out of a swirling ether. It was the size of a horse, shrouded in bright white light; a beautiful radiance. But its rider was not wholly human. It was a youth—naked and powerful—who rode the beast. But he had the head of a night bird—a raven or crow—black as pitch with shining black eyes. The scent of many flowers came to me as the thing drew closer. He had a burning sword in his hand."

"What happened then, Holiness?"

Kodoris opened his eyes and turned to look at them. "It was as if a canvas tent was riven behind the thing, ripping and falling away, and I saw what lay beyond. A blasted, withered landscape, lit by the glow of raging fires on the horizon. A landscape peopled by horrible twisted things. Mockeries of man and beast. And moving from the distance towards me, I saw another youth, naked and fair of face, driving a golden chariot pulled by two black horses. Next to him, another, upon a pale horse whose bones I could see through its skin."

"Did the creature speak to you?"

Kodoris shook his head. "No, not with words as such. But somehow, I heard him. The raven man said, 'The light comes'. *Light.*"

"The light of Andras," said Volpe. "You were afforded a glimpse of the other side of the divide. For it is the demon Andras who appears as the raven man upon a white wolf. His companions are Belial and Belith, demons of a slightly lesser order. We know this from the ancient scrolls of the Old Faith, when their followers in Valdur elevated them to so-called gods."

Kodoris took a breath. "I fell back as it raised its flaming sword. A screeching filled my ears—a terrible wail. And then I felt as if I was falling. I remember nothing more until I awoke again."

Volpe's voice was low and urgent. "They are at our gates; the gates to our plane of existence." He turned to Acquel. "We must find Lucinda della Rovera and kill her before she opens them further."

"She has a duke to protect her now," replied Acquel. "And the army that goes with him. How could any of us get to her?"

"She may come to us first," said Volpe. "Which would save us the trouble." He started to speak again and then fell silent.

"What were you going to say?" asked Acquel, touching the monk's sleeve.

"There are ways—a middle path, neither black nor white—that could afford us a means to surprise her. Such means do carry great risk for the practitioner and those with him."

Kodoris pushed himself up. "I forbid it!"

Volpe bowed his head. "We have not yet reached that point, Your Holiness. God willing, we will not have to."

Acquel was not so sure but held his tongue. If Lucinda came to the Ara, it would be a time and place of her choosing, not theirs. Volpe's words made sense to him: take the fight to her, before she had a chance to strike.

"And what word from the High Steward?" asked Kodoris, wincing and setting his head back down into his pillows.

"He has summoned me to dine with him. To inform him of our plans to defend the city. And also, his letter says, to deliver some intelligence that his men have gleaned of late."

Kodoris nodded. "Yes, you go. But you must not mention any of this talk of incantations. Is that understood? Only martial means of defence. Tell him about the training of the Order."

Acquel bowed. "He would scarce believe it anyway, Holiness. Of that I am sure."

DRESSED IN THEIR black robes and white linen tabards bearing the ten-rayed sun in splendour, Acquel and Ugo Volpe made their way up the winding rock-hewn steps of the palace of Marsilius, High Steward of Livorna. The palace, a fortress in its own right, was nestled into the cliff side at the north-eastern corner of the city. It was a gloomy place, despite the bright orange-red tiles of its many roofs and turrets, and Acquel found himself choking back emotion as he thought of his mother. For years she had toiled at the washing tubs of the palace while he had lived the life of a street thief. It was at her urgings that he had taken holy orders. And then, the murders at the Ara, the blame falling upon him, and ultimately, her death from a broken heart.

Volpe paused, puffing, halfway up the stairs. "There had better be a generous spread laid for us after this effort. A few pitchers of decent Milvornan wine I hope at the very least. A count can afford his guests that, can he not?"

Acquel frowned. "I did not bring you here that you could sate your appetite. I want you to see what we're up against on *this* side of the walls, at Livorna. And why the defence of Livorna is down to you and me."

They reached the gates and were ushered inside by retainers who looked more bored than anything else. Their large green and white check livery made them look like acrobats at a fair rather than a household guard. Yet they bore short, double-edged swords at their hips to give proof of their martial purpose. The monks were led along long corridors of marbled floors and high ceilings illuminated by chandeliers, a blazing constellation of beeswax candles. The great hall of Marsilius was modest compared to the one he had seen at Maresto, but it was impressive nonetheless. High dark beams crossed the ceiling with a large carved golden rose at each intersecting joint. A tapestry thirty feet long and twenty high graced one wall and the long table could comfortably seat a hundred. Acquel watched as Volpe's greedy eye scanned the table top, admiring the platters and the much hoped for tall ewers of wine.

They were left standing there some time, drinking in the beauty of the chamber, while they, in turn, were stared at by the guards. At length, another door opened and in came Marsilius and his councillor, followed by a retinue of servers. Marsilius was old but not ancient, yet Acquel noticed how he leaned on his castellan's arm for support as he slowly shuffled across the inlaid floor in his robes of mulberry red. Kodoris had been right: for whatever reason, age had not treated him well. The councillor, no young man himself, guided Marsilius to the end of the long table and helped manoeuvre him into the high-backed chair. Marsilius waved a hand, motioning for the monks to join him at table.

"Magister Acquelonius, please sit and take some repast. Your companion monk too."

Acquel bowed and took a seat, as did Volpe, on opposite sides of the count. Acquel briefly studied the man. His thin, wispy grey hair fell to the nape of his neck but a large bald spot shone brightly at the crown. He had a proud nose and brow, thin lips and strong chin. His eyes were dark and somewhat sunken, though from age or by birth Acquel did not know. No sooner had they seated themselves than servants began attending on them, first Marsilius, then Acquel and Volpe. Brother Ugo's eyes lit as he quaffed a mouthful of wine, obviously to his taste. The castellan, not known to Acquel, hovered at the arm of the Count's chair. Marsilius twisted himself with difficulty to make the introduction. "This is my advisor, Paolo Voltera. Lord Paolo and I have just returned from Perusia—to pay our respects to the departed king."

Voltera nodded and smiled. "Welcome, brothers of the Ara."

"This is Brother Ugo Volpe," said Acquel as he gestured across the table. "He is… someone who has long experience of martial matter, despite being in holy orders."

"I welcome you both to my house," said Marsilius reaching for a chunk of roasted fowl. "I must say that I am exhausted from our travels. Still, I did not want to delay our talk. Better that we discuss these urgent matters now."

"That is most gracious, my lord," responded Acquel as he watched Marsilius attack the guinea fowl with the rapaciousness of a starving man.

Marsilius swallowed and reached for his silver goblet. "And how fares the High Priest? I have heard he was somehow injured in the crypt. Not more to do with the earlier attack on the Ara I hope?"

"No, my lord," lied Acquel, "He was bitten by a spider as his hand swept over a column. The creature had made its web there. He received good physic from the brethren and is recovering from the wound."

Marsilius nodded. "That is good. Luck runs very ill of late. What with the murder of your predecessor a few weeks gone by... not to mention the unpleasantness of last summer."

Acquel felt himself blanch at the mention. Marsilius gave him a long look. "I fully accept your innocence in that matter, Magister. An awkward time. And we also fully accept your revelations of the holy mysteries. Of the will of Saint Elded." The Count's eyes fell to the chain around Acquel's neck. "May I see the amulet, Magister?"

Acquel shot a glance to Volpe, who in turn gave a slight shrug. Acquel lifted the golden disk from out of his robes. The count's unsteady hand reached across the table and gently took it up, still about Acquel's neck.

"A pretty, if somewhat rude, piece of craft. But to think what it has afforded you." He released it, nodding thoughtfully to himself. Acquel tucked the amulet back into his robes.

The count dug into his meal again. Volpe was enthusiastically wolfing down his own, his plate now piled high with meats and cheese. "It was a sad business in Perusia," continued Marsilius. "To see the queen so distraught by such an unexpected tragedy. Brought tears to my eyes. But it was instructive to see that not only was Duke Ursino absent, he sent no one else from Torinia either. Not a man. Milvorna sent only two from Duke Ridolfo's council. A clear insult as the Duke himself should have been present. Mind you, Ursino's insult was far worse...." The Count trailed off, as if lost for words, his face frozen, eyes looking straight ahead. Acquel leaned forward, waiting for the Count to finish his sentence. But as the moment lengthened into more than just a pregnant pause, the Count remained still and silent, stuck on his last thought. Volpe stopped chewing, his eyebrows raised in bewilderment.

Finally, Voltera cleared his throat nervously and stepped forward, leaning over the Count who now appeared as if he had been dropped in aspic. Voltera extended his right hand which held a round silver pomander with a red ribbon and carefully waved it under the nose of the Count. "Brother monks," he said quietly, "I apologize for this. The count is often afflicted by this disorder."

A few moments later, Marsilius blinked and closed his mouth. His brow furrowed. "Ah, what was I saying?"

"You were speaking of Duke Ursino sending no delegation to represent him," reminded Acquel. Volpe was looking at Acquel to see what he had made of the episode.

"Yes, that is correct. Torinia's slight is as good as a declaration of war against the crown. He will announce the throne his by right of blood despite the existence of the young prince."

"But on what grounds?" asked Acquel. "The prince is the rightful heir. Perhaps he manoeuvres to be regent."

"I know he is kin to the late king. Cousin of some degree. Just what scrap of law on which he would base his claim is..." And once again Marsilius stopped as if enchanted, mid-sentence. Acquel winced and looked up to Voltera. The advisor leaned forward and waved the strong smelling medicine once again under the Count's motionless face. But this time, it did nothing. Volpe pulled a sprig of rosemary out of his teeth and watched, frowning.

"Ah gentlemen," said Voltera, in a tone of sadness that Acquel was not entirely convinced was genuine. "Sometimes these spells do last some time. The scent normally brings him around. Doesn't seem to be working though." He shook his head and then gently pulled the Count back into his chair so that his head rested against the carved back. "Allow me to continue for the Count, if I may. I was in attendance with him."

Acquel sat back and raised both hands in acceptance of the offer.

"The intelligence we gathered upon our return was more alarming," began Voltera as he leaned upon the trestle. "A great army is heading north from Torinia city to join the forces already at the border near Persarola and Palio."

"How do you know this?" demanded Acquel. "Did you see them?"

"No. But we met travellers who had come from the south of the duchy. They told of a vast force, several thousand strong, moving northwards. Mercenary companies, the Duke's own army and guardsmen, perhaps even Ursino himself among them."

Acquel was not surprised. "Perhaps they will turn east and try and invest Perusia."

Voltera shook his head with certainty. "No. They are too far north for that course, Brother Acquelonius. Their objective must surely be Maresto's northern reaches. Or us. Livorna."

"Or both," said Acquel, looking over to Volpe. The old monk inclined his head in agreement.

"There's more I am sorry to have to relate," said Voltera. "We ourselves saw a second great force coming from Milvorna. It was at a distance, but it was sizable, horsemen and infantry. We did not linger to learn more."

"Across the Duchy of Torinia? Then Duke Ridolfo must have right of passage."

"Worse. He is an ally of Ursino now. It must be so."

Acquel looked down at his plate, untouched. The war was coming and just as quickly as he had warned. Maresto had to be informed. Strykar would have to return without delay.

"I know the Count wanted to know what your preparations are in the event of a siege," said Voltera, somewhat awkwardly. He glanced to his lord and then back to Acquel, grimacing. "Perhaps this should wait for another time…"

"You are the castellan, sir. Does not the soldiery fall to your command? I was told that the count had confirmed that all of your militia—all his men-at-arms—would now be under command of the Ara?"

Voltera frowned. "Ah, yes. He did mention that a few weeks ago. Nothing since, I'm afraid."

Volpe shook his head and reached for his wine goblet again.

"Well," said Acquel, "How many men do you have at your disposal?"

Voltera rubbed his chin. "I would have to summon the captain of the guard for the exact number. I am, you see," he gave a nervous twitter, "in more of a *ceremonial* capacity. But, if you press me for a rough count, I'd say two hundred… thereabouts."

Acquel watched as once again Volpe's brow raised in a mixture of disbelief and derision. He turned back to Voltera. "We must get the folk that dwell in the hamlet, just outside the east gate, inside the walls. Can you give the order to bring in all forage and livestock from the surrounding area? There's nothing we can do about the crops in the field. They will be torched."

Voltera looked again at the Count and raised his hands. "When he's like this it's hard to know when he will return. Do what you think best, Magister."

Ugo Volpe wiped his mouth and pushed back his bench. "We should leave now, Magister," he grumbled.

Acquel bit his lip and then too got to his feet. He gestured over to Marsilius, whose eyes still stared upwards, as good an impression of death as Acquel had ever seen. "Should we leave him... like this... Is there nothing—?"

Voltera smiled, remarkably composed thought Acquel, and waved his hand. "No, worry not. He won't even know you've left. Be on your way. I can summon you when he's in a better state for conversation."

Their escort left them at the palace gates and they made their slow progress back down the stone steps to the courtyard and the gate which led out into the city. "Worse on the knees going down than it was going up," said Volpe pausing for breath halfway. "Now I see what you meant by letting me see 'what we're up against' as you put it earlier. How long has he been addled like that?"

"He was worse than I last remember. Sweet Elded save us. I have never fought in a battle. Never defended a town under siege. I barely know where to begin."

Volpe leaned against the rough stone face of the cliff. "Well, you started off right. Getting folk in from the outlying villages with what food they can carry. Imagine we have another week yet, God willing."

"We need to send a rider south, to reach Duke Alonso—or at least get word to the Black Rose and Strykar." He grasped the old monk's shoulder. "Brother Ugo, I cannot lead this defence on my own. I can't. Maybe Lieutenant Poule..."

Volpe smiled and laid a finger aside his crushed medlar of a nose. "You're forgetting that I know a thing or two about war too. We'll sort out the rest as we go along!"

Caught between an advancing army and the black arts of Lucinda della Rovera, Acquel began to feel the world close in upon him.

Fourteen

STRYKAR TORE OFF his gauntlets and quickly ripped open the seal on the letter he had been handed by a courier of the Count's retinue. He re-entered his tent, its gaily coloured flaps now tied back to allow in the afternoon light, and dumped himself into a field chair. He gestured to his server for his goblet and then unfolded the message, hastily scrawled in a thick hand, ink smudged and spill-stained.

It was from the apothecary.

Messere Julianus, my honoured patron,

I have felt compelled to write to you rather than wait until you are next in Maresto (and knowing full well of the exigencies of the battlefield). Since your departure, the reception of our acqua miracula *in the town has surpassed all expectation. As fast as I could distil the precious liquor and bottle it, it is spoken for. All stock is sold, and alas I have but one sackful of the prime ingredient which you alone can provide. I have collected 372 ducats in toto thus far having found that the wealthier sort of Maresto are willing to pay huge sums for our elixir, given its remarkable qualities.*

Strykar's mouth split into a wide grin as he read. His pay as a commander was not insignificant he knew, but an added source of income was welcome indeed. Why should the nobility get all the sinecures on wine, silks, or spice? This was his monopoly: *acqua miracula*. His black-rimmed fingernails ran across the page as he read further.

Yet it is with heavy heart and much dismay, good sir, that I must relate the most difficult of news regarding our venture. News of the elixir has reached the Duke's exchequer and, alas, it has been adjudicated (most cruelly I fear) that our liquor is in breach of law regarding tax and duty owed upon it, for you were never given the right to sell. I have now settled with the exchequer men, having paid the levy and the fines which leaves the enterprise still in profit I am happy to report. I will hold the remaining ten ducats for you when next we meet. Given that you still must obtain a warrant, I shall refrain from distilling any further until you return. May I enquire of your next expedition to the northern reaches that we might obtain more of the leaf?

Strykar balled the letter in his fist and flung it across the tent.

"Money-grubbing bastards!" He kicked over the tripod table for good measure, sending his serving boy dashing out of the tent for fear of his life. He retrieved his goblet from the grass and refilled it with the pitcher that had thankfully been set down upon his blackwood chest near his camp bed. He took a long swig, topped the brass goblet up again, and walked out. The walls of Istriana were just visible above the makeshift stockade of the encampment: palisades of hacked-down saplings rising up over a hastily dug three-foot ditch. Wagons had been pushed into position too, helping to create a wall around the encampment where some four thosand soldiers— whether knightly men-at-arms, spearmen, swordsmen or bowmen—went about the business of preparing for war. As one of three Coronels for the company, it was his captains who directed the rank and file of the *rondelieri*, spearmen and bowmen that were in his column. His duties were to work with the quartermaster to arrange food and billeting and to help devise strategy along with the other Coronels and with Malvolio. The Count himself commanded the thousand-strong heavy cavalry of the Black Rose, delegating to one or two of his noblemen friends to lead the lances into battle.

It was no doubt a similar arrangement on the far side of little Istriana where the Company of the Scarlet Ring had made their camp. Six and a half thousand men combined, thought Strykar. More than enough to deal with the Torinian companies to the east. That was if they would only stop digging in like badgers and begin to get moving across the broad rolling countryside. It was terrain that favoured boldness not passivity. He drained his goblet and pulled on the gauntlets that he had looped into the belt of his doublet. It was time to go into town to meet Malvolio and the commanders of the Scarlet Ring. He made his way through the sprawling encampment, the tang of rusting steel mixed with that of leather and horse strong in his nostrils, and fetched his black courser at the paddock. The grooms saluted, handed off the reins and he trotted out of camp and across the field to the main gate of Istriana.

When he entered the hall of the inn on the main square, the established headquarters for the mercenary army, he saw that he was late. The other two Coronels of the Black Rose were present as was Malvolio, and seated across the long oak trestle were the three Coronels and the commander of the Scarlet Ring, Giacomo Bartholomew, along with one or two squadron captains.

"Coronel Strykar, you have deigned to favour us with your presence at last." Malvolio pointed to a vacant place on the benches and Strykar gave him a court bow before taking his place. "Messere Giacomo," continued the count, "you were saying that your scouts had located the enemy?"

Bartholomew nodded and leaned forward, knitting his fingers together. "Aye. They avoided contact but clearly saw an advance column heading west, about twenty miles from here. The standard was that of the Blue Boar."

"Our scouts have not made any contact past the river," replied Malvolio. "At least that is what Calandra tells me."

Coronel Calandra's drooping head popped up. "That is correct, my lord. No sightings. But I understand the Scarlets' scouts arrived back only this morning. Their reports are the fresher."

Strykar hunched over, elbows settling onto the sticky trestle top. He liked the other officers; on the whole they were a good lot. Even the Scarlets were tolerable if one had to work together with them in the field. Most of these commanders were second or third sons of noblemen while one or two others had advanced up through the ranks. But all were hardened to the fight and grown successful upon the fruits of battle. Yet for two weeks they had all been sitting with their thumbs up their backsides outside Istriana, waiting and adding further useless refinements to the encampments much to the pleasure of the quartermasters and the whores. Strykar began to absently tap his thumb on the table. The five Coronels looked bored to a man, eyelids drooping, fingers looped through the handles of their wine goblets and probably dreaming of their evening meal. Malvolio was somewhat more animated but then he was leading the conference, which was the third in the last fortnight.

"So, good my lords," said the Count. "Is it your council to stay and accept the battle on the Maresto side of the river or venture out and take them on the Torinian side? What says the Ring?"

Bartholomew smiled and inclined his head politely. "So long as we toss for who leads the van, I do not mind one way or the other. If we deploy here, we can choose the ground.

Surely they know they won't be marching further unopposed. They are ready for battle, as are we."

"True," replied Malvolio. "But that option lets them dictate the attack. The when is as important as the where, no?"

Strykar sat up slowly and spread his fingers flat. "Well, my lords, our palisades are sprouting roots we have sat here so long. I for one say we get into harness and move east now."

There was a ripple of laughter which Strykar acknowledged with a smile, even if Malvolio returned it with a scowl.

"Looks like Strykar's been eating horseshoe nails again," said Calandra, grinning. "Always up and ready for a scrap."

"So you think we are possessed of enough intelligence of the enemy, Coronel Strykar?" Malvolio fixed him with a harsh stare but Strykar knew very well that the Count valued his advice more than most. "How many cavalry come against us? How many bowmen? You would have us cross the frontier like blind men, holding onto a long rope?"

"My lord," said Strykar, his voice taking on a tone of insincere pique, "I am counselling that we ride straight into them and shatter their host such that they ride naked and two-up back to Torinia city to tell the sad tale. If *I* were in the Blue Boar *I* would be thinking that the enemy would hold their ground—defend this town—choose the ground as Messere Giacomo suggests. Wait and draw in an attack. And that is precisely why we should not. Because they are expecting it."

Bartholomew laughed. "He *is* an iron-eater, your Strykar! I'll give you that, my lord!"

Malvolio's eyes scanned the faces around the table. He reached into his belt pouch and drew out a ducat. "The win is for the vanguard, my lords. Messere Giacomo, do you call heads or tails?"

The commander of the Scarlet Ring shrugged. "Discussion over it seems. Aye then. Tails for me."

Malvolio flipped the coin, snatched it on the way down and slapped it on the top of his opposite hand.

He lifted his palm away. "It is heads. The Black Rose will lead the force." He turned to Strykar. "And Coronel Strykar's not inconsiderable nose will be out in front of us all."

LESS THAN TWO days later, the combined mercenary armies had crossed the wide but shallow Taro where a ford had reduced the flow to an invigorated trickle over glass-smooth white pebbles. That morning, priests had held prayers and a blessing for the company, a large banner floating over the proceedings. It bore the sun in splendour with ten golden rays, not seven. A ripple of protest soon thereafter spread out among the more religious of the soldiery and Strykar had laughed to see the scrambling priests hastily unfurl a second flag next to the first: the old seven-ray sun blaze of the One Faith. A brawl averted, the prayers had recommenced with mutual nods and grudging acceptance of the two confessions.

The gently undulating plain made the march into Torinia easy, the infantry laughing and swearing as they made their slow progress eastwards, passing between the small stands of oak and beech that were scattered across the frontier. The Black Rose marched in three columns, each twenty men across. The mounted men-at-arms, lances raised skywards and butts resting on stirrup cups, covered both flanks while crossbowmen were burrowed in among the ranks of the spearmen, their weapons slung over shoulders. Groups of free-floating *rondelieri*, round shields on their backs and swords on their hips, roamed across the vanguard between the main infantry and the cavalry.

Strykar kicked his courser as he cantered between two of the columns, making for Malvolio's battle wagon which trundled behind the rear guard. Arrayed from head to toe in polished white harness, his bevor lowered to give him welcome air, he squeezed his knees in tight against his mount as he pounded forward, eager to make his report. One of the company's trumpeters followed in his wake, grimacing as he ducked to dodge flying clumps of sod. The great flat-topped *carroccio*, a massive cart on four oversized wheels, creaked and rattled as it made its way, drawn by four horses. The huge battle standard of the Black Rose was lashed to a pole at one end: a white field upon which the heraldic flower was drawn, sable petals surrounding a stamen of gold. Malvolio stood as if on the prow of a vessel, his baton in one hand and the other resting on the rails of the shaking and wobbling vehicle. He and his personal guard were dressed, like Strykar, in full plate armour over which they had draped their white emblazoned tabards. A complement of crossbowmen were aboard and even two gunners for the cast-iron falconets that were mounted either side and loaded with nails—last ditch defences should they be needed.

Strykar reined in and raised his visor. "My lord, scouts have sighted the enemy. They are dead ahead, one mile distant. Still on the march."

Count Malvolio smiled. "The weather holds fair and the ground is hard. Looks as if you will get your battle this day, Strykar." He motioned to one of his retinue at his side. They moved to unfurl a red signal flag mounted on a glaive. This was waved at the back of the *carrachio* towards where the Scarlet Ring followed the Black Rose at a distance of 500 yards. Moments later, Strykar could see a red flag sprout up in reply.

"Double up your column, Coronel, and deploy the divisions. Here is as good a field as any we could hope for." Malvolio turned to a steel-encased nobleman who stood nearby. "Messere Lucan, if you would mount up and prepare your men for a charge on the right flank. The Scarlets say they will hold their lances in reserve on our left."

Strykar twisted around in his high-backed saddle to give the order to his trumpeter, remembering too late that this was not an easy task in full plate armour with bevor and sallet. He cursed and tugged on his reins and spun his mount around instead. "Relay the order to deploy to the other columns and then rejoin me on the left with the *rondelieri!*"

The sweating trumpeter saluted, reached for the long silver horn slung about his back, and kicked his horse forward. Strykar wheeled again to face the Count. "My lord, may Elded and God be with you! This night it will be boar's head on the table!"

"God be with you, sir! And a feast in Istriana on the morrow!"

Soon after the trumpet blasts reverberated across the plain, the long and fraught manoeuvres began. Slowly, Strykar's column of infantry broadened to two hundred men across, several ranks deep, as the files redoubled again and again into battle lines urged on by shouting sergeants. Across the front, the columns of the Black Rose did the same, forming three divisions. Deep in the rear, Malvolio's cavalry, over a thousand strong, were jostling into position waiting for the enemy to come into view through the scattered trees a mile distant. Strykar moved among the *rondelieri* skirmishers, sword drawn, and sought out Captain Cortese, also mounted and yelling encouragement to the men as the vast caterpillar turned onto itself, tall spears glinting in the hazy sun.

"Cortese! Need you in with the spears and bowmen. I will play with the *rondelieri!*"

The Captain smiled as his horse drew alongside, lightly armoured swordsmen streaming around them where they stood. "Should have expected that, I suppose. You know them well and they know you even better! No matter. I am sure of finding a Blue Boar no matter which ground I hold."

"Fear not, Cortese. I will pay your ransom so long as it is no more than fifty soldieri."

The captain swore and laughed. "And I shall return the favour."

Strykar looked up as the *doom-doom* of kettle drums reached him, floating across from the east and followed by the distant blast of trumpets. He could just make out the enemy as it approached across a front as wide as their own. The men of the Blue Boar were deploying into battle divisions. Two huge silk standards became visible as the lines cleared the trees.

Cortese followed Strykar's gaze and saw for himself the force arrayed against them. "Big," he said, adjusting the chinstrap of his barbute helm. "Maybe bigger than we thought?"

"Depends how many of the White Company are with them. Don't worry, Cortese. You won't have time to lose sleep over it."

Cortese nodded and brought up his slender cruciform-hilted sword in a salute. "I wish you luck, Coronel. God be with you this day!" And he turned his mount and picked his way through the sword and shield men as he called out to the soldiers who turned their faces up to him. "Have a care, lads! It's a blade. Likely to hurt someone! You there! Wrong way. They're coming from *that* direction."

Strykar sought out his old sergeant, Gillani, and found him as he was tongue-lashing a group of fifty *rondelieri* into a semblance of formation, shield edge to shield edge, armoured spearmen at their backs to afford them some protection from an enemy charge. "You are damnable lazy bastards, every a one! The first wave will be the arrows so get those shields up!" The men exchanged worried glances but complied, jostling each other into position even as they saw the specks beyond coalesce into lines of armoured spearmen, moving at a slow walking pace towards them.

"How goes it, Gillani? Are we ready to take them?"

The sergeant turned and saluted, a gloved hand to his sallet. "Aye, that we are, Coronel!"

Strykar raised his voice, deep and booming, that the swordsmen men around him could hear. "You are the fastest runners, the strongest blades of the Black Rose. We'll have to take a few salvoes from their crossbows before we can let you off your leashes. But hold fast! The sergeant will give the word for you to break ranks and flank them."

Strykar looked at the faces around him. Some he knew from years gone by, others not. Some were smiling, others eyes-wide in nervous apprehension. In his heart, he worried. The Black Rose had not seen an engagement this size in years. This was no scrap against a roving band of brigands on the frontier. For many it would be their first great battle. And he knew well, that mad dash across the gap between the armies—full pelt and your armour draining the strength from your muscles—was always the most terrifying. But once you were stuck into the enemy, sword and shield constantly moving and striking, there was no time to feel fear.

The first volley of crossbow bolts sounded like the whispers of dark angels as they arced in low, a black cloud emanating from within the lines of the Blue Boar. The quarrels pinged off shields and armour, some ricocheting and others biting through leather or striking unguarded faces. Instinctively, the *rondelieri* bent knees and leaned in, huddling closer. From within the centre division of the Black Rose, a storm of iron bolts was launched in reply from crossbowmen rising up among the rows of spearmen who had lowered their shafts towards the enemy. Strykar flinched as a spent bolt bounced from his pauldron and tumbled away. He heard a deep thud —Malvolio's small detachment of field serpentines had come into play from deep in the rear, firing over their heads. He pushed his bevor up into place, the spring lock finding its hole with a click. With the pommel of his sword he slammed the visor of his sallet shut, his vision now restricted to a thin slit. It was a most peculiar way to see the world but one he was now long accustomed to.

A second volley of crossbow bolts came raining in and he heard a lamentable scream from in front of him, a *rondelieri* falling and clutching a leg. The sharp sound of iron bolt heads striking steel shields lasted but a few seconds as the attack came and went. The enemy were closer now: rank upon rank of spear and glaive, banners flying in the stiffening breeze. Strykar could also see ranks of cavalry forming in front of him, on their right flank; heavy men-at-arms, lances couched, their horses nervously bucked and started, anxious to break into a trot. The ranks of spearmen among the *rondelieri* lowered their long shafts of stout ash ten feet in front of the shields, forming a hedgehog of blades to throw back the impending charge of armoured horses and riders.

Another gun sounded, a deep chest-thudding boom, but Strykar saw nothing of its result. By the time the gunners had ranged the enemy they would already be locked into the clash of pole weapons. *Bloody useless in a field battle*, he mused as his horse skitted sideways at the sound. His mouth had dried up, his tongue thick. He swallowed and scanned the enemy centre. There was a ripple among the spears and upraised glaives and halberds. Something was coming to the front. He watched as a gap appeared and a shield wall of *rondelieri*, perhaps a dozen men, came out. Behind them, he saw a tall wooden pole with a platform at the top rise up skyward. Something metallic glistened upon this high perch, too far away for him to see. But a banner was draped also: the seven-rays of the One Faith, unsullied by the new commandments of Elded, those rejected by Torinia. A loud cry rose up among the Company of the Blue Boar. Indistinct at first, Strykar soon recognized the words that rolled across to them, a hundred yards away now.

"The Hand! The Hand!" came the cry.

The volleys had now stopped on both sides—a strange tactic in itself, he thought. He raised his sallet's visor up to get a better look at whatever the Blue Boar was taunting them with. Below him, a *rondelieri* (obviously an ardent follower of the Faith) cried out: "It is the Hand of Ursula! They have the Hand!" And like a saltpetre fuse, the news travelled in fits and starts, sparking its way across the front lines and making its way back into the ranks. Strykar had never been an overly religious man but even he had heard of the sacred hand. And he knew it was kept at the Ara, to be delivered up only to the king of Valdur when he went to war. If he knew this, then most of the men of the Black Rose would probably know it too. Was the boy prince with the Torinians? An instant later he felt a tingle run down his neck and spine as he realized the only possibility: Ursino was claiming the throne, and he was there, somewhere in the enemy ranks. How he had thieved the Hand was not important. Ursino possessed it now and Strykar could see doubt moving across his company like a dark cloud covering the face of the sun. Who were they fighting now?

"We must engage!" he shouted. There was no way to signal Lucan to launch his cavalry as he was clear over on the right flank. But as if in an answered prayer, he heard the pounding of earth behind him on his left. He yanked the reins of his horse and looked behind. Hundreds of heavy lances of the Scarlet Ring were thundering across the fields, headed straight for the right flank of the Blue Boar.

Strykar laughed and turned to find his trumpeter. "Those impetuous bastards! Those beautiful impetuous bastards! God love them!" He urged his mount through the throng of spears, sighting his mounted trumpeter three ranks back. "Blow damn you! Blow and sound the advance!" The trumpeter fumbled with his cord and managed to bring the long horn to his lips. The blast sounded out and was soon relayed by the trumpeters of the other divisions.

"Come on, you bastards! Forward!" cried Strykar, waving his sword and urging his horse through the ranks of spearmen and *rondelieri*. In front of them, there was a tremendous crash of steel and the frantic neighing of horses as the Scarlet Ring drove into the serried spears of the Blue Boar. Strykar could see the enemy absorb the charge, falling back yet holding their lines. All across the three divisions—left, vanguard, and right—his men walked briskly forward, ten foot spears levelled and shields raised up to deflect the unlucky arrow shaft or short quarrel. Fifty yards from contact, another volley flew at them, answered immediately by the crossbowmen in their own ranks. Death, fickle as always, sprinkled his reward sparsely all around as men screamed and fell with quarrels in their faces, necks and arms. The Black Rose kept moving, stepping over and around the fallen, whether dead or wounded.

The two sides met with an enormous clatter of wooden hafts as the spearmen shoved, hauled back, and shoved their weapons again, darting eyes searching out a gap or a stumbling man pushed from behind by a comrade. All was a cacophony of yells, grunts of exertion, or cries of pain as each side attempted to force its way through the other. In his eagerness to push forward, Strykar's horse quickly was out into the front rank of spears. Realizing his exposure, he pulled back on his reins but not before the horse screamed and reared, a spear thrust coming in fast underneath its steel chanfron and taking it in the throat. The beast came down again on its front legs and then sagged forward, crumpling. Strykar swore and pulled his feet out of the stirrups as it fell, rolling out of the saddle and onto the ground. A swordsman grabbed his upper arm and helped lift him as the ranks surged and ebbed around them.

"I'm all right, get back in," Strykar mumbled as he staggered up, still clutching his sword. His horse, a mount that had seen him across the breadth of the duchy half a dozen times, coughed blood and lay its head down. "Shit!" Strykar stood back as another rank of spearmen passed him, streaming around the dead animal. He swore again and pushed his way forward and into the scrambling mass. He spied a few *rondelieri* working to give cover to the spearmen with their shields and he waded in to reach them, his sword held high. He saw one of his own jab out with a spear and take a soldier opposite in the mouth, the spear blade ripping his cheek wide open as it continued to pierce throat and neck. The man slumped away only for another to lower his spear and take his place. Two places from where he stood, urging on his men, a sergeant with a pole-arm took a spear thrust in the belly, groaned and collapsed onto his knees.

Strykar reached him, and seeing he was already as good as gone, awkwardly bent down, his gauntleted hands grasping the poor man's weapon: a six-foot war hammer. Six *rondelieri* realised that Strykar had now gathered about him in the swirling, clattering press of pole weapons.

"Coronel Strykar!" said one veteran he knew by sight alone. "Stand behind us until we can get you mounted again!"

Strykar looked at them, faces already red-flushed and streaming with sweat even though they had not yet made their dash into the fray. "Come lads, no time for that. We're going in for the skirmish now." He hefted the war hammer, spiked at top and rear. "You there! To me, *rondelieri*!" He gathered a few more of his sword and buckler men as spearmen cursed and filtered around them. "We get in past their spear points and they're as good as dead where they stand, lads." He looked forward to see where the heavy mounted men-at-arms of the Scarlet Ring had wheeled after their charge, broken lances lying around the trampled ground, the enemy hedgehog shaken yet still intact. Strykar could see the Scarlets were heading in again to take on the spearmen. That tied up that enemy division he thought. There was a gap of twenty yards between them and the division he faced. If he could run his swordsmen to that flank, he might be able to tear it up from the inside. He would need about forty men.

More *rondelieri* joined him, the numbers swelling as they massed, still within the spearmen but near the far left edge of the column, ready to make their sprint towards the enemy. Old Gilani pushed his way through, huffing and puffing.

"Coronel, sir, you are doing my work! Should I mount your horse and play the officer?"

"Are you ready to make another run?" asked Strykar, his eyes wide with the lust of battle. "We shall hit them hard in the flank, get inside their spearheads and cut them up nicely until they collapse like dead wood!"

Gilani nodded enthusiastically despite his wheezing chest and Strykar slammed down his visor over his face.

In threes and fours, they ran out. Strykar followed close on his three chosen men. The dash across the field was short but in the time it took them, the Torinians saw what was coming and awkwardly tried to move their spears to protect their flank. Strykar could see glaive men pushing their way through their comrades to move to the flank to defend the formation. There was a crash as the three *rondelieri* hit the levelled spearpoints with their shields, deflecting them and pushing forward. Strykar was right on their heels and they burst into the midst of the Blue Boar. Swords began to rain down on weapon hafts as the spearmen instinctively drew back, raising their weapons to the vertical to defend themselves. Strykar stepped into a gap and brought down the flat head of his war hammer towards the helm of the spearman before him. The man parried the blow with the haft of his spear but Strykar had already pulled his hammer back and jabbed it forward horizontally, the wicked spike striking the man's unprotected face. It collapsed inwards like the clay head of a child's doll. There was a spray of blood and he fell without a sound, stone dead.

From the corner of his eye, he caught the glint of a glaive arcing down and he brought up the studded haft of his war hammer to block it. A *rondelieri* shield flew up to assist his defence and he deftly used the curved spike on the war hammer to hook the shaft of the glaive and lock it. That gave the *rondelieri* the opportunity to land an overhead blow upon the man's head, rending his helm and sending him to the ground, dazed, dying, or dead. Strykar had entered the strange place in his mind when one fought the melee. It was as if time stood still, all energy focussed on what lay beyond the narrow view of his eye slit. Even the sounds around him seemed to diminish as his concentration deepened, his arms moving without conscious effort. Killing what stood in front of him and staying alive was all that mattered. Something he had been long accustomed to.

They had cut their way deep into the formation, more of the *rondelieri* following them in. The Torinians now found themselves fighting on two fronts and their division was a seething, moving mass, slowly losing its cohesion. The Black Rose spearmen redoubled their efforts, yelling encouragement to each other as they saw their *rondelieri* comrades cutting through the ranks of the Blue Boar. Strykar now saw a large white standard waving among the halberds a few files beyond; a great charging blue boar was painted upon it. He pushed forward for he would have that ensign and the man's flag. The thought of slaying Coronel Aretini rushed into his mind even as his war hammer rose and fell. He prayed that the man who above all others he wished to destroy was there, leading the division. A *rondelieri* next to him let out a cry of pain and groaned, sinking down, a spear thrust in the groin. Strykar lashed out with the top of the hammer, striking the enemy whose blade had done the deed. And then another image flashed into his mind. His wife, Cara. His daughter. Taken from him more than a decade ago by the Blue Boar. *Aretini*'s men. Maybe Aretini himself.

A sword glanced off his pauldron, sending him off-balance. He recovered, parrying a second blade that came down towards his head. Another blow, this time from behind, brought stars to his eyes, staggering him briefly. But his helm had deflected the blade and he threw himself backwards into his opponent even as he whirled to lash out with the war hammer. A spear shaft shot in towards his belly and he jerked his war hammer to parry the head as it came in. He was exposed now, the other *rondelieri* having either fallen back or fallen down. For the first time, he scanned the faces in front of him, full of intent, curses on their lips, eyes wide in the excitement of battle; ugly in their rage. Some looked terrified but others had teeth clenched in grim determination. Strykar saw one bearded halberdier smiling.

"Strykar!" It was his sergeant, Gilani, sidling up to him and holding his shield out to defend them both. Behind followed half a dozen swordsmen, shield edge to shield edge. "Where the hell do you think you're going!" he shouted as a halberd glanced off his shield with a loud ring. "Get behind me!"

Strykar took a deep breath realizing his foolhardiness at his one-man drive to reach the enemy standard. He would be cut down in minutes. He dodged a thrust, lashed out with his hammer spike and fell back behind the *rondelieri* shields. The banner of the Blue Boar seemed to drift further away, still waving, antagonizing him. They began back-pedalling now, beating off the fall of glaive, halberd and spear as they tried to break free of the enemy formation.

A loud screech like the cry of a great bird of prey, but louder than any bird Strykar had ever heard, rent the air. A second cry followed quickly, just as urgent and shrill. Trumpets sounded from somewhere deep in the enemy formation and instantly Strykar felt the push of spear lessen and become hesitant. Something was happening further back and the Blue Boar was pausing.

Strykar and his band found themselves clear of the throng, between both sides in the churned-up field. He hooked a thumb under his visor and wrenched it up. He was nearly winded though it had been but a few minutes of melee. A screech rolled across the field again, so loud that he flinched. He looked to see the top of some enormous siege engine moving slowly through the army. Then, with disbelief, he realized it was something else entirely. It was not a wooden tower, it was alive. Tall as a house, it was moving through the lines, the Blue Boar giving way to either side as it made its steady progress to the front.

"Sweet God!" said Gilani softly. Strykar saw now what it was that advanced towards the Black Rose. It was a griffon, the royal beast of Valdur. It had the head, wings and front claws of an eagle and the body and tail of a lion. Its proportions were enormous: the length of a merchant's cog and as high as the mast. The long tail whipped and twitched above the soldiers like that of an irritated cat. Strykar found his feet frozen where he stood. Such a thing had never been seen in his time except in the pages of a manuscript. From behind, a murmur of disquiet floated to his ears from the ranks of the Black Rose. Strykar now saw that a second griffon was following in the path of the first, its head tossing, beak clacking in anticipation. Muscles rippled along its flanks of shaggy, dark brown fur. The lead beast screeched again, wings spreading wide. The Blue Boar soldiers in the path of the creatures now broke and peeled away, some dropping their unwieldy poles, others not sure whether the beasts were friend or foe.

"Quick, back to the lines!" Strykar said, shaking a glaze-eyed Gilani from his stupor. The small band folded back into the ranks of the Black Rose, practically unheeded since every eye was turned upwards to what now faced them. The griffons stood side by side, proud and magnificent as their huge dark eyes scanned the troops arrayed before them. Two figures on horseback slowly made their way forward stopping in between the giant beasts. One was in full white harness, a ducal coronet sitting upon the brow of his polished helm. The other was a woman, her long flowing blonde hair cascading down upon a silver breastplate. She rode as a man, firmly in her high-backed saddle—every inch a soldier in spite of her sex. Strykar knew she could only be Lucinda della Rovera and that the situation was now far, far worse than he could have imagined but a few hours ago.

An unreal silence fell across both armies as the fighting ceased—totally. The front rank of the Black Rose had now folded back on itself, a concave row of spears and glaives. The woman's voice rose up, clear, confident and commanding.

"You stand in rebellion to the rightful king of Valdur! Ursino, Duke of Torinia!" She raised a gloved hand towards the Duke. "You have seen the Hand of Ursula before you! Now you see the favour of the immortal throne of Valdur itself—these royal beasts!" She raised both arms, gesturing to the creatures that towered over her either side.

Ursino's horse advanced a few feet. "I am your rightful king!" he shouted "Lay down your arms! Join me and your lives will be spared!"

Strykar's gauntleted hands tightened on the haft of his war hammer. He was unhorsed, with no way of getting to the rear to bring word to Malvolio or the Scarlet Ring. Around him stood hundreds of infantry—confused, frightened, and liable to break and run at any moment. He could only pray that one of the trumpeters had galloped back to tell what was happening. Delay would be the end of them all. He watched the Lady della Rovera sitting high in the saddle, back bolt upright. Already playing the new queen. Brother Acquel's warning rang in his ears, a warning he had taken only half seriously. The truth of the monk's words was now terribly obvious.

Two crossbow bolts flew across the distance between the armies. Fired by the Black Rose. One struck the foreleg of one of the griffons while the other shot past the duke's shoulder. An instant later the world fell apart as the griffons cried out simultaneously, a horrific deafening screech of rage. They leapt forward into the front ranks of the Black Rose, a hundred yards from where Strykar stood, and swept men away like so much standing straw. Their giant talons raked across half a dozen soldiers in one swipe, while the huge beaks darted down to snatch and crush armoured men and toss them through the air. Long tails, as thick as the chains of Palestro, cleared swathes of soldiers with every lash, sending men and spears sprawling. Strykar felt his mouth gape as he watched in horror. One of the griffons reared up, golden wings spread, talons clawing the air in triumph. It came down again, crushing a dozen men as it hit the ground. Strykar felt the earth tremble under his feet. The men in the ranks further back now turned and ran. Around him, he heard the sound of dropped weapons and yells as men headed for the rear.

He turned at a new sound to see hundreds of horsemen now cantering in towards him from the far left flank. His heart lifted. Surely it was the rearguard of cavalry of the Scarlets making a new attack. The ground thundered with their arrival but as they drew near, he now saw their blue plumed helms and tabards. A large square battle standard whipped furiously from its staff, carried by a man-at-arms in jet plate armour.

The flag of the Duke of Milvorna. The first wave swept past him and he raised his war hammer to deflect a lance aimed at his chest. The force of contact as he parried knocked him backwards. A second horseman's lance missed him by a hair's breadth, the rider sailing past without slowing. The remains of the Black Rose now bunched up, spears out, a roiling mass. The Milvornan cavalry hit them hard, recoiled, and wheeled away to trot off for another pass. Strykar fended off an axe-wielding horseman, struck him with his hammer and then yanked him from the saddle with the spike.

All around was chaos: screams and the cries of the griffons, the frantic neighing of terrified horses. The Milvornan he had struck was hanging upside down, one foot stuck in his stirrup, and struggling to reach up to his saddle. Strykar hauled back and gave him a tremendous blow to the helm, crushing it and killing the man instantly. He leaned against the neck of the prancing horse, desperate to free the man's boot from the stirrup. It would not budge. He cursed and then flinched as he felt another cavalryman thunder past him. At last, he freed the dead man's foot and threw the leg away as he reached up for the reins. Before he could raise his own boot to the stirrup, he felt his whole body lift with a crash. He was hurled to the ground, sharp pain surging through his shoulder. He rolled over onto his chest, armour jangling, and tried to push himself up. As he raised his head, blue sky came into view. At the edge of his vision, he caught a fleeting glimpse of the russet and black griffons rearing high. Pulling himself up onto his knees, he found he could not lift his arm: the last blow had dented his pauldron so badly it had jammed into his breastplate. He watched dumbly—as if in a dream—as a Milvornan nobleman trotted towards him. The swing of the sword was never seen. He felt the shock through his helm—a moment of roaring, ringing pain—and then he knew no more.

Fifteen

DANAMIS LEANED OVER the larboard rail and scanned the wide piazza of Perusia's harbour. To a new arrival, all might have seemed as it should be: merchants and their goods-laden carts making their way up into the city; seamen congregating at the row of slant-roofed taverns that lined the far side; fishermen stacking their willow baskets near the docks of the quay. Even so, Danamis could tell that a dark, uncertain mood hung over the seafront. It was quieter than at any time he had visited. The boisterous banter and rowdiness had evaporated leaving a flat, sullen stink to the place. Far fewer people and no laughter, no joy. And he had never seen so few vessels sitting at the docks as now. Perusia was a city on the edge of quiet panic, poised for the drop of the axe.

He could hear his men remarking similar thoughts as they hoisted a large triangular sail to serve as an awning over their post at the foot of the gangplank. Danamis had ordered a dozen swordsmen and archers to guard the ship from the quayside. He wasn't taking any chances with this visit as the last had proved so memorable. The *Royal Grace* sat lashed alongside his starboard, a walkway established so that men could cross quickly between the two vessels. And tied just astern of the *Vendetta* lay the unlucky royal galley they had recaptured from its mutineers. These unfortunate men sat chained and roped to their benches, overseen by a prize crew Danamis had set on-board. Their fate would be in the hands of Cressida's royal guard. He doubted very much that mercy would be on the cards for them. Captain Alandris's rotting head had been wrapped in a piece of oilcloth and was bobbing in a small wine cask ready to deliver up to the palace should they wish to give it a proper burial. Bad business all around he thought as he turned to meet Captain Bassinio who had just bounded down to the main deck from across the *Royal Grace*.

"Hell of a welcome so far, eh Nico? When do you intend to go up to the castle? I'd just as soon be rid of that galley scum as soon as we can." He wiped the sleeve of his doublet across his brow and burn-scarred cheek and neck, a lasting souvenir of his defeat aboard the *Salamander* against the mutinous Captain Tetch.

"I go up there today," Danamis replied. "I'll take a dozen men as an escort—you choose the sharpest among the soldiers. Skilled with a blade in a tight situation." He glanced up to the quarterdeck and to Citala who stood by the taffrail looking down at him. He flashed her a smile and nodded. "The merfolk stay here though. At least for now. Until I find out what is happening is Perusia. Until…" He gave Bassinio a knowing look. "Until I find out what Cressida has in mind for me."

Gregorvero, who was standing two paces away, raised his eyebrows. "Citala won't like cooling her heels on ship while you're up at the palace. And that Necalli cove… well, I don't trust him no ways. Always skulking about. Nobbling the crew about everything under the sun and always with that damned ugly grin. He makes a monkfish look beautiful."

Danamis turned back to the railing and leaned on his elbows. "I haven't made up my mind about him just yet. That said, he's in a foreign land on his own—a place where merfolk aren't particularly welcome. I reckon he'll keep his head down."

"And your lady?"

He looked up again at Citala. She was still staring down at him, and by the expression on her face, a hundred questions must be running through her mind. "She will just have to trust me for what lies ahead."

"Damned curious that there's no soldiery to be seen down here since we arrived this morning. Not even a half-drunk militiaman. What do you suppose that means?"

Danamis shook his head. "I don't know, Gregor. But my gut tells me they're all hunkered down. Up there." And he gestured towards the red sandstone walls, some forty feet high, that rose up where the city's houses ended and which enclosed the sprawling royal palace of Valdur. "And if that is so, the people will already be smelling the fear. I need to get some answers from the queen and that weasel Raganus."

Bassinio joined Danamis at the railing. "I daresay that is what they are looking to *you* for."

As THE MID-afternoon summer sun beat down upon the deck, Citala watched as Danamis—dressed in his finest doublet and hose, a wine-coloured cloak about his shoulders and a velvet cap upon his head—left the ship in the company of his men-at-arms. The latter were armoured—brigantines and barbutes all, with swords at their waists. She felt she needed to swim if for no other reason than to clear her head. But the scum-coated waters of the harbour, filled with flotsam and dead fish, deterred that impulse. She would need to immerse herself within another day—or risk the onset of dry-death—but for now she was in no danger.

Four days earlier she had been elated, almost smug, with her victory over the galley and her rescue of Danamis. She had proved her worth. And that first night after the battle when she had announced she would accompany him whether he wished it or not, they had made love as if it was the first time for both of them. She knew then, in the tightness of his embrace and the intensity of his kisses, how deep was his passion for her and her for him. Yet something in her mind was quietly warning her off. It may have been nothing more than the age-old taboo of dealing with landsmen: deep seated warnings of her elders inculcated from childhood. But it was there nonetheless. She worried that perhaps it was something more. That her love was doomed to fail, broken on the rocks of Valdurian wars and human treachery. A forlorn desire that would lead only to sorrow. Now she watched him as he made his way across the piazza, past its tall stone columns and arches, and into the warren of Perusia. She felt a lump grow in her throat and her chest tighten as an impending sense of danger almost overwhelmed her. Why had this queen sent for *him*?

"You fear for his safety, Citala?" Necalli was standing near to her, his shimmering blue silk-like tunic billowing in the hot breeze that swept the quarterdeck. He spoke to her in the mer tongue. It was the dialect of the land of Atlcali, a language new to Citala which she struggled to understand despite the similarities to her own.

"I fear for his future, Master Necalli. What can he do to help save the throne of Valdur for this queen? He has no armies, only his ships. And it is an army—a great many men—that are needed to save a crown from falling off a head." She folded her arms. "He would not take me with him." She turned towards him. "Nor you it would seem."

"Understandable given the years of mistrust betwixt man and mer in this land, wouldn't you agree? Why should he stir up the people when there are enough challenges at the moment?"

She gave Necalli a thin, cold smile. "And why do you bother to speak words when you can talk with your mind? It was you who reached out to me before I left the ship to return home. And you know full well that is a gift that only she-mer possess among my people."

Necalli's huge eyes glistened as she spoke to him. He blinked slowly, nostrils flaring, and lowered his head. "It is an intrusion to push into your thoughts, I know. But I felt compelled to do so before you left the ship. I did not know when we might meet again. I wanted you to know my true feelings."

Citala raised her chin slightly. "Even before we left Palestro I felt a presence—something lurking just beyond sight. Something watching and waiting. Was that you, Master Necalli?"

The merman blinked again, his transparent inner lid moving upwards quickly followed by the outer, pale grey one. "That was not me, Citala. Perhaps you have picked up the sense of some other being. Or merely the echoes of your own thoughts."

She knew that what he said could be true. "It is an uncertain gift and one not always… dependable. Do all of your people possess this, mermen and she-mer both?"

Necalli nodded. "I did not mean to alarm you by reaching out. I want you to understand that I have the interest of your people at heart, whether you believe it or not. Your interest too, Citala."

She laughed. "You hardly know me—even after months in Palestro."

Necalli's wide mouth opened in a grin, filed white teeth flashing. "I feel I have known you for a long, long time, Citala." His long hand reached over and gently touched her wrist. "I would counsel that you must be patient. With him. There is more at stake than his service to the throne. The queen has known him for some time. There are emotions to deal with."

It was now Citala who blinked in surprise. Her reply tumbled out in Valdurian. "What do you mean? Emotions? Between them?"

"He has not told you? It is as I feared." He moved his hand away and placed it upon the railing as he looked out over the docks.

"You will explain yourself, Master Necalli," said Citala, her voice assuming a darker tone. "What of his past dealings with this queen?"

Necalli looked down. "I am told—by Lord Danamis's father—that the two were once lovers. Shortly before she was betrothed to Sempronius and when she was still only the daughter of the Duke of Colonna." He paused as Gregorvero ascended to the quarterdeck of the caravel and gave him a long glance before silently moving to the stairs and ascending to the poop deck.

"He never told me," Citala said.

Necalli moved closer to her and she did not react. "You see," he said, voice low, "some believe the parentage of the young prince is in question."

"What are you saying? That Danamis is the father?"

"That is what *some* say. Now with the king dead, more are saying it. *That* is the problem, Citala."

She turned away. "He never told me. It would be madness to return here with that rumour upon the wind. If war is on its way…"

"If it was your child in question, would you not return to save it from capture or death?"

She looked out across the rows of distant houses, the temples, the piazza, and up to the walled palace nestled in the hills beyond. Searching for answers as her mind raced. "He will tell me all when he is ready. I know he will." But there was little conviction in her voice.

Necalli gently grasped her shoulder. "He is a good and loyal creature. And know that I am here to help him—and you—and all the mer of this land. I owe my life to the father of Nicolo and my blood debt is to his house. But I am mer—like you."

The implications of what Necalli said washed over her, made her dizzy. *The queen is a widow now. And she wants him back.*

DANAMIS WATCHED AS the drawbridge descended. In all his journeys to Perusia he had never seen it raised during daylight, until now. As the chains and weights rattled their progress, his eyes scanned the battlements above. Crossbowmen at every gap, bows cradled and ready. He turned to his man, Talis, and gave a knowing look. Talis nodded in return. Someone was very nervous inside the palace. As the bridge hit the ground with a muffled thud, the portcullis began to rise. Beyond, Danamis could see an array of soldiers, weapons at the ready.

The captain of the guard stood forward, glaive in hand. "Admiral Danamis! You and your party may enter!" The soldiers opened their ranks before him and Danamis and his men passed into the gate tower and the first courtyard.

Danamis recognized the captain as the same who had conducted him through the palace a year before. "Captain Caluro, it gladdens me to see you still in command."

The man nodded but that was as far as his welcome extended. "Your men will be refreshed here while you accompany me into the palace."

"Per usual," said Danamis, grinning good-naturedly. Caluro's face remained as stone.

Danamis turned to Talis, his captain of the fo'c'sle on *Royal Grace*, a man whose confidence was never in short supply. Talis gave him a knowing smirk. "We'll be fine right here, Captain. Wine and a few games of dama for everyone I reckon."

Captain Caluro, nearly as tall as a merman, led him into the damp sprawling palace of Valdur, two guardsmen following close behind. His thoughts turned to one year ago when he had walked with Strykar along these same grand corridors, floored with marble and hung with gaudy tapestries, when he came cap in hand to beg aid from the king. Now that king was dead, felled by the same cockatrice that had followed him around the place like an overexcited dog. There was a lesson in that somewhere, he thought.

Their boots echoed across the wide halls and chambers, dark oak doors creaking open as they made their progress towards the royal apartments. At last they entered a receiving chamber—not a public chamber as it was neither grand nor spacious—but still not a space of intimacy within the royal apartments. A long dining table lay at the centre, laden with all manner of delicacies upon silver chargers, tall wine ewers shining in the light of a hundred candles. "Wait here, my lord," whispered the captain to Danamis. A moment later the door at the opposite end of the hall opened and two of the palace guard entered and took up station either side.

Baron Raganus entered, hands clasped in front of his long black, pleated *cioppa*. His expression was as sour as the last time that Danamis had seen him; a face filled with resentment for having to deal once again with the pirate of Palestro. Raganus walked to him slowly and stopped. Both men gave the faintest of bows, the bare minimum of respect. "Admiral Danamis," said Raganus softly. "You have come as the queen asked. I am not sure that was the wisest course as I have tried to discourage her from further involvement of your… services."

"I appreciate your honesty, chancellor. A refreshing change."

Raganus scowled slightly despite the wry smile that appeared on his lips. "I do not know what she has written you, but I assure you that she and the prince are safe here in Perusia. We have an army. Your flotilla would be of little use against any rebellion."

"The queen has asked nothing of me yet. But whatever she asks, I will do my utmost to comply."

"Commendable, I dare say. But it is the council's opinion that your ships are better employed keeping the seas safe from Southlanders—and those vessels that would rebel against the crown. *If* a rebellion should occur, I might add."

It was now Danamis who smiled. "'If' you say? You might tell that to Captain Alandris who is now a little shorter of stature than before his crew mutinied in favour of Duke Ursino. I have returned his galley to you, and his head."

Raganus visibly started.

"I suppose no one on the council told you," added Danamis. "Then again, how many are left on the council with you?"

Raganus recovered himself, shaking his head. "That changes little. It only proves the point that you should be out at sea and patrolling the coast."

"I would say you already have a war at your doorstep. And the queen is right to summon her loyal commanders to her while we have the time to make plans."

Raganus's voice lowered. "We have all the allies we need in the event of rebellion by Ursino. Of this the queen is fully aware. As an admiral of Valdur you have a role to play to be sure, but it is not here in Perusia."

Danamis closed the remaining distance between them. "I came back once when you had me done for dead, old man. You put your purse on the wrong horse that time. I wouldn't make the same mistake twice."

The thump of a halberd staff brought both of them around. The dowager queen of Valdur floated into the room, her dark silk gown, the deepest shade of indigo, covered in a hundred embroidered stars of spun-gold thread. Danamis bowed low to her, his bonnet in his hand. Even in mourning, she was as beautiful as ever, a shining sun at the centre of such a dark and ancient pile of wood and stone.

"Lord Chamberlain, you may leave us."

Raganus bowed low, straightened himself, and shot Danamis a look of malevolence that the Palestrian returned in full. He hurriedly left, his ridiculous pointed shoes scuffing along the polished marble as he retreated.

Cressida gave Danamis a weak smile and motioned for him to move to the table—there were only two chairs, one at the head and the other close by its side. She took her seat first, a guardsman pulling out the oversized monstrosity of gilded wood and then sliding it in as she seated herself.

"Messere Nicolo, please sit by me," she said as she placed both hands on the arms of her chair. Danamis replaced his hat and walked to his chair, a servant ready to ease him into his place.

"It does me good to see you again, my queen."

She drank him in with her eyes as a servant filled her goblet. "And I am grateful you have survived the dangers of the past few months. And that you have answered my summons."

Danamis nodded. "It is my duty to serve you. As I served the king. We all grieve for him."

"He did little to support you I seem to remember."

"It is the right of a king to support whom he chooses. It is my duty to serve regardless."

"Which I suppose is the correct answer." Now that she was seated, he could see her face was careworn, worry barely concealed, the sign of sleepless nights clear to see. She paused a few seconds. "I am glad you have come as I asked." She raised her arm and another servant came over bearing an elaborate silver goblet the cup of which was fashioned from a nautilus shell and etched with ships, men, and mer. "It is fitting that a man of the sea drink from an appropriate vessel, no?" The goblet was placed in front of him and filled by a boy. Cressida lifted her goblet towards him. "To House Danamis. And to Valdur."

Danamis raised the awkward vessel to his lips and sipped. "Thank you, my queen."

The guards had not left but had taken up station at both doors as the servants went silently about their task, bringing sweetmeats to them, never once making eye contact. He studied Cressida as he took another sip of the wine, deliciously sweet. She wore no veil of grief: her long blonde hair was restrained by a plait bound with a ribbon of black silk and a pearl-encrusted golden circlet sat upon her brow. She was older than he by six years but it showed not in the least; age had not yet touched her despite her heavy burdens. "Raganus did not give you a warm welcome by the sound of it," she said.

"I was not expecting one, your Majesty. But I am ready to hear what news you may tell me. And I stand ready to aid you in whatever you ask."

She nodded. "If we keep our voices low then we may speak freely. It would have been dangerous to meet alone. As things stand."

Danamis knew what she meant. Rumours of their old love had been spread to weaken her. But how any had found out about their tryst, eleven years past, he could not fathom. "After all this time…" he whispered, his hand tightening about the stem of his goblet. "Who knew of us? And how did Ursino discover it? Surely it's he who's feeding the rumours. He is the only one with a blood claim to the throne."

"Enough knew. And now, with the throne vacant, is the time to put such a secret to use." She looked wistful for a moment then smiled. "Go ahead, eat."

"I'm sorry. My appetite has waned. Tell me what intelligence you have as things are now. You wrote of the council breaking up. Do you trust Raganus?"

"Five have left the city. To Torinia or to Milvorna, I do not know. Raganus…" She tilted her head. "In my heart, I believe he is loyal. But he is reliant upon Captain Polo who tells him that things will 'blow over'. He also believes his trump card is the Silk Empire."

Danamis leaned forward. "Raganus is proposing an alliance with the Sineans?"

Cressida nodded. "Through Polo, as the intermediary. I have told him no. I won't have my son a puppet prince to foreigners. "

Danamis set down his goblet and swiped his hand over his chin. "The palace guard. I am assuming you have paid them, handsomely."

She threw him an annoyed look. "You think me that foolish, Nico? It was the first thing I did when Sempronius died. I have eight hundred men here behind the palace walls. Another thousand at camps around the borders of Perusia. I trust Caluro and his lieutenants."

"If he betrays you to Ursino they will put a coronet on his head. Probably slice up your land to make a new duchy for him. You cannot trust anyone, Cressida. At least, not completely."

"That is why I sent for you. For your fleet. And so that you can bring in Maresto and Ivrea if need be. Perhaps Saivona too."

"What of Colonna? Surely your father will send soldiers here to aid you?"

Cressida laughed. "I am afraid that my fellow citizen of Colonna—Piero Polo—has blinded him to the need for such a move. He has written to me that I am to trust in my advisors. That the Sineans can be trusted if we need them to defend the throne. Their three ships sit across the bay in Colonna. They could reach here in less than two days sailing."

"Then you have only the walls around you. Until we find you more men to come to your aid."

"It's worse than that. I have just learned from scouts that Milvorna has two armies on the move. One has gone west into Torinia but a second is headed south towards us. And as the Duke of Milvorna sent only a lowly courtier to the funeral, I think it fairly certain whose side he is on."

Danamis sighed, a long exhalation of weary exasperation. He had only just arrived and already found nearly half of Valdur lined up against them. "I've got a few hundred men and two ships. I can get a party here to the palace to form a bodyguard for you and the prince. A dagger in your boot so to speak, if it comes to that. But only if you think that will help your security and not insult your palace guard."

Cressida wet her lips. "It's delicate. You know that. But I will accept your offer. For Sarant's sake."

"Consider it done. Now what of the city—the Decurions, the Prelate and the rest of the Temple priesthood?"

"They are standing loyal so far as I can tell but talk of war is on all tongues. Whether their backbones will stay straight if Torinian and Milvornan armies appear, I cannot say."

"Mother?"

A boy burst into the chamber, an abashed guardsman at his heels. Danamis stood up to greet the prince of Valdur, dressed in a fine dark silk gown with a dagger on his hip. The boy halted at his mother's chair, placing a hand on the ornate carved lion's head of the armrest. Cressida dismissed the guard and stroked her son's chest lovingly. Danamis took in the lad's jet black hair, as dark and full as his own and the large blue-grey eyes. He had been praying the boy was blonde, or even ginger and freckled. Still, the king had dark hair, he remembered. This was no consolation even if the lad's complexion was fair like his mother's.

"Is this the pirate you spoke of?" the prince inquired, staring down Danamis somewhat haughtily with one hand on his golden dagger.

"This is Messere Nicolo Danamis, knight of the Silver Boar and an Admiral of Valdur. He is indeed the one I told you of."

Danamis bowed. "I am your servant, my prince."

The boy fixed him with a steady gaze. "They won't let me be king yet. I don't think that's fair. I am already king now that my father is dead. What can you do about that?"

Danamis looked over to Cressida, who silently seemed to be urging him to give answer. He looked back to Sarant, who was still staring at him and no doubt puzzling out if one such as Danamis could be trusted. "I will do all in my power to see that you sit on your throne when the law says you may. You're right. You are the king now. But you must listen to your mother."

"There. Wise words and the same as I told you before," said Cressida, soothingly. "Now go back to your chambers and wait for me."

His face, innocent and young as it was, already had a hard, determined cast. He remained expressionless as he looked up at Danamis, as if the answer was not the one he had been hoping for. He took two steps back and gave a court bow to Danamis and then another to Cressida before leaving the chamber.

Slowly, Danamis sat down again, one question burning on his lips.

"He took the death of his father very hard," said Cressida quietly. "Probably harder than me. He was in the throne room when the creature lashed out and bit Sempronius. At first I thought that was cruel of God—that he had to witness such a thing. Then it struck me that it was a good lesson for a future king. Never underestimate your enemies. Or overestimate the promises of friends."

"Where does that leave me then?"

Cressida smiled. "I haven't overestimated you."

"You think there was more to what happened to Sempronius than the attack of a wild beast? I saw the cockatrice when last I was here. Thought it was tame."

"Something changed that creature. It was always unruly but never savage. I saw how it went for Sempronius, and no one else. Its eyes had changed from red to black, I swear it."

"Guided by another's hand?"

She shrugged. "And why not? I remember the satyr's prophecy. The priests tell of dark rumblings in the countryside. The Old Faith stirring."

Danamis remembered the horror at Ivrea that he and Strykar had seen; that which had nearly killed Citala. "More reason to gain allies why there is still time. Send word to the dukes of Maresto and Saivona. To Ivrea. Tell them the throne is endangered and that you are calling them to their oaths. Demand that your father send an army from Colonna. Use the Temple messenger birds if you can trust the Prelate. There is little time to lose."

The queen leaned closer to him. "Are you telling me to invade Torinia or Milvorna before Ursino has even declared himself traitor? Before he has even threatened Perusia?"

Danamis studied his untouched plate piled high with food. His mouth was dry. "Yes. I am saying exactly that. Strike before Ursino strikes you. For he surely will."

"They will say I do this because of you. Because Palestro and Maresto are already at war with Torinia. But, even so, I know you are right, Nico. If I wait until the hammer falls it will be too late to do anything."

For a moment neither of them said a thing. Danamis looked past the queen towards the doorway. The guards stood like statues, uninvolved in what was being said and hopefully out of earshot.

"Cressida... is he mine?"

The queen looked at him with neither affection nor anger, her emotions colourless. But her delicate right hand, resting upon the table, extended and settled on his own, gently pressing down on his tanned and roughened knuckles. Her touch triggered old memories. His eyes fell to her hand: very warm, small and pale, so very much unlike his mermaid's.

"No, of course he's not," she replied.

IN THE LIGHT of the huge wrought iron lantern on *Vendetta*'s quarterdeck, Danamis squinted at the smudged and crumpled piece of paper in his hands. Torches on the docks blazed, keeping the darkness at bay as his men stood at the watch on the quay. He had been distracted ever since returning from the palace late that afternoon, fretting over the advice he had given to the queen. Reticence was a trait he was rarely afflicted with, but this time, he was feeling he may have promised too much. What if *all* the duchies, excepting Maresto, were in sympathy with Ursino? And he thought of the boy. To Citala, keen at his return, he did not confide his worry or tell much that had transpired at the palace. He convinced himself this was because he owed his report to Bassinio and Gregorvero first. Then, as the hour had grown late and the crew had gone to their berths, Citala awaiting him below, a street urchin had delivered a note to the shore watch.

"Come now, what does it say?" demanded Gregorvero, pushing his way in over Danamis's shoulder.

Danamis angled the paper anew. "It's in a cramped hand I can barely read, and I am no scholar as it stands." He lowered his hands and looked at Gregorvero. "Someone says they have information for me. About the attempt on my life last summer. They give a place, and a time. Happens to be now. Says look for a man in a red padded coif. A soldier."

"Anything else? Who are they?"

Danamis scoffed. "No, just the usual. A purse of gold."

"Are you meeting him then?"

"I'll take four men. It's not far. Behind the taverns on the quay."

Gregorvero shook his head like an annoyed bear. "No, no, Nico. More likely than not like they're planning on finishing what they botched before. If you must go then take a dozen, me included."

"And frighten them off? No, just a few with me and even they'll hang back, unless there's trouble. But you can come if you're worried."

Gregorvero smiled. "Oh, aye, you can count on that."

Talis and two of his brawniest led them torch in hand as they made their way through the alley at the opposite end of the quay. No less than five drinking houses lay here, interspersed with the bay-front warehouses of Perusia. They found the one they needed—a small pictogram of a grinning dog-ape holding a wine jug had been scrawled on the note— and they slowly made their way into the dilapidated lean-to of the tavern. Out in the yard filled with trestles and benches, perhaps two dozen seamen and traders drank their wine and conversed, a roaring fire pit at the centre sending sparks floating into the lush cypress trees beyond. In the orange glow, Danamis scanned the fringes for the man who sought him. It wasn't difficult to find him. Down at the back, only a few lone souls—either drunk or asleep—were thinly spread near where a tall stone wall snaked its way through the neighbourhood.

The man was leaning up against a tall gate post, a close-fitting soldier's cap, scarlet red, upon his head, tapes untied.

Danamis motioned to Gregorvero and the others to hold back and he alone went down into the yard. The man had not yet seen him, standing motionless with his chin drooping slightly, as if in thought. Danamis gently swept back his cloak and reached across his belly to put a hand on his falchion's hilt. He stopped a sword length away from the man.

"Hail, friend. Are you looking for a ship from Palestro?"

The man's eyes seemed to look past Danamis and no reply came. Danamis raised his voice. "If you have intelligence for me you'd better spit it out and be done."

Just above the man's high-necked doublet, and what he initially mistook as a button, he now saw to be the small silver pommel of a blackened dagger. It was protruding from the hollow of the man's throat above the collar. Danamis swore an oath and stepped forward. The long stiletto had been thrust in up to the hilt and out at the man's nape, deep into the wood post. It was holding him upright—dead on his feet.

Sixteen

THE SILVER ARM stood upon the table, the delicate female hand raised in greeting. Every detail of the sleeve, from wrist to flattened elbow serving as a base, was finely etched, a bracelet of emeralds and garnets rendered in astounding relief circled the wrist itself. Saint Ursula the martyr gestured skyward, frozen in time. Halfway down the forearm, a glass window revealed a gruesome fragment of yellowed bone.

"One must admit he was right."

The High Priest shook his head at Acquel, a look of mild disgust on his face. "It will fool no one. It looks too new for a start."

"We can rub it down with ash and soot. Make it appear old." Acquel reached out and touched the cold metallic limb. "We are lucky to have this in just a week."

Kodoris was in no mood to compromise his scepticism. "Volpe's beautiful deception won't save Livorna. That old goat's cynicism knows no bounds. All this will accomplish is to cheapen the One Faith and lose us the confidence of the people."

"Volpe's logic is sound, Holiness. The people will see that one side is lying and they are more likely to believe that the Torinians have the changeling—not us."

Kodoris moved around the table and stood at the high arched window that looked out on to the inner gardens of the monastery. "It will do us little good regardless, Brother Acquelonius. I have yet to hear from the dukes of Saivona or Maresto. They have abandoned us it seems. Perhaps they take the side of Duke Ursino, that he is the true protector of the Faith. Not us."

Acquel's hand rested on the pommel of the sidesword that hung from his waist, an accoutrement he still found awkward. "Duke Ursino is a *pretender* of the Faith. At best he is being bewitched into his actions. At worst he has gone over to the old religion and embraced it."

Kodoris's voice became soft, almost plaintive. "I cannot rid my mind of what I saw when I burned with the fever. Those terrible riders, destroyers of worlds. They are coming."

"And we will fight them."

Kodoris turned back to him. "With what? A metal arm such as this? A few spells from Ugo Volpe's book of plants?"

Acquel's heart sank. His fate was in many ways tied to that of Kodoris: he had concealed the man's role in murder to ensure the new commandments would be adopted by the Temple hierarchy. But in the days following the attack in the Temple, and his wounding by the hell wasps, the High Priest had grown increasingly dejected and detached. Now, Acquel worried that the leader of the Faith was losing his mind. "Elded chose me as his vessel to carry the new Word. The amulet guides us, quiet as it may be. The Saint will not abandon us to the horrors we have seen."

The High Priest fingered the ten-spoked golden medallion, a blazing sun, that hung from his neck. "You are right. But he has chosen separate paths for each of us. The enemy appears to have direction and guidance in full measure. I wish Elded's revelations were less obscure and his help more obvious." His eyes fell to the silver arm upon the table. "You may take that away. Do with it what you will."

"Do you not wish to hear of our preparations? At the walls and the gates?"

"No, that is your jurisdiction, Magister. I go now to pray at the Temple. For all our souls."

"Prayer and battle are both needed, Holiness," replied Acquel. "You once wielded a sword. You *know* what war is like. I need your skill as much as Brother Ugo's."

Kodoris's eyes seemed to look past Acquel, through him, as if something else entirely was playing out in his disordered mind. "Battle... yes. I know I will see battle again. But for my many sins, Brother Acquel, my battle will be very different from yours. I have foreseen it."

ACQUEL JOINED UGO Volpe and Lieutenant Poule on the barbican gate of the city, only recently shored up from the earthquake of a year ago. In the past weeks the old monk and the mercenary had become fast friends and fond of a shared pot of wine. As Acquel made his way along the high wall towards the top of the barbican he saw that Poule had already begun to stock the embrasures with barrels of sand and buckets of water. Cast iron braziers on tripods stood every thirty feet, ready to be stoked and fired to light arrows. Where the walkway met the crenelated walls, he saw long forked poles lying at the ready. He was no soldier but their purpose was obvious: to push off and tumble scaling ladders that would be raised against the outer walls.

"Have you seen the piazza down in the town, Brother Acquel?" shouted Poule as the young Magister reached them. "Looking like market day every day of the week what with bullock, cow and pig stockaded from end to end. They're paying five men just to shovel shit from dawn to dusk!"

Acquel nodded. "We must deny the Torinians of as much as we can outside the walls. God knows how long a siege might last."

"A long siege might be the least of our problems," said Volpe ominously, "if the enemy storm us within a few days. The wall at the western end, near the monastery, is low. That's a weakness for us. The barbican here—and at the east gate—I think are strong. The lieutenant agrees."

Poule nodded vigorously. "Aye. Strong enough," he said, "but I reckon we'll be stretched thin along the length of the city wall. Barely enough men even if we put a bow or a bill in every monk's hand. If the Blue Boar and the rest of 'em scale us at the Ara end—as well as here—we'd better hope the saints are watching out for us."

Acquel looked out over the walls, his eyes settling on the dry ditch and drawbridge and then moving out over the broken rolling countryside south. "Will they have guns?"

Poule thrust out his lower lip. "They'll have guns all right. Question is, will they be field guns or siege pieces? I don't rightly know what kind of a pummelling this old gate can take."

Acquel somehow managed a laugh, borne of desperation. "I thought my commanders might have some plans for a defence of Livorna rather than just complaints."

Poule held up his hands. "Easy, brother! I hadn't gotten to that yet! We'll be hard stretched but that useless castellan did point us to a good store of gunpowder and a few hackbuts if we can find any of the militia who know how to load and fire them." He grinned widely. "And I spied some clay fire pots in the arsenal as well. Maybe fifty or so. Fill 'em with pitch and rags and push in a saltpetre fuse and they'll give the Torinians a rain they won't soon forget."

Volpe noticed the dark cast to Acquel's youthful face. "Fear not, we have a strong position here. The walls are sound and we have missiles to last a fair few of their assaults. If we bloody their nose they may leave us for easier prey."

"And how many men do we have now?" asked Acquel.

Poule wiped his forefinger under his nose. "Aye, best as I can figure, the Count can summon a hundred or so—many have seen some service. The militia—next to useless. They've got more experience of tavern brawls than war—we can equip around three hundred of those from Marsilius's armoury. That leaves your Templars on the Ara."

"Four hundred on the rolls."

Poule nodded. "Of which I reckon three hundred and fifty can wield a sword or a crossbow without managing to kill themselves."

"A very thin gravy," muttered Acquel.

"Aye, but the enemy won't know that," said Poule. "We station what we have at the two weakest points on the walls and pray to Elded. At least your Templars can pray *and* fight. You were well ahead of things to begin recruiting your fighting monks when you did, Brother Acquel. Otherwise, we'd be down to tradesmen and merchants holding back the tide."

Acquel's fingers tapped his sword pommel. "And we have six constables to divide up the militiamen and men-at-arms."

Again Poule gave a vigorous nod. "Some good men there. I've met every a one now. They know when the bells sound to gather their soldiers and take to the battlements."

Volpe turned to Acquel. "You know they will ask for the surrender of Livorna first? Are you ready to speak from the walls when their herald comes calling. It falls to you as Magister, if not the Castellan or Count Marsilius."

Acquel had already rehearsed such a moment each night for the past week as he lay abed. If he refused and they stormed the city, they would kill and plunder at will. And every surviving monk would be put to the sword. Livorna would be awash in the blood of innocents. "They want the High Priest, and me as well. Lucinda della Rovera will see to that. It does not benefit them to destroy Livorna. They want to turn it."

Volpe smiled, his deep-set eyes twinkling with fire. "We won't be handing you or the city to them. We will have a few tricks to show them. And mercenaries don't much like sieges from my experience. They hate climbing ladders when folk are pouring buckets of hot sand or shit down on them. Am I right, young Bartolo?"

Poule chuckled. "Most of us would rather wait it out and get paid for sitting outside the walls. You are right in that, brother monk."

Acquel glanced down the grey stone walkway that snaked its way east towards the lower end of Livorna. The late afternoon sun at his back illuminated the rough-hewn stone in a strange reddish hue, long shadows falling across the crenelated walls. It would look very different very soon, hundreds of men, hunkered along the walkway as arrows and missiles rained upon them and they, in turn, loosing their arrows back upon the enemy. A lone figure was approaching them along the cobbled walkway. A woman.

She was clothed in a russet cloak, her hair flying loose in the steady breeze that blew in from the south. Red hair. She walked slowly, as if lost in thought. As she drew closer Acquel looked at her face. His heart nearly stopped, breath taken from him in an instant of recognition. It was Timandra Pandarus. She had paused now, some ten feet from him. Looking straight at him. He had never seen a ghost before yet here she was, standing before him when he had seen her slain one year ago. She wore no expression—did not even give a sign that she saw him—but her eyes took him in nonetheless. It was her—standing before him—her shade, looking wistful and pensive but somehow not really there at all. She seemed to have no depth and her body cast no shadow upon the wall.

"Timandra!" he said, starting to move towards her. Tears filled his eyes and he reached out, longing to touch her. Poule and Volpe exchanged a worried look.

"Brother Acquel? Are you well?" the old monk laid a hand on his arm. "What do you see?"

"She's there. Right *there*. Do you not see her?"

"Who?" Volpe's worry heightened as he saw the tears streaming down the young man's face.

"It is Timandra." Acquel gripped the monk's arm. "Can you not see her? She has come back to me." But as he looked again, she was gone.

Poule swallowed hard. "You saw the Widow?" His hand described a blessing, two fingers to his forehead and then his breast. "Why has she come back?"

Acquel wiped his sleeve across his face. "She is not at rest if her spirit walks among us."

Volpe put a fatherly arm about Acquel. "Come, let us away," he said quietly. "We shall go back to the Ara. I would hear more of this woman." He guided Acquel, still half-dazed, towards the worn tower steps.

Poule stared at the spot Acquel had pointed to. His back felt a chill. He had known the fiery and comely sutler's widow very well, far longer than Acquel, and he had grieved mightily when told the news months gone by. But talk of ghosts before a battle was never a good thing, and far worse if it be one come to call. He blessed himself again, said a quick prayer for the restless soul of Timandra Pandarus, and followed the monks down the winding stair.

"DID YOU LOVE her?" Brother Volpe sat shoulder to shoulder with Acquel, his hands hugging a cup of wine.

Acquel didn't reply, his head hanging and his cup already dry. "Did you break your vow?" Volpe asked.

"No, I did not," replied Acquel quietly.

"Then that saddens me even more, my brother." They had sat for an hour in Acquel's chamber as he had told the story of Timandra Pandarus and his journey with the Black Rose to Palestro and Perusia. Of how she had helped him, guided him, and in the end sacrificed her life to save him. "You bear a burden of guilt that is not yours to carry. It is not your fault she died. It was her own free will that guided her to aid you. Perhaps she was herself guided by the Saint."

"I was her confessor. And I loved her despite that."

"And the woman redeemed sin by saving you. Allowing you to spread the word of the lost texts. This is as the Lord and Elded intended. You may grieve her loss but you are guiltless in this."

"Am I? I lie awake thinking of each step I took. How I might have revealed the Saint's secrets without getting her killed. Or if I'd been faster, better skilled, maybe killing Captain Flauros before he killed her."

"She confessed to you her sin of murdering her husband knowing you loved her and she you?"

Acquel nodded. "But that happened by circumstance. She would have told me eventually, though. I see now she tried to tell me from almost the very beginning."

Volpe frowned. "What circumstance?"

Acquel turned and faced the old monk. "Something that happened in the wood west of here when I returned to the Ara. When she abandoned the Black Rose to follow and join me."

"What happened?"

Acquel hunched and stared into his empty cup. "I am loathe to speak of it."

"But you wish to. That is clear."

"Timandra and I slept rough that night, the first night after she had found me on the road to Livorna. We were a short distance into the trees. Something found us where we lay near our fire: a *mantichora*."

Volpe drew back slightly. "That you're alive to tell me is a wonder in itself. Such creatures are rare."

"I was terrified." Acquel gave Volpe a half-hearted smile. "But Timandra was brave. Told the thing she would take its eyes out before she was eaten. It spoke to us. It sensed I was a greyrobe—even sensed Elded's amulet. And it said that Timandra smelt of another's blood. It called her a she-killer. Said we were both too foul to bother eating. It took our mount instead." He swallowed hard as the memory washed over him.

Volpe grasped Acquel's arm. "What else did it say? A telling?"

"A telling? You mean a foreshadowing?"

"Do you not know the *mantichora* is a creature that has great power? The power to see beyond the present, to look deep into the past. They are ageless, among the first denizens of Valdur."

"It spoke of change. Something that was sleeping but that now awakens."

Volpe lifted his cup and drained it. "We must needs find this creature and speak with it."

Acquel stood up. "Are you mad? Even if we found it out in the forest it would tear us to pieces. It was evil. Rank."

Volpe refilled his cup, spilling the wine on the table. "The absence of good does not always signify the presence of evil. Remember that. And we need all the allies we can get if we are to deal with what stalks us. A *mantichora*'s knowledge could help us. Maybe save us."

Acquel pushed back his bench and stood. "You want to go on a hunt into the forest to find this thing? When the enemy is practically at the gates? Are you drunk again?"

"Sit down," Volpe growled. "This war will not be won by steel and shot alone, no matter what I said up on the battlements. We need other weapons. And we two are the only ones that can obtain them."

"I think you're mad."

Volpe glared at him. "Sit your arse down, brother."

Acquel took a breath, shaking his head in frustration, but resumed his place. Volpe grabbed Acquel's cup and refilled it from the jug. "Brother Acquel, my friend, I do believe you saw the ghost of your Timandra, and I think it was no accident. She wanted you to tell me what you just have." His eyes bored into Acquel. "Things do not happen without a reason. And you must learn to see what others do not."

Seventeen

STRYKAR OPENED HIS eyes. Lying on his stomach, his cheek was pressed to trampled grass and mud smelling distinctly of piss. His head throbbed and as he tried to move he realised his hands were bound behind him. He had been stripped of his armour and as his eyes focussed he saw he was in just his quilted arming jacket, shirt and hose. He looked down and saw that his boots were still on his feet. Not a bad sign. Those were usually the first things to go.

He was in a makeshift paddock of sorts; a paddock for prisoners. Three other men had been incarcerated with him: one looking dead, two others sitting forlornly against a fence. Strykar looked about him, his vision swirling. An encampment. Milvornan cavalry. He was either in their camp or with the Blue Boar. If the latter that was decidedly bad, but he was alive.

"Saints above! He's come around. That's twenty soldi you owe me, fool. Told you he was strong as an ox!"

Strykar struggled to his knees as the guards came for him. Laughing, they hauled him up onto unsteady feet. One slapped his cheek and then poured into his mouth what he quickly realized was *acqua vitalis*, the fiery liquid burning his parched throat but reviving him. "Come on then. *You* have an audience with some people of quality. Been waiting for you to wake up." They half dragged him out of the paddock to face a bearded soldier, corpulent and pock-faced, a chain of office around his neck. The master of the stocks looked at Strykar and shook his head with either admiration or wonderment.

"Almost left you for dead with the others, you know that? Some old sergeant of yours made us pull you out of the muck. Said who you was before he coughed up his guts and died. My my! To think what a ransom we would have lost leaving you out there for dead with the rest of 'em."

Strykar managed to find his voice, rough as it was. "Not much of a fair fight though, was it?"

The gaoler laughed. "Nearly shit myself just watching what happened to your lot." He motioned for the guards to move him along and he was pushed along towards the forest of tents and poles. They guided him to a camp within the camp, roped and guarded, the tallest striped tent at the centre. Led through, Strykar found himself standing before the commander of the Company of the Blue Boar: Coronel Lupo Aretini, whom he had but glimpsed once before. A handful of other officers came out of the tent as well as a few noblemen. Aretini looked Strykar up and down and pursed his lips in disgust.

"Cut his bonds."

The gaoler slid his knife between Strykar's wrists and snapped the rope. Strykar pushed back his shoulders and stared hard at Aretini. His captor then motioned for a cup to be brought over.

"Here. Have a drink."

Strykar took the cup and put it to his lips. It was water. The sweetest he had tasted.

A nobleman, a young man of the sort that Strykar knew well—vain, pompous, and probably of dubious mettle—moved forward, a smile on his face. "So this is a Coronel of the infamous Black Rose. Brought very low indeed from the look of it."

Strykar lowered the cup. "I've known better days, I confess."

Aretini chuckled. "He deserves your respect, Messere Claudio. He was taken at the van—the very front of it. Where were you this afternoon? The baggage train?"

"Unfair, very unfair my Coronel. I saw a fair share of the fight." The nobleman's hurt looked unfeigned.

Aretini turned to him. "Weren't you ordered to shovel-out the griffon's pen?" The assembled captains roared with amusement and Claudio swore and wandered back into the tent.

"Who has put poor Claudio into a rage?" It was Messere Lazaro who had emerged from the pavilion, a large leg of roast chicken in his hand. He saw the dishevelled soldier in front of him and waved the drumstick towards Strykar. "Ah, he's decided to re-join the living."

Aretini turned to the knight. "And you're still interested in paying his ransom?"

"I am indeed. Paying what this knight of Maresto is worth. Have you changed your price?"

Aretini smiled then turned to Strykar. "No. Same price, Messerre Lazaro. Ten soldi."

"Fair as fair can be, Coronel." Lazaro threw the drumstick to the ground, wiped his fingers on his leather doublet, and reached for his purse. The captains roared their amusement to see the transaction done. A few small pieces of silver for a Coronel of the Black Rose. Even through his throbbing pain and fatigue, Strykar felt his face flush with rage. "Send back those beasts that the witch has summoned. We'll finish what we started."

Aretini chuckled and exchanged glances with his men. "You have nothing to finish it with. Your army is fled. As fast as their little legs could take them back across the

Taro. So fast we couldn't catch them up. Not even with the griffons." The chorus of guffaws rang out across the enclosure. "And you insult the Lady della Rovera? The canoness has the blessing of God—she's delivered us the Hand of Ursula. By Elded's balls, she's brought back the royal beasts of Valdur!"

"She will deliver you all to Hell," replied Strykar, his voice rasping. "Yet that is where you all belong—butchers of Caglia."

Standing beside his commander, Captain Janus swore and slowly pulled his long slim rondel dagger from his belt. "I'll pay you twelve soldi now, Coronel, just for the pleasure of gutting him here."

Aretini raised his hand. "Nay, let him speak. I'm intrigued. Caglia?"

Strykar took a step closer to Aretini but the master-of-the-stocks behind him grabbed the skirt of his arming doublet and jerked him back. Strykar elbowed the man but quickly had both his arms seized from behind. "Aye, Caglia! How many villagers did you slaughter that day for your sport? Their houses set afire with them still inside."

Aretini snarled. "You're as hypocritical as any canting blackrobe, Messere Julianus. Worse, I think." He turned to his assembled captains and to the Torinian knights—Claudio had now returned from his sulk to join Lazaro— and gestured to Strykar. "A lecture in morals from one aventura to another? Have you ever heard of such boldness?" Aretini shook his head slowly. "Caglia… Have not heard that place mentioned for a few years." He stepped in close to Strykar. "We had twenty of our men murdered by townsmen *after* Caglia had surrendered and opened their gates. And were we supposed to have rewarded that? The law of war is clear. We punished those responsible. The butchers were those who murdered my men after their lives had been spared."

Strykar did not shy away. He leaned in even closer. "Children too? Don't tell me of the law of war."

Aretini reached up and pinched Strykar's cheek. "We'll have to find a black robe that fits you somewhere in camp." He stepped back and shook his head again. "If we're going to play a game of remembrance... I have one for you. Cast your addled mind back to... *Pernato*."

"Hah!" exclaimed Lazaro. "Let us see how his memory serves him there."

Aretini took a few steps to the blackwood field table and refilled his wine goblet. "Yes, Pernato. Little garrison town on the border. Not far from here I recall. Seven years ago the Black Rose set upon it as the Torinian soldiers were changing deployments. The garrison was smaller than usual and your company found that out."

Strykar's gaze followed Aretini as he ambled among his men, sipping his wine. He did remember the place, an event he had long forgotten. He managed to stutter a reply. "I was not there. But that town lies inside Maresto, always has."

"Debatable point, sir, but we will leave that. Wherever it may lie upon the map the Black Rose swept it clean. Over a thousand dead I recall. Soldiers, townsmen. Women. Children. And I *was* there."

Strykar remembered. Dully, through his pounding head, he remembered the tales that came back with those squadrons which had been at Pernato. Muttered stories told by men ashamed of what had spiralled out of control. Other stories told more loudly by braggarts with a smile on their lips. And he knew then that Aretini had him, hoisted by his own sanctimonious outburst. He poured the last drops of his cup into his mouth.

"I see that you do remember," said Aretini nodding. "A man who does not recognize his nature is a fool—and is seen to be a fool by others. And you, my lord, are a beaten fool."

He snatched the cup away from Strykar. "Bind him again. Lazaro can then take away his prize."

Strykar flinched as the ropes went taut about his wrists with a firm jerk. "She will be your undoing, Aretini, and the whole of your company's as well. That is an honest warning from one aventura to another. She's not what she appears and Ursino is bewitched."

Aretini gave a short, derisive chuckle. "And now a lecture from a Maresto heretic who blindly follows the usurpers of Livorna and their fish tales! Take him away please, Messere Lazaro, before I change my mind and let Janus here cut him a new mouth from ear to ear."

Lazaro motioned to his men-at-arms, who were still grinning at the sport before them. "Take him! I may end up doing the deed myself before we reach Livorna, if the fellow doesn't keep quiet!"

Strykar was manhandled through the makeshift, rutted passageway between the tents of the encampment and across a field to a second camp which flew the personal banners of half a dozen knights of Torinia. He felt one of his guards grab a handful of his sweaty hair and jerk him to the left, towards the baggage train. Near a wagon and a stack of casks there was an iron stake and chain pounded into the ground, awaiting his arrival. He was thrown down into the mud and felt the pinch of a shackle about his leg. One of the guards stood over him, reached into his codpiece and breeches and pulled out their manhood. A stream of piss covered Strykar's boots, ripped hose, and stained canvas doublet as he bore the insult, his eyes never once leaving his tormentors. The blonde-haired soldier, a beardless youth of no more than twenty, laughed as he shook the last drops from his member and tucked himself back in.

"Always wanted to water the Roses, proper-like."

* * *

By THE AFTERNOON of the second day, Strykar felt for the first time that he just might not make it. His anger had reduced to a smoulder and the pain now had taken over his mind. He had been pulled at the back of Lazaro's baggage cart, trudging to keep up as a grinning boy sitting on the bundles of armour lobbed hazelnuts at him from time to time, aiming for his forehead. His left shoulder and bicep was a throbbing, swollen agony. He had had worse wounds as a younger man, but he was no longer young. Somewhere on the road to Livorna—he had lost focus—they pulled up for another night, the entire army making camp on vast fields on the side of the wide track that led westwards. The tents went up and Strykar's now familiar iron spike went down, down into the ground. A man-at-arms threw him a goatskin of water and later came back with half a loaf of black bread and a half-eaten roasted fowl, covered in black ash.

"Look at the state of you," the soldier mumbled. "You must have done something wicked to merit this treatment."

Strykar reached for the wreck of a meal and wiped off the worst of the ash flecks. "I had the ill fortune to be taken alive. I should have known better. How close are we to Livorna?"

The man looked about him, fearful to be seen talking with the enemy prisoner. "Look here, won't make much difference to you from what I hear tell. But I reckon we will reach the walls tomorrow, after meridian. You won't have any reason to want to get there."

Strykar rearranged himself on the ground, grunting. It was as he thought. He'd always doubted he would be ransomed back to his brother in the south. "Oh, Livorna is a lively place despite the blackrobes. You'd like raising a cup of wine there. Not that you or your lot will ever get the chance."

The man reached down and swept up the now empty water skin in his hand. "You think so?" He smiled. "You'll have a good vantage to see us take the place if talk be true." He shook his head and turned to walk away. "You poor bastard."

The night descended slowly, an eternity of purple skies, and Strykar lost track of time. The noise of the camp subsided except for the laughter and light emanating from where the tallest tents were pitched, those of the noblemen, Lazaro included. As darkness fell totally, a canopy of stars overhead, Strykar gave up trying to free his ankle from the shackle. He'd tried pulling his foot out of the boot, easing it bit by bit, but to no avail. He even tried shifting the iron stake but it was deep and he had only one arm that could stand the strain. He muttered a curse on himself, for his own impetuousness into battle, a thing that had undone them all.

The rowdiness in the tents grew louder as the drink flowed. He had finished his chunk of bread, lying in the shadows, waiting for exhausted sleep to overtake him and his pain. He lifted his head as he became aware of some soldiers making their way towards him through the sea of tents and wagons. Drunken laughter and cursing floated to him, the stuff of every military camp. But he knew they were looking for some entertainment and it became clear very quickly that they were headed in his direction. He scrambled up onto his feet and squatted, hands on thighs, to await their arrival. A torch bobbed in front as the party neared. They were soon around him, a group of some seven men-at-arms, Messere Lazaro at the lead.

"Ah, my wilted Black Rose!" laughed Lazaro as he stood over Strykar. He was almost tottering, the smell of wine and *acqua vitalis* wafting from his blood-red quilted doublet as he waved his arms. He covered his mouth in a gesture of embarrassment. "I'm afraid I let slip to the Duke that I had bought a Coronel of the Black Rose, and he was not best pleased to hear how you had insulted his lady. Not in the least."

Strykar kept silent, taking in deep breaths through his nose, preparing for what might come. The others were laughing again, jostling one another for a look at this high officer now brought low. "So... I'm giving you to him!" announced Lazaro, who finished the statement with a burst of laughter. "My gift to the Duke, soon to be our king." He paused and leaned down towards Strykar. "What are you staring at? You pile of dung!" He gave a backhand blow with all the drunken force he could muster, striking the mercenary across the jaw and sending him down. "Don't you dare look me in the eye!"

Strykar shook his head and struggled back up to his knees. The metallic taste of blood filled his mouth where his lip had ripped across his teeth. Lazaro turned to his men. "To think, I paid only ten soldi for him. As cheaply bought a gift as there ever was for a duke, no?"

Strykar raised up one knee and placed a foot on the ground. There was an unwritten code among the free companies that after hostilities, bloodletting ends. After all, they were all men of business fighting for whom they chose. Ransom was to be honoured and parole granted for those who could afford none. Even between the Blue Boar and the Black Rose, such convention had held. That had now been trampled like his men on the field.

Lazaro reeled and asked for a drink. Quickly answered by a soldier, he drank deeply from the clay bottle. He waggled a finger at Strykar. "I don't think you ever said you were sorry for what happened at Pernato. Did you?" The kick took Strykar by surprise. The boot caught his stomach and his balls and he collapsed with a groan, curling himself as the pain surged through him. The kicks came furious as he lay there, coiling himself tighter in a futile act of self-defence. He vomited up his bread and water, retching away as the men-at-arms jeered. After a minute, Lazaro must have become mindful of his prize. "Enough! Leave off the wretch or I shall have to make apology to the Duke!" He wiped his sleeve across his mouth and barked out another laugh. "That would spoil the show for Livorna. And such a spectacle he has planned!"

Strykar rolled over onto his back, his ankle chain loudly adding its own ridicule. A padded arming doublet was no substitute for body armour and he reasoned, dimly in the swirl of his pain, that he had a few ribs cracked now to add to the wounds of the battle. Not that his wounds were of much consequence now. Lazaro had let slip what his fate would be: execution before the walls of Livorna. A taster before the siege and a warning to the defenders. He watched as his tormentors retreated back to their tent, swearing and laughing. The sky above blazed with milky brilliance and as he stared at the endless firmament he slowly drifted away into an exhausted, fitful sleep.

At some point, the sound of his chain rattling woke him. He rolled over to see a dark figure squatting down near the ground spike. Strykar started, pushing himself into a sitting position, prepared for the dagger that might be about to flash. But the figure instead slowly extended an open hand, warning him to be silent. Strykar could dimly make out the man before him in the reflected torchlight of the camp: a veteran, white-whiskered with a bald head, a short black cloak pulled about his shoulders. As Strykar sat motionless, he saw the soldier muffle the ankle shackle with one hand while he inserted a long key into the lock. Jiggling it, he then gave it a turn and the shackle opened. The soldier looked at Strykar and put a finger to his lips. Strykar pulled his leg back and braced himself with his hands as he tried to gain his feet. Friend or foe, he knew not what to expect next. The man gave indication of neither and he swallowed hard, debating what to do next. But the soldier whispered to him.

"Some of us remember Caglia. Some of us remember Pernato. When you be a soldier, like us, over the years you can have many masters. The wheel goes around. But you never forget your comrades be they Boar or Rose. Now, get out of here!" He stood, scanned the sea of tents and then quickly disappeared around a wagon. Strykar found his feet and rising, swayed. But he was whole even if stiff. He listened. There was none of the earlier carousing now; just coughing, the occasional sound of voices in low conversation, the snoring of tired drunken men. He remembered he was near the road and beyond this, across a grassy meadow, a forest spread towards the north—escape a stone's throw away. He wiped his nose with his thumb and forefinger and looked towards the high tent some yards away. The nobleman's tent.

He entered the tent from the back, crawling underneath where the pegs had not been secured properly. Light from the still burning braziers out at the front cast a dim illumination—enough for him to discern his surroundings. A wooden stand for harness and swordbelt, a table, a bed off to the side, a snoring man in it. A shadow swayed outside the tent: no doubt a guard. Strykar clenched his fists for a moment and then crept across the carpeted ground towards the bed. He peered over Messere Lazaro's slumbering form, the wine stench wafting upwards from him. As he stared at Lazaro, all his rage and his shame welled. Shame for his hubris, his boastfulness, his carelessness, and his foolishness. Foolishness that had led good men to their deaths. Foolishness that had got him captured, the abased plaything of others.

He leaned in, knees on the bedframe, and slapped a meaty hand over Lazaro's mouth. Instantly, the knight's eyes shot open, a muffled exclamation stifled as Strykar pressed down.

And Strykar knew Lazaro recognised him even as his other hand grasped the nobleman's throat. The bedframe creaked with the pressure of his exertions as he squeezed. Lazaro twisted and kicked even as his eyes bulged with fear. Strykar stared back into those eyes, his own face a mask of darkness as he held fast and throttled the life out of his enemy. The sound of the crushing of the windpipe, a delicate crack felt underneath his hand, was audible to just the two of them. Lazaro's eyes lost their focus, looking beyond Strykar as the man's body went limp. The mercenary lifted his hands away and the rattle from Lazaro's collapsing chest sounded like a quiet sigh of relief.

Strykar looked to the front of the tent. The guard had not moved, probably asleep where he stood. He moved to the armour stand and gently lifted off the scabbarded sword and belt. He then spied a long woollen field cape slung over a stool. He flung it on, bundled the weapon in his arms like a small child, and left the way he had entered. Moving at a walking pace, he negotiated the tents and wagons around him, just another man-at-arms looking to relieve his bladder in the deepness of the night. He cast a look over his shoulder a few times as he walked the tall grass of the meadow but the moon had long since set and he was a shadow amongst shadows. The great forest loomed before him and he cast one more glance behind towards the camp of the Torinian host. Strykar leaned against a great beech, his cheek pressing the tree like it was a lover. He knew he had to move deeper into the forest before the dawn. They would pursue him if they could. Buckling on Lazaro's side-sword, the jewels of its hilt glinting dully, he made his way slowly, like a blind man, into the tangled root-strewn maze of the great wood.

His last strength, drained by stumbles in the dark, gave out shortly after the rays of day began to bring light to the forest around him. He was almost too tired now to care if he was caught. He settled into a deep sleep, nestled in the vee of a double-trunked tree. Sometime later he awoke to the sound of birdsong above—a cuckoo's mocking. He raised his head, his throat parched and his stomach groaning. And then he heard another sound. A sound he knew well, and no more than a dozen paces away. The unmistakable creak of a longbow being drawn.

Eighteen

ACQUEL HAD FINALLY found him near the makeshift workman's shack that sagged against the north wall of the Temple Majoris. Here, under a carpenter's lean-to surrounded by planks, stumps, mallets, saw-horses and curly wood shavings he found the old monk labouring.

"Days from attack and I find you here—carving… a tree branch!"

Ugo Volpe lifted the adze from the long slightly kinked length of bough, yellowish-white, the colour of flesh-stripped bone. He sighted down its length, three feet long and flattened now from shaving, almost blade-like. He ignored Acquel's outburst and reached for a curved knife mounted on a long wooden handle. He carved out a notch near one end and reached into his robe for a disc of silver which slid down from the pointed end of the stick pressing it into place a hand's width from the opposite end. Acquel now saw that the old monk had fashioned a sword. A sword of wood.

"If we are to hunt a *mantichora*, brother," said Volpe calmly, "then we must be prepared."

"What? Are we going to play a game of fetch with the creature? This is a tree branch."

"It is sorbo wood. I was not even aware that a sorbo grew up here on the Ara and there is but one. Another sign that God is with us, Brother Acquel."

Acquel reached out and touched Volpe's arm, halting him in his work. "Explain."

The monk nodded. "The sorbo is a tree of protection. Some call it the rowanis tree. Narrow leaves, red berries that bear a five-pointed star. You have probably walked past it a hundred times without realizing its significance."

"And how are we to offend an enemy with a wooden sword?"

Volpe gave an indulgent smile. "Some things fear this wood more than they fear steel. And some fell creatures it will cut like the sharpest blade. The old religion had their trees and we have ours. The sorbo is one of them." He picked up the long brown leather strip that lay coiled on the workbench, slick with wet glue. He began wrapping the hilt, slowly and carefully as if he was a swordsmith of longstanding. "Hand me that pommel, just there" he said. Acquel gritted his teeth and complied, hefting the almond-shaped lump of metal and handing it over to Volpe. The old man's gnarled fingers deftly threaded the pommel with a long metal screw and with a pair of tongs he began to slowly turn it into the haft of the bough, tightening the pommel to the end.

Acquel watched him, still in doubt, as the odd-looking weapon was finished. It looked like the practice swords the aventura used. He decided then that he would be carrying the real thing into the forest and nothing less. "And how will we find the *mantichora*? The wood is vast west of Livorna."

Volpe shrugged as his fist smoothed down the leather grip of the sorbo sword. "How did you find it last time?"

"The creature found us."

"Well, there you are. It will find us again in that case."

"I still don't understand what the *mantichora* can tell us about the Old Faith and della Rovera's plans. That's assuming it will talk to us and not devour us instead."

Volpe set the sword down on the bench. He looked up at Acquel. "You must have more faith in my knowledge. What I've seen. What *you* have seen of late. The *mantichora* are tied to Valdur from time immemorial. They have witnessed the battles between the people of Elded and those of the Death Tree. They sniff out the winds of change and they have seen much over the aeons. I am hoping your creature will share a secret with us. Some weakness of the old ones, of their demons that plague us."

"And what if we make it back to find Livorna surrounded by the Torinians? What then?" Acquel knew he was being peevishly contrary, but to hang their fates on peasant magic of root and branch, crushed flowers and incantations, seemed a fool's errand. His eyes dissected Volpe: his scabrous pig-bristled scalp, heavy brow, bulbous nose, thin desiccated lips perpetually red from wine. Was he truly to set off with just this old man and face down that ancient terror, one that had nearly torn him to bloody shreds only last summer? He barely knew this monk.

Volpe scowled at him. "Elded's beard, my brother! You expect me to have all the answers?" He mumbled something inaudible and picked up the wooden sword. He turned and handed it to Acquel, hilt first.

Dubious, Acquel reached out and accepted it. It was as light as he had imagined but unbalanced by the weight of the silver hilt and pommel. Useless and likely to snap the second it was thrust at something, he thought. "A pretty curiosity. I hope you will not have second thoughts when the *mantichora* is picking his teeth with it."

And then, for just an instant, Acquel thought he felt the amulet upon his chest flash with gentle warmth. But just as quickly, it cooled again, dead metal upon his breastbone.

POULE WAS FURIOUS. Dumbstruck that Acquel could think of leaving the city when an army of siege was on its way. And when he had recovered his voice it let loose a volley of profanity that even made Volpe blush in its raw expression. But, good soldier that he was, he obeyed the Magister's command to continue preparations for the defence of the walls, walls already bristling with wooden shields, stacked rocks, braziers, polearms, and barrels of clothyard shafts fletched in black and white goose feathers.

"We will be gone not more than a day and a night," Acquel had told the mercenary. Poule, puffing his cheeks out, had shaken his head and replied, "Better pray you're not late. You might find yourself hog-tied, put in the sling of a catapult and chucked back to us—alight."

Acquel and Volpe had slunk out the east gate in the low town on horseback early the next morning. Though he wore a breast and backplate, his side-sword at this hip, Acquel felt naked when he thought of the beast they might face. Volpe, confidence brimming as always, rode in his monk's robes which he had hiked-up high to his thighs revealing his pasty white, hairy legs. His ever-present satchel was slung over his shoulder, the sorbo blade that lay tucked in his brown belt looked like some child's toy. At Volpe's urging, they had avoided telling the High Priest of their mission outside Livorna. Volpe with a mischievous grin had reminded Acquel that it was easier to obtain forgiveness than to seek permission. Acquel knew anyway that Kodoris would not have looked kindly on their mad quest no matter how much he could have tried to justify its necessity. He had barely convinced himself.

They had ridden west along the main road, past the point where he had tumbled down from Livorna in his escape the previous year and straight into the arms of Julianus Strykar. After half a day's ride, the insects dipping and diving around them as they passed grassy flower-strewn meadows on their left, rising forest on their right, Acquel thought he remembered landmarks of his earlier passage with Timandra Pandarus. Since he had seen her shade upon the walls, he found it difficult to rid her from his thoughts. In his dreams, she pleaded and beckoned. And he would awake, distraught. *What could she be trying to tell me?*

As the sun baked them in the saddle, Acquel at length halted and Volpe with him. The only sound was the countless drone of grasshoppers in the golden meadow. The old monk threw back the cowl that shielded his balding head. "Well, my brother, have you found your bearings?"

Acquel shook his head. "I cannot remember for sure where we had turned off into the woods. Somewhere along here I think. It is all the same for me now."

Volpe flicked his reins. "Come on. It matters not. *Mantichora* have an unnatural sense of smell. He will find us before we find him of that I am sure." They turned up into the forest of ancient oak and beech, a canopy of light and dark, green, smelling of good rich earth and moss. The horses struggled, picking their way over roots and the undulating vegetation, all hillocks and humps. Acquel's mount began to paw and hesitate and finally he dismounted to lead it by its halter. Behind him, he heard Volpe grunt and land on his feet with a mumbled curse. The ground became steeper, the trees older and thicker. Light pierced the canopy in haphazard patches, the early summer foliage now grown full and lush above. They carried on, breathing heavily in their exertions, their horses snorting displeasure as they dragged them along.

Acquel knew before long that this was not the spot where he had faced the *mantichora*. It was too steep for one. He looked about and discovered a small hollow of ground where the trees thinned, more level than what surrounded them. "Let us make camp over there," he said. "And we shall see if your knowledge of these creatures is accurate."

Volpe nodded. "Sensible. Besides, we've made enough noise in the past hour to let anything within five miles know we are coming."

They tied their horses up a short distance away, close to a trickle of a stream they had crossed. Then, pulling off their sacks of food and their bedrolls, they returned to the spot Acquel had chosen. They threw down their supplies and then set off to gather wood. Volpe set about building the fire after he had first gathered up some rocks with which to ring it. They spoke little as they went about their work, Acquel's mind racing between thoughts of being leapt upon by the *mantichora* and by his remembrance of Timandra and her last confession to him under the trees. Volpe, his work done, wiped his hands on his black robes and found a comfortable spot at the base of an oak. He reached into his sack, pulled out a loaf of bread, and tore off a chunk before offering it to Acquel. "Fetch the wine off the saddle bow, brother. And sit down. No point in fretting."

Acquel knew he was right. He knew in his heart that the creature would come to them. It was as if he had no will of his own in the matter; his life of the past year was but one headlong rush into events that seemed ordained. He unloosed the winesack from the saddlebow and found a place next to the old Saivonan, near last monk of his holy order at Astilona. He heard and felt the pungent bed of last year's acorn cups, twigs, and leaves crush under his weight as he settled himself on the damp earth at the base of the tree, his hand gripping his sword hilt, a small comfort in itself.

"Will Livorna be taken?" he asked quietly.

Volpe took the winesack and uncorked it. "I cannot say, in truth, my brother." He took a long swig and handed it back. "What matters is that we fight. With everything we have."

"Kodoris has changed. Since what happened in the crypt. He has withdrawn into himself. Lost faith somehow. He will not lead us."

Volpe sighed. "He's a conflicted man. Always was. Not centred in himself. Was always afraid of losing control—losing the order of things. It has led him down the wrong path."

"I think he has seen something in his visions. Something he has not confided. Whatever it was it has unnerved him. Drained him."

Volpe twisted his portly torso to face Acquel and waved a chunk of white bread at him. "You are the Magister of the Ara now. Leave the esoteric concerns of the Temple to the High Priest. Your duties are earthly. The defence of Elded's people from those who would raise up that which has been cast down. That is why we are here. If not to find allies then to find knowledge."

"I don't know what I'm doing. I thought I did but Elded has stopped guiding me. The brethren said I was his voice—champion of his will. Even his visions have died away."

"Bullshit," mumbled Volpe, as he chewed and swallowed a chunk of bread. "What do they know. Who says you're a saviour? Maybe you're just a *sentinel*. The one who stands upon the tower. I told you my belief once before. That the Lord gives us the tools but how we use them is down to us, and free will."

Acquel leaned back, his head against the rough bark. The sun was now much lower in the sky, its rays obliquely piercing the forest and casting even more shadow as the evening drew nearer. "I will need your help. All that you can give me."

Volpe chuckled. "And you shall have it, my brother. Fear not. And fear nothing."

They lit their fire with tinder and flint just before the sun, dull orange, disappearing entirely. The smell and crackling hiss, the rising warmth, all lulled Acquel. He drank some wine and contemplated the flames. *Just what was a sentinel to do then, once the enemy was in sight?* Volpe got up and searched through his battered leather satchel. The monk pulled out his coil of strange, thin rope, decorated with ribbons. And Acquel knew what would happen next. Without a word, Volpe uncoiled it and gently laid it around their camp, an irregular circle beginning and ending with the tree they backed up against.

"We must be frugal now with our firewood," said Volpe ominously. "We may no longer forage once the sun has set."

They sat inside the circle, a thin braided cord standing between them and whatever lay outside. The old monk had taken out his comical wooden sword and laid it on his lap. Acquel had drawn his steel and done likewise. There had been the normal increase in birdsong and chittering of small creatures at dusk, falling away to the occasional rasp of crow and coo of dove bedding down above them. They conversed sparingly and in hushed tones of war, of battle. Acquel asked and Volpe answered, the latter's memories coming out in brief but vivid anecdotes that all led to sad lessons.

"And so the Duke of Saivona, having won his war, discarded us. The monastery fortress was seized by his own soldiers and we, we who had bled for him, were scattered to the winds. The rest you know."

Acquel nodded, his grave face lit by the low flames. There was silence again for a minute or two.

"When will the *mantichora* come?" asked Acquel. Before Volpe could hazard a guess, a voice boomed out around them like rolling thunder.

"I am already here, little priest!"

Acquel fell forward, his heart leaping in his chest and Volpe rolled into and across the fire, stopping just short of the edge of the magic rope before righting himself and thrusting out his sorbo blade.

Acquel was still on his back as he saw a familiar face, massive and glistening brown, peer down from behind the tree that he had been leaning against. The *mantichora* silently padded from behind the oak, giving them, for the moment, a wide berth. Dark and mottled brown in the firelight, it warily eyed them as it moved, its huge green orbs glinting, almost human in aspect. Acquel scrambled to retrieve his sword and crouched next to Volpe. The old monk looked grim but not frightened by the sight of such a creature. But Acquel could hardly breathe. It was as tall as a warhorse and longer than two, with a lion-like body, muscular and lithe, ending in a swishing tale. But the monstrous nature of the thing, its great saturnine human head mounted upon an animal body, made it horrible to behold, an abomination. Volpe's words of a few days earlier, that the absence of good did not imply the presence of evil, entered his head again. If they survived the next few moments he would have to put that again to the old monk. The *mantichora* turned to face them straight on and Acquel watched, frozen, as he saw it move a paw towards the rope upon the ground. He could hear Volpe's laboured breathing as they waited. The booming voice of the thing, a rumbling male bass, tumbled out again.

"I smelled you an hour gone by. And I remembered your scent. Not like other men. Different."

Just as before, Acquel's amulet had not warned him. Did that mean he did not face something evil? Suddenly he heard Volpe speak, addressing the beast.

"We have sought you out. We seek your knowledge." His voice was strong but even so it quavered slightly. Acquel looked past the creature to where the horses were tied a short walk from their fire. Remarkably, they were still there, dozing. The *mantichora* had come upwind upon them.

"Fat priest. I don't know you, it seems." The *mantichora* swivelled its shaggy, matted head towards Acquel. "And where is the she-marten you last had with you? I liked her. Probably would not have eaten her. Not straight away."

Acquel could barely find his tongue. "She is dead."

"Ah, cruel news." It lowered its head a little and inched forward. One paw, larger than a bear's, touched the rope. It pulled back quickly, as if it had touched a hot iron. The *mantichora* growled and tensed, lowering the front half of its body, nostrils flaring. "What's this then? A charm to protect you?" Neither Volpe nor Acquel gave answer. The *mantichora* broke into a grin, revealing a wide mouth of many sharp teeth. It then slowly raised the same paw and placed it full upon the rope, leaving it there. Acquel drew back, shocked. "Sweet God!"

The *mantichora* let out a laugh that seemed to well up from some deep abyss, otherworldly and chilling. Volpe stood up straight, holding out his sword. They had no barrier. Acquel gripped his blade in both hands and held it in a guard despite his trembling thighs. But the creature stepped back and regarded them, its eyes filled with mirth. It saw the sorbo sword in Volpe's hand—not shaking as was Acquel's. It snorted and then gave a loud petulant sniff.

"Rowanis wood. Fat, *clever* priest."

Volpe waggled the wooden blade. "I say again. We have sought you out. For wisdom."

The *mantichora*'s thick fleshy lips parted in a smile and it sat on its haunches. "I so seldom converse with other creatures," it rumbled. "So lonely here. But to find two holy men of the One Faith in my forest! What good fortune this night!"

Acquel began to find his courage. "You once told me that which was sleeping was waking. Speaking upon the wind. Gathering strength." He paused to swallow the lump in his throat. "We would know more."

The *mantichora* nodded. "Fat priest understands. I was never young and am yet to grow old. I smell things and I hear things. Sometimes I see things too... far away." Its emerald eyes, the size of a man's fists, grew larger as it spoke, perhaps remembering experiences from its long and unnatural life. "And it is your wish that I tell you what is on the wind?"

Volpe didn't hesitate. "It is. Tell us of the followers of the old ways, of Andras and his servants Belial and Beleth." Acquel shivered at the mention of the foul names.

The *mantichora* tilted its head and its throat issued a noise like a heavy millstone grinding away. "It is customary to bring a gift is it not? For the granting of favours." And it looked sideways towards the horses and made a show of wrinkling its nose and giving a loud sniff. Volpe took a step forward, his sword held out. To his own amazement, Acquel found himself moving forward as well to support the old monk.

"You shall not have our horses," said Volpe quietly.

The *mantichora* lowered its head and narrowed its eyes. "Not even one, holy man? That seems mean of you. Considering I could eat both of them if I choose to. And you both as well." Its tail swayed rhythmically. That would be the signal that it was to pounce. As Volpe had narrowed the distance so too had the *mantichora* slowly moved backwards, its rump brushing a tree trunk. "You, young priest, had a stronger sense of Elded about you when last we met. Perhaps you have washed since. It does still mark you though. I saw Elded once. He had a high opinion of himself. Expected much of others. Maybe too much."

Acquel knew the creature was toying with them, teasing and cajoling. Whether from boredom or maliciousness he did not yet know. "We need our horses to return from whence we have come. What else do you desire?"

The *mantichora*'s wide tongue wetted its lips. "Ah, *my* choice, is it?"

Acquel quickly regretted his haste. Volpe gestured with his sword. "Tell us, then. We will promise it if we can deliver upon it. We seek to know what to use against those that come from afar into our world. That which the Tree of Death gives unholy life to."

The *mantichora* stood up on its hind legs and wrapped its massive paws around a beech as it smiled down on the two men, tolerant and mildly amused. The horses were now skittish, stamping and snorting in alarm.

"Very well," the *mantichora* replied. "I am not particularly hungry having feasted on wild pig this morning. That goes in your favour."

Volpe walked forward again, brandishing the sword, and Acquel saw how the beast recoiled slightly. The sorbo wood was keeping it at bay as much as its own desire for amusement. "Then tell us what we wish to know, and what you wish in return."

"Are you willing to pay the forfeit for the knowledge you seek? If so, I will defer it for the moment. But sometime, sometime in future, I will collect."

"So be it!" answered Volpe.

"Not good enough," teased the *mantichora*. "Your companion must give his bond as well. Swear on the bones of all your saints."

"We swear," said Volpe, cautiously.

The *mantichora* swivelled its huge head towards Acquel. "You must give your oath, little priest."

"I do not yet know your price," said Acquel.

The creature smiled at him. "Does that matter?"

Acquel paused for a moment. "I suppose it does not. I swear. Upon all that is holy."

The *mantichora* gave a great sigh, its claws scoring the tree trunk deeply as it lowered itself. "What you fear is already here in Valdur. That which does not belong. That which disguises itself. That which opens the gate for others to come. Creatures not as beautiful as I but far more terrible."

"How do we slay them?" demanded Acquel. "That is what you must tell us!"

"Brave little priest!" the *mantichora* chuckled. "Your companion already holds one such talisman. Rowanis. Purest of trees. There are others… maybe… better."

"We wish to know them," replied Acquel.

The creature focussed its glare upon him, nostrils flaring. "And my price may grow higher, little priest. Have a care."

Volpe gave a dismissive bark. "You've told us nothing we do not already know. Perhaps that is because you know nothing more."

The *mantichora* was fast. Its paw lashed out at Volpe as the old monk instinctively raised the wooden blade. The *mantichora* batted it aside but the cry of pain that bellowed out was deafening as the crack of cannon.

It drew back, snarling and Acquel could see a wisp of smoke rising up from the creature's claws; there was the reek of burnt fur. When it spoke again all playfulness was gone from the *mantichora*'s voice. "My price will be the higher, holy men," it said. "And I will prove my wisdom to you." It paused, contemplating its singed paw. "Ah, gentle rowanis. It will not abide my touch."

"Tell us what you know," said Volpe, "and we will leave your forest."

It scowled back at the two men. "I know *all*. The second thing that I tell you is another you already know. Your circle.

Such a charm works not upon me but will upon others. You may seek protection also in the endless knot if worn upon your person. The third and final thing that I tell you is a potent weapon indeed against all fell creatures. A leaf evergreen, ever shining, as if soaked in the dew of night. It is as venom to that which does not belong. Litalas leaf… myrra to some."

Acquel felt his heart skip.

"I know it," said Volpe, his voice almost a whisper. "It is exceedingly rare."

The *mantichora* swelled its tangled chest and shook its mane. "But I will not tell you where to find it!"

Acquel found his voice again, stronger than before. "I know someone who will!"

The *mantichora* frowned and Acquel found himself breaking into a sly smile. A moment later the creature tilted its huge head as if realizing something, as if it had seen something in its mind's eye. Its slow nod was filled with dire certainty. "The forfeit is now set. Set hard as stone and as heavy as iron. You will find you have paid dearly for what you seek."

Acquel felt his grin evaporate even before the *mantichora* had finished its prediction.

Nineteen

THE CAMPAIGN TENT of Ursino, Duke of Torinia, had many rooms. Enough to make a rich merchant jealous and a peasant weep. Under the canopy of stout canvas, walls of silk and gossamer in a myriad of colours waved gently in the draught that crept in from outside. Woollen carpets with swirling designs from the finest weavers in Valdur covered the ground, an indulgent comfort for feet tired of road and trail.

And it was delicate, milky pale feet that silently padded across the plush floors of the tent in the dead of night. Lucinda's hand swept open the curtain to the inner bedchamber where Ursino awaited her, naked except for his silk Sinean gown of indigo. She smiled as she saw him and he extended his hand to take hers.

"It seems as if I have awaited you for years, my lady."

She hid her nervousness as best she could, lowering her eyes. He gently grasped her chin and raised her head. Ursino was amused by this sudden coyness on her part but in this he was mistaken. Lucinda had put off this moment for months, enflaming his desire even more, but his advances could no longer be resisted. Soon, in the moment of disrobing, she would face questions, questions that she would have to answer. Worse, she would have to keep Berithas at bay. Even as Ursino gathered her to his chest, her mind raced.

Can He hear my deepest thoughts when He comes to me? Will he take Ursino?

She yielded to his kiss, deep and passionate, losing her concentration, the fear of the Redeemer receding in her mind. In spite of everything—her devotion to the Old Faith, her hatred of the New, her mission to remake the world— she had lost her heart to this man. Would she still be able to make him king and save his soul at the same time? Her arms reached up Ursino's back as she returned his embrace. Her tongue teased his, searching. Slowly, Ursino peeled her away, caressing her long golden locks and running the back of his hand over her cheek. His eyes drank in her beauty, her ankle length gown of green velvet. He guided her by the hand and turned to a long table where silver ewer and goblets were placed. He lifted one, already full, and handed it to her as he took the other.

"To have had you there, by my side, blazing in your glory. It filled my heart." He tipped the goblet towards Lucinda. "To our first victory and to the ones that will swiftly follow."

She swallowed hard and took a sip. She felt powerless as her heart overwhelmed her calculating mind, ever filled with the next steps of her mission. And these melted away as desire filled her. "To our love," she whispered. He smiled and raised the cup again to his lips.

"To our love," he repeated.

Lucinda smiled but she worried that the familiar tingle in her shoulder and breasts would come upon her now. That Berithas would speak, insistent and commanding as ever. She remembered the fate of her rapist the previous summer. The glorious horror as Berithas shrivelled him to a dry husk even as he penetrated her. That must not happen now. And how to explain the wound? She found herself stepping back a little, the cup hiding her mouth.

Ursino refilled his goblet as the walls around them billowed in and out with the breeze. "I am doubly blessed," he said, placing the ewer back upon the table. "Blessed that your gifts have bestowed upon me weapons not seen in Valdur for an age long past, since even my forefathers walked the land. But also blessed that our hearts have found one another." He took her goblet though she had taken but one sip and set it down. "Livorna will fall—the griffons will see to that—and the heretics will be destroyed. Maresto will sue for peace after that. They would not dare take to the field with the combined might of Torinia and Milvorna arrayed against them. To see Alonso's face when he sees the royal beasts and the Hand of Ursula in our vanguard; he will know then the Lord is not with him but with us. More importantly, so will his army."

She felt a tug at her conscience—the memory of her dead sister. The act of killing her, months gone by, seemed like it was a dream now. Sometimes she almost felt her presence in the stillness of her bedchamber, as if her Farsight was working still, from beyond the grave. But Lavinia had betrayed her faith, her gods, and Berithas had spoken His will. She had done what needed to be done. For the faith. Ursino would have to learn soon exactly who it was she followed, and who he followed too by default and by blood oath. "I will do all in my power to deliver you the throne," she said, her voice becoming husky.

He set down his goblet and took both her hands in his. "And I will make you my queen. The queen of all Valdur." He pulled her into him, one arm about her slim waist, the other gently folding back her gown from her shoulder, revealing her nakedness.

"You are truly the most beautiful woman I have laid eyes upon."

She heard herself speak words she had not expected to utter. "And I desire you more than any man I have ever known."

She was almost shaking as he led her to the bed: a humble wooden bedstead but piled high with three feather mattresses and finished with silk coverlets. Goose down pillows lay plumped for them at the headboard, a magnificent Torinian needlepoint tapestry rising above. He eased off her robe from the other shoulder and it fell to the carpet. His eyes took in all of her: pert breasts, belly, long milky thighs blue-white, and the blonde mound of her womanhood. He ran his hands from her shoulders down her lithe arms but then, in the glow of the candlelight, he saw the livid wound that ran under her collarbone.

His fingers lightly traced it. "What is this then, my love?"

She reached across and covered his hand with her own. "I was burned as a child. An uncle who bore me ill."

Ursino nodded sympathetically. "If he lives still I will have him whipped before the cart, be he nobleman or not. Does he yet breathe?"

She shook her head. "He does not."

"Good." Ursino then threw off his own gown and pulled back the coverlet for them.

She slid in and he with her. He instantly sensed her tenseness and unease even as she wrapped her arms about him and placed her forehead against the notch of his jawline and neck. "Lucinda, I have never taken a woman against her will. You know this?"

Her reply was quiet. "I do."

"Then this choice to lie with me is yours, yours alone."

She wanted him more than ever now. What he took to be a maiden's modesty he could never guess was her fear of something far different and far more dangerous. He pulled back and found her mouth, his hand resting against the back of her neck as he kissed her. She could feel his manhood against her as her heart began to beat faster. She then tensed involuntarily as she thought she felt her wound tingle slightly.

Not now, please, Lord Berithas. Not now.

Even as his kisses grew more inflamed, her mind fought to keep away—to wish away—the unwanted arrival of the Redeemer. She did not know if she could prevent Him from possessing her for she had never thought to try. But it was different now, and she knew that Berithas sought more than anything to come back into the world in a new form, a new guise to usher in a new age. She knew there would be a price for the gifts He had bestowed upon her. The sensation in her shoulder ceased.

"Are you cold, my love?" Ursino had paused, genuine concern in his eyes. She smiled and shook her head, stroked his neatly bearded cheek, and leaned in to kiss him again.

She relaxed; the Redeemer had not come upon her as before. Perhaps He knew when she willingly lay with a man and when she was under attack. Or perhaps He knew nothing until she let Him into her mind. She inhaled sharply as she felt Ursino's mouth move across her breast. And she was grateful, joyously grateful, that the Old Ones had granted her the pleasures of the flesh unimpeded by the demands of Berithas the Redeemer.

For the first time it struck her that the price to be paid for her gifts, her powers, might be far higher than she had first imagined it to be. For now she was in love.

JULIANUS STRYKAR CURSED under his breath and slowly raised his arms skyward. He heard a second bow creak as its owner pulled it taut. He had not thought he would be that easy to track so quickly but—as in most things of late—he was wrong. But the expected twang of the strings had not come and slowly he turned to face his pursuers. It was not the mercenary band he had expected. Rather, he found himself facing a dozen *venatori*—huntsmen—clad in moss green cloaks and long-tailed hoods, tall boots strapped tight to their legs.

"You have found a poor lost traveller," he said, lowering his head. "Pray give me shelter."

The closest huntsman kept his bow aimed at Strykar's chest. "A deserter more-like, from that army below which we smelled afore we even saw it. Unbuckle that swordbelt or you'll soon be a hedge-pig for the number of quills in you."

Strykar did as he was bid even as he scanned the band before him, robbers or huntsmen he could not now tell. The sword and belt fell to the ground with a muffled clang and the others drew closer to him. One was taller than the rest. "Take his sword and bind his hands." It was unmistakably the voice of a woman.

Strykar struggled to see her face, obscured as it was by a black scarf within the voluminous liripipe hood. He winced as once again his wrists were lashed tight with a strip of leather.

"So much for the goodness of strangers," he mumbled as he was pushed forward. The band, but one, lowered their bows; the remaining huntsman kept his arrow nocked, bow resting on his thigh.

"It's more than clear you're a soldier so cut the prattle about poor travellers." The woman stood toe to toe with Strykar, no more than an inch shorter than he. She glanced at his sword and smiled. "And you are either a thief or a nobleman in trouble by the looks of that blade."

Strykar shrugged. "Sadly, today, my lady, I'm both. And who is it that has made me prisoner? Those who wear masks are usually hiding from someone themselves, no?" Strykar felt the smack of an open hand on the back of his head.

"Settle down, Bero," commanded the woman as she raised the strung bow over her head and seated it over her back and shoulder. "He's entitled to know who we are and we will damn well find out who he is soon enough." She pulled back the green woollen hood to show a silken coif that covered all her head and the right half of her face. It looked like an executioner's mask that had been cut away to reveal only a hazel eye, proud nose, and left side of cheek and mouth, a diagonal slash of shining black. An oval cut-out gave her sight in her right eye. "I am Demerise, Forester of the Duchy of Maresto, and this..." She reached into her satchel and pulled out a wide blue silk ribbon and suspended wax seal the size of a fist, "is my warrant. Now... *your* turn."

Strykar surveyed the faces of the men arrayed around him. They were shadowed in their hoods, unreadable. He knew of the royal hunters, an ancient guild and the only one to hold the right to take game in the forests of the land, for which privilege they provided meat to the tables of the king and his dukes. Each band held closely to their own forest respecting the territory of other *venatori*. They not only held the right to hunt stag and boar, they had royal warrant to hunt men: those that were caught poaching. Given his state of disarray and the fact that he was armed with but a sword, Strykar knew he was unlikely to be considered out to steal the king's venison. He held up his tied hands in a gesture of futility. "I am Julianus Strykar, a company commander in service to his grace the Duke of Maresto. Of late a prisoner of the Company of the Blue Boar and, it would seem, a prisoner once again. Thanks to you." He finished with a sheepish grin.

"The Blue Boar?" said Demerise, more than a hint of interest in her voice.

"Aye. That army your noses have already sniffed out. As always, they fight for Torinia. Which—you may not yet know—has just invaded the duchy. They're bound for Livorna now."

Demerise gave a long look to Bero. She then motioned to two other bowmen. "Take him," she said.

Strykar eyed her warily as her men came to him, one firmly seizing his upper arm and urging him forward. "So I'm coming with you, then?" he called back as he started up the slow incline of the forest floor.

"For the time being," she replied. "Unless I tire of you. But I would rather put more space between us and those mercenaries than remain here to interrogate you, my lord Strykar."

They headed north, to higher ground, the rooted forest floor giving way to outcrops of granite and white boulders covered in fine moss. The wood became thicker and darker as they walked, oak, beech and a few sombre stands of fir all rising up high. Strykar, more than dead-tired now, seemed to stumble every few yards while his companions negotiated branch, root and stone effortlessly, footfalls all but silent. Inwardly, he was relieved. There was little chance now they would sell him back to the Blue Boar and, indeed, Demerise's tone told him that the *venatori* had probably had dealings with them before that had gone bad. It was enough for now that at least they were headed in the opposite direction. His mind suddenly flew back to the tent he had escaped and to Lazaro's purpled and bulging face, the life squeezed out of the popinjay knight. He then remembered Coronel Aretini's cutting words, finally settling upon the sickening remembrance of the calamitous battle.

I brought it upon the Black Rose. By my own pride. My own recklessness.

After an hour they came to a small clearing, wisps of grey smoke from a small fire curling up through the canopy. A man stood as they approached, hefting the stick he had been using to prod the flames.

"So you've caught another one then?"

"Not quite," called back Demerise. "This hare had sprung his trap before we found him!"

The fire-tender bent and tossed a log onto the flames while the huntsmen fanned out. Strykar saw an enormous stag hanging from a tree on the edge of the encampment, bleeding out.

"Put him over there near the fire," said Demerise to Bero. "And you can free his hands. I think he knows we're his best gamble if he is to live."

Demerise shrugged off her bow and quiver and sat on a stump near the fire. She leaned forward and placed her forearms on her thighs. Big lass, thought Strykar as he watched her. She dressed exactly as her men: woodsman's tunic and hose, long boots strapped tight from ankle to mid-thigh.

"So, now you can tell me how you came to be captured by the Blue Boar. Even better, how you managed to escape."

Strykar rubbed his chafed wrists. "Mind if I take off this gambeson? I've had it on for three days."

She shrugged. "Just as well that we're outside. Do as you wish."

Strykar grunted as the sweat-soaked, stinking garment peeled away from his arms leaving him in an equally grim-looking and reeking linen shirt. "I am a Coronel of the Company of the Black Rose. We were defeated two days ago by a combined Torinian and Milvornan army led by Ursino. He has declared himself the rightful heir to the throne of Valdur." Strykar grunted in pain as he pulled his shirt off over his head.

Demerise sat back and swore. "We have been out here three days, and you say war has begun?"

Strykar nodded. "Livorna is next and I fear my army—what's left of it—has retreated south."

Demerise saw the welts and black bruises along his right shoulder and bicep. "But you survived it seems, Messere Strykar."

"Milvornan lancers ran me down but my armour saved me. Almost wish it had not. They took me to the commander of the Blue Boar. He ransomed me to a Torinian. Ten soldi."

Demerise smiled. "So hardly worth my while getting anything for you then. Livorna you say?" She pointed to the hanging stag. "That is expressly destined for Count Marsilius's table. I mean to get it back there, war or no war."

"You'll have to cross siege lines to do it. Unless you're faster than they are."

A huntsman proffered a wooden cup to him. Strykar took it, nodded thanks and drank. The watered wine was reviving.

"When I had heard that Sempronius was dead I knew no good would come of it," said Demerise. "How many towns have been burned so far? How many villages? What is *your* tally?"

Strykar set down his cup and looked into her eyes, intelligent and spiteful. "The Black Rose has no tally. As for the Blue Boar, Persarola is taken and now Istriana is undefended. And they are in league with a sorceress though they may not know it. She guides Ursino. Gives him rare monsters to wage war with. It was these that defeated us."

She was silent.

"Huntress, I need to make it to Livorna to warn them. If there's even still time."

"A sorceress who conjures monsters you say. But you didn't tell me how you managed to escape the Blue Boar," she said. "I would hear that story first."

Strykar held her gaze. "I learned they were going to execute me before the gates of Livorna. Last night someone freed me, out of pity. Or out of guilt for past misdeeds. Who knows, maybe both. I ran from the camp into the forest and escaped them."

"With a noble's blade in hand."

Strykar swallowed and looked into his cup. "There was a slight detour first. A short visit to my tormentor."

She nodded. "Understandable. I did not escape the Blue Boar quite as unscathed as you." She lowered her chin and slowly pulled off the black coif and mask. Her mouse brown hair was cropped short like a man's. As the coif fell from her face, Strykar came to see her meaning. From right temple downwards across cheek, jaw, chin, and neck her skin was flayed scarlet, rippled and furrowed like a farmer's field. Her upper lip sagged on the right such that her face was two halves: the left fair, the right a seared ruin. Strykar tried not to wince as he beheld her.

"Caglia," she said. "I was twelve years old."

Strykar lowered his head. "Caglia," he repeated. "Sweet Elded's mercy. I am heartily sorry for you. It was there I lost my wife and daughter."

Her eyes widened. "At Caglia?"

"I was far away when the Blue Boar attacked. I never found them when I returned." Strykar seemed to look past her for a moment as the images came to his mind's eye. "I was told they had all perished."

Demerise pulled on her silk mask, adjusting her eye-hole. Strykar studied her face as she did so. Did all women with hair of brown and hazel eyes remind him of Cara or was there something more with this one? The shape of the eyes and the nose, features still unblemished. *Twelve years old.* He put the idea out of his head. *Foolishness.* "Will you take me to Livorna?"

She looked at him as she pulled up her liripipe hood once more but she did not answer.

"Or at least point me in the right direction and give me a flask of wine."

She shot a glance to Bero who stood close by, leaning against a tree. The man raised his eyebrows as if to say 'your choice' and shrugged. Demerise looked back to Strykar as she adjusted the scarf around her mouth. "You have an army between you and the gates of Livorna. You'd never make it there before them."

Strykar grinned. "So how do you and your band plan to get there? You don't seem too worried by the prospect."

"There's a small path up in the cliffs above the city where the walls and rocks border the forest. About half a day's march from here. There's a pass there—only wide enough for single file. An army would never get through, even if they knew of it."

Strykar nodded, enthusiasm building in him. "That's it, then. We could make it back to the city before the Torinians arrive and begin the siege. We need to warn them, I have a man there."

She stood and brushed bits of bark from her tunic. "And what makes you think the High Steward will defend the city? Have you seen him? A scallop has more backbone. And that castellan of his—slimy little toad—don't put much stock in him either."

It had not crossed his mind, at all. That rather than risk a massacre Marsilius would surrender, recognize Ursino's claim to the throne. Surely Acquel and Kodoris would never agree to that? "Livorna will defend itself. Whether Marsilius wishes it or not. The Temple monks won't surrender."

She laughed lightly. "I wouldn't either if I were them. Not with what the Torinians are doing to *Decimali* when they catch them." She took out her knife and squatted down to saw off a chunk of meat from the rabbit that lay skewered over the fire. "Seven commandments. Ten commandments. Just another excuse to fight one another. Again."

"Take me. I will carry your stag."

Demerise popped the morsel into her mouth. "I was still thinking about ransoming you, Messere."

Bero spoke up from behind them as he retrieved his satchel from a makeshift lean-to. "Take him back, Demerise. We might even get a reward from his friends for saving his hide. And I don't fancy carrying that stag on a pole the whole of the way through the cliffs."

"Don't get your hopes up," she replied. "He's in no fit state to shift that beast on his shoulders."

Strykar stood up, slowly, knees cracking. "Try me, huntress."

THEY GAVE HIM back his sword, and the march nearly killed him. Or at least the last part of it. Climbing the cliffs that surrounded the east portion of Livorna proved more than he had bargained for, especially since they held him to his word to help bear the dead stag. By the time they had reached the red sandstone pass his knees were bruised black and blue. Jagged outcrops rose all around them but Demerise and her men knew the trail well. They tromped along, the ground breaking downwards, the path strewn with gravel and sand. Boulders and grassy slopes followed, the rooftops and towers of Livorna finally coming into view as they began their descent.

The clanging of bells reached their ears soon afterwards. Those from the low town were echoed by those from the Great Temple higher up on the Ara at the west end of Livorna. Strykar had handed off his end of the pole to another of the huntsmen and had been given a nod of thanks by the others for pitching in to carry the burden of the prize. He stopped at the upper terraces of the city, listening to the bells and the cries below. It seemed he would not be the bringer of the news after all. The Blue Boar had beaten them to Livorna.

Demerise sidled next to him. "You're stronger than you look, Strykar." She nodded towards the great grey turreted palace that rose up just below where they stood. "We go to the palazzo to deliver what was asked to get our money. While we can."

"And what about me? Am I your prisoner?"

She smiled, the good half of her mouth turning up and creasing her cheek. "I reckon you have enough problems as things stand. Besides, you weren't a poacher as far as I can tell."

"I'm coming with you," said Strykar. "The count and the High Priest must be told that it is not an army of mercenaries alone that they face."

Demerise tilted her head. "Your choice. I would not wish to be the one to bear tidings of monsters and dark magic."

"So, once you have your silver you'll be skulking out the way we came in? While you can."

"I don't relish eating cats during a siege. And it might come to that if we get stuck here. We'll make our way east again, stay in the forest until... until it's all over."

Strykar shifted his sword belt on his hips. "They will be in sore need of your skills upon the wall. You and all your bowmen. Don't you want to pay back the Blue Boar for what they did to you?"

She scowled. "Pay back? One man did this to me. A man I can't remember and who may well be dead now. I would rather have the beauty of the greenwood than revenge."

"Every Blue Boar soldier you put an arrow through is one less chance that another girl will suffer as you did."

She looked at him. "Is that what drives you to fight? Regret that you were off killing somewhere else while Caglia burned?"

Strykar nodded slowly. "Fair enough, my lady, fair enough. But you swore your oath and warrant to Sempronius. If Ursino takes the throne, that royal seal you carry might as well be candlewax for all the good it will do you."

"I'm going now to find that oily shit Voltera and get what's owed me. And I expect Marsilius will want to hear what you have to tell him. Not that it will bring him any cheer. But at least he'll have fresh venison to chew on while he's thinking about it."

Strykar extended his hand. "I owe you my thanks. For finding me... and letting me go."

She took it in hers, scarred and rough. "You're no enemy to me, Strykar, and by your tale you've had it hard enough this far. Besides," and she gave him a wry, crooked smile, "we share Caglia, don't we?" She shifted the bow upon her back and resumed her march down the slope.

Twenty

DANAMIS STARED AT the crumpled note as Citala's long blue hand lay upon his wrist.

"No one knew him? And he wore no badge of service?"

Danamis shook his head. "Gregorvero asked around the tavern. He was a stranger to all, or at least no one wanted to own up to knowing the man. But it proves that Tetch was telling the truth. It wasn't him who tried to have me killed. It was someone else."

She gently ran her finger down his cheek. "You must be on guard now lest they try again." They were alone in his cabin, the sounds of the crew above and below growing less as the hour drew late. "So, what do you do now? What is it the queen asks of you?"

He tossed the note across the trestle table and reached for his cup of wine. "I'm probably giving her more problems than I'm solving. I've told her to rally the other duchies to stand up to Ursino. Not wait until he is here at the gates of Perusia. Trouble is, Raganus and Polo are telling her to hold back. To depend on the Sineans for muscle if it comes to a direct challenge by Torinia. Muscle that would come with a steep price."

"So, the queen is conflicted then?"

Danamis turned and looked at her. "Yes, she is. And I have offered a bodyguard for her and the prince."

"Is she conflicted about you?"

"What do you mean?"

"Does she still have love for you?"

Danamis smiled and placed his hands on her shoulders. "Love?"

"Necalli has told me that you were once lovers, years ago, that the prince is a bastard is what is behind this war for the throne. It is said that you are the father."

Danamis frowned. "Well... the rumours are certainly not helping."

He felt her tense. "Are you saying it is true, Danamis?"

"No. No it is not so. The queen has told me herself."

"But she still has feelings for you."

Danamis sat back slightly. "I do not believe that. We *were* lovers, I will not lie to you, but that was more than ten years ago. Put a stop to before it had barely begun. Since when did you share such things with Necalli? I thought you did not trust him."

"He is different than we. Perhaps I underestimated him. But he listens, to everyone. That is how he learns things."

Danamis grunted in reply.

"But why has the queen sought your help?" continued Citala. "You have no armies to offer her."

"Because she trusts me and not the counsel around her."

Citala nodded, knowingly. "That is because she loves you still."

He could not deny it. Nor was he sure that Cressida wasn't teasing him for her own ends. "I would see it if that were true," he lied. "She trusts me because she knows me, and knows that Palestro has no vested interest here other than a continuation of Sempronius's seed." He gave her a reassuring smile. "The boy isn't mine. And all I need is here... in this cabin."

She blinked slowly and returned his smile, her little teeth gleaming in the lamplight. "Maybe you don't know women—or she-mer—as well as you think you do." She grasped both of his hands. "I am here to stand by you. I have no other choice."

"No other choice? You could return to Nod's Rock whenever you wish. War would never follow you there."

"No, I cannot. What I did not tell you, after the galley fight, was that my father has banished me." She saw Danamis's brow furrow and she nodded.

"What? But you brought him more myrra."

"Not enough. And he has guessed that we are lovers. He says you have enslaved me and broken your word to bring the myrra as you did before, in great bundles. His warriors have told him tales of degradation of the merfolk in Palestro. He is furious."

Danamis rubbed his temples and groaned. "What has he threatened?"

"To take the myrra from Palestro by force. Though he has not the means to do this. Or else it is the leaf talking, or his thirst for it. I do not think he will act for now. My people are doomed to die out there, I see that now. The colony in Valdur is what matters now. That is why you must stop Torinia and save the prince and his mother."

Danamis put his arms around her. "Tomorrow, I must face the queen's council and also Captain Polo and the Sineans. If I'm right in thinking what is coming then we'll have little time to act. They will want Cressida to put Perusia's defence into the hands of the Sineans, and the prince in a gilded cage. If they defeat Ursino then the kingdom will be in thrall to the Silk Empire."

She whispered into his ear. "No more of these things now. Let us to bed while there is still night. In the morning we begin anew."

*   *   *

SHE SAW HIM off the *Vendetta*, he and two dozen of his men, as the strong morning sun climbed into a clear blue sky burnishing the walls of the Perusian citadel. She felt weak as she watched him move across the columned piazza, sun glinting off his harness and that of his chosen men. Not from worry, but from a body that was yearning to be in the sea again. She had already waited far too long but the noxious waters of the quayside had made her put off the necessary ablutions. Necalli, too, seemed slower—and crankier—than he had of late. She noticed that his race, these Xosians, seemed not to be as exposed on land as did her people.

The merman came up to her as she stood at the railing. "Are you ready?"

She nodded. Necalli had arranged for a small longboat, rigged with a sail, to take them down the bay a few miles to where the water was cleaner and deeper. But Gregorvero had insisted they were not to go alone and he placed on board a pilot and two soldiers to escort them. She wore the yellow silk robe that Danamis had given her months before and although a sailor held out a hand to assist her over the side and down, she had made the leap effortlessly, before he could protest. The single lateen of the fishing boat billowed out and, hand on tiller, the Palestrian sailor eased them out into the harbour and southwards.

Necalli was staring at her. He seemed to stare at everyone but more often at her it seemed. "You have been fading, Citala. These past two days."

She took in a deep breath of the salty air as they sped through the water, the sail snapping. "I've dealt with worse. In Ivrea once."

"The humans have told me the tale." He spoke to her in the mer tongue but he was using more of her words of late, copying her dialect. "I admire you the more I hear." He smiled, his wide mouth curling up. He wore his usual knee-length gown, a shortened version of the Valdurian *cioppa* but far simpler, tied at the waist with a black eel-skin belt.

She looked out over the bay, dotted with vessels large and small. "The prince is not his child. He has told me."

"That would make matters easier, if others believe it. But that does not answer the problem of what this queen wants of him."

Citala turned to face the Xosian again, the ropes of her snow white hair flying about her long neck. "I trust him. I trust what is in his heart. Do not seek to put doubt into mine, Necalli."

The merman inclined his head. "That was not my intention, princess. Forgive me. I am here to aid the mission of Admiral Danamis, not to hinder it. I would that we trust each other more to make that possible, no?"

"Trust is earned, Master Necalli. Give me time."

As they sailed Necalli told her of the land of Atlcali, the seas that surrounded it, the cities that prospered there. All mer. She found it hard to conceive of a place as large as Valdur that was wholly inhabited by merfolk; merfolk that built as humans did and sailed as they did. It was to her like some dream land only existing in the imagination but for the presence of Necalli—different yes, but also like her in so many ways.

"Mistress! Don't want to sail clear to Telos!" The boat's pilot called. "Haven't we gone out far enough?"

She told him they had and as the sail dropped she and Necalli made ready for their swim. The two sailors grinned with more than a hint of lasciviousness as she threw off her robe and slid over the side. Necalli swiftly followed her.

"Well," said the pilot to his comrades, "suppose we'll just drift about getting sun-addled until they decide to come back, but I did manage to smuggle us some *acqua vitalis*!"

Citala kicked down and down into the pale blue water, so clear she could make out the bottom some twenty fathoms further: white sand studded with rocks and little forests of kelp in which grouper and dogfish prowled. She turned to see Necalli following, a stream of bubbles coursing upwards behind him. At once she felt invigorated, enlivened, the fatigue and burning skin vanishing. She rolled, again and again in her joy, as she went deeper. A green turtle came up to meet her, playful, and she let it pull her where it wished.

Better?

It was Necalli, probing her mind. She had been expecting this once they were under the waves. She decided to open herself, extending that trust.

I am whole again, Master Necalli!

It is good, Citala. Very good.

He caught her up, his smooth grey torso and loins sprinkled with tiny bubbles of air as he sped along, legs propelling him.

So you Xosians can hold your breath after all.

She instantly sensed his mirth in reply. Citala levelled out, releasing the turtle and rolled on her back to observe the light from above, rippling on the surface. She turned again and saw how the seabed fell away into darkness beyond them. She reached the edge of the chasm and halted her progress, head down and gently kicking to prevent her from rising. The light of the sun surrendered to inky gloom when she peered over the edge. She felt Necalli draw near and he placed a hand on her forearm.

Citala?

A large school of sardines, a pulsating ball of living silver, drifted past them and out over the chasm before spiralling up towards the surface. She turned towards Necalli, a small stream of air bubbles escaping her mouth. She could hear his voice inside her head but something else was there too.

Do you hear something, Necalli?

Necalli's lack of response, his unchanging eyes, instantly made her wary. She *felt* something more than heard it, a probing presence. Something that was seeking contact, a primitive incoherent essence but something that was alive nonetheless.

Necalli's thoughts came through to her, insistent.

We should return.

His long fingers gripped her forearm more tightly and she righted herself, brushing off his touch as she did so.

What is it? Something is searching. Seeking.

You hear the deep, came his reply. *The voice of the sea. Let us go back up.*

The presence seemed to be receding now, one last burst of nebulous thought—a sense of loneliness—and then nothing. She nodded to Necalli and gave a kick upwards, shooting into shallower, warmer water. He was close behind her and they rose rapidly together until they broke the surface. As his bald head popped up there was a smile on his face.

"What happened, Citala? Something gave you a fright?"

"*Hahthlxi!*" she cursed, seawater dribbling from her lips. "You felt it too. I know you did."

"It was the voice of the deep. All the life in the sea… its life-force. We who are adept sometimes hear this. You must have before, if you can hear my thoughts."

She shook her head. "Nay, Master Necalli. It was a single creature. One life."

He smiled at her indulgently. "Perhaps your imagination."

Why he refused to admit what she knew to be true she could not comprehend. For days she had been beginning to understand the Xosian, even to like him. Now, suddenly, doubt had crept back in again and her natural wariness was reasserting itself. Necalli was hiding something, that was clear to her. But he was also alone and thousands of miles from his home with not a single ship to call upon. What threat could this shipwrecked merman possibly pose? Treading water, she looked about and spotted the fishing boat bobbing in the swell some distance from them. "I think you are right. We should return now."

DEEP IN THE royal palace, Danamis sat at the vast round table of the council chamber and contemplated the men around him. Though daylight shone through the narrow windows above, the chamber was north-facing and miserly. The lighted candles upon the table threw both shadows and sharp relief across the faces of the council. Fittingly emblematic of the light and dark they each harboured in their souls, thought Danamis. Six of the men he hardly knew at all other than that they were the loyal rump of the royal council, all grey-haired and grey-skinned. Danamis wondered if the half that had fled Perusia might have been any better qualified than this lot: sleepy, doddering, and probably no more than a thimbleful of brains between them. Other faces he knew better. There was Messere Hieronimo, admiral of the galley fleet, a competent sailor and commander with short black hair, a wandering squint in his left eye, and a closely cropped salt-and-pepper beard. He had greeted Danamis with a bear hug upon entering the high-ceilinged chamber. Then there was Caluro, captain of the palace guard, a giant of a man who Queen Cressida swore by for loyalty to her house. He had come from Colonna as a youth, training for the guard that he eventually came to lead. No great friend of Danamis but neither was he an enemy. And any scheme that he might propose to save Cressida and her son would undoubtedly depend on the goodwill and support of Caluro.

Danamis looked across the table to the opposite side, the largest chair still empty; they were awaiting the queen. He scratched at his thin chinstrap of a beard and let his gaze settle on Captain Piero Polo, merchant adventurer and factotum for the Silk Empire in Valdur. He had known Polo his whole life, his father having sailed with the Colonnan explorer far to the east, across the vast inland sea, to open trade with Partha. But Valerian Danamis had not been on the voyage that had gone further, all the way east to the Sinean lands. Polo had returned with silk, spices, and as an agent of the emperor. His father, jealous, had sailed west to explore new lands. But he had come back empty-handed and just as bitter as before he had left Valdur.

Danamis watched Polo, smiling and grinning as he conversed with the Sinean ambassador seated next to him, the *Bo* Xiang Liu. The last man that Danamis had thought of as an uncle had tried to kill him. He wasn't sure that this old friend of his father hadn't tried to do the same despite the loud declamations of support. He still had no proof against him and the man who might have given it had ended up nailed to a post with a stiletto through the throat. Danamis was an admiral of Valdur and Piero Polo still was not. Perhaps that was motive enough.

Polo looked over to Danamis and smiled once he realised he was being intently observed. "It does my heart good to see you my lord! You have indeed had an *anno miraculoso*. Defeating the mutiny against you and then being reunited with your father. Reversal of fortune indeed, yes?"

"I would say that fortune favours those who take charge of their own destiny but I thank you for your sentiments, Captain Polo."

The *Bo*, dressed in a wide-sleeved black silk gown showered in geometric patterns of scarlet, leaned forward, hands crossed upon the polished blackwood table. "We have heard much of your skill at arms, Admiral Danamis. Your *resilience*, too. I wish I had taken more time to speak with you last summer here at the palace. Perhaps we can redress that in the coming days?"

Danamis gave a slight nod. "I remain at your service, my lord. For myself, I would hear of the new arrangements that your emperor has made with Scythiana, a place so far from home. Perhaps it was the tendency there for people of red hair that captured his attention."

Polo's face went hard, the last trace of smile dissolving. But Xiang Lao bowed his head politely. "We could speak of many things I am sure, Admiral. Things of mutual interest and concern."

Danamis smiled. "Of that I am certain, Ambassador."

Doors opened beyond and palace halberdiers entered, rapping their polearms on the wide-planked floors. As one, the men at the table rose, turning to watch the entry of the dowager queen, regent of Valdur. She wore the same flowing gown of night blue and golden stars that she had worn a few days earlier when she had met with Danamis. Cressida floated across the room and took her seat, each of her councillors bowing low as she settled into place, her hands perched confidently on the arms of the high-backed chair. Her eyes moved across the council but didn't rest on any one man, for even a moment. Danamis saw how she barely acknowledged him. Best course, he thought.

"Good my lords!" she began, "Pray, be seated. What advice do you offer me today regarding the threat against the throne."

Baron Raganus cleared his throat and straightened his burgundy felt sugarloaf hat as he regained his seat. "Your Majesty, as advised earlier, we have the ambassador of the Silk Empire, attended by Captain Polo. Would you hear them?"

She turned to Raganus. "I am pleased that the ambassador has returned to court. Will he speak for himself or will Captain Polo make the address?"

"I will begin, at least, your Majesty," said Polo, "but the ambassador is more than capable of presenting his proposal on his own behalf."

Cressida directed her gaze to the aging, elegant seafarer. "Then, Captain Polo, tell us what news you have of the rebellion that swirls around Perusia. For my own sources say that a Milvornan army waits just on the other side of the border. I doubt its intent is benign."

Danamis leaned back in his chair. Now came the moment, he thought. It was time for Polo and his backers to show their cards and in so doing reveal the price of aid.

"It is true, your Majesty, my sources confirm that the Milvornans are building an encampment near Tarolis. It is likely they will invade Perusia in the coming days. It is a formidable force, mercenary companies and militia alike."

"I have asked Maresto and Saivona to send armies and my loyal dukes will not fail me," replied Cressida. "Admiral Danamis has his men and indeed my own guard on the border will add to that force."

Baron Raganus cleared his throat dramatically. "Your Majesty, there is other news that affects the calculus, if I may."

The dowager queen inclined her head.

"I have received word this very morning that Duke Ursino has defeated an army of Duke Alonso's mercenaries in the north of the duchy, south of Livorna. He will now lay siege to the Ara and may even march on Maresto city itself. If Alonso loses the hinterland of Maresto, then he will be busy defending his city and the Saivonans will not be able to cross to get here. If such things come to pass, then the throne is in peril and Ursino's boastful claims are no longer idle ones."

Danamis sat up, watching as Cressida visibly reeled from the import of Raganus's words.

Captain Polo gave an unctuous smile. "With respect, my

queen, nothing is yet lost and the relief force that your father urged is already on its way from Colonna. It is Sinean. Three ships and no more than two days from here."

Cressida attempted to rally. "My lord, it is a gracious gesture of the Silk Empire but three ships will hardly stem a major invasion from the north or the west."

"These are not Valdurian carracks, your Majesty. They each carry one thousand warriors and are the length of ten of your galleys laid end to end. They will defend Perusia and the throne."

The *Bo* nodded and smiled. Danamis quickly calculated the odds of defence if the Sineans decided to impose their will. There were none. With a force that size, if it were true and Polo was not stretching the truth as he often did, there would be no way to resist a Sinean occupation. He could not even begin to wrap his mind around the size of the ships Polo had described. That such vessels could even exist had never even occurred to him. Cressida was looking at him now, almost imploring him to help.

"And under whose command are these ships and their soldiers?" he asked, struggling to keep his tone one of mild interest. "Yours, Captain Polo?"

Xiang Lao let out a bellowing laugh before Polo could reply. "If Valdur and the Sinae are allies then what does it matter? I am sure that we could put you on the quarterdeck of one of them, Admiral!" He looked from Danamis to the queen, his dark eyes twinkling with enthusiasm. "Your majesty, on behalf of my master, the Supreme Lord of the Five Thrones of the Silk Empire, I offer you a formal alliance. One of deep friendship and mutual benefit." He lifted a large folded parchment from his lap and gently placed it upon the table. He slid it towards the centre towards Raganus. "We would wish the House of Sempronius to continue to prosper—and Valdur with it."

Raganus gestured for a guard to retrieve it for him. "And your terms, ambassador?"

Danamis had no doubt whatsoever that Raganus, now chancellor of the kingdom, already knew them.

"I will leave you now to discuss them in private with her Majesty and the rest of her esteemed council," said Xiang with a flourish. "You will soon see that they are the means to a new golden era for Valdur." He rose and bowed low three times to Cressida, his strangely folded silk hat fluttering with each dip. He backed away, and with folded hands concealed in his voluminous sleeves, he left the chamber.

Piero Polo looked about the table, like a fox regarding a yard full of chickens. "Shall we begin?"

Cressida frowned and again cast a glance over to Danamis. Danamis gave her a wink and lifted his forefinger slightly in a gesture of reassurance. He now had less than two days to come up with an alternative to handing over the keys to the kingdom to the Sinaens, and he already knew there was but one.

Twenty-One

WORRY AND FEAR. The two hung over Livorna like a foul invisible fug, from east in low town to the reaches of the Ara plateau high on the west side. Every man of sound body from white-haired grandfathers to boys with but a wisp of downy chin beard had been told their duty. The battlements would be manned, the gates reinforced by cart, barrel and crate, the stones and rocks hauled up in wicker baskets to join the copper vats of sand and pitch already stationed there. Short iron tripod braziers already sat stocked with coal and wood every forty feet along the zig-zagging stonework. Pinched faces regarded one another on the streets across the cramped ribbon of a town, some people hoarding bread and meat, others spending their last silver on dark strong wine should this week be their last.

Now the apprehension had come to an end. Templars along the walls had shouted their warnings below that soldiers had been sighted riding beyond the tree line on the ridge south of Livorna—scouts. They were lightly armoured and bore no banners. Although the portcullis was already down at both stone gatehouses, the order was given to close and bolt the great reinforced wooden gates as well. Like wildfire, the word spread across the town, bells adding to the cries of the militia. Some prayed it was an army from Maresto; others of a more pessimistic nature knew it was Torinia's war dogs that had come.

Lieutenant Poule stood shoulder to shoulder with Acquel on the highest embrasures at the main tower, watching the small groups of horsemen as they cantered along the length of the town, far out of bowshot. They could be seen stopping every so often to confer, as if noting details of the walls.

"Torinia?" asked Acquel, knowing the answer.

"The Black Rose would have already come a-knocking if it were they," replied Poule. "These men are sizing us up for attack. I expect we will have the main army here before the sun sets. Bastards."

Acquel leaned over the wall. "Sweet God. What has happened to the Black Rose? Where is Strykar?"

"If the Blue Boar has got here first then we must fear the worst: that they have already met upon the field, and lost."

Acquel turned to face the mercenary. "You're saying we will have no relief? That we're alone?"

Poule grunted. "Brother Acquel, I'm no Seeker. We will likely have two choices: negotiate a surrender when asked or hold out as long as we can. Duke Alonso will have to send an army north to deal with the Blue Boar. We will have to last until he does."

Acquel took a deep breath to steel himself. "I must tell the High Priest what is happening. And then the two of us must see the High Steward, and find Brother Volpe! I just pray he won't be at the bottom of a wine jug."

"If he is, he'll be in good company," mumbled Poule as he turned to enter the tower stair.

* * *

ACQUEL FOUND KODORIS in a state of deep reflection, unmoved to action by his news of the enemy's arrival on their doorstep. Seated in his chambers, garbed in his purple *cioppa* and surplice, the High Priest seemed oddly detached as he fingered his shining medallion of office.

"I'm going to low town now to inform Count Marsilius that the siege will shortly be upon us. I don't know if he will treat with Ursino personally or if he will delegate to me."

Kodoris looked up at him, his face almost blank. "I shall lead prayer in the Temple Majoris this evening, Magister. That is where my duty takes me."

"Lucius, the walls are sound. The men have been trained and the Order of Livorna stands ready to defend. Maresto will lift the siege if we stand firm."

The High Priest returned a wan smile. "You are the chosen of Elded. You will persevere. And I will do what I must."

Acquel frowned. "You are the head of the One Faith now. Your presence will be demanded, *needed* by the people. Will you stand by me?"

Kodoris seemed to look past Acquel and into the middle distance of his own mind. "I will stand by you, Brother Acquelonius. When the time comes. *This* I know." The delivery of the words sent a chill through Acquel. It was more than a promise: it was preordainment. Acquel stepped back, unwilling to delve into the nature of Kodoris's vision. He would have his hands full leading a battle he was manifestly unqualified to undertake with only one grizzled veteran soldier and an old monk to depend upon. And he knew the strength of the walls of Livorna would have to compensate for the weakness of their skill at arms, and their hearts.

He left the monastery and returned to the battlements to find Poule waiting for him, Ugo Volpe in tow. Acquel could see more horsemen out on the gently sloping plain before the town walls. A wagon and team came into view, halting under a stand of gnarled ancient olive trees: the quartermaster and supplies for the siege, he guessed. The main army would no doubt be hard on their heels. He cast an eye down the long line of the battlement as it wound its way east like a sleeping dragon, the crenulations its spine of stone. Already men were gathering, the constables having rounded up their detachments to man the wall. As Poule had warned him more than once, their defence would be thin and should more than one attack occur along the length of the town, they would be hard-pressed to deal with both. Somewhere below him, a bell slowly and incessantly chimed.

Volpe smiled broadly as Acquel reached him. "Brother Acquel, we are ready. First watch of the brotherhood is on the wall west of the main gatehouse. Lieutenant Poule has tasked the militia eastwards to the gate at low town." He placed an avuncular hand on Acquel's shoulder. "Now we wait for their first move."

"It will be a call for surrender," added Poule helpfully. "That is the usual form in such matters. So who will speak for Livorna? You or the High Steward?"

Acquel felt a strange exhilaration—an almost drunken giddiness—now that the wait was over. He had felt this feeling before, at sea. When about to fight the pirates of Darfan, and it had worried him afterwards. How could a holy monk find rapture in the prospect of battle? This time, he took solace in the feeling. Action was far better than waiting in ignorance, of being afraid. "We will find out now. We're going to the palace."

As expected, it was Voltera who met them in the great hall. He was agitated, face glistening with sweat.

"Magister, we were worried you would not come! Terrible news this day." He turned on his heels and beckoned for them to follow him across the hall and into the meeting chamber. When they entered, Poule let out an oath that carried up to the high-beamed ceiling. Acquel froze where he stood. There in the centre of the ornate panelled chamber stood Marsilius the Count, and Strykar. The mercenary looked as if he had been dragged by a horse. He was filthy and dishevelled, his face the colour of granite.

"Sweet God above!" said Poule as he reached his commander. "Coronel, my good lord, what has happened? Where is the Black Rose?"

"Defeated," said Marsilius, his voice oddly matter-of-fact. "And Coronel Strykar has just arrived to give us the news. Alone."

Acquel joined Poule, who was restraining himself from seizing Strykar in a hug while he stammered away in surprise and shock.

"Strykar, what has happened?" said Acquel, his stomach lurching.

The mercenary looked at Acquel, nodding almost as if to convince himself of the situation. "We were shattered. At the far side of the Taro River. It was the entire force of the Blue Boar and the Whites. Ursino and his own knights. And the Milvornans for good measure. They have joined Ursino."

Acquel's mouth fell open. "Elded save us. Where is the Black Rose?"

Strykar looked behind him and retrieved his silver wine goblet from the table beyond. "They fled. Back over the river and south. I only hope most made it to Maresto. We lost a few hundred I think."

Poule was shaking his head in utter disbelief. "Sir, how did you escape? Are there no others with you?"

"I was struck down and captured on the field. Unconscious. The tale of my escape can wait until later." He took a deep swig of wine. "There is more I must tell you. Of the sorceress."

Acquel grasped Strykar's arm. "The canoness? What has she done?"

"She has summoned beasts to their aid. Griffons. Huge creatures. They tore our vanguard to pieces and when the Milvornans hit our flank we collapsed. The Scarlet Ring was our rearguard but they fell back too and fled."

Acquel released Strykar and stood back, coldly numb as the news washed over him.

"And they carried the Hand of Saint Ursula with them as they attacked. They might have damned well good as carried the crown and throne with them to prove their claim. The royal beasts of Valdur and the Hand!"

Brother Volpe stepped forward. "They do not have the Hand of Ursula. We do. Tell me of the beasts."

Strykar looked at the little round priest and scowled. "Who the hell is this?"

"This is Brother Volpe," said Acquel. "He was a fighting monk of Astilona and has great knowledge of the arcane. He is my... advisor."

Strykar laughed, a derisive guffaw borne of exhaustion and failure. "Your advisor? And Poule here your general?" He turned to Marsilius. "Good my lord, take me to a sickbed that I may sleep unto death."

Marsilius blinked, debating whether to honour the request. But Volpe put his hands on his hips and growled a reply. "I have asked you a question, Coronel, and I expect an answer. It is we who will now face these creatures. I must know what you have seen."

Strykar bellowed and threw the goblet across the room where it struck the hearth with a clang. "Who am I to be *interrogated* by this priest!" Voltera jumped backwards at the outburst and two guards sprang forward and seized the mercenary. Marsilius raised a trembling hand to stay them. "Let him be."

Strykar raised his hand to his brow and lowered his head, instantly ashamed of his outburst. "I must get back to Maresto," he said quietly. "To warn them."

"They will be warned by your comrades who got away," said Volpe, his voice like steel. "We need you here at Livorna."

"He is right," said Acquel softly. "Strykar, we need you. And we may have a weapon with which to fight the canoness."

Strykar looked up, his face a mask of despair. "I lost my command. My company."

"But Livorna will give you back your respect," said Volpe.

"And I will follow you," added Poule, nodding. "All of the militia."

"So will the Templars," said Acquel. "We are ready to fight them at the walls."

Strykar looked up to the garish plaster roses and vines on the ceiling, a cruel reminder of his comrades, now scattered and broken. He smoothed back his greasy hair with both hands and pondered the choice. To stay or to make an escape for Maresto. To return in shame, alone, after the remnants of the Black Rose had streamed back south, was something he could hardly contemplate. He could already imagine the look on Alonso's face when he would enter the palace. Perhaps Acquel and this old monk were right. To stay and fight for Livorna—defeat the siege maybe—that would go some way in restoring his reputation. He looked at each of them in turn.

"Show me what you have up on the walls. From end to end. And I must inspect the gatehouses and towers."

Poule broke into a wide grin, his crooked teeth standing proud.

Acquel turned to the High Steward. "My lord Marsilius, when the time comes, do you wish to treat with the Ursino at the main gate?"

The Count shook his head vehemently and leaned on his castellan who in turn put a hand on the old man's slumping shoulders. "Nay, Magister. I have devolved that duty to you and the Temple Majoris. My infirmities have sapped what strength I have remaining." Voltera fumbled for the silver pomander and tried to thrust it under the Count's nose but Marsilius waved him away.

"Then I will speak as Magister of the Ara, when the time comes. And we will fight them."

"I grant you all that is in my armoury," said Marsilius. "There is the finest plate and chain, good white harness there for you and Messere Strykar. Take what you wish."

"I will escort you there," added Voltera, frowning at his master's generosity.

Acquel bowed. "Then we go to prepare for what is to come. By your leave, my lord."

Volpe coughed, impatient. "And now, just perhaps, Messere Strykar can be so kind as to tell me more of these griffons."

Strykar nodded gravely. "Very well, brother monk. But the tale will freeze your marrow for they kill men as easily as a lurcher shakes a rabbit. I know not how to defeat them."

Volpe nodded in return. "You may be of more help than you believe, Coronel. Let us talk."

Twenty-Two

LUCINDA RODE ALONE. She had left behind the bustle of the Torinian camp with its shouts, creaking wagons, and the harsh echo of axe on tree. Now she had a vantage on the high rise of ground to the south of the camp which took in the sea of canvas below her and the rising walls of Livorna further out. Between the camp and the town walls, soldiers of the Blue Boar scurried, carrying large wicker screens and preparing their emplacements just outside bow range of the defenders upon the battlements. Ursino had demanded she take an escort. She had laughed and then a moment after, he too laughed, remembering her power. She needed to clear her mind, she said, alone, before the siege began.

The canoness sat motionless in the saddle of her white palfrey and gazed on Livorna in the cool air of early morning. She concentrated her thoughts, narrowing to a dagger-point of hard focus: the Ara. Her eyes closed and she willed the Farsight to come to her. Increasingly, it was taking a greater effort to summon the power, with each passing month the Farsight grew dimmer and hazier. Even her dead sister's scrying mirror had gone dull, now just a small useless slab of obsidian. She was but a poor vessel for Lavinia's gift despite Berithas urging her on. She could make men *do* things. Lavinia had been the one to *see* things. Finally, through a sulphurous yellow fog, she recognized the long aisles and massive stone columns of the Temple Majoris, ghostly robed figures processing in prayer. One figure stood alone at the high altar—the High Priest Kodoris. She sought to draw her focus closer, but it could not be done.

A swirl of fog rolled across her view and she found herself in a different place—the walls of Livorna, soldiers streaming past her: boys, greybeards, militia. And there was the meddlesome monk, the new Magister: Acquel, looking tired and anxious but dressed in armour, a sword at his side. With him was another monk, old and corpulent. She had an immediate sense of his cunning, and experience of war. He was practised in the old arts, long forgotten by the smug priests of the One Faith. Who was he? Her vision began to blur and she felt herself pulling away, once again inhabiting the saddle of her impatient, snorting mount.

She was being called. She could feel it welling up inside her. Lucinda pulled down on both reins to steady the horse as she felt Berithas come to her. The voice—calm and strong, decidedly male—seemed to fill her head.

Daughter. The hour draws near.

"I hear you, Redeemer," she whispered.

You have done well. But the tree you gave new life now withers upon the Ara. There are those who know us and work against us. They have poisoned us. Wounded us.

Lucinda nodded. "I will kill them, lord. Grant me the power to find the enemies. To *reach* them!"

You now rule the beasts I have delivered to you. The winged servants I sent once before will come to you again. There will be other allies to come to your command. They will come to you soon. In the dark of night.

"Lord, there is another monk on the Ara. I sense he is a threat."

For a moment there was no reply. But when the voice came it rang with certitude and defiance. *The Three will come soon into the world. The gateway beckons. But the Ara must fall to you first. The tree must be saved. You will destroy those who stand in your way.*

She pushed her shoulders back, head high. "I will, lord."

The time draws near for me to take mortal form once again. You will be my arrow to that end, daughter. Through your lips shall I enter Torinia and thence the kingdom.

Lucinda's heart began to pound. It was as she had long feared. He would possess Ursino's body to manifest himself in the world. In an instant her feelings became confused and she nearly cried out for fear that Berithas might know her thoughts, see her love for the Duke and her resolve crumbling. Mastering herself, she quickly tamped down her emotions.

"Your will be done, Redeemer." And she waited for his wrath to envelop her, ripping her mind to shreds. But it did not come. Lucinda began to breathe easily again as her ears filled with a sound like the gentle tinkling of rain upon stones, the sound of Berithas and his presence.

When you take the Ara the Three shall come into the world anew.

Berithas left her mind. She felt him depart like a thunderclap and then merciful silence, the distant clank and clatter of the camp rising up to her ears once more. She *could* guard her thoughts and her feelings from Him. He was a powerful entity but he had begun as a man a millennia ago. He was not one of the Three. She swallowed hard and cinched up the reins, her mind already spinning with thoughts of how to save Ursino. There had to be a way.

Lucinda guided her horse back down to the camp, the fear and dread rising up in her. She had never questioned her service to the old ones before. Not even when Berithas told her to slay her own sister. The mere contemplation of any deceit made her shake.

Two riders approached her and reined in. The Duke's men-at-arms.

"Canoness!" said one, saluting her. "He requires your presence at once."

They were gathered at the great open area of ground at the centre of the encampment, a makeshift piazza at whose centre flew the banner of Torinia overseen by the Hand of Ursula upon its pole. Lucinda saw Ursino on horseback in conversation with Coronel Aretini of the Blue Boar and Federigo, Count of Naplona who commanded the large army that Milvorna had lent to the enterprise. There too was Coronel Michelotto of the White Company, short and fat, laughing at some jest of Aretini's. She trotted to them and bowed to Ursino and the soldiers each acknowledged her.

"My good lady!" said Ursino, beaming at her. "The morning grows late. Are you ready to treat with Livorna? They're probably wondering what's happened to us by now!"

He was exuberant, confident of impending victory—almost boyish in his enthusiasm and she smiled. "My lord, I am ready to stand by your side."

"And what of the beasts? Will they make a show if you summon them?"

She nodded. "They will come if I call."

"My lord," said Aretini, "The presence of the griffons might even save us the blood and cost of a long siege. They frighten the hell out of me, so God knows what the monks and townsfolk will make of them!"

Ursino laughed. "You hear that, canoness? We may win this without cost. Save the force for the might of Maresto, eh, Coronel?"

"That is a concern, my lord," replied the mercenary. "Alonso has other companies he can march north. Better to get Livorna over quickly so we may turn south before he has time to react. Or find more allies."

The Count of Naplona nodded in agreement. "The Boar is right. And Milvorna must keep an eye to the east as well. The Duke of Colonna has yet to declare against you but his daughter is the king's widow so no doubting where he will come down. He's also playing host to those Sineans and I'd rather not have to deal with them. Not yet, anyway."

The Duke of Torinia lowered his voice. "Gentlemen, we have another card to be played—very possibly a trump—at midnight, tonight."

Lucinda knew his secret and she watched the commanders as they leaned forward in their saddles, eager for more.

"I can tell you nothing else at present but have your best *rondelieri* ready at the east barbican at the hour."

"A spy?" proffered Aretini.

"A hope," replied Ursino. "We shall see. But let us say that the High Steward of Livorna is in no condition to lead a defence of his city. That responsibility has fallen to the holy men of the Ara."

Ripples of laughter spread among them but Lucinda merely smiled, her mind weighed down by what payment would need to come.

"Aretini," said Ursino, "you shall ride with the herald this morning when he delivers the demand for surrender. The lady della Rovera will accompany me, and bring forth her pets when the time is right." He looked over to one of his footmen. "Summon the trumpeters! And where is that damned herald!"

Lucinda could see the nervous exchange of glances at the mention of the griffons. And rumours had already come to her ears across the camp in the last week; rumours that spoke of a deal with unholy powers, for how else could such creatures be brought forth much less be controlled by a woman? She knew that at some point Ursino would have to be told the source of his good fortune and that the price might be both his body and soul. And what would the armies of Torinia make of that? The splintering of the One Faith had helped the cause of the Old, but would it be enough?

The herald, in a blaze of colour, his horse caparisoned equally garishly, made his arrival and the party set out with a guard of four score men-at-arms. Aretini adjusted the strap of his sallet and sidled alongside the herald in his tall felt hat, pheasant plumes sprouting at every side. "You do know what maximum bow range is, I hope," he said snidely.

Unperturbed, the herald glanced over to him. "It is why my man yonder also bears the white flag of truce."

Aretini chuckled. "Oh, magical proof against arrows?"

The broken ground before them levelled out, stands of beech here and there as they ambled at a walk towards Livorna. The sun blazed down in full and a strange breeze blew across the length of the walls, stirring up the dust on the main road into little whirlwinds that danced before them even as it animated their banners. The herald, his trumpeters and Aretini were followed at a longer distance by the Duke, Lucinda and the other commanders. They were flanked by armoured horsemen. At a few hundred yards from the main turreted gate, the herald raised his hand for a halt. He then signalled to the two trumpeters to begin their blast. It carried well, a peal of staccato intensity, demanding attention.

Aretini scanned the battlements. Helmeted heads bobbed up and down its length. He had already noted the shallow dry ditch that ran along the walls, deepening where the bridge and twin towers lay. The right tower of the barbican looked patched and he remembered the earthquake of more than a year ago. But the walls were high—scaling ladders would be difficult to employ and engines would take weeks to build. He muttered a curse. He hated sieges. A waste of men and money. Indeed, a prince was likely to run out of treasure before a city would give in. Open battle was far better. He had already advised Ursino to make a half-hearted attack to gauge the defences once the city had rejected the offer of surrender, as he knew they would. But he still hoped that the High Priest and the Steward could be cowed into some form of surrender before the inevitable bloody shits and camp cough ruined his soldiers. If not, perhaps a culverin could be brought close enough to blow up the wooden gate and portcullis. Or a battering ram might do the trick. He chewed the inside of his cheek as he thought. It came back to the same old thing: more work and time with damned siege machines. And losing more of his soldiers at the walls while Maresto prepared and the Black Rose licked its wounds.

"Give them another blast," he ordered the trumpeters.

It was answered by the sound of a gun being fired up on the walls. And then a voice carried over to them. Young but confident. It came from the embrasures over the barbican and Aretini's round, hawkish eyes focussed on at least a dozen men standing shoulder to shoulder, just visible.

"Who comes to the holy city of Livorna? What is your business?"

The herald, bold as brass (and Aretini had to give him that), urged his mount forward a few yards and answered in a well-rehearsed voice, "His noble grace, the Duke of Torinia, defender of the true One Faith and rightful heir to the throne of Valdur demands your surrender and your fealty! Open your gates!"

A man stood above the parapets, raised up on something below. He wore a thigh length fluted white tabard and an open-faced helm. Aretini could make out some sort of golden device upon his breast, and he remembered what

Captain Janus had told him when they took Persarola: fighting monks. *Decimali.*

"I am Magister of the Temple Majoris and I speak for the High Steward of Livorna. The Duke of Torinia holds no authority here and I suggest he takes his small hunting party elsewhere!" A cheer followed behind him. The herald waited until it had died before responding.

"The Temple has been given over to heretics. We will not treat with you. Show us the High Steward! Let *him* speak!"

There was silence on both sides. Aretini looked behind and caught a glimpse of Ursino sitting stone-faced in his saddle, the lady della Rovera next to him looking equally grim. He turned to the herald. "Bring up the Hand!"

The herald motioned to one of his men and barked an order. Up on the walls, the man yelled down to them. "And we will not treat with usurpers nor with those that harbour a sorceress!" The herald went red and shot a glance over to Aretini. But by this time a soldier had come running forward bearing the twenty foot pole and the holy relic of Ursula atop, shining silver in the sun. The herald puffed up his chest once again.

"Behold the Hand of Ursula! The Duke Ursino speaks for the One Faith and bears this holy relic before his army as the rightful heir to the throne and defender of the true religion!"

There was a pause up on the parapet, a jostling of heads and shoulders, and then a second, taller figure stood up on the wall, plate harness gleaming. Someone thrust something silver into his hand and he held it aloft as he bellowed out to them.

"*This* is the Hand of Ursula! And we shall not be fooled by Torinian market fair fakery!" Another cheer rose up along the wall and Aretini's eyes grew wider. That voice, he knew it.

The soldier bellowed again. "Take your tin hand away and your witch with it! We see her there among you. You will not have this city!"

Aretini laughed and kicked his mount forward to join the herald. He stood up in his stirrups. "Julianus Strykar! More lives than a Palestro cat I see! I salute your good fortune that you have found your feet again—and your mouth!"

The herald turned and scowled at the breach of protocol. The tall man on the wall gave a flourish with his hand in recognition of his name. Aretini quickly looked to the rear again. Ursino's face was turning the colour of a plum as he watched and the canoness had cantered off, her horse just visible through the trees. He faced front and beckoned to Strykar.

"We would have had you down here with us! Giving the city a show as we hanged you, sir! You cheated us of good sport! Lord Renaldo's men might have a few words for you as well!"

Strykar's voice carried strongly on the breeze. "Let them come up and have their say! I will hand them their heads!" A cheer rose up again along the wall, taken up even by those who had not heard the exchange between the two knights. The herald turned to Strykar and snapped "Enough! You are in the presence of the Duke." He jerked the reins of his mount and moved a few yards closer to the walls. "Magister! If you speak for the High Steward then it will be upon your head when this city falls to your rightful ruler. Surrender now, open your gates, and all will be spared."

The other armoured man struggled up again to the parapet. He cupped his hands and shouted down to herald. "The Holy Order of the Temple of Livorna holds this city in the name of the rightful king of Valdur—Prince Sarant! And we will break you upon these walls!"

The herald shook his head and made a sound halfway between a cough and a curse. He flicked his reins and turned his horse back towards the Duke's entourage. A sudden roar of excited men and the neighing of horses made Aretini turn again in his saddle. From the left, up on the hill behind them, he saw the canoness returning on horseback. Behind her, two enormous griffons padded tamely along, following their mistress. The brownish-red fur of their lion bodies, muscles rippling, shone almost iridescent. A steady breeze that blew across the high walls of Livorna animated the white feathers of their enormous heads. Aretini's hands involuntarily tightened on his reins as they approached. He watched as they passed in front of him at no more than fifty feet, heads tossing and their glistening beaks, the colour of ripe oranges, clacking in anticipation. He took a breath as one turned its head to regard him with a steady baleful eye as if deciding whether he was friend or prey. It slowly faced ahead and caught up with its companion. Aretini could feel his horse shaking beneath him, flanks twitching.

A rider plunged past him on his right. It was Ursino. The Duke, oblivious to the giant creatures behind him, reined in next to Lucinda. Cautiously, Aretini followed his paymaster, one eye upon the griffons. They were now within bowshot of the walls and he gritted his teeth at the calf-headed impulsiveness of the Duke. Ursino stood up in his saddle. "Magister of the Ara! All of you!" He thrust one arm behind him towards the griffons. "Look upon the royal beasts of Valdur who know me as their rightful king! You have heard the demands! Open your gates to me and be spared. Or else see your walls torn down around you."

And as Aretini listened, he realised that there was nothing but silence on the battlements. All catcalls and cheers had ceased, mouths stoppered by the sight of the unearthly creatures before them. Not a single arrow came in reply and he remembered his own reaction at first sight of the beasts: barely contained terror. As if in response to the challenge of Duke Ursino, both griffons let out a screech of intimidation that reverberated off the ancient walls of Livorna. And Livorna was, in return, deathly silent. Coronel Aretini allowed himself a small smile. With one bold act Ursino had taken the heart out of the city.

DEMERISE ABSENTLY PLAYED with a pouch of jangling silver coin as she sat at the long trestle of the High Steward's kitchen, sipping from a pewter wine cup.

"You still mean for us to leave tomorrow?" asked Bero, seated across from her. "Even after what we saw today?"

She looked over to him and took another sip. Her scarf she had pulled down from her face to nestle at her throat for she had nothing to hide from Bero. Not after all these years. "We've been paid," she replied quietly.

Bero gave a good-natured chuckle. "But we haven't been here long enough to spend it. The High Steward has given us the run of his household—decent racks for the night. Food and drink. Wouldn't mind another day at least, despite the siege."

"We should be on our way to Maresto. We hunt on the way through the Forest of Sospiri. Deliver to the palazzo when we arrive."

Bero took another drink, savouring the quality of the Milvornan, a wine he rarely sampled. It was late of the evening, but most of the band were still out in low town, making the most of the time remaining before the battle for Livorna began in earnest. "You've been moping all evening. I think you're a little bit torn up. That old knight we found rattled you, didn't he?"

She set down the vessel and leaned forward, aggravated by his needling. "I've told you my intentions. Go find a scullion who will let you mount her—while you can."

"Easy, mistress. No harm meant." Bero gave her a well-meaning smile. There was silence between them for a minute or two. He scratched at his nose and ventured more conversation. "Do you think Ursino is the rightful king? Has the Lord really favoured him sending these griffons to his banner? Claiming to have the true Hand of Ursula and all. I pity the people here if the gates fail. They won't have a cripple's chance in a game of calcio. Not against the Blue Boar, those giant beasts, and God knows what else they have."

Demerise leaned back on the bench. "And what would you have us do? A handful of archers in a fight that isn't ours."

Bero shrugged. "Just saying." He raised his cup to his lips and took another long drink.

She was about to give him another reason when two of her men burst in, throwing back their brown hoods. "Demerise!" said one, the lank-haired unshaven Ricardo whom she could smell the wine on as soon as he reached her. "We were down near the east gate. The castellan is there with four of his men and they've relieved the watch. The *whole* of the watch."

She and Bero looked at each other. "What is that swine up to now?" said Bero. "It's midnight for bloody sake!" Demerise didn't reply but instead walked to the corner and retrieved her bow and quiver. "Let's go, all of you!" Bero's eyes widened but he jumped to and grabbed his own bow while the other hunters ran for their weapons.

They were not far from the east gate, the palazzo being just north of the square where the great barbican was situated. The moon, waxing but not yet full, cast its glow across the lime-washed houses and shops that lined the square. The band moved quickly, silently—as if on a forest stalk—across the deserted cobblestones. Demerise's eyes adjusted to the shadows around her, the great wall and towers rising up fifty feet before them. She could see movement near the gate itself: figures shifting there, ghostlike, busied in some task. Coming from inside the base of the gatehouse of the barbican, she heard the clanking of ratchet and pawl: the portcullis mechanism. A figure was at the right side of the tower, just inside, pulling at the chain that was suspended there. She motioned to Bero to move off and approach from the left while she, Ricardo and two other hunters crept closer from the right. The portcullis was already raised up three feet and as she crept forward, she raised her bow, ready to draw. Two figures rolled underneath the rising massive iron grating and clambered up again, disappearing into the shadows of the cavernous tower. A fourth figure heavily encumbered by ankle-length cloak—and obviously less agile than the others—went to his knees and crawled underneath the portcullis.

Demerise heard Bero give a whistle and she turned. Two militia soldiers were running towards them across the piazza, bearing torches. Demerise called out to the figures inside the gate. "You there! What are you about? Answer me!" She was met with the continuing clank of the portcullis as it ratcheted up higher, someone still cranking at the wheel. Bero returned to her side, his bow already drawn, as they moved forward. "Sweet Aloysius," he hissed, "I think they're opening the gate." Behind them the two militia men came to a stop, chests heaving. "What's going on here?" demanded the older of the two. "Someone said the castellan is taking charge."

Demerise gestured with the nocked arrow of her bow. "Looks like someone has no intention of sitting through a siege."

"My God!" The man leapt ahead and thrust his torch through the portcullis as Demerise and Bero followed behind. The orange flame of the torch revealed three men heaving at the great oak bars that sealed tight the double gates of the tower. One bar had been raised and set down on the cobbled ground, still lying in one of the black iron brackets of the gate. They had the last remaining one in their hands, straining upwards. A fifth man—the cloaked one— was busy pulling at the two large iron bolts of a smaller door set into one of the gates—the night door.

"What in hell's name are you doing!" yelled the militiaman as he struggled to get under the portcullis. Ricardo and two other hunters now were standing at the portcullis and looking back to Demerise.

"Demerise?" proffered Bero, quiet urgency in his voice.

"Take them," she replied.

Bero let fly, his arrow hitting one of the men struggling with the bar. The sound of other whisking shafts followed immediately as each of the hunters took down a man. The cloaked figure sprang away from the door against the stones of the corridor wall, a cry upon his lips, and in the torchlight Demerise saw it was Paolo Voltera. Their eyes met. The castellan was shaking his head, hands raised in a gesture of surrender. Demerise hesitated, her drawn bow creaking as she took her bead on Voltera's chest. "Toad," she whispered. And then she released her fingers to let her arrow fly. The castellan sagged to the cobbles, still clutching at the shaft buried under his sternum.

A mighty crash sounded against the small door and its hinges groaned. Men were pushing it in from the outside and Demerise saw that the lower bolt had been pulled. A steel-lamed foot stuck through the gap as another crash reverberated in the gatehouse, the door shaking again as shoulders rammed into it from without. The militiaman dropped his torch and rushed to put his back against the door. His companion was soon there to throw his weight into it.

"Help them!" shouted Demerise. Her hunters stooped under the portcullis and ran to aid the Livornans. Ricardo, on his knees, drew his dagger and managed to find a gap in the leg armour of the fool who had it wedged at the base of the door. A scream outside was followed by a hasty withdrawal of the limb and, with the backs of all of them straining, the door was shut and the bottom bolt slammed home again. They hefted the oak plank that had been taken off and set it back on the brackets of the gates even as the enemy outside continued to hammer on them.

Ricardo turned and smoothed back his long, dank raven locks. "Elded's balls. That was a near-run."

Bero looked down at Voltera's still-open but lifeless eyes and shook his head. "Saints' blood, Demerise. I think you can now say that we've taken a side. And you've just killed the castellan of Livorna. You know, the one who *pays* us?"

Demerise lowered her bow. Behind her, a dozen militia were running towards them, yelling as they came. She nodded at Bero's words. "Aye, I know what I've done." She let out a sigh so loud that all of them heard it. "We had better go find the Magister and that Strykar."

Twenty-Three

"I HAVE SEEN much in your world, Nico, but nothing such as this." Citala was gazing out over the rail of the *Vendetta*, out over a thousand yards to a ship that lay anchored far out in the harbour, alone. It was the first Sinean warship to arrive at Perusia, a monstrous vessel, its five masts taller than the highest trees. And it could have swallowed whole five ships the size of *Vendetta*.

Danamis, at her elbow, scowled in mock displeasure. "What's wrong with my ship then?"

She put her arm in his. "Yours is a fine vessel. *Royal Grace* too. But it's just that the Sinean ship is so vast. As if out of some dream."

"Probably slower than an old cog."

Gregorvero joined them, having just supervised the loading of supplies in advance of what would be an unannounced departure. "Now *that* is a ship," he said.

"You too?" said Danamis. "Well, the Sineans are our friends of a sort—for the moment at least. What are they mounting?"

Gregorvero leaned over the railing, eyeing the black-hulled monster. "I hear they have guns of bronze. Elded knows how many. Muzzle loading like our orichalcum pieces. There's no one in Valdur casting bronze that big."

"So that will give them long range, like us. Let us hope it doesn't come to a fight."

Gregorvero chuckled. "We'd need a few more ships to even those odds, Nico."

Danamis rubbed his eyes. "How soon can we weigh anchor?"

"By morning if you wish it. Bassinio says the Grace is provisioned and all her men back aboard. We have all we need."

Danamis nodded. "Good. We may only have a day's notice when the time comes."

"Do you see the queen today?"

Citala lifted her head, her violet eyes blinking.

"Aye," said Danamis. "And I pray she agrees to my plan."

"I would accompany you to the palace," said Citala. "I may be of some help to you there."

Danamis smiled at her. "Help? In convincing Cressida to leave with us?"

"That. And if things get dangerous. With the Sineans, or others."

Gregorvero laughed. "You better let her come along! I know that tone well."

Citala shot him a look of annoyance. "You both know how I fight. And I may be able to help convince your queen if she falters in her resolve."

Danamis shook his head, half in exasperation and half in admiration of the she-mer. "You're a formidable warrior, my love. But I'm not as sure about your skill in diplomacy."

"When we enter that place we will never know if we can get out again," she said. "What if her palace guardsmen turn on her?"

"Unlikely," replied Danamis, leaning in. "And if it did happen, you wouldn't be able to make it back to the sea. But, I don't think that prospect will dissuade you, will it?"

"You know the answer to that, Danamis son of Danamis."

Gregorvero rolled his eyes and looked out over the railing. "And while you're both away I shall have a think about just how fast that floating island of the Sineans can make way under full canvas."

CAPTAIN CALURO MET them with folded arms after they had cleared the gatehouse into the first courtyard of the great palazzo. His eyes quickly took in the dozen men that Danamis had with him, armed with side-swords and studded brigantines. Some other fellow, tall and looking like a priest in a long hooded robe, stood close by the Palestrian. "Captain Danamis!" he said with a curt bow as he blocked their progress. "You may take two of your bodyguard with you into the apartments. No more." He gestured to the robed figure. "And who is this then?"

Citala pulled back the hood of her robe and Caluro's woolly eyebrows rose. "What is the meaning of this, Danamis? You bring merfolk here into the royal presence?" He addressed Danamis but could not take his eyes from the mermaid standing right in front of him. The first he had ever seen in his life.

"This is Citala. Of royal blood herself. The princess of Valdur's merfolk."

Citala gave him a slow bow of her head and then pulled her hood back up over her snowy braids. Caluro pursed his lips, frustrated, even as he drank in her strange beauty and the liquid intensity of her eyes. He finally managed to tear his gaze away. "Eh, very well, my lord. But the queen does not like unannounced guests and she expects only you." He motioned to his own guards to bring up the rear.

They walked into the redstone keep, the temperature dropping as soon as they set foot inside the halls. Danamis felt Citala reach for his hand. He quickly grasped it, gave it a squeeze, and then released her. They followed their guide, their swords and harness echoing in the immense corridor as they made their way deeper into the maze-like pile of ancient stonework. The foremost part of the palace was a series of great octagonal structures joined by corridors. As the party passed through the connecting passageways, bright sunlight shone through high narrow stained-glass windows, casting coloured reflections upon the pale flagstones.

The largest chamber followed, a huge octagon with flying buttresses of ancient oak and enough gilding for ten temples. A wistful smile came to Danamis's face as their steps echoed across a floor chequered in red and white marble. It was here that he had first met Cressida as the courtiers played human *dama,* men against the women, in a large as life version of the table game. Instead of jumping a piece to seize it, the capturing player would exchange a kiss with the opponent and then occupy the space beyond. He was still a boyish man then and he remembered his heart pumping in his chest as the beautiful lady from Colonna drew closer, square by square, directed by the old king, Sempronius the First. It was the only time before or since he had ever wished to be captured.

Citala felt slightly ill at ease, the dark memory of the castle at Ivrea still fresh in her mind. These cold, hard human structures filled her with a sense of dread, of impending entrapment. Captain Caluro looked over his shoulder. "She will see you in the gardens today, my lord." Citala felt relieved at the prospect. They turned left and down another great corridor lined with marble walls and floor, the ceiling a riot of criss-crossing rafters shining in gold leaf. At length they came to a large studded oak door. Caluro turned to them and stopped. "Only you, my lord— and your guest."

Danamis nodded and turned to reassure his two guards, men he'd sailed with for so long they had beards of salt-and-pepper and brows as lined as an old chart. "Stay here, and don't pinch anything." He winked and they grinned back at him, ever the Palestrian pirates. The door squealed on its hinges as Caluro hauled it inwards and he and Citala passed through, Caluro at their heels. The brick-walled gardens were immaculate: dark green box hedge, cut in ordered geometric patterns, tall palms gently sagging, beds of tall foxglove of sensual purple and poppies the colour of fresh blood. Stately acanthus spread out along the gravelled pathway. Danamis saw the queen near a white marble fountain, her head down as if in thought or prayer. She was alone.

Caluro increased his pace and she turned as he approached. Danamis held back, placing his hand on Citala's forearm. At length, Caluro beckoned for them to come forward. Danamis went first, making a deep bow, knee bent, his cap swept off as he did so. She nodded and gave him a smile. As he stood again, he took her in. Beautiful as ever but her face showing clear signs of worry and lack of sleep as when she had sat at council. She wore a dress of dark wine damask, cinched tight and high-waisted, a drape of ivory linen over her shoulders to shield her from the sun. Her long blonde hair was coifed and braided, wound into a whorl pinned at the back of her head.

"Good my lord, Nicolo!" she said softly. "I have eagerly awaited your visit. And I thought it better to speak out here, away from prying eyes and eager ears." Her gaze settled swiftly on the hooded figure a few paces behind him. "And who else do you bring with you?"

Nicolo extended his arm toward Citala. "My queen, this is Citala, daughter of the chieftain of the merfolk." Citala stepped forward and threw back her hood. Cressida's lips parted in astonishment but that was the extent of her surprise. She smiled and extended her hands. Citala bowed her head and silently accepted the queen's welcome.

"You are welcome at my court. Would that Lord Nicolo had given me warning that you were to accompany him and I would have prepared a repast for you." She glanced over to Danamis, a look of reproach on her face.

"I am sorry, my queen. It was rather a hasty decision."

"No matter. I have heard tales of your adventures upon the sea with Nicolo. Perhaps we may have time to talk further."

Citala bowed her head again. "I wanted to meet you. To tell you how much Nicolo has risked to serve you and the prince."

Danamis nearly choked as Citala's well-intentioned but presumptuous words met his ears. "My queen, the mer are not used to our customs. Please—"

Cressida raised her hand to stop him. "Do not apologise for her." She smiled broadly. "She is a loyal friend to you... and she believes in you. As do I." Cressida looked down at Citala's hands that she still clasped in her own. "I have not ever seen a mer before today. Your hands are cold, even in the heat of the day, my dear. Is it always so?"

Citala nodded.

"Your race is like ours and then again not like ours. So many stories over the years. I feel remiss in not having met your kind before. Perhaps we can change all that. Let us walk."

"Cressida," said Danamis as they strolled in the burning sun, Citala and Caluro two steps behind, "If you sign that treaty then Valdur will be a vassal state of the Silk Empire. You and the prince must come away with me. To Maresto."

The queen stopped. "What? Abandon the throne? What are you thinking, Nicolo?"

"No, my queen. Not abandon the throne. To lead the fight for it. Against Torinia, the chiefest threat. If I take you to Maresto it will get you and the prince out of Perusia. It will give you time to stall the Sineans because you won't be signing any treaty before you leave."

"Nicolo, this is the old pirate talking," she replied shaking her head.

"No, it's not. The Sineans will bend you to their will as more arrive. Polo can taste control already. You place Raganus and the council in charge while you and Sarant campaign in the west, Raganus will inform the ambassador that you will look favourably on the treaty upon your return. A pronouncement from you, giving your intentions, to be read out after you've left."

Cressida looked at Danamis, speechless.

"Cressida, they need *you*, and Sarant, to give legitimacy to their intentions. If you are at war they cannot act without being the aggressor. I doubt very much the Milvornans will attack Perusia with three thousand Sineans here as your guests. And not before they know the outcome of the war in Maresto. Piero Polo will have to suck his teeth and wait for your return before pressing you to sign the treaty."

She looked down at the flower beds, alive with diligent honeybees oblivious to all else. "He won't let me leave. He will detain me despite my palace guard and good Caluro here. They will never let me get to your ship."

Danamis smiled at her. "That is why I have a plan, my queen. Will you go to the palace temple on the Feast of Saint Giacomo? The day after tomorrow."

"It is as always. The prince and I will attend the temple along with the High Prelate of Perusia who officiates."

Danamis nodded intently. "You must be *seen* to be there. But, you will not be. They will see the queen and the prince but it will not be either of you."

Cressida frowned. "Doubles? A ruse?"

"We need to find those who would take the risk—and who could pass for you and Sarant, at least at a distance. Your man Caluro and the guard will keep the secret and make sure Raganus follows your orders."

She placed her hand over her mouth as the daunting nature of the task hit her. "My God, you are mad Nico...."

"Cressida... there is no other way. You must trust me. By the time Polo finds out we will be on the ship and away."

She looked into his brown eyes; the eyes of the man she had fallen in love with a decade ago. "I do trust you, Nico. But in this we will need far more than trust or luck. We will need Elded's grace."

Danamis gave her a tender smile. "I can provide the luck if you can have a word with Elded and the Lord above."

She grasped his arm. "Then let us set your plan into motion. I will not submit to Sinean blackmail nor Polo's arm-twisting. And I may have an idea on who might help us. With the deception, that is."

"*That* is my Cressida of House Guldi!"

They turned to face Citala, who lingered a few paces behind along with Caluro (who was still transfixed by Citala's grey-skinned features). Cressida caught a look from the mermaid that carried just a hint of mistrust. But she quickly checked herself as she realized that it was not quite mistrust; it was the look of a jealous lover.

"Citala," she said, "I am grateful of your company and also for your rescue of Danamis on the journey here. You are immensely brave."

Citala bowed. "Danamis has been a friend to the mer and believes in my mission to bring our people back to this land from exile."

"He has told me of this before. And now perhaps you yourself can tell me the story of your people."

"It would seem that we will have the time for such things once we journey upon the sea again."

Cressida gave her an awkward smile. Danamis cleared his throat. "My queen, we must plan in detail your steps from the palace to the ship on the day. You cannot bring much with you, and only a few servants at most. And you must bring the royal seal lest it be misused by Raganus."

Cressida nodded. "That had already occurred to me. It will be done."

"And one more thing, Captain Caluro will be key to our deception. For he will have to escort your imposters to the temple. It would be suspicious if he was not there."

Caluro took a step forward, hands spread. "Your majesty! I will not leave your side. It would be too risky. To leave you with this—"

"Pirate?" said Danamis.

Cressida raised her hand. "Enough. The Admiral is right. It would not be believable if you and your men were not at my side as we progressed to the Temple."

Caluro shook his head. "Your Majesty."

"More than that, Captain, I must ask you to stay behind and guard the council. You are the only person I can trust to keep Raganus steady and to keep Polo at arm's length. You will see that everything in my pronouncement is adhered to."

The captain sagged slightly in his disappointment. "Yours will be done, my queen."

"Good," she said, giving him a reassuring smile. "Now, let us plan the details of our little expedition, shall we?

There is a bower over there to take shade in. Citala, you have a part to play in this too and your opinion is valued as much as my two commanders here. Join us!"

AN HOUR LATER, they were back under escort and heading the way they had come, winding their way through the labyrinthine corridors and towards the entrance to the sprawling palace. Caluro, Danamis, and Citala walked in front, the two soldiers from the *Vendetta* behind them, followed by six of Caluro's men.

"She is brave... and beautiful," mused Citala as they walked, her head shrouded once again in the voluminous brown hood of her cloak. "But she is still a prisoner in her own palace. And that is a sad thing."

"That may be so, but no more of that now... or here."

Caluro had been silent, a fixed scowl on his long, mule-like face since they had left the gardens. He spoke up now, *sotto voce* that his men might not overhear. "You had best be right in all this, Admiral. All of it. Because if even one strand unravels you will have me to answer to. She is my charge. She always will be."

"Understood, Captain," said Danamis. "Understood."

They entered that last octagonal chamber before the great double doorway to the courtyard. And coming towards them was another party, under escort by the palace guard. It was Piero Polo and his men. They halted a few paces from each other, Polo making a sweeping bow and doffing his hat. Danamis did the same.

"Captain Danamis, Admiral of the fleet! Well met this day! We are on our way to discuss trade business with Raganus and the council. And you?"

Danamis looked beyond the craggy explorer, eyeing the Sinean soldier who stood tucked between the two crewmen who served as Polo's retainers. "The same," he replied, the hint of a smile on his lips.

Polo nodded. "And good day to you Captain Caluro," turning to acknowledge the towering commander who was clearly irked he had not been informed of the visit to the palace.

"It would have been better had I known of your intentions," growled Caluro.

"Ah, yes, there was no time for the usual protocol I'm afraid," said Polo offhandedly. "I do apologise but affairs of state keep no civil hours."

Polo dipped his head, looking up into Citala's hood. "And who is your escort, my lord? I do not recognize— ah! A mer woman. I had heard of your... *guest* from the sea. It is an honour." He gave a flourish and a court bow. Danamis felt Citala push closer into his side. "We must meet at the harbour—all of us, no? Nicolo, we can give you a tour of the Sinean vessels! Admiral Hieronimo too! You will be fair amazed, my lord, with their shipwright skill. Veritable floating cities."

Danamis looked at Polo's crewmen, their black doublets unbuttoned, hose drooping with laces undone. Their red arming skullcaps, spotted black with tar stains, sat far down over their foreheads, making them look even more witless than they probably were. *Unshaven louts,* he thought to himself. His eyes moved to the red coifs again. The same red arming coif that the dead informant had been wearing when Danamis found him with a stiletto in his throat. He slowly reached behind his *cioppa* and slipped his hand into his leather pouch on his belt. He pulled out the red arming coif from the dead man which he had been carrying around for more than a week. A reminder. Danamis extended it towards Polo in his left hand.

"I think you might want to return this to your quartermaster. For another in your service. Maybe one less careless with his tongue."

He watched Polo's reaction. A moment of surprise and then swift recovery of his expression, the familiar look of joviality upon him. But he did not move to accept the red coif. "My dear Nicolo, what is your meaning? Have you found this on the quay?"

Danamis's right hand moved smoothly across his waist to his left hip, his palm resting on the pommel of the slim Southland blade that had once belonged to his father's castellan. "I think you know where it came from. And who its wearer was."

Polo snorted, but his eyes bored into Danamis's. "I am sure my men lose these upon the docks every week." Polo's two sailors spread apart, sensing the rising tension. The Sinean, a young man dressed in black silk, short straight blade at his hip, stepped off to one side, watching Danamis as he did so.

Danamis's right hand slid from his sword's pommel to encircle the grip. "Why, Piero? Why, after all these years? I can see your eyes give the lie." His voice was like ice. And then he felt Citala's grip upon his wrist, vise-like, telling him that now was not the time nor the place. But Caluro stepped in between the seamen even as the two groups fell back a step.

"Gentles! I know not what score is at stake here but you will not settle it in the palace." His sonorous voice dropped a tone further. "So, stand you down. *Now*."

A large smile broke upon Polo's face, his protruding eyes slightly glistening with false tears. "Ah, Nicolo my boy. You have much to learn about the world."

"Yes," replied Danamis as he stared down the explorer. "I'm learning that loyalty is a commodity in short supply in Valdur."

"Upon my life, I think you are mistaken in whatever accusation it is you make." Polo smiled again, shaking his leonine head in awkward denial. "Captain Caluro, we take our leave of you." He gestured to his men and they stepped off, giving Danamis and his two men a wide berth. Danamis slowly wheeled in place as he followed them, the Sinean casting a distrustful glance back towards him as he adjusted his swordbelt. Caluro looked down at Danamis whose eyes were alight with rage.

"Bad blood must out in the end, my lord. I can see there's no love lost there."

"I am running out of so-called 'uncles', it seems," said Danamis, his anger subsiding as Citala stroked his forearm. She spoke quietly. "It was this man—Polo—that tried to have him killed last summer in this very city."

Caluro whistled softly. "I remember the incident. But a red cap? Your only proof of guilt?"

"It is no proof, I'll warrant that," growled Danamis.

"I'll kill him for you, Captain," piped up one of Danamis's sailors, a broken-nosed veteran of a hundred voyages. "Just give me the word."

Danamis turned and clapped him on the shoulder. "That is good of you, Malaro. But that is a job for me and me alone. One I will savour when the time is right."

Twenty-Four

THE HIGH-PITCHED screeches pierced eardrums and rattled men to the core, rending the air at such irregular intervals that all but the most inured flinched or ducked their heads, eyes clenched in fear.

"For the love of all the saints, don't they ever sleep?" Strykar, sitting against the inner wall spat across the stone parapet and stuck his hands over the glowing brazier in front of him. Seated next to him, Lieutenant Poule jabbed the embers with a stick in frustration. "The creature must be getting a hot poker up its arse every time it drifts off to sleep."

So jangled were his nerves, Brother Acquel found himself chuckling. They were high up near the main barbican and gate on the side that led to the Ara at the western edge of the city. It was late, the chimes for midnight having just sounded below them a few minutes earlier. Acquel pulled his cloak closer for, despite the start of summer, Livorna was cut into the foothills of the great mountains to the north and the air at night was still chilly. Strykar had not allowed torches to be set in the walls lest those patrolling the parapets be struck by enemy bowmen below. All along the wall, groups of Templars and militia huddled together, dozing or conversing in hushed tones.

He sat up as figure approached, having come up the spiral stone stairs of the barbican. It was Volpe. "Hail brothers," he whispered cheerfully as he squatted down with them. Strykar grunted his greeting and Poule merely lifted a hand.

"Did you see the High Priest?" asked Acquel. "How fares he this evening?"

Volpe shrugged. "His body is sound but his mind is disordered still. He has been at prayer since taking his sup."

"Yes, he has seen something... in his mind. A premonition perhaps, but something powerful and frightening."

Volpe nodded. "A vision while he hovered between life and death. He has seen what knocks at the gates to this world."

Strykar looked up. "What are you prattling about, monk?"

"The root of the things that you have seen with your own eyes, Messere Strykar. The Trees of Death that sprout anew. The beasts that you hear screaming up at us even now."

Strykar harrumphed. "That bitch della Rovera has brought this upon us. I shall see to her if God gives me half the chance."

Volpe seized a wineskin that lay nearby and gave it a shake before unstoppering it. "She is but an emissary—a messenger—for what is coming. Those who you call the old gods."

Acquel spoke up. "She is a formidable Seeker. That is how Kodoris first found her and used her skills."

"Perhaps she found *him*," the old monk offered.

One of the griffons out in the fields let loose with a blood-curdling screech.

"Why does it do that?" asked Acquel through gritted teeth.

"It is doing what it is bid to do," suggested Strykar. "Making us consider surrender the wiser of our options before the dawn breaks." Acquel threw him a quizzical look and Strykar smiled wanly. "They don't want to die any more than we do. They're mercenaries. Aretini and his friends would rather end this quickly than suffer a slow bleed against these walls."

"We do not have what we need to fight these griffons," mumbled Acquel. "We have told you that."

"I know," replied Strykar. "Your old friend here has explained how the myrra leaf could help. But until we see what cards Ursino plays out, we must sit tight. We have an army between us and Maresto in case you hadn't noticed."

Poule stopped poking at the orange coals. "And suppose those beasts decide to fly up here onto the battlements? Then what? You told me what they did to our army on the far side of the Taro."

Strykar gave him a look of grim determination. "You stay out of their way and pray the crossbowmen get lucky."

Acquel threw a glance to Volpe and the old monk looked down, for he knew not what to say. Nor did anyone else after that, and silence fell among them. They heard the scuff of feet on the spiral steps of the barbican and Strykar raised his head. Two cloaked figures emerged from the archway and scanned the parapets.

"Hail!" barked Strykar. "Who are you after?"

The pair turned at his voice and approached, dropping back their hoods. Strykar hauled himself to his feet as he recognized the two figures. "Demerise. You're still here?"

"You have a problem," said Demerise.

"*We* have a problem," mumbled Bero at her side.

"Who is this… woman?" asked Acquel, stepping forward.

"We are searching for the Magister," Demerise said. "We were told he is up here somewhere."

"I am the Magister of the Ara," said Acquel. "And who are you?"

"This is Mistress Demerise, a venatora of Maresto," said Strykar. "It was she who brought me here after I escaped the Torinians."

She nodded in acknowledgement. "Magister, I must tell you that there was a traitor in your midst."

"But not anymore," added Bero helpfully.

"What are you talking about?" Strykar stepped closer to Demerise, their eyes practically level.

"The castellan—Voltera. We caught him opening the east gate with a few of his men. He was about to give the city away."

Ugo Volpe shook his head at the name and mumbled something dark, his suspicions confirmed.

"Sweet Elded." Acquel breathed. "What happened?"

"We killed him. And his men. They nearly had the bar off the gates by the time we got there. Not much choice for us at that point."

"Take us there," said Strykar quietly. "Poule, keep watch up here!"

EXCITED MILITIA WERE milling around the gatehouse at Low Town as they arrived, their constable herding them like a fretting mother hen. Near the edge of the square they had laid out the bodies of Voltera and his four henchmen, all retainers from the palazzo. Strykar whistled as he surveyed the corpses, his eyes resting on the features of the castellan, frozen in shock at the moment the arrow struck his heart. "You're sure he was trying to let in the enemy?

"There was no doubt," said Demerise quietly as she stood next to the mercenary. "None at all."

"And we fought off the raiding party that nearly got through the night door," chimed in Bero.

Acquel was still in shock at the sight. He had thought Voltera more than odd and a touch unctious, but never had suspected he would aid Ursino and try to surrender Livorna. "What of the Count? Where is he? You don't think he's thrown in his lot with Torinia?"

"He may need our aid," said Volpe urgently as he turned and trotted off towards the palazzo. Acquel cursed and ran after him. Strykar turned to Demerise. "I suggest you leave your men here and come with me. You will either have an apology to make or another man to kill. I'm not sure which yet."

Demerise nodded to Bero and they crossed the square and headed uphill to the palazzo. When they entered the great hallway it was quiet, candles guttering in the draught. They proceeded up the wide staircase and entered the apartments, Strykar with drawn sword and Demerise with an arrow nocked. They walked down a long tapestry-lined corridor smelling of oak and lime-plaster, and as they slowly reached the end they heard voices coming from one of the apartments. When they reached the room they found Acquel and Volpe attending to Marsilius, who lay propped in his bed.

Volpe turned at their arrival and held aloft a small glass phial. "Voltera was administering this to the Count. It is a solution of night jasmine. It would explain this." He gestured to Marsilius. The Count, listless and pale, was speaking in a rambling whisper, spittle dribbling down his lower lip. Volpe jiggled the phial. "Over time this will kill."

"Will he live?" asked Strykar, scabbarding his blade.

Volpe shrugged. "I can attend to him, but I don't know for how long Voltera was poisoning him."

"Brother Volpe," said Acquel. "do what you can for him. I must go back to the wall. And try and find the rest of his household, unless they've already run off."

"Looks like now you're the ruler of Livorna, brother monk," said Strykar. Acquel felt a tug in the pit of his stomach as that realization sank in. "Come, Magister," Strykar said quietly, "I will accompanying you back to the barbican gate."

Outside, Acquel approached Demerise. "Mistress, I owe you thanks for stopping what could have happened. I know you did not expect such grim work when you came here. I'll see that there are no repercussions against you and your men."

"Repercussions?" she laughed. "I should hope not. You might be hanging by your neck over the walls by now had I not loosed that arrow. But," and she gave a little nod of her head, "I acknowledge your thanks."

"I will see that you're paid."

"Nay, save your money. I'll accept no coin for taking a man's life even if he was so base."

"You should get some sleep," Strykar said to her as they resumed walking back towards the square and the gatehouse. "I imagine you and your men will want to be out of the city at first light."

"About that, Strykar," she said, slowing. "I think we might stay a bit longer. Maybe lend a hand or two. Up on the walls."

Strykar turned. "Stay? Elded's balls! What's changed your heart, huntress? I thought this was not your war."

"I've thought upon what you said about oaths. And of the honour implied. It seems there's precious little loyalty left in this kingdom. After what the castellan of Livorna tried doing tonight, I cannot give up on an oath I've sworn to uphold. Even if it is to a dead king."

Strykar smiled. "A mercenary giving lessons about loyalty to a forester of Valdur. Who could have sung that tale, eh?"

"No," she said, slinging her bow over her shoulder and nodding to herself. "You were right when you told me that my seal would be worth candlewax if Ursino usurps the throne. That is the truth. I just needed to hear it from someone, maybe from a mercenary like you."

"A dozen more marksmen on the walls could help the odds. But I'll tell you honest, Demerise. If the Boar and the Whites breech the gates I don't know that we can beat them back. What with these monks that barely know one end of a sword from the other and militia hardly any better. But the choice is yours."

"I've made the choice. The others will follow me."

ACQUEL DREAMT OF serpents that night. A hundred serpents winding past him on either side as he lay upon cold ground, their hissing seeming to grow in intensity. He found he could not move a muscle, a hapless victim as the snakes roiled around him, tongues flicking. In unison, the writhing reptilian knot would suddenly quiet only to then hiss again.

He opened his eyes, still half asleep. He was propped up on his back on the parapet, a straw-filled mill sack for a pillow. Blinking, he heard a hissing sound streak overhead, and then another. A small fiery flash soared across his view, trailing a tail of black smoke. Then Poule was leaning over him.

"Brother monk! Get up. It's started."

He rolled over onto his knees and stood gingerly. Having slept in his armour, his body was a ball of pain.

"Steady there," cautioned Poule. "Don't get too close to edge or you'll end up with an arrow in you."

Acquel watched as the fire arrows arced overhead, flashing over the walls and falling into the town. "For the love of God! The roofs."

Poule nodded. "Livorna's greybeards had the good sense to use clay tiles and not thatch. The constables have womenfolk down there to douse anything that catches. Our

worry is keeping the bastards from coming up the walls."
Acquel watched as militia and Templars alike crouched like
bent old men as they scuttled along the parapets, arrows and
crossbow bolts whizzing past their heads.

An aged brother came past bearing an enormous brown
canvas sack and Poule tapped him roughly. "Come on
then, you have the Magister to feed over here!" The monk
reached in and pulled out two round loaves of black bread
and handed them to Poule then blessed himself and carried
on down the walkway. Poule handed a loaf to Acquel.
"Now, if we're lucky mind you, we might get some cheese
to go with this before the enemy throws the ladders up."
Acquel smiled thinly. He found it remarkable, if somewhat
calming, that these mercenaries could remain so unaffected
given that the odds of repelling a massed attack were almost
laughable. Poule was accoutred as when he had first met
him more than a year ago: a velvet-covered, brass-studded
breastplate that looked like it had mange, a rusty gorget and
a barbute helm that had more than its fair share of dents.
Underneath, he wore a long chain mail hauberk, hole-shot
with broken links, extending over his thick biceps and
protecting down to his thighs.

Acquel, on the other hand, had benefited from the
largesse of Count Marsilius in a moment of the unfortunate
man's lucidity. His shining breastplate, pauldrons, cannons,
couters and vambraces were a sharp contrast to Poule's
battle-worn and bedraggled attire. Steel cuisses and tall
leather boots had been thrown in as well, and except for
the tabard he wore, no one would know he was a monk. He
felt as awkward as he probably appeared, although Strykar
had remarked that he was lucky to have been a good match
for the pieces in the armoury. But now in the dewy morning,
he could feel the dampness of his quilted arming doublet
sticking to him as he clanked along the wall.

"I want to have a look at them," he said to the lieutenant, his voice quiet.

"Look through the arrow loop there—no, not between the crenels."

Acquel stooped to peer through the long narrow slit of the stone merlon, the front of his visor-less sallet helm ringing as he bumped the wall. It was an astounding sight that met his eyes. Far below, and out to a distance of perhaps a hundred yards, dozens of wicker screens had been erected. Interspersed, long wooden shields leaned at an angle, supported by soldiers behind. It was from behind these barriers that the rain of arrows was being thrown at them. A soft whisking sound floated to his ears as each shaft was loosed. Soldiers were cautiously darting from wooden shields to the wicker screens and then re-emerging with more arrows and pails of pitch with which to set them alight.

Further behind this hidden army of bowmen stood serried rank upon rank of soldiers, large shields at the front. They were waiting for the order to advance. The glint of steel helms sparkled across their lines. But there was no sound and more importantly, no griffons.

Acquel turned and leaned his back against the merlon. "Hundreds, you reckon?"

Poule chuckled and tore off a chunk of the heavy bread. "At least. And that is just one division. There is another army down in front of the east gate. And another further along below the Ara. But... there is one thing in our favour."

"Which is?" Acquel cautiously moved along the wall, away from the ledge. As he did so, two arrows struck the top of the battlements and bounced inwards, clattering off the stone. Acquel ducked and reached Poule again, somewhat alarmed at his first experience of coming under fire.

"Which is," repeated Poule, "they have yet to bring up any siege cannon to the gate below us. Either they ain't got none or they haven't arrived yet. Let's pray for the former."

A much thicker cloud of fire arrows whispered overhead, arcing high into the city. He could hear distant screams and shouts somewhere off between the rooftops and stone towers behind them, random pain and death playing upon Livorna. Strykar's plan of defence seemed simple and though he was no soldier it seemed hardly a plan at all. Poule would lead the men on the far western flank to the main gate, Volpe and himself would lead the Templars and militia in the centre from the main gate east, and Strykar would command the defence of the eastern wall and barbican gate. The latter point the Coronel had deemed the weakest though Poule cautioned how low the walls were opposite the Ara plateau and the Temple. Strykar had replied laconically that was why he wanted him there. Simultaneous attacks would be the biggest threat.

Acquel watched as their own crossbowmen, near to a man all newly trained, fumbled with their bows and windlasses, arguing with each other as to the best way to wind them. He saw militiamen with little clay pots slung in a shoulder satchel, the burning match in their hands protected by a tiny hood of chamois leather lest they accidently touch off their petards and set themselves alight. But the waiting for the real attack was killing him. He thought of Timandra; of her ghost that had walked towards him along the very spot he now stood. Had she been trying to warn him of this moment? He imagined her alive, with him on the wall, carrying arrows and fire and pitch, encouraging the men with her rough cutting tongue. And he suddenly felt like weeping at the loss.

Two hours passed, the volleys of arrows and bolts having stopped once the enemy had realised that the city would not burn. Someone gave a yell and drew their attention to a new development below outside the gate. Acquel carefully peered through an arrow slit and saw a strange contraption on cart wheels being pushed forward towards the ramp of the gatehouse. Those pushing were sheltered behind a wooden wall of hoardings, covered in cow skins. The wooden tent-like structure concealed something. Acquel angled his head downward to get a better view of the front of the machine and could just spy the tip of a large tree trunk that was suspended inside on chains or ropes.

"Shoot them!" he ordered, his voice breaking. Three bowmen made ready and lit their arrows which had been dipped in pitch. Leaning over the parapets, they loosed, but the arrows fizzled harmlessly on the cow skins. One of the petardiers had better success, managing to drop a lighted pot just in front of the machine, splattering it with burning pitch. But then the Torinians returned the favour, their crouching archers loosing arrows upwards towards them. The petardier jumped back as a bolt whizzed past him. Acquel grabbed a clay pot and got a militiaman to light the fuse as he handled it gingerly. The saltpetre wick sparked and he wasted no time in flinging it over and down. But the ram was still inching forward towards the wooden gates. He could smell the burning pitch below now, hear the yells of encouragement of the Blue Boar soldiers as they strained to move the machine.

"Keep at them!" yelled Acquel to the men above the gate. "Aim for the bare wood! Aim for them!" He had no idea what he was doing and his stomach sank. A petardier cried out and fell back as a crossbow bolt bounced off his breastplate before he could throw his pot. Undeterred he crept forward again, shot a glance through the crenel, and then hurled his weapon overhand. A scream this time as the flaming pitch covered a soldier below. It wasn't enough to slow the machine. It was still making its tortuous way up the inclined earthen ramp. Once it reached the wooden gates underneath them, they would not be able to engage it except through the murder-holes on top of the barbican. He looked up to see a soldier tearing across the parapet towards them, shoving aside Templar and militia alike. It was Poule.

"I see 'em!" he yelled as he reached the barbican. "Sneaky bastards were quicker than I gave them credit for!" He looked around him. "Right, you and you!" he said, pointing to two Templars. "Down to the loopholes below on the stairs. Fire at those men pushing the ram."

Acquel's eyes fell to the smoking caldron of black pitch tar bubbling on its brazier. "Poule!" he shouted, pointing to it. "We can pour it down the murder-holes as they reach the gate!"

The lieutenant nodded. "Aye, but we'll set our own gate afire. Got to do it before they reach it." He jumped to the long forked pole lying against the wall. "You lot! Out of the way!" The nine foot pole he put through the wire handle of the cauldron. "Brother monk, take the other end!"

Together they lifted the entire cauldron—a good sized cooking pot—the pole bending precariously under the burden. "Sneaky bastards," repeated Poule, spitting out his words. "Managed to cobble together a war engine in a day. They shuffled the few feet over to the gap between the merlons on the battlements and luckily the iron pot just fit in the space, scraping loudly as they pushed it on the ledge with their gauntleted hands. "Get me a taper!" shouted Poule. Arrows were whizzing past over their heads as the attackers took aim at them. There was a scramble as a crossbowman found a lighted stick and brought it to Acquel. The two half-crouched, cheeks pressed against the cold stone of the battlements as the cauldron rested on the ledge. "Now brother monk, as soon as I tip this up, you reach over and light it. Understood?"

Acquel nodded vigorously, his heart pounding in his chest. He could see Poule's greasy brown leather gauntlet gently smoking where it rested on the cauldron's lip. The lieutenant looked at him again and grinned broadly. "Ready? Then... now!" Poule grunted as the cauldron tipped up and Acquel rose up slightly and threw his arm over, touching the tow-covered burning stick into the pitch. Poule threw the whole cauldron over the edge as the waterfall of black liquid and dancing blue flame cascaded over the barbican. "And you can have that too!"

The screams rising up were terrible as the burning liquid spattered and covered the ram and its crew, instantly setting alight the tree and its hoardings despite the protection of the still bloody animal hides. The men on the parapet let out a roar of triumph and defiance. Acquel moved down the barbican to get a sidelong view of the havoc below. Through the arrow loop he could just see the machine gently rolling backwards down the incline of the ramp as its crew abandoned the burning wagon. His own men wasted no time, bringing their spanned crossbows to bear on the fleeing men of the Blue Boar, the clunking sound of the bow trigger nearly simultaneous with the whisking noise of the bolt as it flew.

A beaming Bartolo Poule clapped Acquel hard on the shoulder, rattling his armour. "There's one for us, eh, brother monk."

Acquel felt exhilarated as the thrill of the little victory coursed through him. He grinned back at Poule and turned, nodding at his Templars, sweating faces grinning back at him. A runner came towards them from the east, his chain mail shirt jangling rhythmically. He reached the barbican parapet and halted, staggering and almost breathless.

"Magister! They have a gun—a big gun—coming up to the East Gate!"

Poule craned his head skyward, his gloved hand rubbing hard against the bristles of his unshaven face. His eyes accusingly scanned the cloudless lapis sky overhead. "You couldn't even answer that *one* prayer, could you!"

Twenty-Five

JAW CLENCHED, STRYKAR watched as the men of the Blue Boar moved their siege cannon forward under the cover of wicker screens, wooden mantlets, and oversized pavise shields. They had advanced past the line of scattered trees, hedge and thorn and into the clear open ground before the city walls. Now they were close to firing range of the gatehouse, the bravest and fastest of their soldiers hunkered down out in front to set up the mantlets while the others tugged the thick ropes to pull the gun along on its carriage. Demerise stood up on the battlements next to the Coronel of the Black Rose with her arms folded across her chest, an unconscious display of self-protection.

"Having second thoughts?" said Strykar.

"Not yet," she replied calmly. "But *that* is likely to do some damage, I'd venture."

Strykar grunted. They had few options. It was at long range for the bowmen on the walls and the hand-cannons would not have the accuracy at this distance. A surprise sally might work to storm the enemy and spike the gun but with barely trained militia the odds were poor. Crossbowmen around him were cranking their windlasses, setting their weapons on the wall, and loosing their bolts, but the Blue Boar were well protected. Their wooden mantlets soon resembled hedgehogs from the number of protruding arrow shafts and quarrels.

"Fire arrows," said Strykar. "We've got to burn that gun."

Demerise nodded. "But not at this range."

"Don't worry, they'll be coming closer." Two hundred yards further west on the wall, they could hear a rising chorus of alarm. Strykar moved along the battlements, instinctively dodged his head at the whisper of an arrow, and tried to get a view of what was happening. He could see a few hundred of the enemy—*rondelieri* and bowmen—making a dash for the wall, scaling ladders in hand. "Elded's holy bollocks!" he whispered to himself. Demerise was again at his elbow and straining to get a view herself.

"Bastards! Aretini knows we're stretched thinner than a sausage skin up here. He must reckon he'll get lucky and break in at least one point along the walls."

"Is that where the Magister commands his troops?" asked Demerise.

"Aye," replied Strykar rather flatly. "That's where the Temple priests hold the wall. God help us."

"We should go there. They will need more help."

Strykar turned to her. "We can't be everywhere at once. They'll have to fend off the attack on their own. Poule will keep his head. We've got to destroy that siege gun or it won't matter in another hour."

Demerise adjusted her slipping black mask. "Your decision, Messere Strykar. But I can send Bero and six of my men to help them. If the enemy gets up onto the parapets it might make a difference."

Strykar nodded, placing a bear's paw of a hand upon her forearm. "Very well. Come back and join me here at the gate. I'll get the pitch and tow ready for the archers."

Bero gave her a look of reluctant acceptance when she gave him the order. But he whistled to the others and they made their way west along the wall, their green and brown doublets, hose, and cloaks in sharp contrast to the armoured militia and white tabards of the fighting monks. Strykar gathered a dozen longbowmen (the crossbowmen were to pin down the gun crew) and set about preparing pitch-soaked tow braids to secure below their arrowheads. But he doubted there was a marksman among them. He paused amid the commotion on the parapet to take another look below. They were stopped at a hundred yards, just within range of the gates. The whole situation was very unlike the Blue Boar. Starting an assault on the first day of a siege was impetuous. It even spoke of desperation. Aretini ought to know better, so what was he trying to do?

He hurriedly tied a long, braided piece of flax around a shaft and handed it up to a waiting bowman. "Show the others. And remember, you'll have to aim up and drop it behind the screens!" The bowman nodded sheepishly, knowing that before today he had only ever shot at a straw target at the butts—straight on. He dutifully squatted down and with shaking fingers copied Strykar's technique. Soon half a dozen of the archers were on their knees like weaverfolk, hurriedly making their fire arrows. When he had them assembled, several arrows each, he yelled to the crossbowmen to ready themselves on the parapet. Before he could put the longbowmen in place, ready to set their arrows alight, a tremendous muffled explosion sounded, followed instantaneously by the sound of smashing wood beneath them. Frantic shouts rose from the gatehouse below. Strykar didn't know if the gates were still on their hinges but he wasted no time.

"You four, up you go!" The bowmen dipped their nocked arrows into a brazier, setting off the black liquid into a beautiful orange and blue flame. "Shoot!" The shafts arced upward and then down. Strykar poked his head between the merlons and watched as they sailed. And fell short. He mumbled a curse. A large wooden shutter, probably ripped from a house in the nearest village, was mounted on the front of the cannon's cart to shield it. It had slammed down again as its crew hastened to reload. That gave them another couple of minutes at most. "The rest of you, stand ready! Judge your distance! We won't get many more chances."

Demerise had by now returned, bearing her slung bow in her hand. "What can I do?"

"How good are you at dropping an arrow down behind a barricade?"

She scowled back. "I shoot game, straight through the heart. I'm not a soldier."

Strykar rolled his eyes. "Alright then, pretend it's a stag hiding behind a boulder."

The fire arrows sailed again from the top of the barbican, this time several landing beyond the gun, a few perhaps among the enemy position. Strykar handed Demerise a tow-wrapped arrow, dripping pitch. She looked at it dubiously. "You don't know how an arrow flies, do you?" She pulled one of her own from her quiver. "It must be clean, clean like a diving hawk." She moved to the parapet and dipped only the barbed iron head into the pitch bucket. Strykar's brow furrowed as he watched her take her position, bow not yet drawn, her eyes looking out towards the gun emplacement. One of the other bowman shouted for Strykar. The wooden shutter was opening again. Strykar put his hand on the ledge and saw the gun crew behind it, one man placing his smouldering linstock on the touchhole. There was a flash and the detonation. This time the sound of splintering wood was joined by the tinkling of falling stone as the gatehouse itself was struck by the massive stone shot, the size of a man's head.

But Demerise had loosed her arrow at the same time. Strykar saw the cannonier stagger back, shot through. He also saw little wooden barrels and a bucket—gunpowder— sitting next to the gun cart. Then the shutter came down again, bouncing on its frame. He looked up at Demerise who was giving him a half-smile from the unmasked side of her face.

A militiaman with bulging eyes reached them, sputtering and gesticulating like a mad fool. "There's a hole big enough in the gate to crawl through! The second shot has struck the arch and broke one of the hinges!"

"Shore it up then!" barked Strykar. He moved next to Demerise, seizing her shoulder and leaning his face close to hers. "When that shutter opens again, look for the little barrels. Put your arrow into those!" She nodded, understanding his meaning and pulled out another of her long white-fletched shafts. She dipped it into the pitch and twirled it, the sticky liquid covering the vicious barbed head and dripping like adder venom. She nocked it and stood ready, one booted foot on the step up to the parapet and the other on the ledge between the merlons. Strykar took a position in the next embrasure, watching, biting his thick lower lip. A volley of crossbow bolts came flying past, clattering and bouncing off the parapets but he didn't move, his eyes fastened tightly on the gun cart. Then it opened.

"Demerise!"

She dipped the arrow into the brazier next to her, setting it alight. Her well-muscled arm drew the creaking bow back, back until the string touched her ear. And she loosed. Strykar could not see the arrow fly, but he saw the barrels rock and a white wisp of smoke. The gunner was about to touch his sparking linstock to the cannon when Demerise managed a second shot just as he leaned over the gun. Strykar saw a white cloud puff out, a yellow flash, and then an explosion that blew the gun and its crew to pieces, the detonation reverberating off the walls around them.

Straight through the heart.

THE TEMPLAR BESIDE Acquel leaned over to fire his crossbow and then his head had snapped back. Acquel could see the fletched end of the quarrel protruding from the monk's chin like a grotesque beard. The man had slumped to the walkway, stone dead. Other Templars were scrambling to load and fire their bows over the edge and one of the two hackbut men awkwardly brought his hand-cannon to bear while his comrade lit the touchhole. A whoosh and crack and the gun fired off the wall.

A loud clack of wood on stone brought Acquel around. He saw the top of a scaling ladder, still vibrating, on the embrasure next to where he stood. He made a dash for the forked stick that was nearby and with the help of a militiaman, angled the ten-foot branch so they could engage the fork against the ladder. They grunted and shoved, pushing it off the wall and running the stick outwards. The ladder tipped sideways and fell. But others were slamming onto the battlements to take its place. And while Acquel and his comrade pushed them back, the others kept up their firing of bow, gun and petard. He had no time to think or to plan. He just kept moving. He turned to see a dazed Templar stumbling towards him. Behind him were other men, half-obscured. As his eyes fell lower, he saw the protruding spearhead in the monk's side, having pierced the leather gambeson. The monk dropped to his knees and Acquel found himself face to face with a mercenary of the Blue Boar. The soldier calmly and quickly extracted his short spear and hefted it to thrust at him. Acquel heard something whistle past his ear and saw an arrow take the mercenary square in the face, dropping him like a hammered ox in a butcher's yard. Acquel looked over his shoulder to see one of the huntress's men reaching for another arrow. He quickly bent down and seized the spear as other mercenaries came towards him, advancing quickly along the walkway. Sadly, it was not a weapon that Poule had yet taught him how to use.

Two militiamen bearing glaives joined him, flanking him. They now blocked the walkway, the *rondelieri* of the Blue Boar inching forward, shields and swords raised. Acquel counted six and further behind he could see a confused tangle of white tabards and armoured heads and limbs. And then the *rondelieri* were on them, their shields held high as they delivered lightning fast wrist snaps with their side-swords. Acquel thrust out repeatedly with the spear while the militiamen held their glaives straight out and thrust to strike the faces of the mercenaries. Acquel was aware of someone standing behind him and then again he heard the twang of a bow. The arrow caught one of the enemy in the throat and the man froze, clutching at his neck, retching and coughing. One of the militiamen timed his thrust and struck the man's comrade in the face, a splatter of bright blood pouring forth. The Blue Boar wavered and then an arrow took down another. The remainder started retreating only to bump into more Templars, Lieutenant Poule at their head. With a cry on his lips Poule rammed into the lot and the monks behind piled on. The mercenaries, cut off from further aid, were overwhelmed, bludgeoned and stabbed until there were a heap of corpses along the walkway of the parapets. Bright blood was already beginning to run out in small rivulets among the stones, with its peculiar metallic odour.

Acquel looked at the gasping militiaman next to him and realized he was old enough to be his grandfather. The man looked up at him shaking his head in both relief and not a little disbelief. "Never thought I'd live so long... fighting at my age, and alongside a holy father of the Temple!" Acquel managed a smile for him, his heart still pounding. He had a strange, familiar feeling in his breast, the same sensation he used to feel when brawling as a youth on the streets below them, knives and clubs their usual weapons. Yet this time there were no watchmen to separate the gangs and send them packing into the alleys.

"A piss-poor assault!" laughed Poule, a slight wheeze in his voice. "Would have expected better of the Boar." He stepped over a mercenary and joined Acquel, after quickly poking his head between two merlons to see what the enemy was up to.

Acquel wiped his face with the back of his gauntlet and surveyed the dead. "We beat them back," he said, softly. "By Elded's grace, we did it."

"They were only testing our defences, brother monk. Don't begin the revels just yet." Acquel suddenly remembered the huntsman who had helped even the odds with his deadly accurate aim. He looked up and saw him standing a few yards down the walkway.

"Huntsman! I give you thanks!" he shouted. The man looked at him without expression but raised his bow in acknowledgement. "Funny lot, aren't they?" mumbled Poule.

"Maybe they just don't like killing men," replied Acquel as his eyes fell back to their own handiwork sprawled on the cobbled walkway.

"And how about you, holy man?" asked Poule, his sweating face serious for once.

"It's getting easier... particularly when they're trying to kill you."

Poule nodded. "Aye, that's the good and the bad of it, brother monk."

"I know they'll come again. This siege has barely begun. But where are the griffons?"

Poule stooped to wipe his sword on the tabard of a boarsman. "Oh, I reckon they have something special planned for us before long. And thinking how Strykar fared against them, I'm not sure I want to see it for myself."

THE LUXURIOUS FIELD tent of the Duke of Torinia sat upon a hill south of Livorna, lit by lamp, candelabra, and brazier. Its walls of red and gold damask billowed almost rhythmically as if it was some great living creature drawing breath. Ursino sat in his carved chair, balancing his wine goblet on the arm as he listened to his commanders plead, argue and cajole. His cheek had developed a twitch from clenching his jaw the past two days, annoyance steadily rising with every failed sortie against the walls.

Coronel Aretini, arrayed with the other mercenary commanders, as well as Ursino's own captain of the ducal guard, took a step closer to the chair that was all but a throne in name. "Your Grace, I've lost sixty men in the past five days. Michelotto here has lost at least that number. I will not speak for the good Count of Naplona—"

"Forty-one killed at the wall," answered Federigo, the irritation in his voice clear to all.

Aretini gestured with open palms towards the count. "And for what? For *what*? Without machines or more siege guns, we cannot get over the walls. It is a waste of my men. A slow bleed." He was feeling confident as he eyed his employer—and possible future king. He knew that it was the Blue Boar and the White Company that held the winning hand, not the Duke, even if he was the one who paid the gold. The Count of Naplona too was expecting reward for service. Nothing was free when it came to war. Without the companies,

Ursino had only a palace guard to fight his battles. And that was never going to get him far. "I had expected more in the way of help from the canoness. As promised."

There were nods all around. Lucinda della Rovera stood at the left side of the Duke, hands clasped at her waist. She had been waiting for that moment, waiting in certain knowledge that the mercenaries would call her out. She saw how Ursino slightly turned his head towards her at Aretini's cutting words. Perhaps he too, was starting to doubt. Doubting her help, maybe his love too. How could she tell him that she barely controlled the beasts that had been given over to her? The griffons could scatter men like frightened rats, render them to pieces as a lion does a lamb, but they could not climb the walls nor batter down thick oak doors and an iron portcullis. She was running out of time.

Ursino leaned forward, the bloodstones in his ducal coronet sparkling in the candlelight. "Are you dictating strategy to me, Coronel? I seem to recall it was your idea to probe the defences by trying to scale the walls."

Aretini was undeterred. "And we did discover their defences, your Grace. It appears that they are not that untrained in the ways of siege warfare. They have some number of mercenaries in there among them."

"Then make yourself plain, sir."

Aretini gave a bow. "Your Grace, the matter is plain. We can sit here for weeks... months perhaps, build towers and trebuchets. Find more cannon and a few master gunners. But we will also pay a price. More sickness and more casualties. And all the while Maresto gains time to prepare an attack on us as we sit here outside these walls."

Ursino held Aretini with his stony gaze, his reply measured and cold as frost-laced iron. "Do not prevaricate in my presence. If you have a plan to propose then do so."

Aretini nodded slowly. "Very well, your Grace, for that is what you pay me for. We should decamp and head south. Leave a token force to maintain the siege of Livorna and march to Maresto city and meet Alonso's armies in the open field. Or"—and he inclined his large bull-like head—"there is one other course we may take."

Ursino sat back. "Go on, Aretini," he growled.

"One last sally against the battlements, but *led* by the griffons. Surely these miraculous creatures show we are favoured of Elded and the Lord?" He looked from the Duke to Lucinda. "Order them to take the gates down or have them fly over the walls. I do not pretend to know of such things... of the ways of these gifts from the Almighty. That is your purview, my lady. If your beasts can break the gates, then we can take the city."

Ursino reached over and gently grasped Lucinda's wrist as he turned his head up to her. He had already asked her about using the griffons in such a manner, and she had made excuses, excuses that the creatures should not be wasted but rather saved for the right moment. And she had distracted him with lovemaking, a task easily accomplished. Now, as he looked up at her, all his hopes as transparent as if they had been scrawled in ink onto his square-jawed face, he expected an answer. As did they all.

She took a deep breath and raised her chin. "My lords, you are masters in the ways of war. But not in the ways of signs and portents. That is my domain. And now the moment has come. The beasts of Valdur will stand ready on the morrow to lead your assault, and I will join you." She glanced down to Ursino. "At dusk, assemble your forces beyond the west gate and await the griffons. I have told them what must be done. If the Divine favours me, then you may win without even losing a man. And Livorna will surrender to your will."

Aretini looked to his comrades, rather surprised by the response. But Lucinda could tell by the nods and smiles that she had not yet lost her skills. Nor did she have to enter Aretini's mind to sway him. But that would have been her next move if doubt and derision had met her words of bravado. He turned back to the canoness and fixed her with a perplexed look. "By the conventions of war that is an unusual time of day to launch a battle." His face then split into a grin. "But—I must say—not unknown to my experience."

"And I have my reasons," returned Lucinda. "Your soldiers will at least appreciate that the enemy will have the setting sun in their eyes when you attack."

Ursino rose slowly from his seat, the better to show his majesty. "You have heard the words of the canoness. She has earned my faith and trust." His eyes settled upon each of his commanders in turn. "Now is the time to make ready for the assault. And may God give us victory." Aretini looked as if he was to make another statement, but his expression faded and he gave a bow before fixing his eyes on Lucinda briefly. The other commanders followed his lead, filing out of the pavilion with courtly bows, whispering to each other.

The Duke handed his goblet to his server and then dismissed him with a gesture. Once they were done, he gave Lucinda a hard, unblinking stare. "You say you love me as I love you. So why is it you lie to me?"

Lucinda moved close to him, her long satin dress rustling. She looked into his eyes. As she did so, she saw his stony expression dissolve and reshape to one of hurt, even loss. "My love for you is unchanged, you know that. But the knowledge I bear is a heavy burden. One I wished to shield you from."

He gently grasped both her hands, and she studied his aching face, ruggedly handsome, his oiled black locks flowing down to his velvet collar. "Do you think I do not know that you do not always face the light? I am old enough to know that darkness and light are but two sides of the same coin. But now is the time to tell me what it is we have sworn to serve."

She moistened her full lips with a flick of her tongue. His thoughts were unguarded now and pulsed forth from him and into her mind. The kernel of truth was already there. The Old Ones gnawed at the back of his consciousness, insistent on bearing witness. He had to be told now that time was running out. Told something at least, if not the whole truth of the threat that Berithas posed to his soul and to her future happiness. She nodded gently.

His voice was soft, almost childlike. "It is not Elded whom you serve."

She answered him even as her mind probed his. "No, it is not."

His mouth opened but the words remained frozen in his throat. "Say it," she urged. She felt his fingers tighten slightly.

The words came off his tongue in a whisper. "The ancient Ones. The old gods. Dread Andras and his brothers."

"And He who leads their way," she replied. "The Redeemer. Berithas." He had known it in his heart for weeks, she could see that now, but not the price. That had not yet entered his mind.

"And it is to them I will do homage if I become king?"

She raised a delicate hand to stroke his lightly bearded cheek. "There will be a price, my love."

"If it makes me king of Valdur then I shall pay it. I have put all my trust in you. Gambled with the loyalty of my troops to give you my trust. The power of command equal to them. You must not fail me."

She nodded and he reached out to lightly touch the flaxen hair that framed her long face. "Then you must trust me further, my love, my prince. My beasts cannot fly over the walls. They may not even be able to burst the gates of Livorna, but they will not have to."

He scowled. "What do you mean?"

"They will be but a diversion. For me. I will deliver you the city by the time the moon rises. I will deliver you the High Priest himself. Not just a captive but a willing partner in proclaiming you the rightful king of Valdur. The world will change!" And she knew there was no other course. She had to take Kodoris in order to save Ursino from paying the ultimate price to Berithas—his very soul. She had summoned Berithas to her hours before, telling him of her plan that he should possess the High Priest instead of Ursino, the faster to bring down the One Faith. With her true thoughts concealed, the Redeemer had agreed. Indeed he had praised her among all of her sex.

The Duke tilted his head, eyebrows knitting together. "You can do this thing? Make the High Priest surrender?"

"Berithas has given me the power to do many things. He has given me servants other than the beasts you perceive as royal griffons. A means to attain the Ara mount. All you must do is be ready when the gates open."

"And what of the young Magister?"

Lucinda's eyes flared. "He will be dead before the sun rises."

Ursino stepped closer and enveloped her in his flowing robes, his lips upon her neck and ear. "Together, my queen. Together we shall reign." He pulled away slightly. "The griffons. What do you mean by *perceive*?"

She smiled. "Berithas has many creatures at his command. Things that have slumbered an age." She tilted his chin up and spoke like a mother to her child. "There *are* no more griffons in the world, my love."

Twenty-Six

IT WAS AN odd council of war. Probably the oddest ever seen in Valdur. Acquel, Brother Volpe, Strykar and Poule plus half a dozen city constables and a drooling High Steward carried into the chamber on a litter. All were tired and dirty, the rank smell of stale sweat lying heavy in the small room of the palazzo in Low Town. Acquel had called the meeting at Volpe's urging since no attack had come during the whole of the day. Exhausted, the men now gathered around a large oak table, taking the opportunity to feast on bread, cheese and roast fowl, while arguing about what should happen next.

Acquel stood and raised his hands to silence them. He had removed his helmet and the armour from shoulders and arms, but still wore his breastplate and tabard, the latter now stained with blood and streaks of green from the moss on the battlements. "We've held them off for nearly a week now. The beasts of the witch have not shown themselves. If we can hold on another week I know that Maresto—maybe even Saivona—will send a force to lift the siege. We must keep up our courage. Trust in the Saints and the wisdom of Elded and the Lord above."

Bartolo Poule nodded his agreement. "You must tell all your men that we are winning this siege! Keep up their spirits! Liberate the *acqua vitalis* if you must to those deserving of it. The Magister is right—we have beaten back every assault upon the walls from east to west. If that is all they have then they will move on to easier prey."

Ugo Volpe rubbed his pudgy hand across his mouth and pushed away his wine goblet. "I would like nothing more than to believe that. But they are at our gates for a reason. They want something from us and Coronel Strykar flatters himself if he thinks it's just his head."

Strykar chuckled.

"Then tell me what it is that they want," said Acquel.

"You, perhaps. Or the High Priest. The witch of Torinia is ambitious and this is about more than destroying the *Decimali* heresy they are railing against. Do not forget what lies dormant in the crypt of the Temple Majoris—the old Tree of Death. Remember what the High Priest has seen in his dreams. They seek the overthrow of the One Faith and the resurgence of the Old."

"She will not prevail," answered Acquel, the quietness of his voice betraying his lack of confidence.

"There is more," said Volpe. "Kodoris has *felt* it. Lucinda della Rovera carries the spirit of Berithas within her. And Berithas seeks to take human form again, here in Livorna."

No one knew what to say. Somebody guffawed and it was joined by one or two others among the less religious.

"Fools!" Volpe said, muttering. He leaned back and folded his arms.

Strykar pushed back his chair and noisily dropped his vambraces on the table as he leaned forward. "There's something not right about all of this. Something *stinks*."

"It's us," remarked Poule, rolling his eyes, making two of the constables snicker.

Strykar ignored them. "Consider that I have seen these monstrous beasts tear through an army like they were scattering so many chickens in a farmyard. Why have they gone quiet now? The Blue Boar and the Whites have just been pricking us—testing our mettle. But they're waiting for something. Maybe it's siege engines or a wooden tower on the way. More cannon. But we can't fool ourselves. This isn't over yet."

"Are you suggesting a sally *out*, Coronel?" said Acquel. "Before they gain momentum?"

Strykar snorted. "I would, brother monk, under different circumstances. A sally might take them unawares. Such things have worked before. But not with untrained militia and holy men magicked into soldiers. No insult intended," he added, raising his hand.

Acquel inclined his head, patient. "We are what we are."

"I've been thinking about what Ursino's mercenaries must be contemplating," said Strykar, his eyes looking around the table, settling on Acquel. "And I would wager they are reluctant to lose men against walls as strong as these. That means they're doing their damnedest to convince Ursino to either lift the siege and move on—before trouble arrives—or to try something we're not expecting."

"The canoness," said Volpe, nodding. "Using her infernal skills."

"Possibly," replied Strykar. "But that does not explain why the griffons have disappeared."

"Not so much as a squawk," said Poule thrusting out his lower lip.

"So what would you counsel, Strykar?" said Acquel. "If not to open the gates in the dead of night and rush forth."

"For now? Nothing we are not already doing. Keep rotating the militia up on the battlements, watching the scrub and tree line below the walls at the Ara mount. I say...

if there is no great attack from the enemy in the next few days then we may have the edge. They will want to head south to attack Maresto, leaving us for the moment. Maybe leaving a token force outside the walls."

"What are our stocks of arrows like?" asked Acquel. "We've loosed hundreds."

Poule waved away his concern. "Not to worry, brother monk. We're in no danger of running out. But the hackbut men are running low on gunpowder. For all the good it's done them firing those things. Couldn't even hit a griffon at fifty paces."

Acquel turned and addressed Marsilius, lying propped up in his litter. "My lord, have you understood what has been discussed? Do you agree we must sit tight and wait things out?"

The High Steward's eyes widened. "I have heard the counsel," he said in a reedy voice, "and... you are in command of Livorna. It is your decision how we best defend." He pulled his *cioppa* closer about his neck as if to ward a chill when there was none.

Acquel winced and turned back to the men around the table. "Well, my lords, we carry on and wait to see what the fates will bring. You constables will continue the rounds. Punish all who sleep on watch. And pray to the Saints."

There was barely a murmur as they all looked from one to another, rose, and shuffled out of the chamber. Each took their leave of the High Steward, giving awkward bows to the invalid who, if he was recovering of his poisoning, was taking his time of it. The sun was hanging low in the sky as Strykar and Acquel began the descent down to the market square, Poule and the rest out in front. Strykar glanced over at the Magister walking by his side. The gormless youth he had known one year ago had become a grim-faced soldier and a leader, if not yet a confident one. And it seemed he himself had aged half a lifetime in just months. For that is what facing an unwelcome truth can do.

"I judged you unfairly," he said, stopping at the bottom of the winding stone steps.

Half a pace ahead, Acquel halted and turned. "Strykar?"

"I should not have blamed you for Timandra's death. That was not right. I was hurt, and prideful." He broke into a wistful smile. "No one could ever tell her what to do. Not even me."

"You put me on my feet a year ago. Trusted me. But when I needed your help these past months you practically washed your hands of me. And you—better than most—knowing what it is I carry around my neck."

Strykar found he could not look Acquel in the eye. "If I could roll back the months I would have listened to you then... Tasting defeat makes you think differently. I know that I have grown very arrogant these past days."

"So how am I supposed to believe that you won't give up on the Templars of the Ara? There really isn't anything holding you here since you know the way out is the same way you came in. Maresto and the Black Rose is where you would rather be."

Strykar hung his great bear-like head, one he knew he was lucky to still have sitting on his shoulders. "Yes, I'll give you that I warrant your doubt. But my reply to you is that I will help you defend this place. Come what may. The world has been turned upside down, brother monk. I know my path back to the Black Rose goes first through Livorna."

Acquel placed his hand on Strykar's forearm. "Then let us work together to save it from destruction."

Strykar again looked at the young Magister of the Ara. "You have changed much in the past year. I did not see that until now."

Acquel smiled. "We may not have all of the Black Rose with us on the walls but we have the best of it. I must go now to the Temple to see how Kodoris fares. Tonight I man the walls at the Ara while Poule will command the gate."

"Then I pray a peaceful evening's watch for you and the brethren," said Strykar. He cleared his throat, gave a respectful nod to Acquel, and then turned, hand on his sword hilt, to descend the remaining steps. It was time to look after someone he had rashly roped into defending the walls. Someone who was no soldier and more used to shooting than being shot at. Demerise.

THE BARBICAN OF the west gate of Livorna, built by the good Count of Polzano five hundred years earlier, had taken many a hammering over the years. Betrayed twice, cracked by earthquake once, but never breached by force of arms, the gate had seen off every ingenious attempt to take it: ram, tower, mine, and catapult. Those who kept an eye to the future foretold that gunpowder would soon spell its end but that day had yet to come. But as the sun flared huge against the horizon that early evening, the main gate of Livorna came under attack once again, and by an enemy the like of which it had never faced before.

Acquel was nearly at the confines of the Temple Majoris and well past the west gate when he heard the shouts and cries behind him. These were rapidly followed by the sound he had come to dread: the deafening screech of the griffons. He pulled up abruptly at the sickening shriek before spotting Ugo Volpe waddling towards him from the Ara, where the wall met the broad green of the Temple mount. As the griffons shrieked again Volpe hastened his pace. When he reached Acquel he grabbed him with both hands.

"We're under attack again! I saw the beasts from the wall. It looks like half the enemy is following in their wake."

"The gate," said Acquel. "They are after the gate."

With Volpe struggling behind, Acquel jogged across the cobbled pathway, his armour giving noisy complaint. By the time they had reached the barbican, all was chaos. Militia were hurling large stones over the battlements, crossbowmen were struggling to angle their bows down while others fumbled at their winding mechanisms to reload. A rain of arrows came arcing overhead, clattering against stone and tile. Acquel felt his heart skip as a tremendous thumping sound echoed up from below, followed by the rattle of ironmongery. And then the griffon's screech came again. He carefully mounted the stone step of the battlements and placed his cheek against the stone of the embrasure. Daring to look out and down he saw them. Their fur was glistening golden brown, almost as if it were wet, the feathers of their skulls and neck bristled and shook, pure white. And then he leapt back as one of the beasts reared up, its huge yellow talons scraping the barbican no more than a few feet below where he stood. Before he fell back, he had seen the glare of its huge, bulging jet black eye and a purple tongue flicking from its beak.

He swore he felt the whole barbican tower shake beneath him. Frantic militiamen were yelling for more stones, for hot sand, for anything to throw down over the walls. Acquel saw two of his brethren turn and run, dropping their weapons as they headed down the stairs. Brother Ugo had jumped up to take Acquel's place at the embrasure. He quickly slid back down and turned to Acquel.

"Why don't they fly?" he said. "They possess wings but do not use them."

Acquel seized him by the shoulders. "They will break down the gates better than any ram! How do we stop them?"

Volpe shook his head then muttered, "Myrra."

"We don't have any! What charms do you have in your book?"

The look Volpe returned nearly staggered him. A look of utter helplessness. Another crash sounded below them mixed with the loud creaking of wood. One of the griffons was putting head and shoulder into the gate again. Then the rasping of talons on the gates carried up and the looks of abject terror from man to man made Acquel begin to turn in on himself, paralyzed with indecision. His ears seemed to ring louder and louder. Acquel took a few steps back and saw Strykar moving towards him, sword in hand.

"Magister, get below and see to more pitch! We must burn these things back to hell!"

Acquel nodded and mumbled agreement, looking slightly lost in the mad scramble of cursing men around him. But Strykar was there now, gathering the militia, his booming voice restoring order. He felt a hand shaking him.

"Brother Acquel, we must go!" It was Volpe, tugging at him. "Coronel Strykar will lead them. We must do as he orders. The pitch!"

Acquel took a deep breath. "Let's go."

They moved to the archway and the spiral stone stairs, bouncing like skittles off the rough-hewn walls as they flew down the staircase. By the time they had reached the bottom, Acquel had found his wits again, embarrassed that he had panicked on the battlements. They moved across the inner court and towards the forge where the huge copper vat of bubbling pitch was propped up over the brick fireplace. He yelled for men to come to him, Volpe following his lead, ordering them to retrieve iron cauldrons to start carrying the tarry liquid up to the barbican parapet. Another crash sounded and he turned to see the portcullis rattling upon its moorings, its chains shaking. Through it he could just glimpse a jagged strip of blonde wood on the black oak doors; it was slowly being sundered. Only the portcullis would stand between them and the Torinian army and Acquel could already imagine the giant horny beaks of the griffons twisting it into a ruin and tearing it from the stonework track.

For a moment he thought he had taken a crossbow bolt to his chest. His knees buckled as the agony of the burning sensation throbbed under his steel breastplate.

"Brother Acquel!" Volpe was at his side, pulling him up from under his armpits.

"The amulet!" gasped Acquel. "It's on fire!"

He frantically dug his hand under his breastplate to pull the amulet up by its golden chain. And then his head was spinning as a wave of dizziness overcame him. Despite the old monk hauling on him, he was quickly upon his knees. His vision went black for a moment and then came back into a blurred swirling view of the world.

He could see the soaring stone columns of the Temple Majoris, the burning torches in the sconces. He could glimpse a robed figure near the dais. Kodoris. And then his head was filled with her—Lucinda. He could feel her power, smell her hair, her skin. He saw Kodoris turn at the approach of someone or something. Acquel felt his mouth gape as Kodoris's face twisted in horror at what his eyes were drinking in. Then Acquel saw her face: beautiful and angelic, lapis eyes blazing, her full lips parting as some dark power filled her from within. The vision pulled back and behind her he saw two tall winged figures, masked in shadow. A wave of the blackest despair filled his head and chest like something had passed right through him.

"The Ara," he gasped. "We must get to the Temple. She is here. Here *now*!"

Volpe's large eyes bulged. "The witch! Sweet Elded save us." Acquel felt himself lifted back onto his feet as if by a miracle, the old monk finding new strength. The burning amulet had cooled a little, though pulsing hot still, yet tolerable on his chest. The Saint had gotten his attention.

"Hurry!" shouted Acquel, staggering across the courtyard and running up the wide street to the west. The old monk was at his heels, puffing and wheezing as they flew past the houses, knocking folk out of the way and gaining a few Templars as they ran until they had four monks in tow.

"Magister!" cried one. "Where are we going?"

"The Temple is under attack!" yelled Acquel without turning back.

The monk, wearing a brigantine made for a far larger man, cast a worried glance to the one jogging next to him whose bouncing sallet helm had all but obscured his vision. "It's just us going?"

STRYKAR GRUNTED AS he and a militiaman stooped to tip the steaming cauldron down the murder hole at their feet. Their effort was rewarded by an ear-splitting screech of pain from one of the griffons beneath them. "More!" bellowed Strykar, tossing the iron pot behind him. He took a few steps back, his hands burning with pain through his leather gauntlets and looked up to the dog-toothed parapet of the barbican. And he stopped. Standing up on the ledge was Demerise, bow in hand. Shafts flew past and over her as she took a bead and loosed one of her own, aimed downwards at the griffons.

"Goddamned foolish bitch!" He was on his feet, scrambling to reach her as she drew another arrow from her quiver and set it in her bow. She wore no armour at all and it was only blind luck, or some heavenly mercy, that she had not yet been pierced by bowshot. "Get down! Give me your hand!" Strykar was on the ledge reaching up but she only glanced back at him, determined to take her bead on the screeching monsters beneath her. Strykar's mouth gaped as he saw her lean over to better her aim and then she was down, her lead foot slipping off the mossy stone. The rest of her followed in a heartbeat as Strykar scrambled up onto the ledge. "Demerise!" He peered over and saw her, one foot on a corbel, the other dangling while one hand gripped onto a rusty old chain that had been left from the old drawbridge mechanism, long ago dismantled. She was still clutching her bow as she kicked to bring up her other foot. Strykar roared and threw himself over the parapet, his armour scraping the stones, straining to reach for her. Demerise's scarf had unwound and he could see her whole face, scarred and now twisted with exertion as she hung on. One of the griffons had seen her and it reared up, claw stretching for the corbel ledge. Strykar bellowed, reaching for her wrist. His head rocked: a spent bolt had glanced from his helm. Two others struck the barbican within feet of Demerise, snapping as they struck the stones.

Strykar felt hands on his legs and feet and a moment later he was being hauled up, still clenching Demerise's wrist. A giant yellow cockerel-like claw brushed her boot, scraping furiously as the beast tried to latch onto her. Strykar's face contorted as he felt his arm wrench. Yet his eyes were locked on hers, her mouth moving wordlessly in shock. Somehow, she lifted her boot, gained the corbel, and Strykar threw his other arm down to get another grip of her. Soon he had her by the shoulders, hauling her up onto the ledge between the merlons. "You damned stupid cow!" he shouted into her ear as he pulled, and with a yank from two militiamen they both fell backwards and onto the walkway. She was on his chest, in his arms, breaths coming fast.

"I hit it... I hit it!" she said. "But... but it bounced off like it was steel."

Strykar rolled her off, sputtering. "What in hell's name made you do that. If the arrows didn't strike you those things would have!"

She was on her hand and knees, trying to regain her wind. "They need a shaft to the eye. That damned black eye." She grabbed Strykar's arm. "They bounce off the fur. Ain't right—it *shimmers*. I had it dead in the neck and it could have been a stone wall for all the hurt it did!" She leaned back and felt for her black scarf, hands shaking.

Strykar scowled and helped her, winding it around her head again. He clamped both his hands on her either side of her head. "Don't do that again!"

The good side of her face managed a smile. "I've bagged boar the size of oxen but never a griffon. I wanted that."

Strykar shook his head and growled. "It almost bagged *you*, huntress."

And the barbican shook as the griffons crashed again against the gates below.

ACQUEL AND VOLPE had gained the parapets at the Ara, the great grey edifice of the Temple Majoris looming to their right. But it looked to them that the Templars had abandoned the wall to aid the defence of the main barbican. There was not a soul to be seen on the parapets or the green itself. The amulet was still throbbing intensely against his chest when the old monk finally caught him up, heaving for breath.

"The Temple," said Acquel. And he dashed across the green, heading for the side porchway. Volpe reached it too and bent over, retching a little, before following Acquel in a limping gait, his wooden sword in his right hand. The sky had turned purple now as the last light of the evening sun faded, giving a sinister look to the ancient and twisted flat-topped parasol pines that grew near the west portico. Inside the temple all was dim but his eyes quickly began to adjust. A few braziers burned near the altar and half a dozen torches were also lit in their sconces on the massive stone columns holding up the great vaulted ceiling. His side-sword rasped as he drew it from the scabbard. There was no sound within. His heart thumping, he looked for Kodoris and the woman he knew was already there.

His sword in a low guard, he advanced from the archway into the first aisle even as he heard Volpe push the studded oak door to join him. By the time he heard the scrabbling sound it was too late to react. He felt himself flung across the aisle from the kick of the harpy. Dazed, he pushed himself up only to be slammed to the flagstones and then lifted off the floor. The harpy had dug its talons into his tabard, having failed to find flesh and instead only steel. Clinging to his sword, Acquel rose up and over the benches as the great flapping wings lifted him higher. But the tabard ripped apart and he fell crashing into the pews, luckily not from a great height. Again he scrambled to gain his feet, the cries of Ugo Volpe echoing in the cool vastness of the Temple.

His opponent rose up, hovering, its rapidly flapping wings generating a stinking gust as it looked again for him. But, as last time, it could not see him. It let loose a furious high-pitched howl of rage and made for Volpe instead. Behind him, at the main portico, he saw two figures half in shadow. One was the High Priest, the other smaller figure had to be Lucinda. Volpe cried out again and Acquel pushed his way along the pew to regain the aisle. In the light of a wall torch he saw the little monk holding off two harpies near the side entrance, his wooden sword slashing the air as the creatures darted in towards him.

Looking past Volpe's fight, Acquel saw Kodoris and Lucinda standing a few paces apart as if in conversation. If he ran now for the sorceress, Volpe would die before he could get back, that was certain. He hefted his blade and ran towards the harpies. They turned at the sound of his clanking armour and in that instance, Volpe struck one in the flank. The creature screamed and Acquel could see wisps of smoke rising up from the wound as it staggered back. Then it turned, its companion joining it, and the two creatures hopped and loped down the aisle straight for him. Their large clouded eyes, like silvery moons, could not see him but the invisibility afforded by the amulet was now negated by the very thing that protected him from an enemy's steel— the sound of his plate armour. The unwounded harpy leapt on its rippling feathered legs and took wing while the other came on, its grey hands flexing and unflexing, wings drawn back. Acquel didn't wait to receive them but rather ran to one side, swinging a blow as he passed them and so joining Volpe.

"Ugo! With me!"

"We must save the High Priest," shot back the monk. "Leave me to hold these things. You must get to the canoness. Stop her."

But now there was no time. The harpies were upon them again. In the poor light, Acquel could see one held a shining black obsidian dagger in one hand. Along its bare arm the raised jagged welt of a badly healed wound could be seen; the wound he had inflicted weeks gone by. The harpy's head tilted as it listened for him, a long red serpent's tongue flicking out from its mouth. It was an infernal travesty of woman with its long flowing locks and sagging breasts. Hag-like but immensely strong and filled with hate. And it remembered him.

A puddle of black blood was forming around the other harpy's legs. Yet its pain only increased its rage and again it made a leap for Volpe, razor talons shooting straight out to rake the old monk. His sword beat the foot aside but the force sent him down on his backside. Acquel moved in front to cover him, his own sword slashing. The harpies jabbered and screamed abuse in a tongue that seemed to scorch his ears, the unknown words driving deep into his mind as if they themselves had the power to wound. The creatures fell back, hunched and gesturing with clawed hands. It was stalemate.

"We must get to Kodoris before she works her enchantment upon him. Can you move to the right? I will be at your side."

Acquel threw a quick glance over his shoulder, and saw Kodoris and Lucinda nearly toe to toe, as if in intense conversation. "Let us try, brother!" he said as he moved his right foot out to the side and closed with the other. Volpe sidestepped too, closing the gap. The unwounded harpy saw the game though—it flanked Acquel and again thrust with its long black dagger, forcing him to parry with the sword he wielded in both hands.

LUCIUS KODORIS STARED into the eyes of Lucinda della Rovera. Despite every attempt to hold her off, she was in his mind now. Pushing deeper and deeper, opening doors that he had struggled hard to keep shut even from his own awareness. It was if he was in a dream where he could not move or speak. She was beautiful. More beautiful than any woman he had ever seen in his long life. Her blue eyes and full lips pulled him in and he wanted her, a dreamer lost in the world of his own mind. He felt her hand upon his cheeks, cradling his face and then her face moved closer. He wanted to fall inside of her. Her lips touched his own and for a moment there was immense pleasure. Then a dizzying rush struck him. Lucinda was no longer in front of him but instead, the vision of his fevered dream returned in its full horror.

The giant white wolf ridden by the naked raven-headed man was coming towards him, the rider stretching his open palm forward, reaching for him. Andras. A bright light emanated from behind, nearly blinding him. And then another vision as that one faded: a man's face, long doleful and clean-shaven, black hair falling to the shoulders. He had never seen this man but somehow he knew him. The visage filled his entire field of vision. Another voice, not his own, came into his head—Berithas the Redeemer. The Trickster, the Deceiver! Berithas had joined with him. He could feel him inside, becoming part of him. His thoughts were Berithas's and Berithas's were his.

Kodoris became aware again of his surroundings, of Lucinda holding his hand as they walked. He was outside on the green, and a cool breeze swept over his face. In the sky he saw two great chariots borne by a black horse and one by a horse translucent. Beautiful naked youths drove them across the firmament from out of the blood red sliver of sun that remained upon the horizon. Belial and Beleth were coming. He knew this and was not fearful anymore. Kodoris was dissolving, growing fainter in his own skull. He was Berithas. He knew all that Berithas had been and had done.

Someone was yelling his name from far away. It distracted him even as Berithas spoke to him. He found himself rising up as if out of a dark well.

"Kodoris! Fight her!"

He knew the voice. Brother Acquelonius. He saw Lucinda next to him smiling as she led him across the grass. But Berithas was taking him as if he was being swallowed feet first. He fought. He wilfully recalled his sins, the murders laid at his doorstep, the innocent blood spilt for the One Faith. And suddenly, what was left of Lucius Kodoris understood what had to be done. As if bursting through the surface of a dark lake, he gasped and released Lucinda's hand. He raised his own and struck her, hard. And then he staggered across the green towards the walls that overlooked the fields far below.

"Lucius, wait for me!" Lucinda's voice filled his head but he did not stop. Already it was becoming harder to move his legs, Berithas was absorbing what was left of his self-awareness. He was on the walkway, mounting the stone ledge and then hauling himself up onto the wall itself. He turned to see the glory of the Temple Majoris, bathed in the orange light of sunset. He saw Brother Kell and the novices waving, the men he had slain. He smiled and then turned again, tottering on the wall, looking out onto the fields below, fires in the distance.

"Climb down," said Lucinda, her hand outstretched. Inside his head, Berithas said the same and he began to bend his knees to comply. He *was* Berithas. And he began to forget his own name. Suddenly the Temple bells rang out. Once again he drifted upwards, fighting the invader. He lifted his head and spoke.

"I am Lucius Kodoris, High Priest of the One Faith."

He raised his arms, the purple silk flapping in the wind. And then the High Priest launched himself over the wall, falling and falling until the final mystery was unveiled to him.

UGO VOLPE WAS losing strength, already winded. But his opponent was weakening too, its blood pooling and smearing across the flagstones. It screamed at him again and aimed a vicious kick at his chest. He dodged it and thrust out his sorbo sword. It went deep into the harpy's naked belly, practically igniting it in a red flame. A little puff of stinking smoke poured forth and the creature collapsed with a pitiful, almost too human, moan. Seeing its companion slain, the other harpy drew back, screeched, and stretched its leathery wings. With a tremendous single flap it launched itself upwards into the air and flew to the beaten copper doors of the temple, now wide open.

The purple sky was streaked with red as Acquel entered the green, sword at the ready. He saw Lucinda near the parapet wall gesturing up to Kodoris who was balanced upon it. And with his mouth open in silent horror, he watched Kodoris jump. Behind him he heard Volpe let out a cry of despair. Lucinda turned and saw him and in the same instant the amulet sparked to life upon his chest. He strode towards her, hefting his blade. It was time to end her life. He was close enough to see her face, strangely animated, her eyes boring into his. A lance of pain filled his temples. The amulet warmed him and the pain faded. As in the crypt months before, he saw a look of astonishment come over the sorceress. Acquel brought up his arms into a high guard, ready to cleave her in two.

A grey flash blew past him, unbalancing him. He stumbled, caught himself, and saw the harpy catch Lucinda della Rovera in its arms, effortlessly lifting her up and out, over the wall in one swift pass. The sword fell from his grasp.

When he reached the wall and looked down he saw soldiers gathered about the spread-eagled form of the High Priest some sixty feet below. As he looked on, still dumbfounded, he saw them pick up the body and carry it off back to their lines. Acquel lowered his forehead against the cold stone. When he looked up again a figure stood where Kodoris had stood on the ledge. It was Timandra. Bright and glorious, her auburn red hair flowing behind her, she looked down at him and smiled. Then her arm extended, pointing straight ahead. Towards the enemy encampment and beyond: to the south. She looked at him, filling his heart with warmth, and she gave him a deep nod, affirming her counsel. Her voice filled his head, telling him that all was not lost. The final battle would come in the south. *Maresto.*

Twenty-Seven

DANAMIS SHOOK HIS shoulders to settle the leather and plate brigantine onto his frame and then jiggled a bit more as Citala stood watching him impassively. She reached out to begin fastening the buckles at the front and he did not protest. He looked into her face as he held his arms loosely at his sides.

"You sure you haven't been squire to someone before?" he said as the *Vendetta* gently rocked at the quayside.

She smiled. "Just because we don't wear armour doesn't mean we can't figure out how it's put on."

They stood outside his stern cabin near the helm and the whipstaff, just out of the way of the crew further forward, those who were part of the landing party also donning harness and weapons. He took a deep breath—nervous—as Citala worked her way down, her long fingers dexterously doing up the buckles that went down to his hips. He would look a fool if the queen didn't turn up where she was supposed to. Worse, he might be arrested as a traitor if the council had betrayed her and said he was abducting her rather than merely conducting her to Maresto. Once inside the palace with just two of his men, he'd never be able to fight his way out. And that would be that.

"She still has affection for you... your queen," said Citala quietly, her eyes focussed on her task.

Danamis gave a small groan. "I do not believe that. But she is desirous of my aid when few others can oblige."

"That is closer to the mark, my love. You should not confuse love or fancy for appreciation. You are a valuable retainer to her. A means to an end. If you think she has other ideas you will be disappointed."

Danamis reached up and grasped both her hands. "Jealous? For something Cressida and I shared a very long time ago? Or is it the boy? She said I was not the father. And that is that."

"It is true I would not wish to lose you to her. But to lose you to her for the wrong reasons—perhaps a lie—that I could not bear."

"You know I am sworn to her royal house. I hold warrant at the court. I have a duty to fulfil."

She gently untangled their hands and resumed doing up the last two buckles. "Duty. You swore an oath to my people—to me—to help the mer. What of that promise?"

It cut him, for she was right and he knew it well. He had fobbed her off despite her worries about her father, myrra and the colony at Nod's Rock. And the way the new colony at Palestro seemed to be sinking into listlessness; that was an image he had tried hard to wipe from his mind. She had asked for help and he had deferred her. Again and again. He reached up with a chafed hand and cradled her cheek. She leaned into it.

"Citala. I promise you again, here, that as soon as we reach Maresto then we will go to your father, come to an agreement. Do what must be done." He leaned forward and touched his forehead to hers. "I have no wish to lose you."

"And I will stand by you all the way there," she said quietly.

He smiled. In his heart he was not really sure whether the queen still had feelings for him. Or whether she had lied about Sarant being his. Or, deep down, even whether he still harboured feelings for Cressida in spite of the love he knew he felt for Citala. He suddenly felt as if the old Danamis, the callous and selfish fool of a year before, might somehow rise up again to rule him. And he hated himself.

The she-mer blinked slowly and clapped him on both biceps. "There, you are ready! Where is your blade?"

"Hey ho! Heads up!" It was Gregorvero who had come around the deck into the helm. He gave a nod to Citala. "Captain, we're laden, lashed, and ready to shove off when you return. Assume you're still expecting a hasty departure?"

Danamis nodded. "The quicker the better, my friend."

"Captain!" shouted Talis from across the main deck, "The landing party is armed and ready on the quay."

Gregorvero lowered his voice. "Nico, be careful up there. I'd sooner trust the word of a Darfan merchant than any behind the walls of the palace. If the queen does not appear where and when she said she would then you must get out. Straight away."

"I hear you, Gregor. It's dicing with the Devil, but Cressida won't lose heart. She'll see this through." He turned back to Citala who held out his Southlander blade and scabbard. "We will be in and out before anyone even notices," he said, winking.

She placed a hand on his wrist. "Elded will watch over you, Danamis son of Danamis," and Gregorvero gave a cough and hurriedly blessed himself.

BRIGHT MORNING SUN blazed through the leaded windows and painted coloured patterns upon the grey flagstones of the royal temple. Situated in the middle terrace of the palace grounds, the temple was not particularly large and now it was crammed full of the nobility and the royal household, cheek by jowl and none too happy for it. The High Prelate of Perusia in his tall, square felt hat of ultramarine blue stood near the altar, waiting for the chorus to finish their song—the signal for the dowager queen and the crown prince to enter. The feast day of Saint Giacomo required the Saint's skull to be brought forth in its silver casket where, up upon the dais and the unadorned altar of white marble, the queen and her son would kneel, kiss the casket and offer prayers.

Captain Piero Polo stood in a side pew, looking bored but less bored than the Sinean ambassador whose eyes were nearly closed like some dozing cat. The ambassador's guards stood behind him, impassive, while one of Polo's sailors picked his nose. Polo looked around him again at the sea of faces, most of whom he knew: the council, the barons and counts, the wealthier merchants of Perusia, the honoured guests from the outlying duchies and free cities that weren't currently warring. Baron Raganus sat fidgeting on his bench as if he had boils on his rump. But one face was missing—Nicolo Danamis. That struck him as odd given his special relationship with the queen. Perhaps a problem aboard his vessel, he thought.

The last echoes of the choristers having died away, a trumpet fanfare sounded the entry of the royals. The palace guard entered at a slow marching pace with their red tasselled glaives, and in their wake came the queen, veiled in blue, her son at her side wearing a hooded cloak of penitence like some common monk. The long tubular bells began to clang, dirge-like, while the royals made their stately way down the aisle towards the altar. The queen seemed to float along, her face hidden under a gossamer veil. Prince Sarant was at her side, walking—or rather *ambling* thought Polo, with a rolling gait—like some sailor fresh from sea. Behind them came Captain Caluro, tall and self-assured, dressed in gleaming breastplate, tall black boots and a red cape that reached the floor.

All eyes were upon them at the altar, the High Prelate bowing with clasped hands. As the queen leaned forward and began to bend her knees down to the wool sack kneeler on the steps, her veil was pulled off from behind. Polo's eyebrows raised as he watched the young prince step backwards for he had apparently trodden on the long veil. Polo now focussed on Sarant, and saw that the boy appeared slightly shorter than he remembered. Alarmed, he pushed forward to the annoyance of the nobleman in front of him. Polo then saw the stunned look on the Prelate's face. A murmur rose up, starting nearest to the altar and then rippling outwards, a wave of voices. Someone shouted, "Where is the queen!" and that was when Polo saw that it was not Cressida who knelt, scrambling to retrieve her veil. The prelate pulled back the prince's hood to find Nanino, the court dwarf, staring up at him rather sheepishly. Confusion erupted and the decorum of the temple evaporated in an instant. Caluro, expressionless, gathered up the woman and began to lead her out of the temple, the dwarf in tow. Polo's eyes narrowed when he saw Caluro's brisk but rather calm reaction. *Unsurprised.*

"Elded's balls," he muttered as he turned to his retainers. "All of you! With me!"

DANAMIS AND TWO of his men waited just inside the inner gatehouse. He had left the better part of his forty-strong party outside the palace walls, milling about as if awaiting entry. An act not itself exactly unsuspicious but there was little he could do about it. Now he leaned against the wall, watching the great oak doors of the palace and waiting, praying, for the queen and the prince to arrive. It seemed like an age. A hundred ill thoughts crossed his mind, each one chipping away a little more of his confidence.

It was the small side door that opened at the palace and Danamis sprang up as two rather tense looking young guardsmen emerged. Behind them, three women and a child. Cressida was dressed in a long undyed woollen cloak, a hood obscuring her face. The boy, dressed as a page, had on a wine-coloured beret two sizes too large that flopped over his brow, offering some concealment. The two other women bore large wicker baskets and he was pleased that Cressida had borne his advice in mind to take only what was necessary. A queen could always buy or borrow whatever she needed.

He and his men moved to meet her.

"Captain Danamis," said one of the guardsman, "Here are your charges."

Cressida raised her head and he saw her smile deep inside her hood. Danamis noticed the prince watching him, a look of deep scepticism on the boy's face.

Danamis gave him a reassuring smile. "Are you ready for an adventure?"

The prince's hand moved to rest upon the hilt of the short dagger he wore. "I would rather be staying here, Captain. A king belongs in his castle. This whole course of action strikes me as most unwise."

Cressida's right hand smacked the back of the boy's head. "We are ready, Captain Danamis," she said, voice firm. "Lead the way."

Danamis nodded. "The rest of my men are beyond the gates. We must waste no time."

One of the guardsman spoke up. "Captain Caluro has ordered us to stay with you—right to the ship."

"I am grateful for another two swordsmen. Shall we?"

Outside the gates a small crowd had formed near the Palestrians, who themselves were doing their best to look like they were lost and looking for a tavern. Talis gave

Danamis a look of relief when he saw he and the passengers appear. Danamis put an arm around him and spoke into his ear. "Form the men up into a square. The women and boy in the centre." Talis put thumb to forehead and began to muster the sailors. Danamis turned to Cressida. "My lady, we must proceed at a brisk pace. I don't know how long we will have until the ruse is discovered."

"Did you think I've forgotten how to run? I used to run well enough when you were chasing me," she said. She seized Sarant's hand even as the boy began to protest and moved into the jumble of rough soldiery, her handmaidens following. Danamis saw another two cloaked and hooded figures approach. Both with walking staffs. It was Citala and Necalli.

He stepped forward, his head shaking. "You should have stayed at the ship. This is no time for the merfolk to be implicated if this all goes wrong."

Citala was unchastised. "And if it all goes wrong you will need all the help you can get. Necalli insisted on it. His promise to your father, you remember?"

Master Necalli nodded. "She is right. We must stand by you."

Danamis pulled at his mouth. "There was a time when I used to give the orders. Very well, you are both with me here at the rear."

Their small army set off down the wide cobbled street that led back into the centre of the city, the harbour visible below them. They walked quickly, purpose undisguised. The merchants of Perusia darted into their shops fearful of a riot or raid. Danamis knew if his men had attracted unwanted attention on the way up, they were certain to have even more on the way down as they jostled and clanked. At the tail end, flanked by Citala and Necalli both looking tall and sinister in their dark cloaks, he would every so often glance behind to see if there was pursuit. The fifth time he cast a glance back he was rewarded with more than the looks of distrustful townfolk and whispering housewives: there was an armed party storming towards them at a fast trot.

He let out a curse. "Talis! Ho there!" The forty of them came to a halt, line slamming into line. "Get back to the ship with the passengers! You men here in the last line. We stay and fight."

Talis swore an oath and urged the rest of them on at a jog, the sailors grabbing the queen's baggage, one of them roughly seizing the yowling prince and trotting along with the heir apparent under his burly arm. Cressida kept up, a hand on each side of her hood to safeguard her identity, and the band dashed pell-mell down the long sloping terrace of white-washed houses and shop awnings. As his eleven remaining men turned to face the newcomers, Danamis drew his sword and threw back his cloak over his right shoulder. Necalli slowly pulled back his hood, eyes blinking in the strong midday sun. Citala did the same and hefted her staff in both hands.

Closer now, he could see who his pursuers were. It was a gang of Piero Polo's men, reinforced with a few sword-wielding Sinean soldiers. He couldn't quite make out their number but the odds were not good.

"Citala, my lovely. Would it be a waste of my breath to tell you to get behind us?"

She laughed.

He called back to his men. "If I fall, you all make a run for it. Understood?" He was met with a ripple of grunts and "ayes" as the line tensed ready to receive what was coming their way. Polo's men slowed and spread out to cover the width of the street, all wearing the now-familiar scarlet red arming cap and gripping their side-swords and axes. Two black and red satin-clad Sineans pushed their way to the front, brandishing their own unique weapons: short double-edged swords with miniscule guards. And behind them was Captain Polo himself, red-faced and barking out commands.

Instinctively, the Palestrians spread out to prevent the enemy from flanking them. And before another second had passed, Polo's men sprang upon them. It was as nasty a street fight as Danamis had ever seen. The clang of steel and desperate yells echoed between the tall houses on either side as Danamis fended off a gap-toothed and curse-spitting sailor while trying to keep an eye on Citala. It nearly cost him his head as another one of Polo's henchmen aimed a side stroke at him from off to one side. He jumped back and parried before flicking his own blade with a shot from the elbow. As the first opponent stepped in and threw another blow, Danamis sidestepped and grabbed his sword arm with his left, just for a second. It was enough for him to thrust the man in the throat, dropping him to the ground in a brief spray of blood.

He saw Necalli swing his staff with both hands and lift a sailor off his feet, sending him sprawling across the cobbles. But his heart flew to his mouth when he saw Citala square against a Sinean soldier. He needn't have worried. The Sinean wasn't sure what manner of creature he was fighting and it showed when he raised his sword up into a hesitant guard. Citala didn't wait. She was on him, raining down furious blows with the staff and it was all the Sinean could do to parry and step back from her attack. Before Danamis whirled away to deal with another problem, he caught a quick glimpse of the Sinean's jaw parting from the rest of his head as Citala's powerful swing struck the man. Danamis bumped into one of his own who was backing out of a vicious sweep of a blade and then he turned to catch an incoming blow aimed at his skull.

The fight rapidly became a confused frenzy as of wild dogs set upon one another. As fate would have it, Danamis turned to find himself staring straight into the bulging brown eyes of Piero Polo. He paused for an instant, swore to himself, and moved in.

"You'll have to do your own killing now," said Danamis, raising his blade in both hands.

"Abducting a queen, Nicolo? You're nothing more than a corsair after all. And you'll not be mourned." He gave a yell and lashed out with his long blade. Danamis held his ground, beat it aside, and cut downwards in a riposte. Polo twisted out of the way but Danamis managed to clip his shoulder as he moved.

The old explorer grimaced and shuffled back a few feet. "Did you really think that you could get away with this? Fool me? Fool the council?"

Danamis waved his sword, looking out to either side for the rush of another foe. "You lying bastard. You know I serve the queen. Unlike you—a whore for the Sineans."

"Nicolo!"

At Citala's cry, the instinct of a hundred fights took over and he instantly voided his head and shoulders away to be rewarded with the swishing sound of a sword as it cleaved the air. The sailor pressed forward and Polo seized his moment to rush in. But the new attacker found Citala and Necalli at his back and twisted around to face the mer. Danamis wheeled and parried the close-in thrust of Polo's blade with a downward beat, his left hand moving fast to grip the *ricasso* of his sword. A second later he had pushed forward and driven it deep into the meat of Polo's right thigh. The captain collapsed with a howl of pain and Danamis stepped back to survey the scene before him. Men lay sprawled all around, blood running in rivulets across the cobbles. But those on the ground were more Polo's men than his. As the great explorer and discover of the eastern oceans rolled into a ball, his men rushed in to pull him out of harm's way.

"Back to the ship!" barked Danamis. Two of his men hauled up a wounded Palestrian and started moving down the street. Citala grabbed his arm and pulled him away even as he watched Polo's twisted mouth spew a steady stream of curses at him. Remembering his own agonies of a year ago, *gratis* Piero Polo, he was glad he hadn't killed the man. Yet.

Twenty-Eight

VENDETTA'S PROW CUT deep into the waters of Saint Blasius Bay, white foam tossing either side and bubbling furiously along its strakes as the ship raced southwards. Portly old *Royal Grace* ploughed on through *Vendetta*'s wake, her master Bassinio piling on as much canvas as the ship would bear. And just a speck on the bay from the vantage of her stern rail, another ship followed them, one far larger.

Citala, wrapped in her silk robes, stood with Danamis in the high bow of *Vendetta,* as the caravel, dipped and bucked in the rolling swell. On the far side of the mast, two sailors hauled on lines through a deadeye, tightening the canvas of the square foresail while Necalli—brooding as usual—stared out over the shimmering waters.

"Nicolo, what are you thinking?" she asked, her voice soft.

He turned to her, taking his eyes off the horizon ahead.

"You mean other than when the Sineans might catch us up? In truth, I was thinking about Strykar, and what awaits us in Maresto. I hope the fight has gone well for the Black Rose."

"He is a cunning warrior from what I have seen. He will serve Duke Alonso well."

Danamis chuckled. "Aye, that he is. And a keen eye for business too." He paused a moment. "Used to think I was clever. Like Strykar, a schemer. But what if the situation is changed when we arrive? I'm bringing Cressida and the prince into the unknown. No news from Maresto in weeks. God knows what has happened there or Livorna."

She reached for his arm. "Who expects you to know the future? She should be grateful she has your loyalty when those cowards around her either fawn and scrape or try and gain their own advantage."

"She has stayed in the cabin all day. Not ventured out on deck."

"Perhaps she is ill. Or does not want to draw attention to herself."

Danamis nodded. "Or she is having second thoughts. About the plan. About me."

Citala made a strange growling sound as she often did when annoyed. "Enough of that. It will be Alonso's problem once you deliver her to his palace."

Gregorvero tramped up the ladder to the foredeck, negotiated the mast and swung around a shroud line to reach them. "Nico, they're gaining."

Danamis scowled. "We had at least four hours lead on them. But if Polo is on board they won't give up the chase. They're bigger than a whale. So how can they be out-sailing us?"

"They can throw out ten times as much canvas as we can. And though they're big they've got a narrow beam. That gives them speed despite their size. But I'm more worried for the *Grace*. They'll catch her first, even if we can run on."

"Best guess?"

Gregorvero scratched his hairy cheek. "If we sail through the night—everything close-hauled—probably after first light. That's assuming that Bassinio can keep up with us."

"Feed them all well tonight but no wine. And rouse the ship before sunrise to make ready for battle. I will advise the queen."

Gregorvero nodded. "Aye, Nico." He gave an awkward nod of encouragement and left them.

Danamis placed his hands on the steep railing that ran at chest level. "Even if we outrun them, we can't stop until we reach Maresto. Not Nod's Rock. Not even Palestro."

"I know."

"If it was your wish... I would understand if you and Necalli choose to return to Palestro. To return to the colony."

She pulled his arm away from the railing and turned him to her. "I have vowed to stay with *you*. If for no other reason than to keep you from wallowing in self-doubt." He did not know what she knew, that Necalli's interest in her went beyond the salvation of the Valdur merfolk. And she shuddered at the thought of Danamis confronting Necalli at swordpoint. "What would it benefit me to return to Palestro without you?" she said. "Outnumbered by your father and—" She shot a glance across the deck to Necalli. "No, Nico. We shall see this through together. First Maresto, then Palestro."

He smiled in unfeigned relief, his eyes drinking her in. "My Citala," he said quietly, "my love. You're worth more than rubies and emeralds, worth more than all the treasure that could ever be raised from the depths." He brushed her locks with the back of his hand and then turned to make for the stairs. She had not been honest with him. Already, guilt was welling up inside her, guilt for abandoning the colony she had begun. She had left them with no one to face up to the worst of the Palestrians or, more worrying, the fickleness of Valerian Danamis. This was heaped upon the anger and despair she felt now that she was banished from Nod's Rock. The only home she had known. It seemed that the chances of saving her father from his own demons had now slipped even further.

As Nicolo pounded down the stairs to the main deck, Necalli slowly faced Citala, and then made his way across to join her.

His large round eyes, black pupils gleaming, did not blink.

"You heard his words?" she said in the mer tongue.

He nodded.

"What chance do we have in this world? With war upon war by the landsmen, devouring themselves. I have left my people in the midst of them. Like some dying whale set upon by sharks who will then feast upon each other when all is gone."

"They are a strange race. But you already know that. And your hope is to change them. I know that is what you think. It will not happen. They will change *you*."

She stared at him, half-accepting that he was right. The other half of her could not give up on the promise of mer and man in Valdur. "There is hope, Necalli. Always that."

"You need not worry if the Sineans defeat him tomorrow."

Citala raised her chin, eyes narrowing. "You mean that you and I can always slip over the side and disappear if that happens. Leave them all to their fate."

He shook his head and raised his hand. "I mean to say that I do not believe they will defeat him." He looked away from her as he struggled for words, reluctant to go on.

"What are you saying? How would you know such a thing?"

His long, thin nostrils flared and twitched. "If the battle goes ill, I may be able to help him."

"How? How can you help?"

He suddenly changed his mind and drew back. "I can say no more. Pray that Danamis will outrun the enemy." He drew his shining blue garment about him and turned away but then stopped. "I beg you, say nothing of this to him. Please."

She frowned and did not answer, her mind straining to remember something that had happened days before; something that had touched her consciousness from a great distance and then just as quickly, had withdrawn.

THE LONG LOW rim of orange spread a tentative light from the east, the sky yet purple over the duchy of Torinia off the *Vendetta*'s starboard. Danamis and Gregorvero stood on the stern poop silently watching the gigantic ship that was now drawing closer. So close now as to be able to count all seven of its towering masts.

"They'll have us," said Gregorvero. "And there's not a goddamn thing we may do to change that."

"Hoist my personal standard and the royal pennant," growled Danamis. "Perhaps if the Sineans see that they will leave the *Grace* and make for us instead."

Gregorvero sputtered and rounded on him. "What? Are we to surrender or try running some more? We should give them iron from the orichalcum guns! They haven't seen the likes of that before."

"No surrender. But I will wager they won't fire on us for fear of harming the queen and the prince. That would not help their cause in Perusia and they know it. And if Polo is on board, he will most certainly know that."

"And then what?"

"We fight them close in if we can without grappling, and then try and run south by east and lose them in the islands."

Gregorvero's eyes widened. "You don't have the faintest scrap of a plan, do you?"

"Just raise the standards. And run out the guns." He saw Gregorvero swallow his protest, salute, and turn. What could he do? He had never before faced a Sinean warship and he knew nothing of their crew. But he had already underestimated their speed and that could yet undo him. He cursed himself and headed down. It was time to see Cressida, and it would not be pleasant.

She was already fully dressed when she bade him enter the cabin. Sarant had his nose pressed up against the diamond panes of glass at the stern, watching the large ship draw ever closer.

Danamis gave her a little bow, his lips pressed tightly together.

"Polo and his friends are fast approaching," she said in her regal voice. "Or have my eyes deceived me and that is not a Sinean warship bearing upon us?"

"And it seems a faster vessel than yours, Admiral Danamis," observed Sarant with an almost scholarly detachment. "Will we have a battle?"

Danamis spread his hands. "I am sorry. I thought we might outrun any pursuit but they are swift sailors. But I'm not giving up yet. We're smaller and we can outmanoeuvre them. They won't harm you or the prince. They need you alive."

"That is your consolation? That we will be captured alive?"

"If they take the ship you two will be the only ones to live. The rest of us will fight to the death."

"I trusted you, Nico," she said, her voice bitter.

Sarant was watching him, a look of derision on his round dark face. "Your other ship is turning away, Admiral. Maybe they have had enough already."

"Stay inside the cabin," said Danamis, curtly. "No matter what happens. Do you understand?"

Sarant bounded off the bench and stood tottering, hands on hips, caught off balance on the ship's roll. "I want to fight on deck. Give me a sword!"

Danamis gritted his teeth and gave another bow to the queen. "If they fire upon us, I will have to have you taken down to the hold."

"I will not be treated as cargo, Nicolo Danamis!"

But he was already out the doorway.

GREGORVERO HAD HIS eyes firmly fixed on the Sinean vessel, its bizarre trapezoid sails billowing and rippling, the foaming water churning under its high blunt-nosed prow. "Bassinio's a crafty devil. Breaking away and making them choose which one of us to follow."

"Looks like they have chosen us," said Danamis, his knuckles white on the railing. He was right. The massive vessel had kept its course, bearing down upon them and ignoring the *Royal Grace* as the latter made a lazy turn to larboard. Easy prey should they try and take it. But it was clear now they knew exactly who their quarry was.

"You do realize we can't raise our guns high enough to reach their main deck. Do you reckon we can hole them below the waterline?"

Danamis had already realized that was the only tactic he could pursue in bringing his guns to bear. But he had no idea how thick the Sinean hull was. He kicked himself for not accepting Polo's offer of a tour when he had the chance. "Gregor, this will be a dance to end all dances, and we must avoid it ending in an embrace."

The master nodded. "Manoeuvre. Play the breeze and get them becalmed in a turning game. They're fast with the wind at their back but how do they sail into a stiff breeze, eh?"

Danamis shielded his eyes and could just make out the mouths of two large cannon mounted up on the box-like fo'cscle of the Sinean ship, itself almost as large as a river barge. "If we find we can't hit them with our guns then we can shower them with our arrows.. Tell Talis I want every man who can fire a bow ready and armed." Gregorvero too was watching the Sineans draw ever closer, his eyes taking in the brass guns and the bobbing heads of the sailors who stuffed the foc'scle.

"If they catch us Nico... if they catch us, we can fight it out. But we can't win."

"I know, Gregor." He turned to his friend and smiled. "But *Vendetta* hasn't been caught yet. When the archers are ready on deck and on our foc'sle, we'll ready to come about, close to the wind. North by east nor'east."

No sooner than he had spoken than a rolling boom sounded, a cloud of white smoke blossoming from starboard foc'sle gun of the Sineans. They were still out of range. It was an unsubtle demand to lower sail.

"Well, at least we know their intention," said Gregorvero.

"Those bastards have no right to demand anything of us. Ready the decks."

A QUARTER OF an hour later they were within range. Necalli and Citala now joined Danamis on the long quarterdeck of the caravel, watching the gargantuan vessel dip and rise, it huge sails the colour of yellowing parchment. They could now see the glint of many steel helmets on the enemy deck. Citala leaned against Danamis's shoulder. "I am ready to fight if it comes to that." Next to her, a Palestrian loaded the small iron swivel-gun on the railing. Against what was bearing down upon them, it was little more than a toy.

Danamis leaned over and whispered in her ear. "If we are boarded you go over the side. Back to Palestro. Necalli will go with you. Understood?"

She looked into his eyes. "Do not ask me to make that choice."

"I pray you do not have to. But your duty is to your people. Not to me." One of his soldiers had brought up his falchion and swordbelt. He accepted it and wrapped it around his waist, slinging the scabbard over the back of his left hip. He looked up to his mainmast. Overhead his dolphin pennant streamed out in the wind for fifteen feet. And on the mizzen mast spar, a great square flag: the griffon standard of Valdur, fluttered wildly, animating the beast upon it into a fury of movement. He moved forward and called down to the helm. "On my mark, come about to larboard, hard as you may!" He was rewarded with a reassuring holler from Gregorvero and he turned again to face towards the stern, waiting for the moment and gambling that the Sineans would not dare fire upon the royal family they had been sent to retrieve.

His shoulders involuntary flinched as the sound of the detonation rolled over the deck from the Sinean warship. It was followed a heartbeat later by a furious buzzing whir, the tearing of canvas and a long drawn-out cracking and groaning of wood overhead. Black hail bounced on the deck around them: small thumb sized cubes of iron shot. Danamis rushed forward, swept up Citala and rolled to the deck near the railing as the long mizzen spar of the lateen sail collapsed. There was a scream as a sailor was crushed and then a mountain of red canvas sail swept over their heads and then out over the side into the sea. The *Vendetta* listed and slowed.

Danamis lifted up Citala, her eyes huge with shock at the suddenness of the attack. "Get below," he said, shaking her and then pushing her towards the stairs. His crew staggered to their feet. "Cut it away! Cut it all away!"

His falchion drawn, he was soon hacking away at the tangled lines. The great spar, nearly the length of the ship itself, was lying diagonally across the deck, trailing its canvas half in and out of the water. *Vendetta* was still making headway, but painfully slow now, despite its other sails propelling them forward. More canvas was soon dragged out over the side by the movement of the ship, the spar groaning as it shifted on the deck. Gregorvero had already yanked the whipstaff back, straightening the vessel lest the turn set it over. *Vendetta* crawled on, stricken, and the Sineans closed the distance. Danamis paused at his wild hacking and saw long hooked poles sliding outwards from the Sinean vessel in preparation for grappling the *Vendetta*. They were barely a hundred yards behind. His fist clenched tight around the grip of his sword. *So it has come to this.*

In the confusion of yelling, cursing men, Necalli stood near the rail and closed his eyes. His mind began to call, a silent call as loud as a trumpet blast. So shrill and urgent was it that on the chaotic main deck Citala clapped her hands to her ears. She understood then, in Necalli's call—his demand—what it was he had tried to tell her earlier. What it was she had sensed under the sea with him a week before. Her hand reached out unsteadily for the staircase to the quarterdeck. She must tell Danamis: something was coming.

She pushed her way across the deck, fighting the cursing sailors that were struggling with the massive spar. Necalli stood as if frozen at the corner of the deck, his blue robes fluttering in the breeze, eyes shut. But she could see his eyes moving underneath the lids, seeing. She made her way to Danamis who was assembling the small party of bowmen to fend off the boathooks that now dangled just yards away. "Danamis!"

He turned to her and gestured for her to retreat but she fought her way to his side. "You must get us away from here," she said, her voice twisted and hoarse with alarm. "Away from that ship!"

Danamis waved his falchion, dumbfounded. "My love, that's what I'm trying to do! Get below!"

"You don't understand. It's Necalli. He's summoning something."

Danamis shot a glance across the deck. Necalli's whole frame was shuddering, convulsing even as his eyes remained firmly shut. "What in the name of God...."

Citala's mouth fell open. "It's too late," she said.

An enormous fountain of seawater erupted at the stern quarter of the Sinean ship, sending a cascade over the deck and knocking the breeze out of the great sails. First one, then several gigantic black tentacles lashed out from underneath the surface, the largest with a girth that made the ship masts look like twigs. A wave of seawater crashed over the stern of the *Vendetta*, sending men off their feet. As the stern pitched up and then down with the unnatural swell, Danamis held onto a line from the broken mizzen, transfixed by what was rising from out of the sea. Whipping tentacles ripped the Sinean canvas, shrouds, and stays, and their masts bent under the strain, the whole ship now listing towards the thing that was hauling itself up towards the churning surface.

Danamis wiped his arm across his face, recovered his senses and turned back to his men who were frozen in horror. "Cut, damn you! If you want to live cut it all away!" The Sinean ship now had nearly stopped dead under the weight of its assailant, putting more distance between it and the *Vendetta*. Danamis hacked away with his falchion, severing rope and wood, and then the last of the massive lateen fell away over the side. The *Vendetta* righted itself effortlessly. Danamis staggered to Necalli who had now collapsed motionless upon the deck.

"What have you done!" Danamis raised him up and shook him like some mischievous child. "A kraken!"

Necalli's eyes opened and he reached up and placed a long fingered hand on Danamis's chest. His words came slow and slurred. "My *ihiyolcatl*. My spirit beast." Citala helped

Danamis get the merman to his feet. They saw the kraken, the monstrous oily lump of its head having now cleared the surface, its tentacles wrapping around the masts of the Sinean vessel. Its huge white bulging eye, a square black pupil showing every sign of intelligence, goggled the ship. And now, only for the first time, they could hear the pitiful screams of the Sineans. An enormous cracking sound echoed towards them as one of the seven great masts was snapped by the largest of the tentacles, mast and sail tumbling into the swell.

"I cannot control it," said Necalli softly. "The rage is upon it now that I have called it."

"What are you saying?" said Citala, pulling the mer by his collar.

"We have been paired since childhood," said Necalli. "In Atlcali. It protects me."

Danamis threw Citala a look of unadorned fear. "What does he mean he can't control it?"

Citala shook her head and Necalli closed his eyes again, as if drifting to sleep.

Danamis took a few steps back and whispered, "Sweet Elded." He turned and yelled to his crew, all staring out across the water. "Clear the mainsail of that broken spar! We need all speed with what canvas we have left!"

Sineans were jumping and falling into the sea as the greatest ship ever seen in Valdur was torn apart by the kraken. Another mast came down, broken halfway, its sail of many internal slats folding up like paper. Citala left Necalli, still swaying, confused, and walked to the railing. The tentacles now contracted, pulled, and Citala watched as the great ship heeled hard over and the sea rushed in over the side, obscuring the creature except for its mighty arms which yet hugged the Sineans in a deadly embrace. Citala closed her eyes and concentrated. She could feel the kraken in her mind, a lumpen angry inchoate voice that cried out with blind rage.

She probed, probed and bid as she did with whales and dolphins, as she had in Ivrea with the mastiff that saved her life. Gently she pushed, trying to penetrate the roiling sense of its primitive mind—telling it to be still, to surrender its anger. That Necalli was safe now. She opened her eyes then drew in a sharp breath as she saw the tentacles release the shattered ship which slowly righted yet listed drunkenly still. And then she froze in horror. A large dark wake, olive green against the blue of the sea, was coming towards them. Larger than the entire ship. She stepped backwards, and into Necalli's arms.

"Citala, what have you done?"

Her mouth moved but words would not come. She had lured it not away but towards them.

Necalli moved to the railing. He raised up both his arms and stood motionless. Citala felt his presence, stronger than ever before, as the ripples of his thoughts touched her and continued out and towards his *ihiyolcatl*. She felt dizzy and reached for the railing, watching the sea foam and bubble as the submerged bulk of the kraken approached. Her head throbbed with the creature's reply, a blurt of questioning emotion. And then, the kraken slowed, its wake dissipating across the azure waters. The black shadow under the surface disappeared and she knew, she felt, the creature return to the depths. Necalli lowered his arms and turned, unsteady on his feet. His head drooped and Citala moved forward to hold him up.

"It heard me," Necalli said, his voice weak and tremulous. "It *heard* me."

"You HAVE TAMED this sea monster?" asked the queen. "It does your bidding?"

Necalli dipped his head. "Your Majesty, it is not as simple as that. It has followed me across the *Mare Meridies*. I can summon it... but controlling it is sometimes a different matter."

Cressida nodded, eyeing the merman with a look that contained more than just admiration. More like studied calculation, thought Danamis. He thought that Necalli's colour was still a paler shade of grey after the kraken's attack, not his normal hue, whatever normal was for a Xosian merman. Out on deck the sound of axe on wood and Gregorvero's bellowing carried through to them in the great stern cabin. For two hours they had drifted, the returned *Grace* roped alongside as repairs were begun. Now that the terror had passed, sailor and soldier alike jabbered like washerwomen about what they had seen. Even now, the great Sinean ship lay floundering, half sunk and drifting a mile away. A ship of death.

Cressida turned on her cushions and looked out the diamond-paned glass. "If they make it back to Perusia, none can say that we were the cause, now can they? A convenient weapon, your kraken." Behind him, Danamis could almost feel Citala's eyes boring into him. Looking over his shoulder, he found he was right. A look of warning. Worry that Cressida was getting ideas.

"I wanted a battle," chirped Sarant. "And a sword."

"There will be others, my prince, rest assured," replied Danamis. The boy was annoying after not even two days and Danamis now wondered how he ever thought the brat was his.

Sarant's mouth rounded in a pout and he turned and climbed onto the bench near the windows to obtain what he hoped would be a better view of the Sineans' final plunge beneath the waves.

"Captain," said Cressida, "is it your intention now to continue to Maresto as planned? It would seem any obstacles have been fortuitously removed."

"We get under way as soon as we hoist the new spar and sail. If the weather holds and the wind follows then we shall make Maresto in a few days." She was either playing regal for the sake of the mer in front of her or else she was changing towards him. He wasn't yet sure. As for Master Necalli, he was still furious that the merman had kept such a deadly secret from him, though he couldn't deny that Necalli had made the difference between death and deliverance. And now he understood his father's insistence that Necalli accompany him.

The Xosians are an ally of Palestro now. Some day you might find out why.

Twenty-Nine

HE WATCHED. WATCHED as he stood surrounded by his smug mercenary commanders, the captain of his ducal guard, and his noble knights. Watched as the griffons of Valdur paused their attack like pack hounds responding to the call of an unseen master. And he had watched as they bounded away for the tree line west of the walls of Livorna, leaving only the sound of cheering from high up on the battlements.

He felt his face flush even as his men, who were gathered behind the protection of straw and wicker bastions, looked one to another, bemused by a retreat in the face of near victory.

What has she done?

And but moments after, his darkness changed to sweet elation when a runner, breathless and wide-eyed, made his way to where he stood. "The canoness! The canoness has captured the High Priest!"

Minutes later he stood at her side in a ragged mud-stained field tent on the edge of the encampment, looking down upon the broken body of Lucius Kodoris. Coronel Aretini and Messere Claudio crammed in from behind, craning to get a view of the High Priest.

Ursino leaned forward cautiously in the miserly lamplight. "How is it that he yet lives?" The body of Kodoris was shattered. He had fallen a great height to end up in a twisted heap in the rough gravel, stones and wild lavender of the ditch below the wall. Torinian soldiers had dragged him out, thinking he was surely dead. But Lucinda had detected breathing—faint as a sleeping newborn's—and Kodoris unconscious but alive was better fortune than she could have hoped for.

Lucinda's gently restrained the Duke from getting too close to the cot. "He is stronger than most of his age. You have a victory my lord. You have the heretic High Priest of the One Faith."

"I have half a victory."

Claudio piped up from the corner of the tent. "Finish him now, my lord. That we may put his head on a spear to show the *Decimali* on the walls. Then they shall know their game is finished."

Lucinda slowly turned and fixed Claudio with a look that would wither corn. "The prisoner is in my charge and I shall decide, with the Duke, what shall befall him. And when. He still has uses."

Claudio scowled and disappeared outside, thrashing the tent flap in anger. Aretini seemed unfazed by the prisoner. "Well, without their High Priest Livorna does not matter," he said, throwing up his hand. "And what happens to this old man isn't important anymore. All the more reason to head south, your Grace."

Lucinda looked up at Ursino and gave him a glance that wordlessly gainsaid Aretini's pronouncement. Ursino turned to Aretini. "The canoness decides Kodoris's fate. If nature doesn't in the meantime."

Lucinda studied Kodoris's face, covered in dried blood, nose and lips swollen black and purple. "See that the High

Priest is not touched or moved from here. No one is to get near him. And set a strong guard on this tent." She knew that the man who was Kodoris was gone, his soul flown. What lay before her was a vessel for Berithas, and he was now trapped inside it like a wasp in a bottle. So long as the body took breath he would remain there and Ursino would be safe from possession. It was the power of Berithas alone that gave this broken old mortal shell the flicker of life.

After all had left, Lucinda watched the old man as his chest rose and fell with shallow irregular breaths. How long he could remain this way she did not know. He might die that night or even wake come the morning. But he would never walk out on his own. For all her devotion, the Redeemer was her prisoner now and she did not regret it. When she joined the Duke in the private chambers of his field pavilion, she found Ursino in a reflective mood, dining in silence. Lucinda tore off the leg from a roasted pheasant, dropped it into her trencher, and wiped her delicate fingers with her napkin. "What is it that vexes you, my love? Have I not delivered to you what I promised? The city's resolve will crumble. It is only a matter of time. Aretini is partly right. Livorna doesn't matter—for now."

Ursino's reply was measured, his voice quiet. "Why does he live still? It is not natural. And more to the point, why do you wish it to be so?"

Lucinda took up her goblet and put it to her lips, sipping the sweet wine. "Because Berithas is there, it is not Kodoris anymore. Do you understand me?"

"I find such a thing difficult to believe, that I will tell you. But what of your desire for Berithas to take form again so that he can... help us. Help *me*."

"My love, fate has been kind to us with this turn. We do not need Berithas if *I* have his power to summon and raise servants of Andras. For the moment, Berithas is trapped.

If he awakens I do not know what he would do. To me...
or to you."

Ursino's hand splayed upon the table. "Did you push him
off the wall?"

"I did not. It was Kodoris who jumped and took his own
life. But now *you* are safe for the moment."

Ursino studied his plate, still piled with meat. "For the
moment, you say. If he wakes, what then? Or if the body
dies. Are you saying that your Redeemer will come for
me?"

She fixed him with a look of dark determination. "I will
not let that happen. We will find another vessel."

Ursino had the look of a man who had just discovered he
had bought a lame horse. He exhaled deeply and scratched
his temple. "And what of the Magister? The young monk
who has caused you great worry. Did you slay him?"

Lucinda shook her head, irritated. "His will is broken.
He is no threat to us anymore."

Ursino slowly pulled his wine towards him. "Let us
hope so. I care little for prattling monks that play at war.
That is for you to deal with." He raised his goblet but
then changed his mind, his fingers playing on the silver
base instead. "But, I tell you, Aretini's counsel is indeed
sound. I received new intelligence even as the griffons were
attacking the gates."

Her hand stretched across the table to touch his. "What
news?"

"The Duchy of Saivona marches east. There is a new
alliance between them, Maresto and Palestro. The city of
Ivrea too, the message says. Calling themselves the Western
League. We must march south tomorrow. Engage Duke
Alonso's army before any aid can come his way to worsen
our odds. And I will need your help. *All* of your help,
infernal or otherwise."

"We shall defeat them all, my love. Each in turn."

Ursino looked into her cornflower blue eyes. "I've given you more than my love, Lucinda. I've handed you my future."

ACQUEL LOOKED AT each of the six wizened men seated before him in the chapter room, the rump of the Grand Curia. He felt ashamed. Ashamed and no better than a mountebank who peddled potions and relics in the market square of Low Town. Bad enough he had not saved the High Priest but what he was about to tell them would go down hard, that he knew full well. Brother Volpe stood at his side. Not especially a great help as the Curia thought little of him or his suspect beliefs. But it made Acquel feel better to have at least one of the brethren who believed in what had to be done.

"Your war has cost the Faith much, Magister," said the First Principal, Brother Dromo. "Brachus, then Magister Lodi, now Kodoris. Do you expect one of us to step up now to be the next sacrifice? Is this the price of our accepting the revelations you have brought forth?"

The words stung him. Volpe had managed to find his belt under the roll of belly at his waist and dug his thumbs in. "This war is all of ours, my brothers," he said, before Acquel could defend himself. "Born of human avarice and lust for power but fostered and spurred by infernal powers. Whether we wish it or not this war is laid at our door and we must act."

Dromo scowled. "So what would you have us do? Elect another High Priest in the midst of this turmoil?"

"No," said Acquel. "I expect that the Curia do nothing until this threat is defeated. That is why I must leave Livorna. You all know what it is that I carry—Saint Elded's will. I must find and destroy the witch of Torinia before she succeeds in destroying the One Faith, and that I cannot do behind these walls."

Dromo laughed. "So now we are without a Magister as well? To be abandoned?"

"The war is moving south," said Acquel. "The Torinians have left but a token force outside the walls and Livorna is in no longer under imminent threat. Lieutenant Poule will stay to lead the defence of the city."

One of the other principals shook his head in disbelief. "So you're leaving a *mercenary* to run things?"

Why had he even bothered to brief the council when he could have just left them to their own pointless deliberations? "The Count is recovering his health as we speak. You may rule the Ara as you see fit. I suggest that you brethren continue…" His mind raced for the right word, his hands flailing. "Continue arguing," he blurted. Volpe sniggered while the principals exploded into righteous anger, fingers wagging and bearded heads bobbling to one another in shared outrage.

"Let's go," said Acquel, tugging at Volpe's robe. "We need to speak to the people that matter."

"I AM LEAVING Livorna, Strykar, and I need you with me." Acquel stood on the barbican battlements, the splintered gate below them trussed with beams and reinforced by cart, bedstead and cupboard dragged from the houses of protesting merchants.

Strykar did not look too surprised. "So who will lead the Ara? You wanted my help in defending this place, and looking out over these walls I still see the camp of the Blue Boar."

Strykar was right—to a point. But the many tents of the enemy, like whitecaps on an imaginary sea on the plain below, had now diminished to just a few. Curls of smoke from a handful of cooking fires coiled lazily up into the sky.

"Their siege is all but done," said Acquel. "They are moving south, to Maresto. You know that."

"If those griffons return, what then? That pile of kindling underneath us won't hold them for long."

Brother Volpe stretched out his legs from his seat on the steps of the tower. "They are not griffons, Coronel Strykar. Any beast with wings as prodigious as theirs ought to fly. By which means they ought to have wiped us from these parapets. They did not."

Strykar turned to Volpe, mildly amused. "So what are they then, a figment of our imaginations? The end result of a jug of bad wine?"

"They are *viverna*—great worms that have slumbered for countless years under the earth. And they lie under an enchantment that gives them the shape of griffons. But these are fell beasts, long banished by Elded. The canoness must have summoned them from the stagnant holes in which they slept. Plenty of those in the forest hills around Rovera, where she's from. Did you not see how their fur seemed to shimmer?"

"He's right." It was Demerise, who had been standing just beyond them, leaning on the far wall of the barbican. "I watched my arrows bounce from their hides, as if they were hard. Not pelts of flesh and fur."

"Scales," said Volpe, nodding.

"And they are now heading for Maresto with the witch that commands them," said Acquel. "And God knows what else she has summoned to aid Ursino. We cannot stop her from here. Maresto must be warned what is coming."

Strykar scratched his cheek, salt and pepper stubble now prominent after a week on the walls. "Aye. Never expected to hear military sense from a monk but I cannot argue with you. You want me to lead you back then? Somehow outflank them back to Maresto?"

"I need more than that. I need the myrra leaf you still hold there."

Strykar's chin fell. "Myrra?"

"It is poison to these creatures, maybe our only means of destroying them."

Strykar laughed. "And how are we to convince them to eat myrra? Stuff a dead goat and present it to them?"

"I don't know," said Acquel, discouraged. "I only know we must try. We can do them little hurt otherwise. And you have not seen the harpies she can invoke. Or the wasps. This myrra gives us a means to fight back. That, and a few tricks that Brother Ugo has up his sleeve."

Strykar rubbed his right eye with the heel of his palm. "Elded's bollocks... even if myrra is the wonder weapon of the saints, well... I do not know if my stash even survives in Maresto."

Volpe turned to look at Acquel.

Acquel stuttered. "It's... it's gone?"

"Well, most of it was... distilled. Makes a very good *acqua vitalis*. But far more potent."

Acquel turned to Volpe who in turn shrugged. "Distillation? Could make it stronger against them," said the old monk.

"Look," said Strykar. "I will give you the myrra, or the *acqua miracula* if the apothecary hasn't drunk or sold it all. But we have to cover a hundred miles to get there with the Blue Boar, White Company, the Sables—God knows what else—between us and Maresto."

Acquel nodded. "I know that. We will have to travel light and fast. Find horses, maybe change them along the way."

Strykar smiled and shook his head. "Sweet Aloysius. I've seen you ride before. And who's carrying the venerable Volpe?"

"You're a Coronel of the Black Rose," said Acquel quietly. "You'll get us there."

"Shit, you reckon that, do you?" He paused. "That still leaves the question of who will stay on to defend this place?"

Strykar saw Lieutenant Poule making his way towards them along the walkway from the western side of the walls. He joined them, harness a-jangle and a half-eaten brown fig in his right hand. "Coronel! All quiet on the wall. Most of the Boar has well and truly buggered off. No more than a few hundred left."

"Poule. You're promoted to captain. And as of tomorrow you're leading the defence of Livorna." Poule stopped, jaw slack, and looked around at the others not knowing what to say. "Hell, if you succeed at that they might even make you the next High Priest," added Strykar.

Poule stuck out his lower lip as he contemplated the possibilities. "If there's pay in it then count me in."

"Can we leave in the morning? Or do we travel by night?" asked Acquel.

"We'll be doing both, Magister. If you want to get there at all."

Acquel gave a weak smile. "Thank you, Strykar." He gestured to Volpe whose knees cracked audibly as he rose, dusting off his bottom. "Let me know what you need of me, Strykar. We'll be ready."

Volpe looked behind as he reached the barbican steps with Acquel. "And I do know how to ride, Coronel Strykar."

"Not worried about you riding, Brother Ugo," said Strykar. "Just worried about you falling off."

Poule watched the monks depart and took another bite of his fig. "You're leading them back to Maresto? Now? Holy hell!"

Strykar didn't answer. He shuffled over to the wall and rested his elbows on the ledge of the embrasure, looking out onto what remained of the enemy camp. Demerise moved beside him.

"You're afraid to go back, aren't you? To face the Black Rose after what's happened. And your brother."

"Maybe."

"But they probably think you're dead. It was you that saved Livorna, they will learn that."

Strykar turned and gave her a tired, thin smile. "It was you that saved Livorna, mistress."

"And it was you that saved me, right here where we stand."

Strykar looked out again over the plain and the lonely stands of ancient twisted olive trees. "I need you with me. You know the ways south off the main road. And I need bowmen who can actually hit something if we run into brigands or scouts from Aretini. I don't know if I can beat the enemy to Maresto. In time, or at all."

She did not answer for what to Strykar seemed an eternity. "I do not like this killing. Nor do my men. Bero has told me he still sees the ones he shot, up close here on the wall. It is one thing to kill an animal, another to slay a man."

"What do you think would have happened to the folk in this town had the enemy breached us? To the women. The children. This isn't just about a duke who wants to grab a crown, it's a fight against the goddamned Devil himself. "

She nodded. "That is why I stayed. And to safeguard my honour, my oath to the crown."

He reached over and grasped her wrist. "It will all happen again, in Maresto. Unless the holy men stop this sorceress who leads Ursino around by his nose. I do not understand all of the things they say. This *magicking* they do. But I believe it."

She stayed silent.

"It was my damned prideful arrogance that undid the Black Rose. At the Taro. I cannot undo that until I help defeat Ursino, if I can save the crown, save Maresto…" He squeezed her wrist and turned her to him. "I need your help to get us back. I want you with me."

She pulled away her scarf, revealing the sad ruin of her face. "Even if it comes with this, Messere Julianus?"

His hand touched her fairer side, gently cupping her cheek before falling away. "Mistress Demerise, of all the women I have met in my miserable life, I would follow you to the gates of Hell itself."

Demerise looked into his eyes but her voice betrayed no emotion. "Well then, sir. What am I to say to that?"

"Say you know a way south, and that you will take us by it."

She nodded and began to wrap the scarf around her face. But Strykar gently pulled it down so it lay around her shoulders. "You don't need that anymore. Not with me."

Poule, still standing behind them, raised what little eyebrows his scarred forehead still possessed and reached into his pocket for another fig.

Thirty

THE RECEIVING CHAMBER of the Duke of Maresto was a swirl of glorious silks and brocades: nobles, soldiers, officials and the servitors who scrambled among them, the latter clothed in bright red livery of the finest Maresto wool. Three of the Duke's favourite lurchers quietly threaded their way through the throng, snapping up morsels that had fallen on the vermillion tiled floor. It was a long chamber, high-ceilinged and ornate, decorated in terracotta, black and gold. At one end was Alonso, resplendent in his velvet *cioppa* and golden chain of rank, a feathered hat of the blackest silk tilting over one ear. He was stepping down from the dais that held his ducal throne, palm extended to take the dainty hand of Cressida, dowager queen of Valdur.

Some way down the *salla*, somewhat behind the ambassadors from Saivona but not as far down as the guild masters of Maresto, Danamis stood watching the pageant, Citala at his side. He noticed that they had given them a wide berth, those around them uncomfortable with such an exotic creature in their midst. Danamis looked at her and thought her most beautiful while those that gawped he reckoned as base fools, chained by superstition and poisoned by tall tales. Alonso had by now conducted the queen to his throne, vacated for her, while the young crown prince bounded up onto the dais to seat himself in the smaller gilt chair placed there just for him.

A blast from the herald silenced the burble of the court and Alonso, still standing, addressed them. "We give thanks for the safe arrival of her Majesty and our noble prince, Sarant!" There was spontaneous applause and scattered cries of "*Vivat!*" Cressida inclined her head to accept the acclaim. "We go to war in the coming days, to face a foe both arrogant and overconfident. A would-be usurper!" There were growls and groans of outrage and Alonso held up his hand. "But we in Maresto are not alone. Our new league unites us—Saivona, Ivrea, and Palestro. And more than this, our prince will join me in battle, at my side as we throw back Torinia. And this I swear to you all, his Highness will be not a year older before we are standing in Torinia itself!" More applause and Danamis watched as the boy on his throne smirked and nodded to the crowd.

Cressida sat back, head high, looking regal. After Alonso had made his address, she joined him at the foot of the dais as the noblemen converged like needles to a lodestone, all seeking notice from the queen and the Duke. Danamis watched as twenty halberdiers took up positions cordoning what had become a more intimate reception separate from everyone else further down the hall. Danamis noticed quickly that Alonso's face transformed each time his eyes fell upon the queen. A look of more than admiration. No one could fail to see that he was smitten by her. Once more, it looked to his eyes that Cressida was returning the fascination.

A bumptious merchant in a rich wine velvet cloak jostled him as the fellow struggled to move closer to the inner sanctum, the fount of patronage. He had to admit to himself he was hurt by it all. Hurt by the fact that she had not thanked him, though it was he who had liberated her from Perusia. Hurt that he had seemingly been denied a place at the top even though he was still the senior representative from Palestro this day. Somehow, he was now on the outside looking in and the fires of resentment kindled to life in his breast. He turned to glance at Citala and found her looking at him with such a sad indulgent smile that he realized his face had betrayed his emotions. He swallowed and reached for her hand.

"Come, it's time we found Strykar somewhere in the central courtyard as he bid. I long to see that ugly face of his again after so long."

She lifted his arm and entwined it around her own. "We may walk among them but we are not of them," she said quietly, her large almond-shaped eyes holding his. "You have done your duty to your queen."

He strove to crack a smile for her. "Am I so plain to read?"

Danamis cut a path towards the double doors of the *salla* and guided Citala down the wide marble staircase to the ground floor and the sprawling courtyard that was encompassed by a seemingly never-ending loggia of sculpted arches. It was filled by armoured men of the ducal guard as well as hangers-on, but Danamis spotted the old mercenary straight away in the southwest corner—and he was not alone. A tall fellow, another of the Black Rose he assumed, dressed in boots and hose with a leather doublet and long cloak and hood. He saw Strykar open his arms wide and Danamis's heart lifted as the mercenary enveloped him in a bear hug.

"The sea dog returns!" Strykar laughed, patting Danamis hard on both shoulders. "And with the beautiful Citala at his side!"

"Seems you've been busy since last we met, old friend. Brawling by the looks of you."

"Worse than that, Danamis. And I shall tell you more over a jug this evening." Strykar turned and gestured towards the figure who stood a few paces behind. "This is Mistress Demerise, a king's Forester in Maresto."

Demerise threw back her hood and bowed her head smartly. Danamis returned the greeting, barely concealing his look of astonishment. "Mistress Demerise, Nicolo Danamis at your service," he said. He looked at Strykar. "A holder of the royal warrant and somehow in league with you? That begs a story as well, Strykar."

"One you shall soon hear. It concerns Livorna and our mutual acquaintance, the monk. It is not altogether a tale to raise your spirits."

Danamis scowled. "That sounds ominous coming from you." He extended his hand to Citala and brought her forward. "Mistress Demerise, this is Citala, daughter of the chief of the merfolk of Valdur. My consort." Citala pulled back her hood, revealing her snow white locks. She inclined her head, curious about this female who dressed as a man and who bore upon her face proof of some terrible fate.

Demerise bowed. "I have heard much of your kind, my lady."

"For better or worse, mistress? We are much maligned these days."

"Have no fear on that account. I am *Decimali* and follow the new commandments of the Saint."

"Then I welcome you as a friend," said Citala, her violet eyes shining.

"Good," said Strykar. "Now that we're all friends you both must come with me. I have something to show you."

"What are you on about, Strykar?" said Danamis. "Something here at the palace?"

"No," replied Strykar, his voice low. "Beyond the town walls. And we have little time. I shall tell you the whole story as we walk."

"More conspiracies? I just managed to get out of one in Perusia with my skin intact."

Strykar fixed Danamis with a heavy look. "Danamis, I am now the black sheep of the Black Rose. But I've been given a chance by the Duke to win back my honour. And I will need your help."

He told them of the battle near the Taro River, the arrival of the griffons, his capture and his humiliation. And how through his own overconfidence a third of the Black Rose expedition had been lost. He told them of his escape, of how Demerise and her band found him, and how Livorna was saved. Danamis had guessed that Torinia was bearing down on Maresto but he had no idea just how bad the situation was. Nor had he known what kind of infernal powers had joined forces with Duke Ursino. He knew that Julianus Strykar was not inclined to exaggerate. What was bearing down from the north was a mortal threat.

The four of them looked a strange sight as they negotiated the warren of streets and made for the north gate: a dark nobleman in fine clothes, a soldier in half armour and black cloak, and two figures equally tall that defied description. Those merchants that caught a lingering glimpse even lost their bartering patter, necks craning, as the party swept by them at a rapid pace.

Danamis gestured to interrupt Strykar as they neared a massive gatehouse, under heavy guard by the militia. "So again... why are we paying visit to a *painter* for the court?"

They all pressed against the wall of the stone tunnel as a great laden oxcart came through, its wheels liberally spraying road muck. "He is more than a painter. My brother swears by his skills, he's actually a craftsman of sorts. He thinks of useful things and then builds them."

"Strykar, you sound like you've lost your wits."

"What he makes are war engines. My brother has commissioned him."

"*Half*-brother."

"Yes, goddamn it, my half-brother."

"Sounds like he's just trying to get rid of you since you cocked things up out in the field."

Strykar swore under his breath. "I had expected more in the way of support from the few friends I have left."

Danamis raised his eyebrows and nodded towards Demerise who was furthest behind, bringing up the rear. "What's all this then?" he whispered. "A *woman*, Strykar?"

The mercenary gritted his teeth. "Later... if I don't end up throttling you beforehand."

Strykar led them to a sprawling wooden lean-to built against the town walls, a workshop scattered with timber beams and uncut marble slabs. Beyond the workshop there was a great tent-like structure built from what Danamis instantly recognized as canvas mainsails, all roped and pegged to protect—or disguise from prying eyes—what lay behind. Strykar pulled back a flap. "As a man of the sea you might appreciate this."

They entered. Danamis took a step then stopped, his eyes grown large. "What the hell is it?"

Strykar folded his arms across his broad chest. "It is a land ship. Impervious to attack."

Danamis still wasn't quite sure what was in front of him. It was a wooden war engine of some sort, maybe a siege machine, but its shape was, of all things, circular. It was like two enormous deep platters, one placed inverted on top of the other. He could make out what appeared to be square ports at different points along the outside. The machine was completely round with seemingly no front or back. It sat close to the ground, perhaps two feet above, and Danamis bent down to try and look at the underside. Wheels. Four enormous wheels were holding the craft up. He stood back and shook his head. The engine had to be at least forty feet wide and nearly as high.

Workmen in short tunics, carrying bits of timber and tools, paid them no heed as they went about their tasks, disappearing underneath the wooden contraption. A voice bellowed out from somewhere on the other side of the land ship. "Halloo! Messere Strykar!"

A short, wiry, grey-bearded man emerged from around one side. He had crows' feet deep as road ruts and a beard that nearly reached to his navel. The man had hiked up his tunic into his belt, revealing two pale bandy legs, his green hose sagging unceremoniously around his ankles. Sweating profusely from his exertions, his right hand still clenched what appeared to be a wood auger for boring holes.

Strykar smiled. "Master Elanordo, this is an old ally of Maresto, Captain Nicolo Danamis."

The old man pointed a bony forefinger. "Ah, the admiral of Palestro. I seem to remember your father turned me out when I was a younger man. Didn't like the painting I did for him. Never paid me for it either."

"Valerian Danamis never was much of a patron of art," said Danamis. "But he might have changed his mind had he seen... this."

Elanordo grinned. "I expect you'd like to have a look inside. That is the true marvel." They followed him around to the other side as he jabbered away about his creation. "This is a wooden tortoise with some bite, my friends!"

Large double doors were cut into the machine, fixed by strong iron hinges. They hardly had to stoop to enter. A round hole in the top of the land ship let in light and Danamis's trained sailor's eye took in the details. A raised platform ran around the circumference of the structure and he counted six hinged ports. Two great wheels, which he was convinced were modified water wheels wide and flat, were mounted amidships. The whole structure seemed to sit on uprights and lateral beams tied into the wheel-boxes. Two smaller wheels taken from gun carriages were fore and aft to balance the machine. There was no floor. Enormous cogs like the inside of a clock were mounted higher up on the platform. Elanordo whistled to two of his workmen who were working on the hatches. "Giorgio! Give the visitors a demonstration of the traverse." The workmen moved to the largest of the toothed cogs and grasped a long handle as they stood side by side. Slowly and with effort they pushed it, cranking it. It thumped as each peg moved around interlocking with a matching wheel. The entire top of the structure, platform and tent-like roof, began to rotate around. Another workmen pulled a rope and one of the hatches opened upwards and inwards. And Danamis knew at once this was a firing platform. A fortress on wheels. If the beasts of the witch were as big as Strykar had told, crushing men like ants, then he understood why Strykar had taken to the land ship.

Citala threw Danamis a look of complete bafflement but Demerise had already clambered up to the platform to walk around it, her tall frame stooping as she did so.

"It is moved by a few oxen placed here between the wheels, plus a bit of muscle from the crew when it's needed," said Strykar gesturing. "Crewed by as many as you can fit in. Gunners and archers. You hear that, Demerise!"

The huntress turned to him, her voice measured and assured. "I made you no promises, Strykar."

Danamis ran his hand over a cog, sanded smooth and newly oiled. "So where are the guns?"

Strykar smiled and nodded at him. "That is where you come in, my friend."

BROTHER VOLPE, PARTIAL to brewing an elixir or a tincture himself, beheld the apothecary's work table with envious eyes. He picked up a long clear glass vessel and sniffed. A solution of agrimony, a plant difficult to come by these days this far south.

"Brother Volpe, I would ask you again, sir, not to touch anything." The apothecary scuttled around from the far side of the table and gently retrieved the glassware from out of Volpe's pudgy hand. "If you insist on this then I will have to ask you to wait outside." Volpe harrumphed and moved away.

"Coronel Strykar has told you what we require," said Acquel. "I would ask that you deliver it up to us that we may leave you in peace."

The apothecary grimaced. "But he has not explained why you need *all* of it. And you do understand that the Duke's men have put it under a tax so punitive as to make it dear as gold?"

"We're not selling it. Or buying it."

"The Coronel wasn't specific about whether I was to hand over the leaves or the elixir," the apothecary protested.

"Both," said Volpe, relishing his authority from Strykar. The apothecary sighed. "Well, that is a shame. I was going to distil the last of the leaf this very week. But the lord Strykar is the one who calls the tune and I may but only dance to it." He guided them further into the recesses of the cramped shop. There was a dusty cabinet of blackwood at the very back and from this he pulled forth a linen sack of no great size. "Here is the last of the myrra leaf. I pray to the saints that Messere Strykar is granted the good fortune to bring back more."

Acquel took the sack from him. It weighed almost nothing. He pulled forth a leaf, bright green even in the dim light of the room and put it to his nose.

"It is myrra," said the apothecary, annoyed. "The very last few handfuls."

"And the elixir?"

The little man turned, bumped into Volpe, and mumbled as he made his way over to another cabinet. He fumbled for his ring of keys and opened a locked cupboard at the top. He brought forth three flat bottomed leather flasks each the size of a large wine goblet. They were stoppered with a cork and chain. "Here you are Brother Acquel, the very last ounces of it. *Acqua miracula.*" The little cupboard door squeaked as he began to close it. Acquel passed two of the flasks to Volpe then leaned over and stared into the apothecary's froglike eyes.

"All of it, sir? Or will I need to return with a few *rondelieri* to make a thorough search."

The man blinked a few times and reached again for the cupboard. He pulled out a silver pocket flask and reluctantly offered it up. "My personal supply," he said, giving a disingenuous smile. "Offered up for the cause."

Acquel nodded and took it from his hand.

"But you have still not told me, nor did the Coronel, why the Temple Majoris has need of this mixture. I mean, it is, after all, his property. However, I am the one who distilled it. Is it so important to the One Faith?"

"It is a cure for many ills," said Volpe. "Both big and small."

Outside, Volpe gently tucked the three flasks into his own satchel, making sure each stopper was firmly seated. Acquel hefted the linen sack of leaf. "Do you reckon we will have enough to do what is needed?"

Volpe looked tired. "Brother Acquel, we are both now deep into terra incognita. We must pray that Elded is still our guide."

IT WAS DARK when they returned to the villa attached to the great temple of Maresto. Acquel was flagging, still exhausted by the wild ride down from Livorna nearly two days gone by. The High Prelate had given them rooms, asking few questions of their mission, trusting in Acquel's high office as Magister of the Ara. Volpe thought the fewer details given the better but Acquel knew this only raised more concern in the Prelate.

Volpe's eyes fell to the sack that Acquel carried. "I'm going to find a drop of wine in this place. Are you coming, brother?"

Acquel shook his head. "I am off to bed. Strykar wants us down at the harbour with the myrra after dawn. So don't get over-friendly with the bottle, brother."

Ugo scowled. "Give me the benefit of knowing my limits with the noble grape."

Acquel closed the door to his chamber and set the precious sack down on the floor next to his bed. He threw off his cassock and fell onto the narrow mattress and pulled up the coverlet. He was asleep almost as soon as he drew up his legs, huddled, fatigue dragging him down into blissful oblivion.

His sleeping mind took him on several journeys, into his past and his present. And then he found himself standing in a sun-blazed meadow of high summer, filled with wildflowers. The sky shone an almost unnatural shade of ultramarine, unblemished by cloud. It was glorious and he knew immediately this was no ordinary dream.

He turned and saw her. She was standing six feet away from him, long blonde hair falling about her slim bare shoulders, a white gown that was high-waisted with full sleeves bedecked in red ribbons. Lucinda della Rovera, fallen canoness of Saint Dionei, regarded him with gentle curiosity.

After all that had befallen him in the past year, he had never truly spoken with her, their few encounters always too brief and bloody for conversation. She smiled at him. "Brother Acquel, the one who struggles so hard for so little."

He wasn't fearful. She was in his mind but not probing him. She was toying, studying him. "You have found me, murderess, so speak your piece while you may." Her face glowed with unearthly beauty: high, rosy cheeks and perfect lips, her eyes almost matching the vivid sky.

She crossed her hands over her belly. "We are coming for you, Magister. The forces of the rightful ruler of Valdur who is aided by Berithas and the true faith of this land. You will not prevail in the coming days. You know that, don't you? In your heart." She delivered the last with a voice of almost tender concern.

At that moment, Acquel felt a great weight upon him, with a determined grimness to match it. He knew he was dreaming but somehow not dreaming. "Your demons will not save you or your usurping Duke. I will seek you out and deliver the justice of Elded and the true saints."

She laughed lightly and looked down her nose at him. "Really? Brother Acquel you have misplaced your faith and you squander your bravery. Elded will not save you or the Ara. You're running out of High Priests."

Now and only now he felt her inside his mind and he pushed back, casting her off. "Why?" he asked. "I want to know why. Why all of this?"

He saw her brow crease at his words and she seemed to struggle for a reply. Suddenly, her perfect features relaxed. "*Why* you ask me? Let me tell you a story, Brother Acquel." She floated towards him until they were but a pace apart.

Her pale skin seemed to shimmer. "When my mother was delivered of her last child a fever took hold of her. As I watched her sink closer to death, Lavinia and I prayed upon our knees. We beseeched the Lord to save her. I begged the sky god, *your* god; offered my life instead of hers. For two days. He did not deign to answer my prayers."

Acquel watched her eyes look beyond him and into her own past. A small smile came to her lips. "But Berithas heard me. He came to me and promised help, if we would serve Him... and if he could have the babe. My mother lived and the child was taken."

Acquel felt a deep chill flow through him.

Lucinda nodded. "I saved her, through Berithas." Her eyes moved again to focus on Acquel. "But my father found out my secret, later, months later. When he caught me at my prayers. Told my mother, he did. They beat me for a sorceress, an unholy witch they said. He would have turned me over to the elders to have me condemned and burned." Her eyes bored into him as another smile spread upon her face. "But Berithas saved me... He took them too." She gave a girlish shrug. "I have been chosen. As you have."

Acquel could almost feel his blood freeze in his veins. "You have chosen emptiness and death, Lucinda. Over life and hope."

She raised her head, her chin as sharp as her tongue. "I might say the same of you if you wish to prattle about motives. It will change nothing. Can you not feel it on the wind? The old gods are returning. Berithas leads them to Valdur once again." Her eyes flared and he felt a stabbing in his chest. "There is nothing you can devise to stop what is coming. Bow down while you can."

Acquel summoned all his will and silently invoked Elded. He felt her recede, as if her icy hands had slipped away from his body. He stared back at her image. "Look into your own heart. They are not gods. And they will fail you in the end—just as they failed your poor sister, Lavinia. Have you forgotten her?"

Her eyes narrowed. She seemed to hesitate before recovering with more bluster. "We will meet soon, Brother Acquel. And your blood will then nourish the great tree under the Ara. What marvellous fruit it will bear!"

Her last words seemed to echo around him and he felt himself falling into blackness. He gasped and sat up, face and chest slick with sweat. The lone candlestick near his bed still burned. He lay back and let his head sink into his pillow. It was she who had pushed him away and broken their contact. Then he prayed, prayed fervently that he had shielded from her his knowledge of the myrra and the guns that would deliver it straight into the bellies of the beasts of Berithas.

Thirty-One

As THE GULLS screamed overhead, Gregorvero's voice boomed out over the *Vendetta*'s main deck. "Watch out there! You, keep both hands on that line. That gun is worth more than all your miserable hides."

The orichalcum cannon swung drunkenly out over the quay, suspended from the boom of a braced crane on the dock. The seamen managed to steady the copper-coloured piece, lowering it until it made contact with the flatbed cart to join its mate already bedded down. Danamis stood silently, watching from the long quarterdeck, arms folded, as two of his precious guns were offloaded. He turned to Strykar standing next to him, equally grim-faced. "That makes four, as you asked." Two hours earlier, he had had to shout down Bassinio on the *Royal Grace* when he demanded that two cannon be taken off his deck for Strykar's mad scheme. And to hear his own doubts thrown at him from the mouth of Bassinio was hard to bear. True, he still had four guns (and the *Grace* the same) but should Torinia mount an attack by sea he would need everything he had.

Maresto harbour was practically an open invitation to attack with but one long mole virtually undefended and no towers or chains. He had decided that he would anchor both *Vendetta* and *Grace* end to end at the mouth of the harbour to form a floating battlement. It was the best he could do to honour his promise to the Duke but he prayed that he had intimidated the rag-tag Torinian fleet enough to keep it in its port. If he was right, it looked as if the battle for Maresto would be a landward one and he would be but a distant onlooker.

"Thank you, brother," said Strykar. "It will give us the chance we need and God knows we have precious few of those."

"Did that lickspittle Malvolio strip you of your command yet?"

Strykar grumbled. "No, not exactly. But now Captain Cortese commands the *rondelieri*, the spearmen, and the horse. I've been afforded *this* unique opportunity to show my prowess instead. Sure my brother twisted his arm on that."

"Half brother."

"On that horse again are you? Well, at least he knows damn well I've fought on land and at sea—with you. Who better to fight and command a ship on wheels?"

"It's likely to be slow as a snail under the weight of those guns. If the ground is muddy…" Danamis shook his head.

"Aye. It's a fool's gamble, I know that. But I've seen those beasts that the witch brings with her. We need to take the fight to them, not wait and be slashed to ribbons as we stand. Your guns—and the stuff that the monks are brewing below us as we speak—is the only thing that we've got to do them hurt."

Danamis threw an arm around Strykar's shoulders. "I can think of no better fool than you to show them how it is done."

Strykar nodded. "If it works it may make a Temple-goer of me yet."

Across the length of the ship from up on the fo'c'sle, Citala and Demerise watched the old friends converse. "You have much regard for Coronel Strykar, don't you?" said Citala.

Demerise looked to the mer princess at her side, her equal in stature. "I do."

"You have followed him here even though you are no soldier or mercenary."

Demerise gave an awkward smile. "I could say the same for you... and Captain Danamis."

Embarrassed, Citala lowered her gaze.

"Messere Strykar," said Demerise, "is the first man who has ever asked for my help, or valued me for something other than bringing game to the feast table."

"You have an understanding... as I do, with Danamis."

"It is clear that you are lovers. I see it in both of you, when you speak."

Citala had known her for but two days but she had found that they shared much—including a certain bluntness of speech. She gave a slow nod. "I do love him, though that is a risk for both of us. And I sense something more than respect in your regard for Strykar."

Demerise's open hand smoothed down the black scarf that wound about her neck, buffeted by the strong breeze that blew across the ship. "We share things too. My scars I wear on the outside, his are on the inside."

In the gloom of the ship's hold, another altogether different labour was under way. Near the cramped quarters that contained the *Vendetta*'s tiny brick forge, Acquel steadied an iron cannonball, the sixth thus far, as master gunner Tadeo Verano bored the soft lead with a screw auger. "Brother Ugo," said Verano, his face muscles tight with the exertion, "I cannot guarantee these won't disintegrate upon firing. Never drilled out shot like this."

Volpe, who was crushing more myrra leaf with mortar and pestle by the flickering light of a lantern, wiped the beads of sweat from his lip with his sleeve. "So long as it does not explode the gun, I am willing to take that chance. Even a spray of iron should give those cursed *viverna* something to worry about."

"There, that is deep enough," said Verano. "Are you ready, brother?"

Volpe scooped up a glob of myrra paste in his fingers and leaned over the rough-cast iron. He pushed the mixture into the hole and tamped it down, adding more as Acquel straddled the cannonball between his legs. He then reached for a fat tallow candle that perched on a bench next to him and tipped it over the hole, dripping wax until it had sealed the opening. He looked up at Acquel smiled. "Why so glum, brother? Our arsenal grows."

Acquel's reply was almost a whisper. "What if the *mantichora* lied to us?"

Volpe leaned back on his haunches, knees cracking loudly. "So that's what's bothering you then. Here, Master Tadeo, fetch us another round to drill if you please, I have enough myrra for three more shot."

Verano shrugged and grunted. "My guns on their own should blow any griffon back to hell, magic potion or not. These are orichalcum! But please yourself."

Volpe tugged at Acquel's sleeve. "Here now, boy! Now is not the time to doubt our purpose. *Mantichora* relish showing how much they know—and they always keep their word, leastways that is what I know of them. That creature was no different."

"The Saint has not spoken to me. Nor shown me visions. But our enemies benefit from signs and powers from the other side. Does not Elded and the Lord want us to defeat Berithas?" He set the cannonball down with the others in a wooden crate. "I am so low, Ugo. I almost can't see a way out."

Volpe sat, rubbed his knees, and sighed. "Let me tell you a story, of the last Dukes' war. I was newly ordained—a greyrobe as you were—at Astilona. The Order was young but our monks were good swordsmen, competent men, and the Duke of Saivona honoured us by placing us in the vanguard against Torinia. When battle was joined on the plain, we found we were outnumbered. The fight was bloody, started to go badly—after one hour it was looking bleak for us all."

"But you're here to tell the tale, so you won."

Volpe put a forefinger by his nose. "Aye, I survived. But at the turning point, standing on the edge of defeat, twenty-five of the brethren decided to call upon Elded to intervene. They knelt in fervent prayer, right there on the field, steel and death a whirlwind around them."

Acquel listened with increasing interest. "Holy intercession? Did they succeed?"

Volpe snorted. "Succeed? They were cut down to a man where they knelt. The rest of us fought like devils until Saivonan horsemen drove off the enemy. I learned that day that God helps those who help themselves."

Tadeo Verano stepped between them and thumped down another cannonball on the planks. "Enough tall tales, holy men, here's another waiting for your magic."

ON DECK, ONE of the crew gave a long shrill whistle and Danamis and Strykar both looked out to the piazza to see a large armed party of halberdiers approaching, a palanquin trailing them drawn by liveried attendants. Danamis wiped his palm over his brow. "For the love of the saints, why she's made a game of surprising me like this I don't know."

Strykar made a rumbling sound. "Well, they're the Duke's men. They could be here to arrest me for all you know."

Danamis shook his head. "It's got to be both of them. I'd better go down."

"Think I'll stay up here. Holler if you need me."

Danamis pounded across the gangplank to the stone quay. The fifty-strong guard fanned out while the red and gold brocade palanquin was gently set down a short distance from the ship. He glanced down at himself and yanked his short linen tunic down over his loins and adjusted his belt, pouch and dagger. Sure enough, as the curtain was pulled away on the palanquin, out jumped Alonso who brushed off the attempted aid of his footmen. He turned back and extended his elegant, velvet clad arm to the other occupant.

Cressida emerged, shining as brightly as the sun overhead, dressed in a flowing silk dress the colour of saffron, her pearls and earrings brighter still. Danamis cleared his throat and moved to meet them as they approached, hand in hand. He halted at a good distance and swept off his black felt cap before bowing deeply. "My Queen, your Grace!" Those sailors on deck and working on the quay followed their captain's example and went down on one knee. Strykar cursed under his breath and followed suit.

"Admiral, rise, please!" said Alonso, grinning broadly. "We know we have interrupted you in your preparations. I apologise."

Danamis stood and replaced his cap. Although he was loath to ask, he had to. "How may I be of service?"

"I wanted to make sure you have what you need to defend the port," said the Duke, still grinning. "My men are at your disposal if you give the word."

"That is appreciated, your Grace. But unless we are overrun at the end of the mole, I am confident we can beat back any attack." He wanted to add *unless it is the Sinean fleet* but thought that inopportune.

"Excellent! I see Coronel Strykar is managing the transfer of some of your ordnance, as arranged. Master Elanordo informs me the land ship is ready to receive and mount the guns. But I first must redress a wrong, for I..." and he extended an open hand towards Cressida, "*we*... have not sufficiently thanked you for bringing the queen and the prince safely to Maresto. And for staying to guard the city when I know you must be concerned for Palestro itself."

Up on the quarterdeck, Gregorvero had sidled up to Strykar. "What's he so cheerful about?" he whispered. "What with the combined armies of two duchies about to knock at his gates."

Strykar harrumphed and whispered back, "Can't you see? The poor fool's in love."

Gregorvero blinked and stuck out his lower lip.

Danamis had just completed another bow and doffing of his cap. "To serve the throne is my joy as well as my duty."

"Well spoken," said Alonso, nodding appreciatively. Cressida released the Duke's hand and took a step forward.

"Alonso is right in giving thanks, but this falls to me as well, Admiral."

From the slash in her voluminous sleeve she pulled out a pendant jewel on a golden chain. The emerald, a hue of moss green and the size of a large almond, caught the midday sun and it dazzled, sparkling white. Her delicate fingers undid the clasp and she moved closer to Danamis, reaching up around his neck. "I ask you to accept this token of my personal thanks." Alonso took a few steps backwards, hands clasped, and watched as Cressida fastened the jewel around Danamis's neck. Danamis felt more than awkward and could almost feel Citala's eyes boring into his back from her vantage up on deck.

Then Cressida leaned in towards him and spoke so that only he could hear her words. He could feel her warm breath on his ear. "If the battle goes ill and Alonso falls, you must get the prince and me out of Maresto. I am depending upon you, Nicolo."

Danamis gave a slow, almost imperceptible nod.

She paused a moment, then leaned in again close, her lips brushing his earlobe. "Sarant... he *is* your son."

Thirty-Two

DAUGHTER, DAUGHTER...

Lucinda could hear him, a voice as if it came from the bottom of a deep well, drifting and disembodied. She was near the wagon where Kodoris lay on his mattress, a canvas tilt over it to protect from prying eyes and the elements. She had to be this near to hear Berithas at all, calling out, trapped inside a dying old man.

The army was camped on both sides of the main road to Maresto and now so close that she could smell the tang of the sea upon the night breeze. She reached and lifted the edge of the canvas. What was once the High Priest of Livorna lay there as he had for four days, motionless, breathing as lightly as a sparrow. And for all her cunning, Lucinda della Rovera did not quite know what she was to do once that mortal husk succumbed, releasing the Redeemer again. Even now she was amazed that she held the powers gifted to her. The *viverna* shadowed her like loyal hounds, keeping to the edge of forest or copse as the army moved south. They feasted upon cattle from the homesteads and villas abandoned at the approach of the Torinian host. The Blue Boar and the White Company gave the creatures a wide berth and the troops of

Federigo, Count of Naplona, distrusted them such that they would march only on the far flank.

Daughter, release…

Still distant, she thought, but more insistent than before. She dropped the flap and retreated to the edge of camp, the snarling and deep bass rumblings of the great worms sounding from the forest clearing where they dozed, not far away. She was worried despite the quiet confidence of the force that surrounded her. Her gift of the Farsight remained intact, but that afforded little against an enemy she could not seem to control—the young monk. An *arrogant* young monk now, she thought, daring to question her motives and her faith. But what caused her wakefulness, her wanderings in the dead of night, was the fear of what Berithas would do when he did obtain release. Would he blame her? Would he know she had worked to save Ursino from him? Would he destroy her?

"Here you are, my lady."

Ursino emerged from the forest of tents clad in a red *cioppa* and barefoot, two bodyguards close behind bearing torches. He smiled at her and she thought he looked ghastly in the harshness of the flames. He had eaten little in the past two days but she could smell the wine fumes from him as he approached and took her arm. "My bed felt cold and then I saw you were gone. Are you unwell?"

"I think better in the quiet of the night… and the darkness. Nothing more."

Ursino turned to his soldiers. "Wait here." He took Lucinda by her hand and walked her further out from the edge of camp and under the canopy of ancient trees. The darkness increased. He folded her into his arms, pressed her frame to his chest and kissed her neck. She closed her eyes and, for a moment, let herself fall into him, returning his embrace and pushing her worries from her mind.

"All will be well," she whispered into his ear. "The stars align for us, my love, and you will prevail."

He relaxed his embrace and stroked her face. "Much could yet go wrong, but I have you."

"The beasts are sworn to serve me. When the time is right."

"We saw scouts from Maresto today, they know we are here, they know our numbers."

Lucinda smiled. "But you know how many soldiers they have behind their walls. And you know that Saivona's army is still many miles from here, making little progress. Because I have seen it."

Ursino let out a small sigh. "Would that I had the power to use your little mirror…"

"You need not with me at your side. It is for you to lead your men, to rule as the uncrowned king."

"So much to… to decide. It fills my head in all my waking hours, around and around."

She placed both hands on his cheeks. "You *will* be king of Valdur. Maresto will fall and the others will follow. Will you do as I ask and command the battle from the rearguard, in the *carroccio*? I will be able to seek you out there upon the field when all is chaos."

"You know I desire the vanguard, that's where a duke who's fighting to be king belongs. But, I will heed your counsel. I've decided that the Count of Naplona will treat with Maresto in my stead. He knows what an honour that is. And the Boar will take the lead—the sharpest point of my spear."

She laid her head on his chest and he stroked her hair. "We should return now," he said, "else my guards will think you've devoured me."

She lifted her head and gave a quiet laugh. And then she remembered. "Ursino, promise me… promise me you will not venture near the High Priest."

"What? The old man is barely alive, what is there to fear of him? But if he recovers, then we might make use of him, if he should renounce the *Decimali* heresy or declare me rightful—"

"No!" She dug her nails into his biceps. "He is still dangerous. He... might..." She trailed off as her mind stumbled for the words to explain something that she had no wish to.

He gently prised off her grip. "What are you fearful about?"

"Just promise me... trust me. Do not go near his wagon."

"My love, he is only a man. A dying old man."

In the darkness, Ursino could not see the expression of heartache that came over her. The actions of Berithas the Redeemer were the one thing she could not predict.

Thirty-Three

CORONEL ARETINI'S VETERAN eye took in the lines of the enemy arrayed before him. Cavalry on their right flank down to the bank of the wide, lazy Taro. Squares of spearmen and *rondelieri* across the centre along the length of the city walls, several ranks deep. On the far left Maresto had placed more horsemen backed by infantry. Bowmen he could not see but he knew they were lurking in the rear.

"What do you reckon, Coronel? An easy meal for the Blue Boar?" Federigo, Count of Naplona, resplendent in his suit of shining plate armour, rode next to him as their mounts ambled slowly towards the Maresto lines under a flag of truce. Aretini grunted. "We outnumber them. And we'll outnumber them even more once the griffons wade in." He could make out the battle flags of the Black Rose, the Scarlet Ring, various devices of what he assumed where the Maresto militia companies.

"Do you see that *carroccio* wagon near their centre? What do you make of that, then? Strangest one I've ever seen, from the size of it looks like they have more commanders than soldiers!"

Aretini squinted and tried to puzzle out what exactly Maresto had constructed. It was nearly as high as the city wall and looked like an inverted wooden bowl. He shook his head. "Well they can hide away inside it if they want but will make little difference to me."

Three heavy men-at-arms rode behind them, bearing the flags of Torinia and Milvorna, snapping smartly in the stiffening breeze that whipped across the open plain. It was the only sound, the two armies strangely silent, expectant as the official preliminaries of war began. Between the standard bearers, one horseman bore upon a long ash pole the dull silver and purloined Hand of Ursula.

Across the field, Aretini watched as a party made its way towards them, the Maresto line opening up to permit passage. "This will do, my lord," he said, tugging gently on his reins. Federigo reached up and steadied the visor of his gold-encrusted sallet helm.

The Maresto men closed the distance between them at a deliberate pace. Aretini's eyebrows raised slightly as he noticed the royal standard—twin golden rampant griffons upon red—borne by a man-at-arms. *Bloody arrogant for Alonso to think he can speak for the palace at Perusia. He'll have a different attitude by day's end.* The five horsemen approached and reined up a spear's length away. Federigo raised a gauntleted hand in salute and sat up in his velvet-clad saddle, straight as an iron rod. "I bring greetings from Ursino, rightful heir to the throne of Valdur. In his name I ask that you open your gates to us and avoid the spilling of innocent blood."

Alonso, Duke of Maresto, leaned forward on his pommel. "And the Duke is not man enough to come here to tell me that himself?"

Federigo smiled. "You would expect a king to treat with you? To request what is his right? And I see you presume much with the royal standard at your side."

"Not as much as the pretender who hides behind your lines."

Aretini chuckled.

The Count of Naplona threw him an angry sidelong glance before shifting his weight in the saddle. "Your griffons are made of baize and golden thread. Ours are flesh and blood. And hungry." He raised his arm and gestured to the holy relic behind him. "And here is the Hand of Ursula, relic of the faithful. Do not speak of royal right to us."

Alonso's voice was ice. "The queen of Valdur watches us from the walls, Federigo. The throne is here. Now. Watching you."

Federigo hesitated as he swallowed the news. Seated next to Alonso, Count Malvolio of the Black Rose, his face as red as a boiled crab, spat upon the ground. "Milvorna makes a choice today as well as Torinia. One that cannot be taken back. If you speak for *your* Duke, my lord Federigo, the one sitting at ease in Milvorna, than you should speak wisely."

Aretini was now looking beyond Alonso and Malvolio, at three riders breaking out of the Maresto lines and moving towards them at a fast canter. One was out in front while the others raced behind. His hand moved to the hilt of the sword at his waist. "My lord Federigo," he said calmly, "... some new arrivals." He flicked his hand behind him and motioned for the men-at-arms on his flanks to move up. Alonso craned his head behind him and then swore under his breath.

The new arrival from the Maresto lines pulled back on his reins and trotted up to join Alonso. "Uncle, haven't these men surrendered yet? This is all taking up too much time."

Alonso smiled and kept his eyes upon the Count of Naplona. "We are just getting to that Your Highness, aren't we, my lords?"

Aretini looked at the boy across from him and shook his head in mild astonishment. He may have doubted the tree of Sempronius in the past but this boy-prince had balls. Sarant glowered at them while sitting tall in his saddle, his filigreed armour polished to a mirror finish. "I hope you have told them, uncle, that traitors this day shall receive no mercy from the crown." One of the prince's minders fumbled for Sarant's bridle but the boy twisted in his saddle and whacked the man's arm away.

Federigo began to stutter, still thrown by the appearance of the heir to the throne of Valdur. "You should get this boy to a safe place, my lord, before he finds himself hurt."

"Boy!" Sarant roared, his high-pitched voice echoing across the open space between the armies. His golden laméd gauntlet flew to his sword grip but Alonso reached out to stay his hand.

Sarant's bronzed face took on a darker cast, brown eyes throwing daggers at Aretini and Federigo. As his glance settled on the commander of the Blue Boar, Aretini gave him a quick wink. If he had ever had doubts about Duke Ursino's bold enterprise, they had been few. Until now. With the queen and the prince on the field, this was no longer a war between two dukedoms. And the boy prince knew that very well.

Duke Alonso choked up on his reins. "I expect you to turn your armies around and make for the border before an hour has passed. Otherwise, the command of the prince will be the word of the day. Traitors will not be ransomed or spared the sword."

Federigo chuckled.

"Amused?" said Alonso. "We know you failed to take Livorna. Surprised at that? Yes, we know now since Coronel Strykar has arrived from there to tell us. With a considerable force at his disposal I might add."

Sarant smirked as Federigo's smile evaporated.

"Deliver that message to Ursino and think well upon it!" Alonso then nodded to Sarant and turned his horse, kicking the animal into a trot. Count Malvolio gave Federigo and Aretini one last look of perfect disdain and then flicked his reins.

"That went well," muttered Aretini. The Duke of Naplona cursed in the lowest dialect of the northeast reaches of Valdur before twisting his horse's head around with a jerk of his reins. Aretini followed and they made their way back to the lines but Federigo continued on to the rearguard and to Duke Ursino's six-wheeled *carroccio*, festooned with red pennons. Aretini meanwhile reached the lines and made his way down to where the heavy cavalry of the Blue Boar stood ready, mounts snorting in anticipation. He carried on until he reached Captain Gheradi, their commander and his comrade-in-arms since they had been scrawny recruits too raw to know the difference between skill and blind luck.

Aretini nudged his horse close to Gheradi and leaned in to clap him on the shoulder; a jingling slap to his pauldron. "Change of plan, old friend. I want your horsemen deployed between our foot and the Naplona foot."

Gheradi gently pushed up the brim of his barbute. "What? Not deploy on the right to take the Black Rose on *their* flank?"

Aretini nodded. "And you will hang back on Naplona's right flank. No charge upon the enemy—*any* enemy—until I give you word."

"I don't understand, Coronel…"

Aretini looked him square in the eye. "Captain, let's just say I'm hedging my bets—for all our sakes. And you, old friend, are that hedge."

Thirty-Four

From the centre of the lines, Strykar steadied his feet on the creaking wooden platform and watched as the parley ended, riders cantering back to their respective sides. He was in a sort of cupola, the crow's nest of the land-ship, a tight fit for even a small man and reached by a rickety ladder that barely supported his weight in armour. Below him in the gloomy confines, six brawny servants of Master Elanordo worked to turn the great wooden wheels that propelled and turned the contraption on its axis, aided by the raw power of four oxen. The presence of the latter was an innovation that Strykar now felt sure hadn't been thought through. The stink that wafted up to him was almost unbearable and the creatures were reluctant to pull at their yokes unless constantly prodded. And as Danamis had predicted, the land-ship moved as fast as a bored tortoise. The machine bounced through a rut on the field and Strykar cursed, grabbing for a handhold; the land-ship shuddered as badly as any carrack wracked by waves at sea.

Six Maresto gunners, chosen for their skill and coaxed by a hefty bounty, worked the orichalcum cannon into place on their new carriages, ready to poke out when the six trap-door hatches were pulled up by their ropes. Although the gunners had baskets of stone shot to fire at the enemy, they had but nine pieces of lead shot, ones impregnated with pretty much the last of his myrra haul. That was destined for the griffons alone.

Five *rondelieri* and the two monks were also on hand to help defend the land-ship should any Torinians have the boldness to crawl underneath on their hands and knees to try and take them. That left little room for Demerise and three of her bowmen but she had insisted on joining him and in truth he was glad of it. A good archer had saved his skin more than once in battle and he wasn't about to trust this shaking pile of carpentry he now dubiously captained. Two of Elanordo's men let out a cry as one of the oxen fired its own cannon and sent a stream of shit spraying out behind it.

Strykar gritted his teeth. *Elded's balls. We haven't even met the enemy yet.* He felt someone coming up the ladder underneath him and looked down to see Demerise, bow slung over shoulder, rapidly ascending the rungs.

"Can't see a thing out of the arrow loops down here! What's going on out there?"

Strykar reached down to give her a hand up and she squeezed next to him on the tiny platform. "Have a look for yourself." She smelt of cloves and leather. He twisted to push his back against the sloping roof-boards to make more room, conscious of her pressing against him.

"Sweet God above," she whispered, taking in the sprawling lines of Torinian soldiers. "So many…"

Strykar could see dismay writ upon her face; perhaps regret too, of her foolish promise to follow him onto the field. And for his part, his heart sank at the realization that he had let it happen. "There are plenty of us lot too, mistress," he said, "with the promise of more from Saivona any hour now."

She nodded, though clearly unconvinced. "Have you seen the beasts yet?"

"No, but the holy men assure me that they will come. Something about the sorceress having claimed Acquel's head for herself. Her pets will be with her."

"If she's still mortal I will put a goose-feathered shaft into her heart."

Strykar smiled softly at her. "Let us hope you get the chance."

He felt her arm rest briefly on his shoulder before she made her way back down the creaking ladder. He turned back to the view outside, grey overcast sky blending into the lines of steel grey soldiery beyond, armour dull and banners nearly lifeless as the wind died. He watched as the van of the Torinians began to walk forward to begin the battle, lance wielding cavalry jostling on the wings as the horses picked up the sounds and smell of the impending clash. He could not rid his mind of Count Malvolio's reprimand when he had returned from Livorna with his ridiculous little war party which included two monks.

You should have died on the field and if you had any respect for your blood you would have done so.

The worst of it was that everything the trumped up sycophant Malvolio had uttered was true. And he felt sick for it.

How many good men did you get killed at the Taro with your goddamned self-pride and arrogance? And you ask me to give you another chance by leading the defence?

The Torinian foot, *rondelieri* shields protecting the long spears of those behind, were coming into range. All along the lines he could not see a single cannon. Now that was arrogance—or stupidity. He may have only had nine rounds with myrra but he had plenty of plain stone shot as well. "Carafa! Are you awake down there! Raise the port on gun two and fire on the enemy centre!" His order was answered by the cries of men below and the slamming of wooden planks as the shutter was raised and the mouth of the cannon pushed out. A moment later the orichalcum gun sang out and he watched as the fist-sized shot ploughed into the front line, sending men crashing to the ground and juddering the entire formation.

He wanted Aretini and the witch to know that the giant wooden machine he was in was more than a big barrel on wheels. Now they did. And he needed them to come and see for themselves. "Well placed, Carafa! Give them another!" The land-ship dipped and rose again over the uneven ground and he clutched at the rail next to him. His own forces were now advancing, cautiously, from the right. The centre, commanded by Cortese and Malvolio, remained firmly planted and he could see that they were trying to draw the enemy in. Turning to get a view behind the land-ship, Strykar saw hundreds of the Black Rose gathered in his wake like so many chicks behind a fat hen. He looked forward again to scan the left of the battlefield and saw the enemy lines beginning to part like a rippling curtain in a breeze. The beasts had arrived. They moved slowly, enormous heads shaking in anticipation; the Torinians were far faster in their haste to avoid being trampled.

No sooner had the pair of griffons emerged from the Torinian lines then the excited burble of a thousand voices of the Maresto force rose up, carrying surprise, wonder and fear. The survivors of the debacle a few weeks before would not have soon forgotten what the creatures could do. Nor had he. He managed to get down the ladder without falling, avoiding the enraged and deafened oxen, and moving to where Acquel and Volpe stood on the circular perimeter of the machine.

"They're coming. From the left." He moved to open the hatch on the first gun, yanking hard on the rope and securing it in place around a wooden cleat. "We've got to get them to come to us."

"She knows where I am," said Acquel darkly.

"Let's just make sure of that shall we?" replied Strykar and he whistled to the gunners to load. He saw that Ugo Volpe wielded his wooden sword, a small buckler in his left fist. He prayed that Acquel knew what he was doing. Wooden blades and brain-rotting myrra leaf seemed the measures of desperate men but then again he had seen that cold steel did no hurt to the griffons—or *vivernas*—as the old monk claimed they were underneath their enchantment.

The master gunner grunted and hefted a piece of stone shot while his assistant rammed a powder bag into the cannon. "We aren't likely to hit them at this range…"

"Plenty of targets behind them if you miss, friend!"

Brother Volpe, dressed in a leather brigantine, his sun-emblazoned tabard belted and cinched over that, leaned out of a gun port. "She follows, behind them, on horseback." He turned towards Strykar. "They will cover the ground fast. You should load the myrra rounds in both these guns… now."

Carafa touched his match to the touchhole and the gun erupted, sending a yellow cloud of powder smoke spilling back into the land-ship. Volpe hunched, hand over mouth and withdrew. "You heard him, Carafa," said Strykar, his ears still ringing. "Load the iron rounds next and may God help us."

From the rear of the land-ship, eye to a loophole, Bero let out a long whistle. "Light horsemen coming across from their right flank." Strykar bounded up to the platform and pressed his cheek to a viewing port. "Shit. Well, I would have done the same thing." He turned to the others. "They are going to try and get underneath us. I need swordsmen down on the ground. Demerise, you and your men could be of good service here."

At the front of the machine, Acquel's timorous voice rang out. "Strykar!"

They watched as four knights of Maresto, lances couched, rushed past them at full tilt, clods of earth flying off their horses' hooves. The griffons, standing side-by-side, stopped and waited. "Valiant fools," muttered Strykar as the knights drew near the beasts. The first two were scattered like skittles in a tavern by the swinging head and neck of one griffon as it batted them away. Acquel said a prayer aloud as he watched the men tumble and spin through the air, hit the ground, and roll to their deaths. The horses screamed as claws raked. The second griffon twisted to avoid a lance and with lightning speed snatched a rider in its jaws, the man's legs kicking in his death agonies. The fourth knight's lance shattered as it hit the flank of the same beast. Acquel could see him hunker down in his saddle, pass behind the griffon, and then ride hell for leather back towards his own lines.

Strykar and Acquel looked at each other for a moment, both thinking the same. Thinking that the guns, the myrra, and prayer were all they had now. Strykar turned to the master gunner. "Carafa, get that second gun loaded! I will manage this one! Brother Acquel, lend me a hand." They pulled the gun back on its carriage and Strykar reached into a nearby suspended wicker basket for a powder bag. As they worked, a commotion broke out below. Strykar soon heard the twang of bowstrings; Demerise and her men taking aim through the loopholes and loosing their arrows. The enemy must have reached them, dismounting to make their approach.

Glancing up towards the open port of his gun, Strykar could see golden brown fur obscuring everything. His heart skipped a beat. Enormous yellow talons reached inside, scraping against the wooden planks and trying to swat him like some cat at a mouse hole. The oxen had caught the scent of the beasts and stopped in their tracks; the creeping land-ship came to a halt, creaking and groaning. Volpe, still upon the platform, rushed to the gunport and lashed out with his wooden sword. A screech like a thousand eagles in unison erupted and the smoking claw was withdrawn. Strykar's jaw dropped as he watched. Volpe hefted the sword, nodded to him and then gave himself a quick blessing, head to chest.

Another great screech split the air outside and the land-ship was rocked on its twisted-rope and beam frame, sending men on the platform to their knees. Strykar shoved a bag of powder down the mouth of the gun, then pulled back on its carriage. "Acquel, hand me a round!" The monk picked up a cannonball, a large wax scab hiding the precious myrra inside. "Let me," he said, his shaking hands pushing the ball down the barrel.

"Stand back," warned Strykar as he shoved in the short wooden rammer. They both pushed the gun forward on it ropes and pulleys, stopping short of the opening. Strykar called for a match and the burning rod was thrust into his hand. The blows of the griffons had stopped now and Strykar held his breath as he waited. Carafa had finished loading the second gun, his scarred hands now held the rope that would raise the second forward-facing gun port. The land-ship rocked anew as one of the griffons brushed against it. Its shining fur again obscured the gun port and Strykar touched match to cannon. It jumped on its carriage with an ear-splitting detonation quickly followed by a scream of agony from the beast. Through the smoke, daylight again could be seen. Strykar cautiously peered out. The creature was thrashing upon the ground, its movements shaking the land-ship as the giant writhed and rolled.

Acquel pushed in to get a view. "Look, it's changing!"

The griffon's head and long neck were raised to the sky as it uttered another screech, this time weaker, and its companion withdrew from the far side of the land-ship to come to its aid. It was indeed changing. The golden fur shimmered and grew even lighter. The creature became a sickly, maggot-like yellowish-white. Fur turned to scales, its head elongating into a lizard-like snout. Its wings had vanished, having never really been there. The enchantment was undone. Where the iron shot had struck it, a black and red wound gaped, tendrils of decay spreading out from its dark centre. It shuddered, the poison taking hold, its head drooping as its demise approached. Acquel saw that its companion was also losing its colour, transforming back to its true nature, a fabled great worm of the northern pools of Valdur, a *viverna*.

Acquel looked beyond the beasts and saw Lucinda. She was trying to control her mount which pranced and side-stepped. She was too far for him to tell if she was panicked but surely she had not seen this coming. Strykar stood and called over to Carafa. "Fire your gun at the other one!" He turned to Acquel, grasping his shoulder. "You and Volpe reload this one!" An orichalcum gun rang out behind Strykar and they both craned for a view outside. Carafa had missed, the precious myrra bouncing its way towards the Torinian centre formation. The unwounded beast began to make its way back to them, belly dragging on the churned-up muddied field, forked-tail lashing.

Strykar dropped to the ground and hurried to the back (if there was such a thing in the circular land-ship) just as Demerise released another arrow. He clambered up next to her and looked out an adjoining firing slot. The enemy cavalry had pulled back under a hail of crossbow fire from the Maresto line, aided by some well-aimed shots of Demerise and her hunters. Two dozen bodies lay on the ground, riderless mounts aimlessly nosing them. The remaining Torinian light horse were already riding back, their gambit a failure.

"We took one down, Demerise," said Strykar, grinning like a mischievous boy. "I don't know if it was the iron or the myrra but it goddamned worked!"

She lowered her bow. "And the other?"

Strykar suddenly looked back. Volpe and Acquel were tugging at their gun with no success as it had jumped its wooden running board. Carafa had just opened his gun port again, leaning in to secure its rope. The land-ship shuddered top to bottom amid cracking timber as the *viverna*'s horned head bulled through the gun-port, exploding the oak planks to kindling. Carafa threw up his arms but in an instant the creature, its red eyes rolling up into their sockets, had clamped its jaws upon him, dragging him outside. He had not even a chance to scream. For a moment, everyone froze where they were, all eyes turned to the gaping hole in the machine and the remains of the dangling trap door of the gun port. And then a tremendous impact sent the land-ship nearly sideways, groaning and cracking. The axle of the oversized front wheel snapped and Master Elanordo's machine collapsed, its lower part juddering into the soft earth. They were immobile, and worse, one gun now pointed down and the other up towards the sky. The oxen began a high-pitched moaning, thrown and driven down under their skewed yokes. Strykar reached for the ladder to the cupola even as Acquel and Volpe managed to stagger to their feet again.

He reached the lookout platform and took in the scene around him. Both armies appeared to be hanging back, hundreds of armoured men transfixed by the duel between the *viverna* and the land-ship. Strykar's eyes moved to the woman on horseback, her long blonde hair flying now in the strange breeze that whipped across the open plain. If she was guiding the *viverna* it was obeying. Hurling its great bulk against the sloped planks of the land-ship, its great pointed teeth gnawing at the opening it had already made. Lucinda della Rovera raised her arms as if imploring aid. Strykar knew that if he couldn't traverse the cannon, they were finished. Done for. They'd have to make a run for it: underneath and out of the back of the machine and pray they weren't run down.

A sudden movement at the corner of his eye startled him. As he swung his body around he had a glimpse of grey feathers, huge yellow bird-like claws and flaring membraneous wings. A second later a kick to his chest sent him backwards, slamming into the platform's railing and knocking the wind out of him. Before he could recover, the thing had climbed into into the cupola from the outside, a scream of rage on its purple lips. The hag-like monster jabbered away as it went for him again, a spindly withered arm wielding a black dagger. Without a thought, he reached to block the dagger, leaning in to throw his weight against the creature. The harpy kicked outwards, its great taloned foot again thumping him and sending him crashing through the railing. He tumbled down inside the land-ship, dropped onto an ox, and rolled off onto the churned up ground.

He was on his back, gasping, still conscious but stunned rigid. His breast and backplate had saved him but his leg was in agony. Above him, he saw the nightmare launch itself down, black wings spread, renewing its attack with a terrible scream. Strykar tried to raise himself, crying out with the pain that ran up his broken leg. The harpy dropped to the top of the great wooden wheel and tensed to pounce upon him. The arrow caught it centre-square in its chest between its pendulous breasts. As it reared up and clutched, a second shaft took it in the neck. In the dim light Strykar could see the wisps of smoke coming off the thing and a stench of rotting flesh immediately filled the already fetid air. The harpy crumpled like a rag doll and fell backwards to land in front of the terrified, twitching oxen.

Demerise leaned over Strykar, cradling his head.

"Are you whole? Sweet Lord I thought it had gutted you like a mackerel!"

Strykar blinked and winced. "Elded's beard, am I still alive?" The land-ship was rocked again by the *viverna*, its roar filling the air.

"You are for now, old man." Demerise hooked her arm around his neck and back to raise him up, their faces close.

Strykar reached for her shoulder and looked at her, her scarred face covered in sweat. He stretched his neck and kissed her full on her lips. She started, her brown eyes widening, but in an instant she returned his kiss, if only for a moment.

"Leave off, you fool! We've got to get out of this wretched coffin."

Strykar nodded and swallowed. "Take the men, make a rush for our lines." His eyes fell to the quiver on her back. He could see two arrowheads covered in bright green paste. "Myrra?" he said, his head falling back.

"Yes. The little priest thought it good insurance." Demerise gave Strykar a tender smile. "Bet you're glad of that now, aren't you?"

ACQUEL AND VOLPE came around the wheels and reached his side, falling to their knees. Strykar tried to haul himself up on his elbows. "The huntress here bagged herself a harpy in the bargain."

Acquel, pale as death, felt his amulet burning against his chest. "Strykar, we must get a gun shifted before this machine collapses. Before Lucinda can summon something more!" As if the great worm outside was listening, it then gave the land-ship another shove, the trusses above them creaking and drooping precariously as the machine contorted.

Ugo Volpe reached out for Acquel's arm. "Brother, fetch my satchel hanging over there, so I may tend to the Coronel." He thrust the point of his sorbo sword into the ground next to the mercenary. As Acquel moved, Volpe reached out and grabbed him again. Acquel saw that the old monk was almost smiling, his face filled with something he had not seen before—a peace of inner grace. The wine-besotted, impish holy man he knew seemed to have become someone else. "Acquel, all will be well. Elded is with us. He is with *you*."

Acquel shot a confused look to his friend and then gave a nod. He stood up and spotted the satchel and dashed around the back of the oxen. Daylight poured in through the hole at the front of the land-ship. A great scaly claw thrust in as he watched, curling about the planks and scratching as it tried to make purchase. The boards squeaked as nails gave way and soon another plank was ripped free of the frame. He reached the satchel and yanked it, his head spinning. Strykar was down, the land-ship finished, its guns unusable. He returned to where Demerise and half a dozen men now surrounded the wounded commander. But Volpe was gone. His wooden sword was still thrust into the earth. Acquel whirled around, and caught sight of the old monk, or rather his sandaled feet as they disappeared under the edge of the land-ship.

"Sweet God!" Acquel reached the spot and dived down onto the trampled grass. Sprawled underneath, his lungs took in fresher air as he turned his head to look for Volpe. The monk was walking, calmly around the land-ship towards the *viverna*. In his hand was a silver drinking flask.

Thirty-Five

URSINO, DUKE OF Torinia, stood on the raised platform of his *carroccio,* his gauntleted fist rhythmically tapping the wooden railing, his body rigid as he surveyed the unfolding battle; the retainers near him hung back for fear of his coiled rage.

"Why is our centre not moving?" he snapped to Messere Iago, a young knight who waited upon him.

"Why, my lord, the griffons are tearing apart their war tower as we speak. When the beasts advance again so will the centre."

Ursino growled in acknowledgment and looked again to the left wing which was pushing slowly forward, a hedgehog of spears and pole weapons. The steady crash of steel and the crack of wooden hafts was distant but clearly audible. He was unconvinced of the wisdom of sitting out the battle when he knew in his heart he should be in the saddle, commanding from the front. Lucinda had told him to let her forces roll over the enemy, leaving the mercenaries to sweep up the field after Maresto had collapsed. That had not happened yet and worse, he could not see her or what was transpiring ranks ahead of where his lonely *carroccio* sat at the rear, safe but impotent.

"And why are Aretini's cavalry sitting on their arses over there! We could roll up the Maresto flank now, griffons be damned!"

"Should I send a rider to him, my lord?" Iago reached out tentatively for the railing next to the Duke.

"Order him forward. Now."

Iago saluted and turned, grateful to be gaining his leave. No sooner had he departed than a rider came pounding up to the wagon, reining in and shouting for the Duke.

"Your Grace! It is the High Priest."

Ursino leaned over the railing. "The High Priest? What of him?"

The messenger worked to control his excitable, slightly maddened mount. "He has awoken, my lord. Regained his wits as if he had just woken from a nap. He's asking for you."

Ursino pulled off his helm. "Asking for *me*."

"Yes, your Grace, he says he has urgent words for you. Something about the Faith and how the battle can be won, that he recants his *Decimali* heresy. You must hurry."

The Duke seized the man-at-arms next to him by his tabard and gave him a shake. "Fetch me a horse this instant!"

Mounted, Ursino whipped the horse underneath him as he and two guardsmen worked their way around the rear of the armies and towards the baggage camp that lay at the north end of the open plain. If Kodoris had regained his senses and had decided to support him, it could turn the tide. If needs must, he could always lash the old priest upright into a saddle so that the enemy could see him. The day would be his all the quicker.

He dismounted and threw the reins to a nearby soldier. "Take me to the High Priest!" War harness jangling, he made his way through the forest of canvas and guy ropes, throwing off his gauntlets and polished sallet helm and leaving them for the fawning guardsmen that followed in his wake. He reached the tent and grasped the flap. There was silence and darkness within. Almost a palpable stillness. Lucinda's warning popped into his head—a foolish womanly warning—but now that the High Priest was awake such timidity had to be discarded. With the leader of the One Faith at his side there would be no doubt he was the rightful heir to Valdur. Either Kodoris or the spirit of a long dead prophet, what would it matter, so long as the old man was his ally. Ursino raised the flap and stepped into the airless gloom.

CORONEL ARETINI BIT the inside of his cheek when he saw the first griffon—or what had been a griffon—fall to the ground dead. He was some distance away from the Maresto war machine but his view was clear: they had fired on it with cannon and had killed it stone dead. Around him, he could feel the lines of the Blue Boar spearmen and swordsmen shudder and begin to bunch as hesitation set in. They, like him, had witnessed a deception, a deception of dark magic. The whispers of "enchantress" and "sorceress" had floated on the wind for days in camp and now, foul white worms that had long been banished from Valdur were but a few hundred yards away. He had felt unease himself for a while but had kept his doubts to himself. Now, his mind weighed options and outcomes even as he watched Lucinda try and regain mastery of her little battle against the wooden contraption. Leaning forward in his saddle he could just make out a figure emerging from the machine, walking towards the beast as calmly as any man out for an afternoon walk.

Aretini spurred his horse out in front of the lead rank of spearmen, guided it left around the corner formation and rode hard for the cavalry that stood massed on the other side. He singled out Captain Gheradi and pounded up to him. "I have new orders for you, old friend!"

"New orders? I just had word from the rear that the Duke himself has ordered us forward. We are forming up for the advance."

Aretini cursed. "Belay that. My orders are if you see the other monster fall then you are to charge the infantry of the Milvornans."

Gheradi tilted his head and sat back. "Change sides?"

"Aye. Roll them up and crush them between yourself and the Maresto spearmen. I smell a change of fortune on the wind, Captain, and we must be ready to act."

"Brother Acquel?"

He hadn't even bothered to reply to Demerise as she tended to Strykar, but just yanked the sorbo sword from where it was thrust into the ground and then dashed to the wall of the machine again. A bellow from Strykar followed him. He knew what Volpe was doing and his stomach rolled on itself, a leaden weight. He crawled out from underneath the land-ship and stood, holding the wooden sword and praying its magic would work for him as well as it had for Volpe. Yet when he saw the *viverna* his legs just stopped as if they had been cut off beneath him. The beast had extracted its head from the land-ship at Volpe's approach, the monk yelling and waving his arms. Acquel wanted to cry out but could not find his voice. The creature shook itself, bemused by the lone man that was walking towards it. Cautiously, it turned to face him full on, lowering itself for a lunge.

Acquel's mouth opened in silent horror as he watched Volpe pour the contents of the flask down his throat and then hurl the empty silver at the *viverna*. It was the last of the *acqua miracula* they had taken from the apothecary. And perhaps Lucinda had realized this too. She was now low in the saddle and pounding towards Volpe, sword in hand. Acquel knew he could not save his friend, but he might be able to prevent the witch from stopping his final desperate plan. He ran toward her as she came on. Lucinda saw him, eyes widening, but did not stop. Acquel reached her, raising his sword arm and clutching at her bridle. The amulet on his chest flared, an agony of white-hot fire, and a pain exploded inside his head as if he had been clubbed. Lucinda lashed out with her sword as he ineptly warded her blows, one hand stubbornly clinging to the horse's bit. Again and again she swung, screaming at him to let go. His foot slipped and her blade glanced from his shoulder, the tip cutting across his face and opening up his cheek in a spray of blood. But he had gained precious seconds, seconds that she had lost.

Acquel spun around, his grip slipping off the bridle. He hit the ground upon his knees and then saw Volpe raise his hand to his forehead and then his chest. The *viverna* leapt forward, jaws wide, and in one swoop clamped down on the monk, swallowing him whole to his knees and then arching its head and neck as it shook and swallowed. Lucinda's horse reared up where it stood and Acquel's eyes filled with stinging tears. He stumbled to his feet, the sorbo sword limply held in his shaking hand. The *viverna* locked its eyes on Acquel and he froze anew. Slowly, playfully, the great worm crept towards him, fifty yards away. It took a few more strides and then Acquel saw a shudder ripple through its massive frame, turning into a frenzy of thrashing. It rolled onto its back and let out a screech and the light greenish-white hue of its underside rapidly began to turn inky black as finger-like tendrils spread. The *viverna* rolled over again, tongue shooting out, its sides heaving rapidly as the poison coursed through its body. Suddenly, its eyes clenched shut, its massive skull lowered, chin hitting the ground, and it died.

Behind him, Acquel heard the cheer of the Maresto soldiers echo across the field. What had been almost a stand-off on the right flank now turned into a melee and he thought he saw horsemen on the Torinian side plough into men on their left—their own—while the Maresto spearmen rushed forward against the same target. He staggered toward Lucinda, his tabard covered in his own blood, and he could feel a breeze playing on the open wound of his face; a deep dull throbbing to accompany the sting of the wind. Beyond Lucinda, the serried ranks of the Blue Boar were quiet. Acquel could see the ripple of the raised spears as men jostled and turned, unsure what was happening. Swaying, he saw Lucinda a few feet away, staring unbelievingly at her dead beasts. She then wheeled in the saddle, fixing him in her gaze. A sharp pain stabbed his temple, instantly doubling him up in agony. Her voice rang inside his head, one word thundering around his skull: *How?*

She lifted her sword and Acquel lifted his in both hands into a guard. He knew the *sorbo* sword would be nothing but a tyro's practice blade against her own steel for she was, like him, born of woman. Sorbo held no power over her. Her horse began moving towards him at a walk, her face contorted into a mask of pure rage. He felt he could hardly hold up the wooden blade. A blast of trumpets shattered the air, louder than anything he had ever heard in his life, almost unearthly in its volume. Lucinda pulled up on her reins and the look on her face suddenly changed. She appeared apprehensive, uncertain, blank eyes looking beyond him, beyond everything. And it had nothing to do with him. Lucinda suddenly kicked her mount and jerked the reins, flying back to the Torinian lines, lines fast disintegrating into confusion. Acquel, dumbfounded, watched her ride away. His feet managed another two steps and then he fell to the ground.

LUCINDA REACHED THE *carroccio* and pulled up hard, her horse whinnying in protest. Men were running away, others standing dumb like confused sheep, all discipline dissolved, the bonds of fealty cast to the four winds. Coronel Aretini was nowhere to be seen. The wagon itself was empty of anyone, its red pennons waving forlornly. Then she saw Ursino, walking towards her, a few of his banner-men and guards tentatively following in his wake. In Ursino's wake, what looked like a bank of pale fog was coalescing and rising up from the ground. She stopped a few paces away and dismounted, dread tugging at her throat.

She could barely get out his name. "Ursino! My lord!"

He stopped and raised his hands out to either side. Again, unearthly trumpets blared and the remaining retainers fell to their knees in fright. The cloud of fog cleared and Lucinda saw in its place a vision as if looking through a clear, rippling waterfall, a hundred feet wide and as high. It was a window on another world. A new sun shone beyond and in the distance she glimpsed riders moving towards the portal's edge, towards her world. She felt a tremor under her feet and the *carroccio* bucked and tipped upwards, driven by a pulsing tree root, a massive beanstalk of shining oily blackness. *The Tree.* Her jaw fell and she dropped her sword, shaking. "Ursino, my love."

She reached him and looked into his face. And it was him. The man she loved. His mouth opened in a rapturous smile as he focussed on her. "Lucinda... my daughter!"

She halted and felt herself fall back a little. "No," she

whispered. Then the tears welled up. "No, Ursino, no. You should not have, my love."

The shimmering window on the other place pulsed with light and now a wind of considerable force blew up, emanating from beyond. The riders could now be seen and Lucinda felt terror, not the joy she had always anticipated. A huge figure, naked, with a raven's head, rode upon a white wolf grown monstrous. It brandished a flaming sword. Andras was about to step into Valdur, summoned by his prophet Berithas the Redeemer. On either side of the raven man, two naked youths— each ten feet tall, shining, golden and beautiful, with tumbling curls—walked as his escort and each held swords that issued tongues of red fire. Belias and Belith, the trinity complete. Glimpsed behind, loping and hopping on misshapen limbs, an army of dark troubles followed.

Lucinda turned to Ursino and screamed at him, the tears coursing down her cheeks. "I told you not to!" But the man she loved was no longer there behind the grey eyes she knew so well.

"My daughter, come to me." It was Ursino's voice still. "Come to me and prepare for the arrival of the Three." Lucinda let out a sob and approached Berithas, now human once again. The ground around them buckled and shifted, the grassy plain erupting as more shoots of the dark tree pushed their way to the surface, each as thick as a man's thigh. Soldiers dropped their weapons and began to flee, what they were witnessing beyond all comprehension. Lucinda stood in front of the Duke. She reached up and touched his cheek with her left hand, stroking his fine trimmed beard. "Oh, my love," she breathed.

The Duke smiled at her but it was more with amusement than affection. "Daughter, you will kneel to receive the Lord Andras and his servants." Lucinda turned to look at the portal. The old ones were still coming, not yet having reached the shimmering curtain between the worlds but now a stone's throw from it. She looked back at Ursino, turned her hand and stroked his cheek again with the back of it. She tried to swallow the lump in her throat as the tears ran down her cheeks. She turned again to look at Andras, the raven's jet eyes were empty of either hate or love.

She shook her head slowly as anger blossomed in full. "No. If I cannot have him then no one shall! Not even you!" Her right hand flew to her belt and then in one swift movement— left palm pressed against Ursino's skull—her right rose to drive her dagger through his neck to the hilt, a fountain of crimson spurting and pulsing, splashing her face. The body of Ursino gasped, shuddered, and dropped to its knees. Lucinda, still gripping the dagger, held his head against her armoured belly. A voice she knew well, disembodied now, wailed in its despair and then disappeared into nothing, borne away. And her mind was her own again, the livid, living wound above her breast silent.

Like a dark curtain falling over a window, the portal instantly clouded over, the wind falling. The ball of fog began to shrink upon itself until only wisps remained and then were still. The roots of the great tree groaned and then stopped their movement. Lucinda tried to suppress the sobs that wracked her, her left hand caressing her lover's head. She pulled her dagger out and slowly let Ursino's body fall away.

Those few terrified men that had remained did nothing, their faces ashen. Lucinda glanced around at them as if she had forgotten where she was. Slowly, she stepped away, not looking at the fallen Duke, the last vessel of Berithas. The dagger still dripping in her hand, she remounted and fumbled with the reins. She then closed her eyes and opened them again. The guardsmen were still staring at her—the sorceress assassin— bloodied and terrible. And their fear held them rooted, petrified.

Lucinda kicked her heels and the horse sidestepped before

recovering and moving forward. A place suddenly came into her head, a place in the north, in the shadow of white-capped mountains. A place she had once loved and called home. *Rovera*. And there would be no gods there in future, no Old Faith, no new. She was done with belief and done with the world.

Thirty-Six

STRYKAR GRIMACED AND leaned back on the trestle bench, his splinted leg thrust out in front of him. "And can you believe they awarded that son of a bitch Aretini a knighthood? Messere *Lupo*! Makes me sick."

Danamis filled Strykar's mug then his own. "Mercenaries change sides. What did you expect?"

"Bah! He should have had his head struck off—like the Count of Naplona. Aloysius on an ass! He even made Alonso a gift of the sacred Hand of Ursula; it wasn't even his to give."

Danamis took a swig and leaned back to admire Citala, who stood staring out the windows of the stern cabin of the *Vendetta*. "Alonso could hardly do that when Aretini's men rolled up the Milvornan army and drove it into the river."

Strykar waggled a finger. "You're playing Devil's advocate, my friend! The queen recognizes that my service in that hellish contraption is what won the day. That and my myrra." He paused a moment. "And that mad old monk. I must give him his due. Damned brave... glorious. Both of them." He raised his cup. "Aye, Brother Acquel took that hard, and blames himself for not killing the witch on the battlefield."

"And did you give him comfort?" It was Citala who spoke up from across the cabin. "He has lost his mentor, and his way. So where are his friends?"

Strykar looked down into his mug as if he had lost something. "He wanted no comfort, mistress. We cleaned him up, tried to cheer him. The Duke received him, thanked him for his fight against the beasts. But I swear, he just wanted to be away with himself."

Citala frowned. "And that is when a friend is most needed."

Danamis gave Strykar a sheepish look.

Strykar cleared his throat. "Aye, I take your meaning mistress. But a man must be his own captain. Brother Acquel's road leads him elsewhere. And... I will miss him."

"What of your road?" said Danamis. "You told me yesterday you've decided to give up your command of the Black Rose. I thought perhaps you were just being... Strykar."

The mercenary gave him a baleful eye. "Is that what you think? Well, I told Malvolio to shove it up his arse. I've had enough of the Black Rose. Cortese can have it all." He sealed his declaration with a long gulp of wine. "Besides, my brother has offered me command of the palace guard—if I want it."

"Half-brother."

Strykar pursed his lips and then grinned. "You're a bastard, Nico."

"Your decision wouldn't have anything to do with a certain royal huntress of the Duchy of Maresto? Would it?"

Strykar issued a low growl and shifted his weight on the bench, prodding at the cushion that supported his leg. "Mistress Demerise and I have an understanding."

Danamis smiled.

"And towards that end," Strykar continued, "it is better that we stay in Maresto for a while. For the both of us to serve Alonso and his household."

Danamis stood up, listening to Gregorvero's roaring voice out on the main deck. Final preparations were under way: the lashing of the guns, the stowing of supplies, sails and spars made ready. "I am glad for you, my friend. But if the Lady della Rovera still lives, you may yet find yourself in harness and on the field."

Strykar shrugged. "So be it. But with fifty witnesses babbling about how they watched her slit Ursino's throat and then ride off as if nothing had happened, I doubt she will be troubling Maresto again soon. That was some lovers' quarrel."

"There's a tangled maze of giant black roots beyond the city walls that say otherwise."

"Whatever evil she helped spawn is dead out there. I have walked it myself. It's hollow, dried out and lifeless. The Witch of Torinia is defeated and so is her magic."

A muffled knock sounded at the door to the cabin. It was a liveried ducal guardsman. He bowed to Danamis. "Admiral, begging your pardon, my lord, there is a summons for Coronel Strykar to return to the palace. His palanquin awaits on the quay."

Danamis turned to Strykar. "Palanquin? Sounds like you've already accepted your brother's offer."

Strykar returned a sly smile. "Half-brother, Nico, half-brother." He shifted his leg to the floorboards and suppressed another grimace. "Come, my lad! Help me up and get me down to the dockside." The guardsman rushed over to the table and hauled up the mercenary, though not really knowing what he should do. Suddenly he paused and turned back to Danamis.

"Begging your pardon, my lord, I almost forgot. I am to give you this." He reached into his doublet and pulled out a letter. "It is from the queen."

Strykar cursed and reached for his crutch. "Hope that damned chirugeon set my leg proper. I'm still waiting to sniff a bit of rot and then that will be the end of it all. So, Nico, will I see you at court in the palace tomorrow? There's talk of the prince returning to Perusia—and Alonso coming with him. To dictate terms of submission to Milvorna for their treason... and to sort out the mess with the Sineans too, no doubt. God knows who will rule in Torinia now that Ursino is crow food."

Danamis touched his friend's shoulder. "Yes, I will see you again soon." He turned to the guardsman. "When you have tucked the Coronel into his palanquin, return to me. I have a message for you to bear to her Majesty."

Strykar took Danamis off guard by throwing his arm around him and leaning in to give what bear hug he could with only one arm available. "We made it through another one, eh?" He gestured for the guardsman to support him and hobbled to the door, his crutch thumping. "And when my brother gives me the rights to distilling *acqua miracula* again, your ships will take it to every port in Valdur!"

Citala moved to stand by Danamis, her arm entwining around his. "He doesn't know does he? You didn't tell him."

"No, he might feel obligated to tell the Duke... or her. He will understand my decision once he sees we've sailed." He cracked open the small, sealed square of parchment that he held and read.

We would hear of your plans for the fleet and for our return to Perusia...

He tossed it onto the trestle and folded his hand over hers and squeezed before moving over to his chipped blackwood sea chest in the corner. He pulled out a large square pouch of oiled leather, opened the canvas tie, and removed a much larger square of parchment than the one he had just received from Queen Cressida. He returned to the table and laid it open, a work of intricate calligraphy in purple and red ink, triple-tailed ribbons and wax seals dangling down. His warrant as an admiral of Valdur.

Citala gripped his forearm. "You are certain of this, my love?"

He pulled her into his arms, their faces just a breath apart. "With all my heart. The throne has had its good service of me and I have shirked my duty to you and your people long enough. Necalli and I have spoken much about this. We don't always see eye to eye, but we agree on one thing. The merfolk of Valdur must be saved. It is time for you and me to deal with both our fathers."

A knock again sounded and Danamis broke their embrace. "Come!"

The guardsman stood before them and dipped his head. "Admiral, your message?"

Danamis folded the warrant and put it back into its pouch. He handed it to the soldier. "Take this to the queen."

"No other instructions, my lord?"

Danamis shook his head. "No. She will know what it means."

Alone again, he swept Citala up into his arms. "So it is for Palestro now."

"And then to Nod's Rock."

He nodded. "We will have a little war on our hands. But we have a kraken. Fathers can be stubborn."

She laughed, that peculiar musical trill that he knew so well.

"Which probably accounts for my mule-headedness... on account that I'm a father too. Cressida told—"

Citala's violet eyes widened. "But I haven't told you yet! The queen could not possibly know." She pulled away from him, her long-fingered hands cupping her belly, a smile taking form on her round, blue-grey face.

Nicolo Danamis, pirate, then admiral, and now pirate once again, blinked a few times. Slowly, he felt the corners of his mouth turning up, mirroring hers.

Epilogue

DEEP WITHIN THE dormitory of the monastery of Maresto, Acquel pushed back his little bench along the rough-glazed and uneven terracotta tiles of the bedchamber floor. Before him on the table was Ugo Volpe's leather satchel, its content spread out before him. His coiled rope of tied ribbons, a few phials, a knotted cord of incredible complexity, and a little book, well scribbled in. The latter was filled with drawings and symbols none of which Acquel understood. Lastly, there was a letter, written in the old monk's crabbed hand and addressed to him.

Brother Acquel, if you are reading this then two things have happened. I am dead and you yet live. If Elded has given you the strength and the power then the old evil has been banished from Valdur. Do not grieve for me. I knew from the words of the mantichora *that the price for our knowledge gained of him would be in blood. I am grateful that it was mine and not yours.*

Take what you find in this sack and learn if you can. It will take devotion. And reflection. I would have taught you myself but the Arrow of Time flies quickly. Follow my path to Astilona: you will find wisdom there in the ruins. Keep too the sorbo blade but give it a twin of good steel and remember that God helps those who help themselves.

Lastly, whether or not the Witch of Torinia is slain, the evil she birthed will live on, always striving to gain a foothold in our world. I sensed a bitterness in the lady borne of guilt. But also, a still-glowing ember of conscience. There is no more powerful a weapon than an enemy turned ally. Remember this. Fare you well!

Acquel folded the parchment and returned it to the satchel along with the book and the other strange amulets of forgotten magic. He found himself smiling as he remembered what he thought upon first seeing the old monk when he waddled into the practice yard on the Ara mount, a fat grizzled fighting priest with a fondness for the wineskin. A living relic. Now he was beginning to see, just glimpse, the rough edges of Elded's wisdom. Outside, bright sun shone through the leaded glass and he rose to go out into the cloister garden. He opened the heavy oak door and entered the fresh air, surrounded by climbing rose, camellia flowers, and olive trees. The rays of the sun covered his face and he shut his eyes.

"Magister?"

Acquel turned to find the High Prelate had joined him. He could see the priest was trying hard not to stare at the black poultice and bandage that covered half of his face and tied behind his neck.

"The brethren have prepared your horse and provisions as you asked. But I would beg you to stay here with us a bit longer that your wound may be tended each day."

Acquel managed a smile. "That is kind but I must be on my way. The wound will heal... I will heal."

"I do understand, magister. The Ara must be told of all that has happened. We will prepare the body of the High Priest and await instructions from the Council. A procession from Maresto to Livorna? In a few months, I mean... when all has settled."

Acquel saw Kodoris's face again, as he had found him, dead and abandoned in the camp of the Torinians. And for all the hurt and harm the priest had done, Acquel knew that Kodoris had atoned. He prayed he had found peace—and forgiveness. He nodded to the prelate but said nothing.

"If you think it not too improper," said the Prelate, his voice lowering, "who might become High Priest? Someone who is destined to heal the rift in the Faith."

"Someone who understands the weakness of men... but also their promise. And may Elded deliver him. It is not I."

Acquel looked past the Prelate to the corner of the garden most exposed to the burning sun. An angel in flowing white gossamer stood there, her face beaming at him, filled with undying love. A face he knew: Timandra, the widow Pandarus. And she was pointing north.

Dramatis Personae

Alonso – Duke of Maresto
Bero – a hunter and companion to Demerise
Lupo Aretini – a coronel of the Company of the Blue Boar
Caluro – captain of the palace guard at Perusia
Citala – daughter of king of the merfolk of Valdur
Cressida – daughter of House Guldi and Queen of Valdur
Nicolo Danamis – an admiral of Valdur and scion of Palestro
Valerian Danamis – explorer and High Steward of Palestro
Demerise – a huntress and Royal Forester
Acquelonius Galenus – monk, Captain-General, and prophet of Saint Elded
Gregorvero and Bassinio – master mariners of Palestro
Lucius Kodoris – High Priest of the One Faith at Livorna
Lazaro and Claudio – two knights of Torinia
Malvolio – commander of the Company of the Black Rose
Marsilius – High Steward of Livorna
Necalli – a merman of Atlcali across the sea and advisor of Valerian Danamis
Piero Polo – explorer, merchant and representative for the Silk Empire
Bartolo Poule – a lieutenant of the Company of the Black Rose
Raganus – chancellor to the Queen
Lucinda della Rovera – noblewoman and sorceress, lover of the Duke of Torinia
Sarant – Crown Prince of Valdur
Julianus Strykar – coronel of the Black Rose, half-brother of the Duke of Maresto

Ursino – Duke of Torinia
Ugo Volpe – an old warrior monk of Astilona
Paolo Voltera – castellan to Marsilius